Louisa Heaton lives on H
Hampshire, with her husba
a small zoo. She has worke
the health industry—most recently four years
as a Community First Responder, answering
999 calls. When not writing Louisa enjoys other
creative pursuits, including reading, quilting and
patchwork—usually instead of the things she
ought to be doing!

Also by Louisa Heaton

Single Mum's Alaskan Adventure
Finding Forever with the Firefighter
Resisting the Single Dad Surgeon

Greenbeck Village GPs miniseries

The Brooding Doc and the Single Mum
Second Chance for the Village Nurse

Yorkshire Village Vets miniseries

Bound by Their Pregnancy Surprise

Christmas North and South miniseries

A Mistletoe Marriage Reunion

Discover more at millsandboon.co.uk.

BEST FRIEND TO HUSBAND?

LOUISA HEATON

FINDING A FAMILY NEXT DOOR

LOUISA HEATON

MILLS & BOON

First published in Great Britain 2025
by Mills & Boon, an imprint of HarperCollins*Publishers* Ltd,
1 London Bridge Street, London, SE1 9GF

www.harpercollins.co.uk

HarperCollins*Publishers* Macken House, 39/40 Mayor Street Upper, Dublin 1, D01 C9W8, Ireland

Best Friend to Husband? © 2025 Louisa Heaton

Finding a Family Next Door © 2025 Louisa Heaton

ISBN: 978-0-263-32496-9

02/25

This book contains FSC™ certified paper and other controlled sources to ensure responsible forest management.

For more information visit www.harpercollins.co.uk/green.

Printed and Bound in the UK using 100% Renewable Electricity at CPI Group (UK) Ltd, Croydon, CR0 4YY

BEST FRIEND
TO HUSBAND?

LOUISA HEATON

MILLS & BOON

To Nick, my Best Friend and Husband. x

CHAPTER ONE

THE AIR WAS filled with the scent of lavender from the fields that surrounded the village of Clearbrook, as Dr Lorna Hudson arrived at work. It was something she loved about the village, as the soft scent filled the air. The calming aroma was normally so good before she started her day at Clearbrook Medical Practice. She used to walk in, as her cottage was only about a mile away on the edge of the village, but now she ran or jogged, as she was training for a marathon and any chance she got, she'd use. Unless she was on house calls and then she would drive in, in case she needed her vehicle that day.

But today, she'd jogged. She'd needed to burn off her anxiety, her nerves, about one of the new doctors starting today.

Dr Oliver Clandon.

Olly.

Dearest Olly. He'd been her everything during her time at medical school. Her rock. Her shoulder to cry on and, yes, she could admit, she'd had the teensiest, tiniest crush on him. A crush that had remained unrequited, because he'd been going out with Jo. And when medical school had ended, they'd both gone their separate ways, promising to keep in touch, but somehow never managing to.

She'd put it down to the fact that she'd been so busy, set-tling into her placement as a junior doctor and beginning her GP training and, besides, she'd then been swept off her feet by Craig. It had seemed wrong to keep in touch with an old crush when she was planning a wedding and so she hadn't.

Wow. So many years have come and gone and now he's coming back.

'Did Oliver say anything in the interview about his family?' Lorna casually asked the practice manager, Priti, as she got changed out of her running gear in the staff-room and put on her work clothes. She'd been invited to Olly and Jo's wedding, which had been a surprise after they'd lost contact. The couple probably had kids by now. Grown-up kids, maybe having babies of their own.

Could Olly be a grandfather?

She felt an ache in her womb at the thought of it. A sense of unfairness and injustice. But it passed quickly. If he was a grandfather, she had no doubt, knowing the kind of man that he was, he would be an amazing one and those grandkids would be lucky to have him.

'I can't remember him mentioning anything specific. He just said he was looking for a fresh start somewhere new, away from the hustle and bustle of an inner-city practice. Peppermint tea, or normal?' Priti waggled a box of mint tea in front of her.

'Normal's fine.' That could mean anything—a fresh start. A fresh start for him and Jo?

She hadn't been able to attend the wedding; it had fallen right in the middle of a holiday to the Maldives with Craig. With regret, she had sent back an RSVP card politely declining the invitation. She'd only met Jo briefly on occasion. Not properly. She'd tended to avoid her back then, knowing that meeting her would make her feel uncomfortable. But she had seen her once, had watched her picking up Oliver from the hospital in her car and she'd been stunningly beautiful. Hauntingly so. Long, blonde hair, the type of face that ought to be fronting an international make-up campaign or skincare regime. But dark shadows beneath her eyes.

Lorna had felt ugly compared to Jo. She'd not yet fully understood how best to use hair product to tame her ginger waves. She was self-conscious about her teeth when she smiled—even though there was nothing obviously wrong with them, she felt they were slightly crooked. It had made her crush on Oliver even more painful, knowing it would always be unrequited—when he could bag women like Jo, why would he ever look her way?

'When do they all get here?' Lorna asked, feeling her nerves set slightly on edge. The lavender scent had abated inside the building and its calming effects were long gone.

'I said nine o'clock, but their clinics don't start until ten. I thought it would give them all time to get settled in, meet you, get their rooms sorted to their preferences...'

Lorna nodded, accepting her mug of tea from Priti. 'Thanks. It's strange, isn't it? With everyone gone?'

Clearbrook Medical Practice had always been a four-doctor practice, but in the last six months, there'd been some changes. Dr Mossman had retired after thirty years' service and was currently enjoying the pleasures of a world cruise with his wife. Dr Bleaker had gone on maternity leave and had recently given birth to her first baby.

And Dr O'Riordan had left to work with Doctors Without Borders. He was apparently somewhere in the Gambia.

The changes had necessitated Priti having to interview to fill the posts. Oliver had gained one place and the other two posts were going to be filled by a Dr Bella Nightingale and a Dr Max Moore, who were going to renting cottages across from one another. Oliver, Priti told her, had secured a place to rent in the centre of the village.

'Just a bit. But we can build another close-knit practice with Oliver, Max and Bella. I really liked them all in their interviews and think they'll fit in with the community. How long has it been since you saw Dr Clandon?' Priti wanted to know.

'Oh, God, years! I dread to think how many. Certainly before I got all these laughter lines and crow's feet!' Lorna joked.

Their conversation was interrupted by the reception supervisor, Saskia, popping her head around the door. 'Dr Clandon has arrived.'

Lorna felt herself tense. She couldn't understand why she was so nervous. She and Oliver had been very good friends and study partners for five long years. There was no need to feel this anxious. They'd no doubt get along like a house on fire and carry on as if they'd not been apart for decades. She glanced at herself in the mirror. The redness in her cheeks from running had gone down now. She was back to being pale and heavily freckled. She straightened her hair subconsciously, smoothed her blouse and skirt and prepared to meet an old friend.

Was it strange to feel as if he were coming home to family? Even though he'd never been to this place? Had only just moved into his cottage and his life was still in boxes? That he was about to start a new job?

She's there. In that building. Lorna.

He'd not known that she worked here when he'd first applied for the position, but when he'd begun his research into the practice before his video interview and he'd seen her photo under the staff page, his heart had begun to pound. He'd known then that out of the six places he'd applied for, this job, the one here at Clearbrook Medical Practice, was the one that he absolutely had to get.

He needed a friend—or at least a friendly face. Quite frankly, it had almost seemed to be a sign.

Oliver had arrived in the village on Saturday and had spent Sunday jogging about the village to get to know it. Running was a new thing he'd taken up recently on his travels. He didn't do it often, but he liked the way he felt afterwards. As though he'd done something good for himself. It blew away the cobwebs. After the long drive to his new place and the hours of unpacking boxes, going up and down stairs, he'd needed some fresh air. A part of him had hoped that he would somehow stumble upon Lorna in the village, but just because she worked here, didn't mean she actually *lived* here.

He knew she'd got married years ago. She'd sent him an invite, but he'd not been able to go. Jo had been having radiotherapy at the time and hadn't been feeling good. Though she'd told him to go to the wedding on his own, he'd felt bad about leaving her alone in the house. And Lorna hadn't made it to his wedding either, so did it really matter? Even though he would have loved to have seen her. She must have looked beautiful in her dress.

Her hair done, her make-up done. He would have liked to have seen her like that.

He tried to picture Lorna with kids. Maybe even grandchildren. Lorna? A grandmother? He couldn't picture it. Didn't want to picture it, because then, wouldn't it mean that they were both old? That half their lives had passed by?

He couldn't wait to see her. Say hello. See that smile of hers. So wide. So bright. She used to say she hated her smile. Thought it showed too many teeth, but he'd always disagreed. She'd had a lovely smile and he wanted to see it again, to pull her into a hug and hold her for a moment. Lorna represented a happy part of his past.

If all he got to do with her each day was hug her, then that would be enough. It would have to be. Surely her husband wouldn't like it if he tried anything else.

Not that he was looking for anything more with Lorna than friendship and a good working relationship. She was married, and as for him? He had far too much baggage, and he was determined now to be a bachelor. To enjoy what he never could before: living a life of freedom, with just himself calling the shots. His years spent travelling had shown him how much he enjoyed doing that.

He walked up to the lady at Reception. A bright young thing in the practice's uniform of a royal-blue blouse and black skirt. 'Good morning. I'm Dr Clandon, the new GP.'

'Hello! I'm Saskia, the reception supervisor. Take a seat and I'll go and fetch Priti.'

He sat down in Reception and placed his briefcase on the floor beside him. It seemed to be a standard waiting room. Lines of empty chairs, walls covered in health information, reception desk off to one side. Behind the desk, he saw a board of names and there was Lorna's, right at the top. He smiled and wondered if she knew he was coming. She had to, right? How was she feeling about it? Was she excited to see him?

She'd no doubt notice a few changes. Nearly three decades had passed since they'd last seen each other. He had a bit more grey in his hair. He wore glasses now. *Nerd glasses*, his nieces reliably informed him, and he was rather proud of his short beard and moustache, even if they were also peppered with grey. He thought it made him look quite distinguished. And though he might no longer have the flat, washboard abs he'd once had as a young man, he kept himself reasonably trim and fit.

How would Lorna look?

It didn't take him long to find out.

As Priti emerged from a door down the corridor, Lorna stepped into view behind her. A broad smile crept across his face at the sight of her.

She looked lovely. As she always had. Her auburn hair was still long and fell in soft, smooth waves past her shoulders. Her blue eyes were as kind as ever and her smile…that broad smile of hers hadn't changed one jot. Once he'd shaken hands with Priti, he looked at his old best friend. 'Lorna! Good to see you after all this time!'

'You too.'

God, it was good to hear her voice. He proffered his arms for a hug and she stepped into them and, just as he'd wanted, he got his hug. He could hardly believe they were back together again. Could he keep on holding tight to her? He felt as though he had thirty years of hugs to catch up on.

She smelt like flowers and some of those sharp edges

she'd once had seemed to have softened. Before, in the early days when he'd give her a hug, she'd almost freeze. Stiffen. She wouldn't relax. But now?

He wanted to just stand there and hold her tight and tell her that he'd missed her, but he felt her pull back to take a good, long look at him. Reluctantly, he let go.

'Well, we've a lot to get through, Oliver, so if you'd like to come with me, I can give you your welcome pack,' Priti suggested.

He wished he could have a moment longer with Lorna. But he was here for a different reason. To *work*. 'Of course. I'll see you later?' he asked Lorna.

'Absolutely. Good to have you here, Olly.' She looked as though she meant it and he was glad. And she'd called him Olly, the way she used to. What was that sing-song name she'd once given him? *Olly-Wally?* Something like that, because he'd used to joke around so much in the early weeks of medical school?

Well, he was different now. He didn't joke around so much. Life had knocked him about quite a bit and though the bruises were gone, they could still hurt.

But being here with Lorna would make him feel better. She already had.

She watched him walk away with Priti, her gaze focused on how Oliver looked.

My God, the years have been kind to him!

How was it possible that he looked so good? Maturity and years had given Olly a touch of class that she just couldn't pinpoint. Was it the fine suit? Dark grey with a hint of a checked pattern? The perfectly white shirt that was open at the neck? The highly polished shoes?

Or was it those glasses? He'd never worn glasses before and they added a sense of distinction that she'd not expected. Maybe it was the beard? Peppered with silver? He'd always been clean-shaven before. Or perhaps it was the laughter lines around his eyes? Those eyes that saw right into her soul. Eyes that had always seen her for who she was: a nervous and naïve young girl who'd been so afraid of stepping out alone into the big, wide world. But someone who wanted to make a difference. To change people's lives.

Or maybe it was simply seeing his smile all over again, after all this time? It had made her feel an intensity that she'd forgotten about—the way Oliver would make her feel, just by being in his presence. It was like seeing him for the first time all over again. Oliver had been young, fresh-faced, almost cheeky-looking, with his floppy hair and natural charm. Everyone had seemed to know him and be his friend. He had been a popular, well-liked guy, and he'd seemed to have an easy confidence around people. A confidence that, she'd noted in some of their early lectures, would *disappear* as he struggled to follow some piece of chemistry or brain function. And then, in one lecture, he'd settled into a seat next to her and she'd felt so incredibly aware of him, but had been too frightened to say anything. She'd sat there, chewing on her pen and then…

Lorna turned with reluctance and headed into her consulting room where she began to boot up the computer and get ready for her clinic. As she sat down at her desk, she glanced over at the picture that had always sat there. Graduation day. The moment when everyone had thrown their caps into the air. She'd stood next to Oliver and though everyone else was looking up with joy, she and Oliver had been caught looking at each other, joy on their faces. Him, thankful for all the help she'd given him—and not just academically. All the extra study hours in the library they'd spent together, long into the early hours. The many hours they'd sat together talking about Jo. Her, already trying to hide the pain that she knew was coming when they'd go their separate ways, hoping he'd keep his promise to write or email. Wondering if that moment would be the last she'd see of him.

Lorna swallowed and looked away, bringing up her clinic listing. She had six patients this morning and the first was to check out a lump a patient had found in her breast. Verity James. She grimaced. She liked Verity. She owned the cheesecake shop in the village. A good woman. Kind.

Lorna called her in and Verity sat opposite her, looking nervous. Apprehensive. 'Verity! Hello. Take a seat. How can I help you today?'

'I found a lump when I was in the shower. Here, on this side of my breast.' She indicated the left side of her left breast.

'Okay. Does it hurt at all?'

'No.'

'You've not banged yourself, or had an injury to that side?'

'No.'

'And you've not had a cold or an infection recently, or felt unwell?'

'I've been tired and I think I'm losing weight, but I've not been trying to. I'm eating the same.'

'Busy at work?' Verity's shop was world-famous for

the lavender-infused cheesecake that sold all over the globe. She'd even made cheesecakes for movie stars and royalty. The kitchen was going twenty-four hours a day, six days a week to accommodate all the online orders that they had to meet.

'It's always busy at work, but no more than usual.'

'And how long would you say you've been feeling tired?'

'I'm not sure. It kind of came on gradually, but a good six weeks or so.'

'And how much weight would you say you've lost?'

'Half a stone? I'm not sure.'

Lorna looked at Verity's last recorded weight. 'Let's get you to stand on these scales for me.' She stood up and escorted Verity over to the weighing scales in the corner of the room. 'Hmm. You've lost more than half a stone, Vee. It's more like fifteen pounds.'

'I didn't realise it was that much.'

'Any fevers? Night sweats?'

'One or two, but isn't that just menopause?'

'Maybe. But it might be worth doing some bloodwork, too. Let me just take your temperature.' Verity's temperature was normal on examination. 'And if you'd like to go behind the curtain, I'll perform a breast examination, if that's all right? I'll just be one moment to fetch a chaperone.' Lorna left the room to look for the nurse or HCA that worked at the clinic and managed to grab hold of Carrie, in between taking bloods.

'You know Carrie?' Lorna called as she re-entered the room.

'Of course,' Verity said from behind the curtain. 'Ready.'

Lorna put on gloves and she and Carrie went behind

the curtain. 'We'll examine both breasts and I'll look at the right breast first, okay?'

'Yes.'

Lorna performed a visual examination first, looking for puckering, discolouration or another sign that might indicate something going on with the breast. She checked the nipples, too, looking for inversion, but everything seemed normal. 'Lie down for me.'

Verity lay and Lorna then performed a physical examination of Verity's breasts. The right one was fine, with no sign of any lumps in the breast, armpit or chest. Then she began the examination of the left breast. She felt the lump immediately and palpated it to see if it was adhered to any tissue, or if she could move it. It was small, maybe half a centimetre. 'I can feel it. We'll definitely need to get this checked out. Okay, you can get dressed for me. Thanks, Carrie.'

Carrie left the room and when Verity emerged from behind the curtain, Lorna talked her through the referral they had to do in instances such as this. 'You'll receive an appointment at the breast clinic within two weeks. You'll see a consultant, have a mammogram and an ultrasound, and should receive the results at the appointment. It's probably just a cyst, but it's best to get it checked out.' Lorna hoped the night sweats and the weight loss were incidental, but you never could be too sure with something like this. 'Any history of breast issues in the family?'

'My mother's sister had breast cancer. She ended up having a double mastectomy.'

Lorna nodded. 'Okay. It's definitely good that you've caught whatever this is early.'

'Let's hope so. Thanks, Lorna.'

'Take care, Verity.'

As she typed her notes, Lorna couldn't help but think of her own mother, whom she'd lost to breast cancer six years ago. It was a loss that should never have happened. Her mother had said nothing about her lump, thinking it would go away, and had been too scared to ask her daughter about it. She'd figured that, as there was no history of any other family members having breast cancer, it couldn't possibly be anything serious, until she started to feel really unwell. By the time she'd made it into hospital, the cancer had metastasised into her brain and bones, and it had been too late to treat it.

Watching her mother die in palliative care had been an awful thing that Lorna wouldn't wish on anybody, and it had been a huge wake-up call to her entire family. Lorna now made sure that everyone did everything that they could to maintain their health. She ensured that her father completed the routine bowel-health tests and prostate exams when they were asked for. That her brothers stopped smoking and began eating healthier and going to the gym. And Lorna? She'd started running as often as she could, and examined her own breasts every three months alongside her regular smear tests and NHS health checks.

She hoped Verity would be okay, but there was nothing they could do now but wait.

A knock on her door interrupted her thoughts. 'Come in.'

Priti opened her door. 'Just popping in so you can quickly meet Bella and Max.' Priti opened the door wide and stepped in, followed by a beautiful young woman with long dark hair and an extremely attractive young man with blond hair and a beard.

Lorna stood up and held out her hand in greeting. 'Pleased to meet you. I'm Lorna.' She shook their hands. 'Did you find us all right?'

'Yes, thanks,' said Bella, nodding.

'It was easy enough. Thankfully the clinic is near the infant school,' said Max, smiling.

'Oh, that's right. Priti said you'd both got young kids. How old?'

'Ewan's four.'

Max nodded. 'Rosie, too.'

'Same age? Maybe they'll be best friends, then? Well, welcome to Clearbrook. It's good to have you both with us. Maybe I'll get to catch up with you both later on.'

'Looking forward to it,' said Bella.

Lorna's computer beeped to let her know her next patient had arrived in Reception. 'We'll let you get on,' said Priti. 'I'll show you to your rooms.' She ushered Max and Bella out of Lorna's consulting room, and Lorna sat back down at the computer to finish her notes on Verity and make the referral.

Bella and Max seemed lovely. She was looking forward to getting to know them both better. They'd had such a lovely clinic when Clive, Tilly and Ben, the outgoing three doctors, had been here. They'd been like a small family. She had been sad to see them all go. Had even begun to question if she herself ought to move on. She'd been here at Clearbrook for eight long years, after all.

But she was happy here. Settled. She loved living in Clearbrook and couldn't imagine ever being anywhere else. And when Priti had offered her the senior partnership, she'd accepted the post gladly.

The next patient to enter her consulting room was Michael Cooper. The only note accompanying his appointment was stomach pain, so she called him through.

Michael came into her room, looking uncomfortable, one hand on his abdomen, as he slowly lowered himself into the chair.

'Morning, Michael. It says here you've got a bit of tummy pain—why don't you tell me about that?'

'It started this morning about two a.m. I'd got up for a wee and felt fine, to be honest, but just as I was flushing the loo, I got hit by these sudden stomach pains. I could barely stand. I think I crawled back to my bed somehow. Took some paracetamol, which helped a little, but my stomach hurts so much!'

'Can you show me where the pain is?'

He rubbed the area above his belly button, but below his ribcage. 'I'm sorry to hear that. How would you rate that pain on a scale of one to ten, with one being barely anything at all and ten being the worst?'

'About a seven. Maybe a six or a five once the pain-killer kicks in.'

She took his blood pressure, checked his SATs and his temperature, which were all normal. 'Any nausea, vomiting or diarrhoea?'

'I feel a little bit sick, but I haven't actually been sick.'

'And yesterday, you didn't have a fall, or bang into anything, or lift anything too heavy?'

'No.' Michael shook his head.

'Did you eat or drink anything different yesterday?'

Michael nodded. 'I did, yeah. I had a couple of pints

down at the pub. I don't normally drink, but my nephew was here visiting. He's come over from Ireland and he kind of encouraged me to have a pint or two.'

'And how would you describe the pain? Is it burning pain? Stabbing? Aching?'

'It just hurts, Doctor. I'm not sure I could describe it.'

'Let's examine you.' She encouraged Michael to get up onto her examination couch, so she could palpate his abdomen. It was soft and he didn't react or show pain when she pressed down. It didn't make him feel worse with her poking and prodding him. 'You can get up now. I think you've probably got a touch of gastritis. That means your stomach is inflamed and irritated. That's causing the pain and the slight nausea you feel. I'm going to write you a prescription for some omeprazole to protect your stomach and some codeine for the pain, okay? I want you to take them regularly for at least a week and if you're still in pain after that, give us another call. Okay?'

'Will do, Doc. Thanks.'

'In the meantime, no more alcohol, no spicy foods. Try and eat simply until this passes.'

'Yes, thanks.' Michael took the prescription and left her room.

Lorna quickly typed her notes, then realised she'd had a couple of blood reports and hospital letters appear in her inbox for previous patients. She checked those, noting further treatments, and got the ladies on Reception to call those that she needed to see again. After that, she worked her way through the rest of her patient list until morning break. She headed off to the staffroom to make herself a quick cup of tea and to grab an apple from her lunchbox.

Max, one of the new doctors, was in there, having just made himself a drink.

'Hey. How's it going? Finding everything all right?' Lorna asked him.

'Yes, thanks. I am. How's your morning going?'

'Not bad at all.'

'I got a chance to speak to Dr Clandon. Oliver. He tells me that you two knew each other way back.'

She smiled and nodded. 'Medical school. Yeah.'

'Must be weird meeting up with each other after all this time. I bet you've got a lot to talk about.'

'I'm sure there are a few stories we could tell each other.' She thought of all that Oliver had missed. Things she wished she could have told him about when they'd happened, but she'd never maintained contact. It had felt wrong to, especially as they had both been with partners, getting on with their lives. Her name was different on her social media profiles to protect her identity from patients. A lot of doctors did it, so if Oliver had tried to contact her, he would have had difficulty. She could have told him about her mum. Her relationship with Craig. The fertility treatments. Then Craig's betrayal. Feeling as though she had lost everything and having to start anew, all alone.

But Lorna didn't normally like to focus on the bad things in life. She tried to always press forward. To be optimistic. What was the point in wallowing? Maybe she'd tell Oliver about these things and maybe she wouldn't. And even if he did find out, what could he do about it? It was in the past and he'd made a life with Jo now.

Briefly, she wondered what Jo was going to do in the village. Did she have a job? Was she going to commute elsewhere? She'd not thought to ask him this morning how his wife was.

I must remember to do that.

Jo had been through a lot. That early cancer scare during medical school had really thrown Olly. His partner going through chemo when she was still only a young woman on the brink of living her life must have made them both re-evaluate what was important.

'Have you managed to get everything unpacked yet, or are you still living out of boxes?'

Max laughed. 'I'd love to tell you that I'm perfectly organised and everything's done, but unfortunately, no. There's still a lot to do, but I unpacked the important bits and my daughter's room is done.'

'Rosie, right?'

'Yes.'

'How old is she again?'

'Four.' He smiled. 'Let me show you a picture.' Max got out his mobile phone and Lorna dutifully looked and made all the right noises.

Rosie was indeed a lovely-looking young girl. Same hair colour as her father, but that was where the resemblance ended. 'She doesn't look like you. Does she take after her mum?'

Max's eyes darkened slightly. 'Yes. She does.'

Lorna wasn't sure if she'd said something out of line, but something about Max had changed. She hoped she'd not upset him, by asking about Rosie's mother. She wanted to make the conversation return to its brighter overall tone. 'And she's going to the local infant school here in Clearbrook?'

Max nodded, putting away his phone into his back pocket.

'I've heard it's very good. One of the teachers there is a patient of mine. Miss Celic?'

'Yes, that's Rosie's teacher.'

'Oh, she'll have a wonderful time with her. Everyone rates her.'

'That's good to know.'

Lorna began to make herself a cup of tea and it was at that moment that Oliver walked into the staffroom. He looked from Max to Lorna and said hello.

'Looks like we're all on the same mission,' he said, grabbing a mug from the cupboard and dropping a tea-bag into it.

It was weird having him so close. Since the hug this morning, she'd tried to keep her mind off how it had felt to be pressed up against him. But his physical presence was having a weird effect on her. She could see his arm muscles through his shirt. He had nicely defined biceps that made her think of strength and safety. That he could be the type of man to protect you if you needed. She liked that, but tried not to stare. 'Tea is essential,' she said.

'Absolutely.' Max's phone began to ring and he pulled it from his pocket and glanced at the screen. 'Excuse me.' And he left the room.

Lorna became acutely aware that she and Oliver were alone together for the first time since meeting again. She'd thought it would be the same. Two friends who would just slip back into exactly how it was before.

Only it wasn't like that at all. She felt incredibly aware of him. 'How's Jo?' she asked, unable to think of anything to say, but feeling the need to cut the tension in the air.

He shrugged. Tried to look nonchalant. 'Fine. I think.'

Lorna frowned, puzzled. 'You think? You don't know?'

'Not really. I haven't seen her for years.'

Years? Lorna swallowed. 'What happened?'

'We got a divorce.'

'Oh.'

She almost couldn't believe it! Jo and Olly *divorced*? The way they'd been together before, she'd thought they were a for-ever couple. He'd seemed so dedicated to her. They'd been through so much! The worst that life could throw at them—a difficult, long-term, life-threatening illness—so what had been the thing that broke them apart? Was he single, then?

No. Not possible. Not looking like that. There has to be someone else.

The second his divorce papers had come through, there'd been a part of Oliver that had wanted to rush off and track Lorna down. Find her. Spend time with her, rekindle a friendship that he'd never been able to achieve with anyone else. Lorna had understood him completely. Probably because he'd been able to be himself with her and known he wouldn't get judged. Because he'd known he could talk to her about his fears and she wouldn't call him out for being weak. When he spoke to his male friends and the talks got serious, they had a tendency to laugh things off. Make a joke of them. Lorna hadn't. She'd sat quietly and listened. He'd felt *seen*.

So much of his relationship with Jo had been all about

her, and rightly so, but sometimes he'd needed someone to check on him. That was what Lorna had done. In those formative years, the two of them had got on like a house on fire. Lorna had helped get him through medical school, when all his mind had been able to focus on was caring for someone with cancer, alongside chemo drugs and their side effects. Nausea. Exhaustion.

Without Lorna, he would have failed his exams. He'd somehow got into medical school by the skin of his teeth and right away he had begun to struggle with the level of work, the assessments, the studying, the revising, the tests—but somehow, she had calmed him down. Got him to focus. Turned him from the joker he'd once been into a serious student who knew how to revise properly. Who made his own set of flashcards.

She'd somehow known what to dangle in front of him, like a donkey following a carrot on a stick. She'd bought tickets to a comedy show after they'd passed their first OSCE assessment. OSCEs were the Objective Structured Clinical Examinations, which demonstrated that a student could carry out clinical skills such as history-taking, physical exams, blood draws, medical knowledge and order writing. She'd bought a ticket for Jo, too, but Jo hadn't gone. She'd been too ill.

At the end of their first-year exams, she'd booked them in to complete a Colour Run around a local park, completing a five-kilometre race over a series of obstacles whilst having coloured powder thrown over them by supporters. He'd taken her to see a film as a thank you after their first successful placements. They'd gone with three others to Brighton for a pride parade.

And all the time, no matter where they'd been, she had

quizzed him on his medical knowledge. He'd present her with case scenarios for her to diagnose in return. It had become a game. One Lorna had seemed to enjoy playing. In short, she had supported him when everyone else in his family had expected him to fail. And she'd been there, long into the night, when he'd called her needing to talk to someone about Jo's cancer battle. Researching with him at all hours, to find him the information he needed to sit in the room with those oncologists and advocate for his girlfriend.

And he'd always felt, despite trying, that he could never give her enough back.

Oliver had met Jo at college, doing A levels. She'd been in his science classes, because Jo had wanted to become a veterinary surgeon. She'd been gorgeous. Funny. Witty. Full of life. They'd had great fun together and started to go out seriously. They'd each applied to neighbouring universities and got in, celebrating with a weekend trip to Paris. It was there that he'd thought he could feel a lump in her breast.

Jo had dismissed it at first, even though she'd told him she would get it checked out, and for months during their first year at uni she'd told him it had been checked out and it was nothing. Only she hadn't. She'd lied to him, because she had actually been very afraid. One day her lies had caught up with her and he'd discovered the truth, so he'd made her an appointment and gone with her to the GP, sitting in the waiting room and praying that it was just a cyst.

It hadn't been, and that was the day their lives had changed. And changed again weeks later when they'd discovered that the cancer was already Stage Three. He'd felt so angry because if she'd just gone when they'd first discovered the lump, maybe things wouldn't have ended up the way they did.

He'd felt bad about being angry with her. She'd had cancer. How could he have been angry? Their relationship had been on unsteady waters for a while after that. He'd stayed by her side, though, because Lorna had helped him process that anger. Made him see that he wasn't angry at Jo, but at the cancer and what it had been taking from them both.

It had taken from Lorna, too. Because he ought to have been a better friend to her, paid her more attention, found out about what was going off in her life, rather than just focusing on his own and yet, selflessly, she had always been there for him. He'd wondered, once, if she'd liked him as more than a friend. But she'd never said anything. Never made any move, which had probably been for the best, because he would have had to turn her down and that might have ruined their friendship, which he'd valued so much.

Lorna had lamented that in all the time she'd been at medical school, she'd not met one guy whom she'd thought she could be with and that she'd end up a lonely spinster surrounded by cats. And he'd tried to help. Had tried to set her up with various guys, whom she'd go out with for one date and then never see again.

He'd be lying if he denied often thinking about whether life with Lorna would have been better, but what was the point in that? He couldn't have walked out on Jo. Not whilst she'd been going through the battle for her life. What would that have said about him? He wasn't heartless. But he'd been able to feel Lorna slipping away.

Medical school had been at an end, they'd both got jobs in different hospitals, they hadn't been going to see each other every day any more. Lorna wouldn't be there and he would miss his best friend in the whole wide world. And she'd told him, right at the end, that she wished things had been different for them, before she'd stepped on a train and out of his life…

A statement that had made him question everything.

But he had not stayed in touch with Lorna. He knew why. He'd wanted to. He'd promised to. But he'd been trying to make things work with Jo. She'd needed him and he'd known that if he'd kept in touch with Lorna, it would have felt, somehow, as if he were cheating on Jo. Even though he and Lorna had only ever been friends.

He was an honourable guy.

He'd done it for his marriage. He'd made a choice to stay with Jo and he hadn't wanted that sacrifice to be for nothing, so he'd given his marriage one hundred per cent.

And still *failed*.

All that work, all that sacrifice, had been for nothing.

Left with nothing. Nothing to show for all the sacrifices he'd made for her, except for divorce papers and no family. He'd never felt so alone. Lost. He'd thought about Lorna then. Missed her soothing words. Her friendship. Had briefly considered getting in touch with her, but had decided not to, because what would she think of him getting in touch only when he needed something? It had felt selfish. Wrong. And he'd wanted her to live her life, without him striding back into it, needing her.

And so instead of finding Lorna, he'd taken some time to discover *who* he was and what he wanted from life now. Years of taking locum posts. Travelling. Globe-trotting. Just sitting with who he was and what he wanted from life. Having experiences. He'd come back knowing he wanted peace. Quiet. He wanted to live somewhere beautiful and so he'd done an Internet search for the most beautiful villages in England. He'd found Clearbrook in the top ten. Then he'd done searches for GP vacancies and there it had been. Clearbrook had had vacancies. And weirdly, strangely, *miraculously*... Clearbrook had Lorna.

And he'd felt as if it was meant to be.

'So, I have a question.' Oliver stood with his mug of tea, looking at Lorna. He knew that she had never thought of herself as beautiful. She felt her auburn hair was unruly and that her freckles made her stand out in the wrong way. She thought her body was nondescript, and she didn't care for fashion, but rather comfort.

But he thought she was beautiful. He always had. And in the years that had passed since they'd last seen one another, Lorna had clearly found her style. Her long, auburn hair was wavy, and cascaded around her face beautifully. Her freckles were as gorgeous as they always had been, but she wore a little make-up now that focused the gaze on her eyes and lips. She looked strong and fit and her clothes were timeless. She was wearing a summery dress in a jungle print, lots of leaves and green and somewhere in there were brightly coloured birds. She'd teamed the outfit with a nifty little pair of heeled ankle boots. And he had forgotten how great she smelled.

'Oh?' She looked at him with curiosity.

'We've not seen each other for a long time. We ought to spend some time catching up.'

Lorna smiled. 'That wasn't a question.'

He loved her smile. It made his heart glad to see it

again. 'I wondered if you'd like to go out for a meal. You can bring Craig—it'll all be above board.'

Lorna's eyes darkened and she looked away. 'Craig and I are no longer together. I'm divorced, too.'

'Oh. Well, okay, you can bring whoever you're with, then.'

She blushed. 'I'm not with anyone.'

Lorna was single? His heart began to beat rapidly. He'd never expected that. Not in a million years! Craig had let her go? Was the man stupid? 'What happened?'

She smiled. 'Maybe we should talk about that over dinner? I've got to get back to my clinic.'

'Of course. Are you free tonight?'

Lorna nodded. 'I am.'

'Know any good places around here? I'm new.' He smiled and winked at her, the way he used to.

She laughed. 'Jasper's is good. Casual dining. Excellent range of food. Decent prices.'

He nodded. 'Then I'll give them a call.'

CHAPTER TWO

I'M GOING OUT to dinner with Olly.

She couldn't believe this was happening. Hearing he was going to join her practice had been one thing. She'd figured, though, that he'd be married still, and that at some point, yes, they'd probably go out for dinner with Jo, as a sort of reunion celebration. She'd psyched herself up for that.

But dinner with just the two of them?

Knowing that he was single? Same as her?

She wasn't looking for a relationship these days. She was quite happy being single. She was good at it, too. Her cottage was exactly as she liked it. Her job was wonderful. She ate out alone quite happily. She let no one down and they didn't let her down. No one said mean things. She went to the movies whenever she wanted. Did whatever she wanted. Took cruise holidays and made friends whenever the desire took her for some time away to see the world. She liked her routines. Her life. Olly being back in her life would just add to that. Having her best friend back. It would be the icing on the cake, but she didn't need any more than that and, besides, he'd never shown any romantic interest in her, anyway. She'd only ever been his friend. That was the box she resided in for him, and that was enough. Even if she had once harboured feelings for him, and even if she did still find him incredibly attractive.

It would be wrong to let it become anything else.

Why ruin a beautiful friendship?

He was never interested in me anyway and why pursue rejection? I've just got him back. He could be back for good. Why take the risk of ruining our friendship?

Lorna had put on a flowing white dress, put her hair up in clips and allowed a few tendrils to fall. She liked how her hair looked when she did it that way. It was showy, yet casual, and she wanted to look a little different from how she'd looked at work all day. Wanted to feel confident. To show Oliver that she was different from the mouse she'd been before. Some strappy sandals and a couple of ankle bracelets completed the look and once she'd spritzed herself with perfume, she was ready to go.

In the past, Olly had always been a little late, but at seven-thirty on the dot, she heard his knock at the door and the butterflies in her stomach began to flutter.

She grabbed her clutch and opened the door. 'Wow. Look at you!' she said, admiring his look. Oliver was wearing dark trousers and a pale blue shirt, open at the neck.

'Look at *you*!' he said in reply, palms outward. 'You look stunning.'

'Thanks.' She tried not to blush, but it was hard when she wanted the compliment. Wanted him to notice that she knew how to dress herself these days. Knew her style. What worked for her. When they'd been in medical school, she'd not known what clothing worked for her and so she'd often hidden beneath oversized hoodies and jumpers, teaming them with jeans or baggy cargo pants.

'Ready to go?'

'Let me just lock up.' She turned and locked her front door, dropping her keys into the small clutch she'd brought with her. When she turned, he held out his arm and she slipped her own through his. 'We're walking?'

'If that's all right? It's such a lovely night.'

'That's fine. Let's go.' They had a reservation at eight. Olly had popped into her room at work in the afternoon to tell her he'd made the reservation and she was looking forward to getting something to eat.

Lorna often ate at Jasper's, but previously she'd always dined there alone, or on occasion with Priti or Clive for a work meeting. It was going to be nice to eat there with Olly. 'This still feels a little surreal.'

Oliver smiled at her. 'Walking?'

She nudged him playfully with her elbow. He'd always been a joker. 'No! You. Being here. After all this time.'

'Glad to be here.'

'Did you know I was here, when you applied?'

'Honestly? Not at first. I sent in the application and figured I'd research the post later if I got offered an interview and when I realised you were on staff...well... I almost went running in the other direction.' He laughed.

'Olly!'

'No, seriously, when I knew you were here, it made me want this job even more.'

She smiled, hearing him say that. It felt good to know he wanted to be back with her.

'I should never have lost touch with you.'

'It happens.' She didn't want him to feel bad. 'I wasn't

great at keeping in touch either. The first few years after graduation are crazy—whenever I got free time, I just wanted to sleep.'

'They were the worst, weren't they?' he agreed. 'I remember this one nightmare shift that never seemed to end. I was triaging minors in an accident and emergency department in London. Started at eight at night and I was meant to finish at eight in the morning. But we were slammed. Short-staffed. The department overrun with patients, you felt like you never made any progress. Eight a.m. came and went. Then nine. Then ten. Then I was asked if I could carry on until five p.m. to cover for someone who'd not made it in and you know what it's like. You're young. Eager. You want to impress and show you're one of the team. Jo was doing okay, so I stayed, and by the time I got home it was around seven-thirty that evening. I think I passed out for almost a whole day.' He shook his head. 'It made me realise that I had to learn to say no, for my own health and sanity. These days I don't think they let you work that long. For safety reasons.'

'I hear you. Those first two years of working as a doctor almost put me off, but I knew that if I could just get through it, then I could begin my general practitioner training and do the job that I wanted to do.'

'Strange how we both became GPs.'

'I know! I always thought that you'd want the adrenaline of being a surgeon, or something.'

'Really?'

'Yes. I remember being on placement with you and we were both observing an appendectomy. You looked fascinated.'

'Never even made my specialism top ten.'

'Was GP training always your number one?'

He nodded. 'Actually, yes, it was. I wanted to be able to build a rapport with my patients. Know them over time. Watch them have children and then treat those children. I liked the continuity of that. I think it's because I remember growing up, when we had this family doctor who I saw all the time. Dr Spencer, his name was. Lovely guy. And I just remember how I used to feel seeing him. Knowing that he knew me. That he'd known me for a long time and how comfortable that made me feel. I wanted to make other people feel the same way about me.'

'That's nice. But you've moved here where you have to start again? Get to know a whole load of new families? That wasn't daunting? Or upsetting, having to leave the families you did know behind?'

'No. I was never able to build that kind of relationship. What with Jo and needing to be there for her, I did a lot of locum work. She did, too, when she was able, and we moved to pursue a big job she wanted. I've never felt settled in one place. Don't get me wrong, locum money is great, but I wanted that community feel, you know? I took time for myself after the divorce just travelling and finding myself and deciding on what I want to do and… yeah…here I am.'

'Here you are. And we're very glad to have you here. *I'm* glad to have you here.'

'Good.'

The village looked very pretty this evening. To be fair, it looked pretty all the time. Clearbrook had been declared an Area of Outstanding Natural Beauty. The scent of lavender from the fields filled the air. Fat bumblebees were still flitting from flower to flower, even this late in

the day. Lorna saw foxgloves and hollyhocks and mari-
golds spilling over walls. Jasmine and clematis climbing
over doorways and trellises. Everywhere was leafy and
green and birds sang happily.

It was peaceful.

It was perfect.

And she was here to experience it with Oliver. She'd
never have imagined that he would come here and yet
here he was. Ready to put down roots, by all accounts,
and that made her happy.

'Here we are. Jasper's.'

Jasper's was an old building, Grade II listed, built of
local stone and adorned with hanging baskets and window boxes. There was some seating outside for people
that just wanted drinks. The dining tables were inside
and out the back, where they had a large garden, the tables were protected by large umbrellas. The garden overlooked the local woods and a small lake, where ducks,
geese and swans would lazily glide.

'Looks great. After you.' Oliver held the door open
for her and she smiled as she passed him, feeling hungry and looking forward to having something nice to eat.
She told herself that this was just friends catching up. It
could never be anything more, because she didn't want
to be a disappointment to anyone ever again. The way
she'd felt she'd been to Craig.

She was never disappointed with Jasper's, however.
The food was filling, local and had ample servings that,
if you didn't finish, they'd let you take home with you.

Inside, a low light, created by wall sconces and mood
lighting, revealed an interior that was classic and comfortable. White linen tablecloths on round tables. A bud

vase, filled with sprigs of fresh lavender, sitting in the centre of each. Wooden chairs, each painted a different soft pastel colour. Walls filled with old black and white photographs of the lavender farmers through years past. People harvesting the flowers. Horses pulling carts, piled high with the lavender in neatly tied bunches. An old market stall, complete with seller in apron and flat cap, his ancient, grizzled face lined with a history untold.

Their host for the evening was Rupert, Jasper's business partner and husband, and also one of Lorna's patients. He welcomed them warmly and escorted them to a table situated near the double doors that led outside to the garden, giving them a fabulous view of the lake and the woods beyond.

'Can I get you any drinks?' Rupert asked.

Lorna, who didn't very often drink alcohol, asked for a fresh orange with lemonade and Oliver joined her.

'This looks great,' he said. 'Look at that view! I had no idea there was a lake here in Clearbrook.'

'This used to be a bit of a manor house in years past and the owner had the lake dug out for him, so it's not actually natural. Apparently, he was into fishing and stocked the lake with fish.'

'Old money, huh? I wonder what happened to him?'

'I'm not sure, but I bet Rupert would know.'

As if summoned, Rupert arrived with their drinks on a tray.

'What happened to the guy that had the lake built here? Do you know?'

'I do! Sad story of unrequited love, I'm afraid. He was the Earl of Witton and legend has it he fell for a serving girl when this place was a manor. Their love was forbidden and the earl's mother wasn't too pleased about it, so she would harass this poor girl and make her do all this menial work to try and break her. Make her leave. But the poor lass wouldn't. She stayed. It's said that the earl's mother wanted to go out on a horse ride around the grounds and made the servant girl fetch her saddle and tack and the horse startled and kicked her in the head. The poor girl didn't survive. People think the mother was hoping something like that might happen but it was never proven. The earl remained single the rest of his life, refusing to marry and refusing to give his mother the heirs she said were his duty and after that the manor fell into disrepair.'

'That's so sad!' said Lorna. 'Imagine not being able to be with the one person who made you happy. Thank goodness we don't live in those sorts of times any more.'

'I guess it depends where you live,' Rupert said. 'Jasper and I weren't allowed to get married for a long time, remember?'

Lorna nodded. 'You two must be coming up on a big anniversary soon?'

'Ten years this autumn.'

'Ten years! Are you going to do anything special?'

'Well, if I have my way, we're going skiing, but you know what Jasper's like. He only wants to admire things from a distance and he keeps talking about this glacier express thing he's seen.'

'Well, that sounds amazing. Can't you do both?'

'Depends if you order the lobster or not, my love! Those things are expensive.' Rupert winked and left them with their menus to decide on what they wanted to eat.

'Friend or patient?' Oliver asked with a smile.

She laughed. 'Both. And neighbours. Rupert and Jasper live right next door to me.'

Oliver perused the menu with a smile. 'So, shall we pick the lobster and send them on their way to Switzerland, or nibble at a garden salad and keep them here?'

'Actually, I'm rather craving their beef wellington. I've had it before and it's marvellous. A singular taste sensation that you'll be talking about for weeks.'

Olly raised an eyebrow. 'That good, huh? Well, okay. I'll be guided by you.'

'And you have to try the local lavender cheesecake with honeycomb for dessert. Or the raspberry and rose ice cream. Or the profiteroles! Oh! Choose anything! It's all good!' She laughed.

Oliver smiled at her. 'You haven't changed at all.'

She looked flustered then. 'How do you mean?'

'Before, whenever we'd go out to eat anywhere, you would love everything. Caramel popcorn at the cinema. Or hot dogs with all the trimmings. Then there was that kebab place we'd go to after the pub and you could never make up your mind what sort of kebab you wanted, because you liked them all and the owner, Christos, would make you a little mash-up of everything.'

Lorna gasped. 'Oh, I'd forgotten about Christos! Oh, he was a lovely guy, wasn't he? I wonder what he's doing now.'

'Well, he was in his sixties back then, so he's either very old, or...'

Oliver didn't need to finish his sentence. She knew what he meant. It made her feel a little sad. 'Well, I'm going to hope that he's still with us somewhere. He did have that ancient grandmother—perhaps they're all long-lived in his family and he's sitting somewhere right now eating a chicken souvlaki. To Christos.' She raised her glass.

Oliver clinked her glass with his own. 'To Christos and his marvellous tzatziki that has never been beaten.'

They sipped their drinks and laughed. It felt good to reminisce. Felt even better to be sitting across a table from Oliver again.

How many times had they done this? Over meals? Over revision books? Flashcards? At a pub? A library? He might have needed her book-smarts at university, but she, in turn, had needed him and he'd helped her for the better. She'd been a mouse to begin with. The quiet one in the corner, who no one had wanted to hang out with. When she'd tried to make friends, she'd struggled, feeling as though she'd never quite fitted in, or had a voice loud enough to be heard over everyone else. And then one day, Oliver had simply slid into a seat next to her and struck up a conversation.

She could remember the shock she'd felt at being noticed by the most handsome guy in the room, feeling nervous at having him so close, but when she'd discovered that he had a girlfriend and that it wasn't some trick, or dare by his friends, she had begun to relax. Becoming study partners had helped her revise, too. She'd admired his easy way of being in the world. His carefree nature. His laughter. His smile. He'd been warmth, when she'd felt cold. Softness, when she'd felt sharp. A welcome when she'd felt alone. And because she'd been in Oliver's orbit, she'd got to know his friends too and they'd become her friends. As she'd opened up and felt more comfortable, medical school had become a lot easier, fun as well as educational, and she'd loved every minute of it. The early starts, the cadaver practice, the tests, the assessments, because throughout it all, Oliver had stayed by her side.

She'd missed him when they'd gone their separate ways. Had felt all alone again as she'd headed out into the harsh real world, without his reassuring presence at her side. Had needed his heart-warming presence when she'd gone through the worst upset of her life.

And now he was here. After all this time. Sitting opposite. Smiling at her.

Why had they ever lost touch?

Why had she allowed that to happen?

She wanted to tell him that she'd missed him. She wanted to tell him that life had not been the same without him. But she knew she couldn't do that. She was too afraid.

As Rupert arrived at their table with a smile and their beef wellingtons, she waited for him to go, then looked at Oliver over the table. 'So…should we catch up?'

'Why not? We've kinda been circling each other all night.'

'Is Jo…okay? After the whole cancer thing?'

He nodded. 'As far as I'm aware she is. We don't really talk now since the divorce, but yeah, she's in remission and has been for years.'

'That's good.' She meant it. 'I'm glad. I know you two went through a lot together. I don't know how you managed to get through medical school with all of that going on.'

'She had it harder than me. And besides, I had you.'

It meant a lot to hear him say that. That she'd been

worthwhile. Of value. 'And she had *you*. So what happened between you two?'

Oliver let out a big sigh. 'What didn't happen between us?' he asked. 'The cancer thing went on for quite a few years. Chemo, radiation, surgery, recovery. Remission. Recurrence. More chemo. When she finally got the all-clear, we were *so happy*. I remember thinking, *Now. Now is the time for us to live*. To live a life that wasn't centred around the hospital and the oncology ward, you know? It was strange, I don't mind admitting. Jo was struggling to accept that for now she was free of it. Every twinge, every pain, every headache, she would worry, but her scans kept coming back clear and we began to think about the next stage of our marriage.'

'Children?'

He nodded. 'Jo had frozen her eggs before treatment all those years ago and so we knew that if we were going to have kids, it would be through IVF. So we started monitoring Jo's body a different way. Temperatures. Blood tests. Scans. Injections. Hormones. It was like we'd swapped one regime for another and it was all we could talk about. It hit us hard. It hit me hard, seeing her go through all of that and each time an implantation failed, I wanted us to wait awhile before we tried again. To recover. Maybe just have some time for us? Maybe go travelling, see the world, enjoy life, before we went into another round.

'It caused arguments because Jo just wanted to try and try again. She felt like she'd already waited far too long and she began to feel that maybe I didn't want a baby as much as she wanted one and, honestly? At one point, I didn't. I didn't think it was worth it, all the stress, all the mood swings, all the upset and the grief each time her period arrived or the test read negative. I was trying to give her a break. I was trying to let her see that there was more to life than what we had and we began to drift apart.

'When the third cycle failed, I said no more. It hurt me too, but she couldn't see that at all. She thought I wasn't affected, but she was wrong. So wrong! I would have *loved* to have a kid, but it wasn't happening and I didn't want to keep going through that heartbreak when we could have just lived instead and enjoyed each other, the way we'd never been able to before.'

He looked down at his plate. Lorna could see that he was hurt and all she wanted to do was reach out and comfort him, as she always had. But events in her own past relationship stopped her. Craig had made her doubt herself. Had told her that she wasn't enough for him and she'd begun to question if she would ever be enough for anyone. 'I'm so sorry.'

He shook his head. 'The IVF didn't work for us and, in her anger, she blamed me for it all and we couldn't come back from that, so we got divorced, years ago.'

Lorna felt nothing but sorrow for what he had been through. 'I wish I could have been there to hold your hand through all of that.'

He sighed. 'Yeah. Me too. But I'm not sure Jo would have liked that.'

'Why?'

'Because I spent all of my time with you at med school and because you never went out of your way to spend time with her, she felt that, well…she was being avoided for a reason. That you had feelings for me.'

'What?' Lorna feigned even more shock, to show that

she was appalled at such a suggestion, surprised at it, but deep down, she knew the truth. Yes, Oliver had been her best friend and study partner, but she *had* harboured deeper feelings for him. Feelings that she could never have expressed because he had been with Jo and Lorna was not ever going to be the other woman. She did not want to be part of some sordid affair, or break up a couple. She'd always wanted one hundred per cent of a guy's feelings, not what he could spare for her when his girlfriend or wife wasn't around. 'But we were just friends,' she protested. 'Study buddies. You told her that, right?'

'Of course I did!' Oliver shook his head and smiled before sipping his drink, as if Jo's suggestion had been the most ridiculous thing he had ever heard in his life.

And even though she'd reacted as if it were ridiculous, to see him react the same way, to imply that the idea of them was stupid, hurt her. But she couldn't show it. She forced a smile and poked at her food.

The beef wellingtons were delicious as always, but Lorna was filled with a strange discomfort. She was a habitual people pleaser, and it did not sit well with her that Jo might not have liked her. She'd always imagined that Jo was fine with her spending time with Oliver. She'd been helping him get through med school. He wouldn't have passed without her. And surely Jo would have *wanted* him to pass? 'I wish I could have spoken with her. Put her mind at rest.'

'I think her doubts came from her mindset that she was missing out. The chemo made her feel so ill, she would barely leave the house most days, but she saw me going out, participating in life, following my dream and

I was doing all of that with a girl? A girl that wasn't her? I could see her point of view, honestly.'

Lorna nodded. 'You were put in a difficult position. I'm sorry if our friendship made your life much harder than it needed to be.'

He shrugged. 'It's in the past. We got through it. What about you? What happened between you and Craig?'

Lorna sucked in a deep breath and then let it out again. In some ways, her history was similar to Oliver's. 'We were great. Until he cheated on me.'

'Really?'

'We went through a similar thing. We got married, everything was great, then we began trying for a family, starting as you do with all that youthful exuberance and belief that it will probably just take a few months, but then a year went past and then another without a single blip in my cycle. My period came every month, on time, as expected. But I lived in hope and kept buying tests and doing them early, only for them to come out negative.

'We decided to consult the doctors. They performed tests and discovered I had a hostile uterus, which is a phrase any woman just loves to hear.' A hostile uterus meant that the mucus that existed in her uterus was not the best when it came to swimming sperm that might want to go find an egg to burrow through. It would prevent the sperm from moving and sometimes be so acidic as to kill them. 'So we embarked on IVF as well.'

'You did?' Oliver looked intrigued.

She nodded. 'They implanted two embryos on the first round we did. It failed. The second round, they implanted two more. We got a positive pregnancy result from that one and we were so excited. Well, *I* was. Craig seemed a little distant, but I put it down to the whole exhaustive process. I finally thought our dreams might have come true, that everything would be all right now and Craig and I would be close again, but we performed an early ultrasound at week eight and there was no heartbeat.'

'I'm so sorry.'

Lorna smiled, refusing to revisit the pain of that moment, and forced herself to carry on with her own sad tale. 'We tried a third time. There was one embryo left and we pinned all our hopes on it. *I* pinned all my hopes on it. We were at work when the blood results came through. I took the call and discovered that we had failed and was devastated, I went looking for Craig to tell him the news. I found him in his consulting room with his tongue down the throat of one of our receptionists.'

Oliver looked at her in shock.

'That kind of ended things on a permanent basis.' She sipped her drink. 'I couldn't stay working in the same place as them. It was humiliating. I served my notice and got a job here. That was years ago and I've been happily single ever since.' She raised her glass, hoping she sounded convincing. She was happy. Mostly. But she did often feel lonely.

He clinked it, thoughtful. 'I can't believe we both went through similar struggles. If we'd have known we could have helped each other through it.'

Lorna nodded. 'Maybe we could have.' She thought of what that might have looked like. Weekly calls? Fortnightly? Jo would probably have hated that too. Lorna remembered all too well what it felt like to have her hormones played with. She'd become so emotional sometimes, not knowing whether she was coming or going.

One moment she could be laughing at something, the next in floods of tears. Her nerves had been on a knife edge and anything could have set her off.

Feeling Craig drift away from her had felt awful. That feeling of suspecting you were losing someone and not being able to do anything about it...it was horrible. Losing a chance of a family every month. Losing her embryos with every implantation. Losing her husband... Especially when you felt as if you were doing everything to keep yourselves together. To try and grow a family for that person. To have a baby in the hope that everything would be right again. She should have known. Should have stopped the process and sorted her *relationship* first, then maybe she wouldn't have gone through so much in the first place? But she'd ploughed on, believing that a positive result on a pregnancy test would somehow set the world back on its axis.

'They're still together, Craig and Anya, the receptionist. They've got kids, so it all worked out for him, at least.' She tried not to sound bitter. Because she wasn't. Not really. Not any more, anyway. It was more of a wry assessment.

'He clearly was not the right person for you.'

'No.' So who was? She looked at him from across the table, her heart going pitter-patter. Once upon a time she'd yearned to believe that Oliver was the person for her, but he had been with someone else.

Maybe I just have a habit of choosing the wrong man?

Oliver felt a strange surge of unexpected anger when he heard what Craig had done to Lorna. Cheating on her when she was trying to get pregnant with their child?

The man sounded like scum. No honour at all. No pride. No moral centre. No idea of sacrifice. Whilst Lorna was going through so much.

Oliver knew what IVF cycles were like. They were long and arduous. Tough to get through. He'd watched Jo go through everything, because most of it fell upon the woman. All the guy had to do was provide a sample and that was no hardship, but the woman? She had to face tracking of her cycle, artificially *changing* that cycle, flooding the body with hormones, enduring daily injections, examinations, scans, procedures.

Jo had once suffered horrendously with a condition called ovarian hyperstimulation syndrome. Her abdomen had swollen, she'd felt sick, vomited, suffered dehydration and fluid had begun to build in her chest, affecting her breathing. When she'd been admitted into hospital and told to stop her IVF for a while, they had been devastated.

But Craig had thought nothing of his wife's sacrifice and cheated behind her back, humiliating her in front of her work colleagues.

If I ever meet that man, I'll have a few harsh words to say.

He wished he could have saved Lorna that pain. Maybe if they hadn't lost touch with one another, he could have? Maybe both of their lives would have been different? He'd never told anyone about how he'd once been thinking of ending things with Jo before they'd discovered her cancer. How their relationship had been flailing and in the weeds for a while. He'd been building up to it. Thinking about how he could do so without hurting her. He'd wanted them to remain friends, if possible.

But then things between them had got a little better

and he'd discovered that lump when they were in Paris...
then she'd been having investigations and been extremely
nervous and worried. He couldn't have left her like that.
What kind of a human being would he have been?

And so he'd stayed. Stuck by her side. Through thick
and thin. Supported her. Cared for her. Advocated for
her. Loved her as best he could and, yes, the fight to live,
the fight against a cruel disease, had brought them back
together. It had made them stronger when it could tear
others apart, and he'd been so happy when she'd finally
got the all-clear, of course he'd said yes to her proposal of
marriage, because they'd been through so much by then,
he'd thought nothing could tear them apart. The fight,
the sacrifices, would not be for nothing. And he had really wanted a child and he had loved Jo.

But now? Looking back? He was glad that they
hadn't had children together, because if they had, then
he wouldn't have gone travelling, he wouldn't have found
himself, he wouldn't have looked for his own happiness,
he'd be continuing to sacrifice it for others. He wouldn't
be sitting where he was right now, and right now felt
wonderful. Because he was back with Lorna and looking at her face and seeing her smile. Hearing her voice
was like a balm to his soul.

The lavender and honeycomb cheesecake was placed
before them and he took a bite, not sure if the two fla-
vours would be a good combination, but, oh, my goodness, they worked! And he polished off the dessert as
quickly as he could.

'Convert?' Lorna asked.

'Absolutely. They make that here? I'm coming back
every night, just for this.'

Lorna laughed. 'Actually, it's from Verity's. She makes all the local cheesecakes. Ships them all over the world. They're famous.'

'I'm not surprised. This ought to be in everyone's staple diet.'

'I don't think that would make for a healthy population.'

'Probably not, but think of all the running you could do afterwards to burn it off.' He smiled.

'You still run?'

'I do. Not as often as I should. In fact, I only started up again recently. I've been meaning to do it more often. What about you? I remember you used to run.'

'I still do. I run to work every day and again in the evenings, if I can. In fact, I'm training for the local marathon. I'm raising money for a stillbirth charity after one of my patients lost a child.'

That had to be awful. 'I'm sorry to hear that. What's the marathon?'

'It's called the Clear Twenty-Six. The route takes you all around the local area, through Clearbrook and all the other neighbouring villages. It's a mix of road and trail running. Lots of elevation, so I'm not sure I'll make it.' She laughed nervously, sounding uncertain. Unsure of herself. 'But if I have to crawl across the finishing line on my hands and knees, which, frankly, is probably going to be very likely, then I'll do it.'

'When is it?'

'Soon!' She took a sip of her drink, nervous of how fast the time was approaching.

'Fancy a training partner? I'm an experienced runner. I

ran a half marathon just a month ago and I've been building up my distances. I could accompany you.'

She looked shocked. 'You mean that?'

'Absolutely! I could do with losing some of this.' He
patted his stomach.

'There's nothing there to lose!' she said.

'I'm wearing a very expensive girdle.' He winked.

Lorna laughed and he couldn't help but smile at her
amusement. She was so lovely. He'd missed her so much.
'I'd love to train with you. When's your next run?'

'Tomorrow evening after work. Just a short one.'

'Then, if you're happy for me to join you, I will. And
I'll sign up to run the marathon as well.'

She looked surprised. Pleased. 'You could run for a
charity, too.'

He liked making her smile. 'I'll pick one.' He raised
his glass for another toast. 'Running partners.'

She clinked his glass. 'Running partners.'

CHAPTER THREE

'I THINK I'M having TIAs.'

TIAs were transient ischaemic attacks or mini strokes. Oliver raised an eyebrow at his patient. An older gent, in his seventies. Walter McCormack. 'And what makes you think that, Mr McCormack?'

'Call me Walt, please. I have these episodes, I guess you could call them.'

'Can you describe them for me?'

'They're all a little different, to be fair.'

'Okay. So tell me about the last one you had.' Oliver glanced at Walt's medical history on the screen. There was a history of high blood pressure. Type two diabetes that was being controlled. He'd had a left knee replacement last year.

'I woke up in the night to use the bathroom. I had a wee, washed my hands and the next thing I knew, I was on the floor. I tried to stand, but my arm and leg on my right-hand side wouldn't work properly. It was like they were weak and I struggled to get to my feet. I had to call my wife to help me.'

'And when was this?' There was no mention of a hospital visit in Walt's records.

'Last week.'

'And you didn't call for an ambulance?'

'Well, no. I felt okay by the time I got back to the bedroom and I didn't want to worry my wife. Sheila? She's not well.'

'Did you bang your head when you fell?'

'I don't think so. I didn't feel any lumps or bumps and I didn't have a headache.'

'And you didn't feel dizzy or unwell whilst you were washing your hands?'

'I think I remember my eyesight feeling weird. Fuzzy. Like I couldn't focus, but it was fine when I was on the floor, because I remember noticing there was a loo roll behind the sink.'

Oliver nodded, thinking. 'How long do you think you were on the floor for?'

'Well, I went to the bathroom about two a.m., maybe just before, and by the time I got back to the bedroom it was ten past, so not long.'

'And do you think you lost consciousness?'

'I don't know.'

'Okay, well, I'd like to perform a set of observations, if that's all right with you?'

'Of course, Doctor.'

Oliver performed a series of checks. Blood pressure. Temperature. Checked Walt's ears using his otoscope to see if he had an ear infection. His vision and eye movements. Strength. Reflexes. Heart rhythm. Everything was coming back normal. Nothing out of the ordinary. 'And you say you've had a few of these episodes?'

Walt nodded. 'I had one at my daughter's a month or so ago. We'd gone to visit the grandkiddies after school.

I was just sitting in my chair, chatting to the youngest, when my daughter said I went blank for a moment.'

'Like you weren't present?'

'Exactly, but in my mind, I'd been there, present all the time.'

It did sound as though something neurological was going on with Walt, but the events had happened last week and before that, so there was nothing Oliver could do right now. It certainly sounded possible that he could be having TIAs, or mini strokes, that were not leaving any lasting deficits afterwards. 'All right, well, it does sound like something's going on. Whether you're having TIAs or not, I can't say for sure. Not without witnessing one personally or getting you into hospital within an hour of one happening. But I'd like to keep an eye on this, so why don't we meet up again in, say, a month? If you have any more then we can refer you to a neurologist for an assessment, but if not, then we can see how we go. How does that sound?'

'Sounds good to me.'

When Walt had gone, Oliver updated his records and checked his watch. Time for a cuppa. He checked Lorna's list. She didn't appear to be with a patient at the moment and so he went to her door and rapped his knuckles upon it.

'Come in!'

He opened the door and smiled. 'Making a brew. Want one?'

'Oh! You're a star! Tea, please.' She passed him her mug. It was red and had words on it that read *World's Best Doctor*.

He raised an eyebrow. 'Gift?'

'From a very grateful patient, not because I'm egotistical and bought it for myself.'

'I would never have considered that. What did you do?'

'I diagnosed her Addison's disease, when her last doctor kept dismissing her symptoms as anxiety.'

'Addison's? Good catch.' Addison's disease was an adrenal insufficiency that could cause stomach issues, weakness, weight loss and sometimes darkening of the skin.

'I can't believe her last doctor missed it. She had classic symptoms. He could have caught it with a simple set of blood tests.'

'How do you have it?'

'What?'

'Your tea. Last I remember, it was milk with one sugar.'

She smiled at him. 'It still is.'

He was glad she hadn't changed. In fact, the more time he spent with Lorna, the more he realised she was still the same woman he had always known. Only age and time had tried to change her. The self-doubt was still there.

'Coming right up.'

He quickly made them both tea, then took her filled mug back to her room and passed it to her. 'How's your morning going?'

'I've seen a nasty abscess, a case of chicken pox, one urine infection and a sore throat. How about you?'

'Back pain, migraines, an ear infection and a possible case of TIAs.'

'Who?'

'Walt McCormack.'

She nodded. 'Bless him. I hope it's not that. He's a carer for his wife, Sheila.'

'I'm keeping an eye out for him. Told him to call if he experiences anything strange.'

'Are you still up for our run tonight?' she asked, looking at him as if she'd expected him to back out.

'Absolutely. Where are you taking me?'

Lorna blushed and he had to admit he liked it. She looked beautiful. The tilt of her head, the soft flush in her cheeks. 'Through the woods and up to the lavender fields and back. It's a nice run. Slight elevation. Five kilometres. Road and trail, which is what we need to practise on.'

'Sounds perfect. I signed up for the marathon online when we got back from our meal.'

'Have you chosen a charity?'

'Yes. It's a group that supports families through infertility.' He knew they'd both had their struggles there. It seemed apt.

'That sounds great.'

'They do a lot of good work. They run a twenty-four-hour helpline that anyone can ring and just be listened to when they're feeling upset or frustrated, angry or confused.'

'I certainly remember feeling all of those things.'

'Yeah. Me too.' He'd wished he had somewhere to reach out when he and Jo had been going through all of that. But back then, there'd been nothing like that. And he'd felt as though all their friends had heard enough about either Jo's illness or their issues getting pregnant and he'd not wanted to lean on them any more than they already had. And so he'd kept a lot of his frustrations and upsets to himself. Trying to be strong for Jo. But because he'd done that, withdrawing into himself, Jo had felt him pulling away and it had simply restarted all their old arguments. The ones they'd had before she'd even begun to get sick. Her jealousy. Her insecurities rising to the surface. Accusing him of flirting with the women at work, which had been blatantly untrue. Oliver was not and could *never* be a cheat.

'Did you ever feel alone with it all?' he asked. It was the one thing he'd felt above all else. Even though he knew that there were thousands, if not hundreds of thousands of people around the globe that faced the same thing.

'Too much. Even though I had all these people focused on me. Doctors. Nurses. Specialists. Family members. All watching me. Waiting. Expecting things. For my temperature to be a certain number, for my hormone levels to be within a certain range. For my ovaries to produce a certain amount of eggs. So much focus and yet... I felt alone. Like I was failing them all when my body didn't respond the way they expected it to. Feeling less of a woman. When I failed month after month to give Craig's parents the grandchild they so desperately wanted, I felt their pity, their sympathy and, after a while, their dismissal. Like they'd given up on me and I was a failure. They'd never been my biggest fans and I felt certain they were telling Craig to look elsewhere. It took me a long time to get past the feeling that I had failed them all. I'm still not sure I have now.'

Oliver stared at her. 'You're not a failure.'

'Thank you. But when you tell yourself something, or hear it from others often enough, it's hard to get past it.'

'Then get ready, because I'm going to start telling you how amazing you are. Every single day. Until you believe it.'

She smiled at him. '*You're* amazing.'

He winked. 'But not as amazing as you.'

Her day began to feel a little better after that. Oliver's kind words, his attentiveness to her well-being, kept making her smile at odd moments during the day. She really could have done with his relentless optimism and cheerleading whilst she was going through infertility with Craig—though she wasn't sure that Craig would have loved her best friend being a guy. She might have got through it all so much easier with Oliver by her side.

She thought about their dinner together at Jasper's. How he'd walked her home afterwards to make sure she got there safely, even though she'd told him he didn't have to. 'Clearbrook isn't exactly filled with rapists and killers, you know,' she'd said.

'What about muggers and thieves? Any of those?'

'Not that I've heard of.'

'How about a really mean cat?'

Lorna had laughed. 'Now you mention it, Mr Penrose's Maine Coon has a bit of a temper!'

They'd reached her front door and she'd turned. Asked him if he wanted to come in for coffee.

He'd glanced at his watch. 'It's late and it's a school night. I'd better go. There'll be hell to pay with my boss and colleagues if I'm late tomorrow, and I need my beauty sleep.' He'd winked.

Of course. She was being too much. He'd probably had enough of her today. She would have liked him to come in for coffee. Just to spend a bit more time with him. He always made her feel better about everything.

'Regrettably, yes. Goodnight, Lorna.' And he'd leaned in to drop a kiss upon her cheek.

Thinking of that kiss now, as she waited for him to turn up for their first training run together, she couldn't help but think about how her body had responded to it. To his leaning in, to his lips pressing against her skin, the casual way his hand had rested upon her waist as he'd done so. The heat of him. The proximity of him. Her body had wanted more. Just as it had when they'd been younger. She'd always been attracted to Oliver and it looked as if that attraction hadn't gone away. Her body had still reacted to him. Her heart had beat faster. Her blood pressure had risen. Her mouth had gone dry. Her skin had tingled to his touch.

But it was probably best that they stayed just friends now. What could she offer him? They'd both wanted to be parents and she was in the thick of menopause now, whereas Oliver could still have children if he picked the right partner, which, obviously, wouldn't be her. And even though both of them were single, she didn't want to risk trying anything and it blowing up in her face. She'd dated and married a colleague before, and look at how badly that had turned out for her.

She was settled here in Clearbrook and it sounded as if Oliver was looking for somewhere to settle too. To create that longevity with patients that spanned years and decades. She couldn't put that at risk. For either of them.

They'd both been through the mill. Both had fought infertility and lost. Both divorced. Both were wary of anything new. But Oliver had a chance now to grab what he couldn't achieve before. The chance of a family. If he still wanted one, even if he would be an older father.

So, best to be just friends.

It was better for both of them.

* * *

Lorna looked amazing in her running gear. She wore a black tee, emblazoned with the name of a band he'd never heard of, and black running leggings that moulded to her form and revealed her shapely legs and rear, the latter of which he only noticed because when he arrived to join her, she had her back to him and was tightening the laces on her trainers.

He'd never seen her in anything tight before. Lorna had always hidden her shape behind baggy oversized hoodies, jeans or scrubs borrowed from the hospital. There'd been hints, of course. A stance, a turn, that had *suggested* a shapely figure beneath the clothes, but he'd never really seen it and to see it now? Well…there was certainly a reaction. He felt it, but hid it behind an ebullient greeting and a great show of arranging his water pouch in his running vest.

'Have you warmed up?' Lorna asked, once they'd both said hello and greeted one another with a kiss upon the cheek. Her skin was soft. Creamy. Her hair smelt of flowers.

'Not properly.'

'We should do some stretches before we begin. To prevent injury.'

And so he followed her lead, trying to focus on her directions rather than the way she looked and most definitely trying to not focus on how much he'd rather admire her. He didn't normally stretch, even though he knew he ought to, but now he actually enjoyed it. Once they were warmed up, they set off on their run.

Lorna led them through the village on the roads, before turning and heading onto the trail that ran through the woods, and she increased their speed to a good pace.

As soon as they left the village and they were surrounded by woods and birdsong and the scent of mulch and greenery, he felt himself relax even more. Even Lorna slowed. This place was perfect. A green canopy above, sunlight filtering through the gaps, the earth sparkling with sunbeams. He saw a squirrel dart up the trunk of a horse-chestnut tree and off to his left he even saw a small group of muntjac deer dart away through the undergrowth. Oliver couldn't help but smile.

'Doing okay?' Lorna asked as they jogged.

'Yep. You?'

'Doing great!' She gave a small burst of speed and he laughed, catching up with her, running alongside her once again. 'This feels great after sitting down in clinics all day.'

'Blows away the cobwebs for sure,' he agreed as they broke into an open glade briefly, before heading back beneath the cover of the trees. 'I don't think I've ever run anywhere so beautiful as this.'

'Just you wait.' Lorna veered away from the main trail and down to the left, following a smaller, thinner path.

He followed, trusting her, and soon he could hear the bubbling of water as Lorna brought them to a trail that ran alongside a small, babbling brook, which in turn led to a small, but ancient set of stepping stones that led across it. They slowed, crossed the water carefully and when they got to the other side, Lorna leaned forward to take deep breaths. Hands on her knees.

'You okay?'

She nodded.

'Didn't set out too hard?'

'Maybe a little. I just need a breather before we head up there.'

The trail led sharply upwards to where he could see a break in the trees and bright sunshine.

'Take a drink. Get some fluids on board.'

She followed his direction. 'Can you believe we're doing this? Sometimes, I think I'm crazy to even think I can tackle a marathon.'

'You've done harder things than this.'

'Like what?'

'Got through doctor training and God knows how many rounds of IVF, in which your body wasn't your own. You're a lot stronger than you give yourself credit for.'

'Am I?'

'Yes. You are. Come on. The secret is to just keep putting one foot in front of the other.'

They set off again, huffing and puffing up the steep track, and when they reached the top of the hill, she stopped again to admire the view. Like a reward.

They'd reached the lavender fields. A mass of purple from the lightest lilac to the darkest plum, in long, neat rows. The flowers covered the fields in perfectly straight lines, waving gently in the evening breeze, and seemed to stretch for miles. These were the famous lavender fields of Clearbrook and they were astonishingly beautiful. His nostrils filled with their scent and he couldn't help but reach out and pluck a stem from a plant and hold it to his nose. 'Wow.'

'Isn't it amazing? I come up here often, whenever I'm feeling stressed. It always helps me.'

'I can see why.' There were lots of bees here. He could see them buzzing from flower to flower, collecting pollen, and he also glimpsed a few rabbits over to the left of the field darting into the low hedgerows. He pulled out his mobile phone from his vest pocket and took a photo to remind him of this moment. 'Let's get one of us together.'

She laughed. 'Really?' And stepped to his side.

He switched the camera on his phone to face view and draped an arm around Lorna's shoulder as they took a selfie with the lavender fields behind them. They both looked happy. Healthy. Hearty. Their faces infused with colour from their run. He showed her the picture afterwards.

'Oh, I love that! Will you send me a copy?'

'Sure. I'll message you. Want to give me your number?'

She reached for his phone, tapped it in and blushed as she handed it back.

He sent her a copy and smiled, sliding his phone back into his vest pocket.

'Over there, behind the hedgerows, are the apiaries. George Shanahan, who farms these fields, keeps bees and sells the honey that they make.'

'I bet it tastes amazing.'

'You can buy it anywhere in the village and Verity uses it in a honey cheesecake that will blow your mind.'

'I'll add it to my list of things to try.'

She smiled. 'Ready to head back?'

'Lead the way.'

It seemed to take less time to make their way back to the village in that strange way that time worked whenever you headed for home and before he knew it they were back at the village, at the green where they'd met, and Lorna was leading him through some cooling-down exercises and stretches. When they were done, they both had a long drink of water. 'One run down, only a gazillion to go.'

'Have you ever run a marathon before?' he asked.

'No. Just park runs and five-kilometre races. This is a huge challenge for me. What about you?'

'I managed that half marathon I told you about and a few charity runs. I discovered it's not just about the physical training you do, the practice runs, but the mental game as well. You hit a wall out there on a long run and you need the mental fortitude to push past it and know that you can keep going, when all you want to do is stop.'

'I hear that. But at least we'll have each other for support. Should be easier than going it alone.'

'Absolutely.' He nodded. 'What are you doing for the rest of your evening?'

'Going home and having a long bath. Then I'll grab myself something to eat and watch a movie, maybe, before heading to bed.'

It sounded great. He would have loved to join her, he realised, in all of those things. And the idea of joining Lorna in the bath flashed into his brain and wouldn't go. That would certainly throw a spanner in the works. He laughed nervously and raised a hand in a goodbye, knowing he couldn't do that. Lorna was his friend. His lifelong friend. He wasn't looking for another relationship in which he had to make sacrifices and give control over to another person again. He still wanted time to be a little selfish. Control his own life, without constantly having to worry about someone else.

'Sounds perfect. Well, I'd better go. You have a good evening and thanks for today.' He leaned in to kiss her goodbye. Closed his eyes to savour the brief moment his lips pressed against her cheek and he breathed her in. But he knew he was doing the right thing in stepping away. He didn't ever want his life to be curbed by anyone else again; it was his time now and he was going to enjoy it. They already worked together all day long and now they trained together. That was enough.

Even if he was still curious about her life.

Her place would no doubt be perfect. Softly furnished. Warm. Welcoming.

The cottage that he'd rented was still filled with boxes that he hadn't unpacked. He'd not yet made the place his home—he'd been working a lot. Maybe at the weekend he could put some effort into getting rid of them, unpacking and settling into his new place?

He turned to check that she was walking back to her place. Saw her reach for her ponytail and release her wave of auburn hair, so that it cascaded over her shoulders and down to her mid-back like a fiery waterfall, glinting and catching the sunlight.

Lorna was beautiful. She'd always been beautiful.

But she didn't know it. Wasn't aware of it.

And it was something he longed to show to her.

To prove to her.

He wanted her to know that he saw her in that way.

CHAPTER FOUR

VERITY WAS BACK and she'd been seen by the hospital. 'It's cancer.' Verity sat in front of her looking pale and numb. Her normally perfect appearance a little off kilter. No make-up. An old sweatshirt with jeans. Her hair falling out of its clip. 'I never thought it would be. I'd convinced myself it was a cyst.'

'I'm so sorry, Verity. Have they said what their next steps are?'

'I've got to have all these scans. Bloodwork. I've got an appointment with an oncologist coming up, but I just feel kind of stunned all the time. Like I can't take anything in at all.'

'You're in shock. I think that's a perfectly reasonable reaction to what you've just learned.'

'Jack and I were going to go on a second honeymoon before all of this, did you know that?'

Lorna shook her head.

'We never really got a first one. I was working hard to get the business off the ground and so we were working all hours, what with the online boom we had after that article in that American newspaper about a little ole cheesecake shop in England. We'd planned this itinerary. We were going to go to Marrakech, Tunisia, North Africa and travel our way down to the south and go on safaris in Kenya and Gambia. Jack wanted to fit in Madagascar, too. We'd spent hours trolling websites and writing down what we wanted to do. But because I felt so unwell, I thought it best to get checked out first. I just figured I was a bit anaemic or something. That all I'd need was a few iron tablets and I'd be sorted. But now we're facing this.'

As Lorna listened, she couldn't help but reflect on how Jo's cancer diagnosis had affected Oliver back in the day. They'd had dreams too. Oliver had already been in medical school training to be a doctor. Jo had been at uni training to be a vet. Jo had insisted that Oliver continue to attend uni, and she remembered one night turning up to the library for a study session with Oliver and how he'd arrived looking stressed and bummed out.

'Hey, what's up?' she'd asked.

'You don't want to know.'

'Oh. Okay.'

He'd sighed, run his hands through his thick, lush hair that had not yet been peppered with grey.

'Jo's just frustrated, is all. What do they say about the seven stages of grief? I think she's in the anger stage.'

'She's allowed. Cancer has derailed all her dreams. She's had to press pause on her life and you get to carry on.'

'But I'm not though. I feel like my life has been paused, too.'

He'd told her then that Jo had trashed her little study area in anger. Thrown her textbooks and folders all over the place. Torn up some of her printed essays. How he'd told Jo that he'd take a break too, if it would make her feel better, and how she'd lost her mind at that. How she'd said that then he'd blame her for putting his life on hold too, and how she'd thrown her keyboard at the wall. How he'd walked over to her, pulled her into his arms to give her time to calm down and how she'd struggled in his arms, crying.

'It's not fair, Olly! It's not fair!'

'If you need a break, you can always stay at mine. There's room on the couch,' Lorna had suggested, blurting it out without even thinking about it.

He'd looked at her then with such longing that she'd felt something shift inside. An awareness. That maybe he'd felt something for her too. Had been seeing her in a different light, the way she'd wanted! But then a darkness had clouded his eyes and her hope had faded.

'Thanks, but me sleeping over at another girl's place won't help. Let's just get on with our studies. Learning about brain chemistry isn't going to happen by itself.'

And the subject had been closed. She'd seen and observed snippets like that through the years they'd studied together. Oliver and Jo would be fine and then there'd be a huge upset. A row. A slamming of a door. Jo would get frustrated with her treatment and the side effects. The way life had been happening for everyone else, whilst she'd felt stuck in limbo. It had been understandable and Lorna had wished she could do more for both of them, but she hadn't known how back then.

Not really. She'd just had hope. That life for Oliver and Jo would get easier. Cancer didn't affect just the person that had it, but those all around them.

She looked at Verity, wondering if she was going through the same thing. 'I know it's hard, but I'm always going to be here for you as you fight this and I know you'll fight hard. Let's arrange a standing appointment with each other. Every month, we'll meet and check in. Just to chat. To touch base. If you need me for anything other than that, you call and make an appointment—I will always be there for you, okay? I'll let the receptionists know to always fit you in.'

'Thanks, Lorna. And thank you for seeing me today.'

'No problem. If Jack needs to come in with you or by himself, tell him I'm just one phone call away, okay?'

'Thank you.'

'No problem. You take care of yourself.' She gave Verity a hug and waved her goodbye, watching her slumped, almost defeated form leave her room.

Cancer. Such a horrible, insidious disease. It wrecked so many lives. Touched so many people. Good people, who didn't deserve it. Young and old. Rich or poor. It wasn't selective. But when it happened, it did make people take stock. Made them realise what was important to them. Made them focus on what they wanted to achieve in life. Places they'd always wanted to go. Sights they'd always wanted to see. People that they needed to talk to. To clear the air. Or apologise, or simply say *I love you*.

Cancer made you realise what was important. It wasn't that you didn't know it before, it was just that the disease gave you *clarity*. Knowing you could die from it. Time became shorter. More important. More focused.

Since Oliver had started here, life had been amazing. It was great having him back in her life. Working together, running together. It was as if they'd always been together. As if they hadn't had decades of being apart. He perked her up. And Clearbrook Medical Practice was getting into a new rhythm with all of its new doctors. Lorna had spent time now with Bella and Max. They were both lovely and she actually suspected that there might be a bit of an attraction between the two of them. She couldn't be sure, but she wasn't usually wrong. They had a lot in common. Both of them single parents, with children the same age, in the same class. They lived opposite one another, having rented the two holiday cottages from Dr Mossman. Both young, working together. Living opposite one another... She'd seen the side eyes. The looks when they thought no one else was watching.

It was easier to see it in someone else than it was to see it in herself. Even though she knew she still held strong feelings for Oliver, they were both keeping each other firmly in the friend zone. The colleague and training-partner zone. It was safer that way. She couldn't be anything else to him and she wanted him to have options. Her childbearing days were over and she couldn't enter another romantic relationship. Not now. Not that she thought that Oliver would want to, but she didn't want to ever make herself small again to fit in with someone else.

He'd never been available to her before and he wasn't now either. He'd always been with Jo and so her unrequited love for him had been something she could secretly treasure and nurture without harm. It hadn't ever been going to get her hurt, because he would never have been in a position to reject her romantically. It was better to have certainty and a deep love through friendship than it was to have *uncertainty* in a relationship.

But she couldn't escape the fact that he was here and they were both single. Both divorced. Both having gone down the infertility track. They had more in common now than they had ever had.

But she was scared to love Oliver again. Scared to open that box. Because she'd been cheated on. She'd been found wanting and Craig's betrayal had made her feel small. It had happened over time. Slowly. Because in the beginning, everything had been marvellous. The early years of their marriage had been the happiest she'd ever had. She'd felt as if her life were charmed, even if she had changed bits of herself to fit in with him and his family.

They'd told her in no uncertain terms that she wasn't Craig's usual type. That he'd always dated buxom blondes, women with hourglass figures, whereas she was slim, small and a redhead. She'd dyed her hair once and Craig had been appalled and made her take it back to its natural tones. She'd always loved going to the theatre or the cinema, but Craig hadn't and so they'd never gone. She'd liked the idea of having skiing holidays, but he'd always wanted sunshine, so they'd always ended up in the Mediterranean.

But it had been little things, too. Changing her choice of drinks. Changing her make-up. Him giving his opinion on her clothes. Her nails. Bit by bit, he'd slowly chipped away at her and she hadn't noticed. Not properly. Not until after the relationship was over.

And then of course he'd had that affair with a curvy blonde and she'd felt second best. Not good enough. And that was a hard thing to get over.

She was ruminating on these thoughts when Oliver knocked on her consulting room door and brought her in her tea. He'd got into the habit. Morning break, he'd make her tea and bring it to her and they'd chat in her room. Afternoon breaks, they'd be more sociable and take their breaks in the main staffroom with Bella, Max, Priti and whichever of the nurses were free.

Lorna loved these moments and tried her very best to keep them work-related as much as she could. 'I had a patient come back in today. She's just been diagnosed with cancer.'

'I'm sorry to hear that.'

'I wish I could do more for her, but it's out of my hands now.'

'Is this the lady who owns the cheesecake shop? I spoke on the phone to her husband, Jack, yesterday.'

'Yes.'

'He said he was struggling. I keep hearing about that cheesecake place, though. I must go one of these days.'

'Yes, we should support them. I could ring and book us a table.'

'You have to *book* to go to a cheesecake shop?'

'Well, yes. It's world-renowned and popular with tourists. The place is always packed, but maybe I'll be able to get a table.'

'Maybe I should run for two charities? Split the donations?'

She smiled at him. 'I don't see why not. That's a lovely idea.'

'I could run for a breast cancer charity. It makes sense, what with my history.'

'Jo.'

Lorna sipped at her tea and decided to change the subject. 'Did you have any interesting cases this morning?'

He shrugged. 'Not really. Run-of-the-mill stuff. Back pain. Headaches. A dodgy knee. I did see a case of pompholyx.'

'Oh. Okay.' Pompholyx was a type of eczema. It caused blisters to form on the fingers and the palms of the hands and sometimes the soles of the feet. 'I've seen a couple of cases of that before. Not often, though.'

'I think it had been caused by stress. The patient had lost her job and was trying to raise her kids, whilst at the same time take care of her elderly parents.'

'The sandwich generation.'

'Mmm.' Oliver sipped at his tea. 'Where are we running this evening?'

'It's a longer run tonight, according to the training schedule. I thought we could run over to Todmore and back, though I might need oxygen assistance for that.'

'The next village over?'

'Yes. It's quite a scenic route. Mostly roads, though.'

'You'll do great. And when do we get the cheesecake?'

Lorna laughed. 'I'll give the place a call, see when a table is free.'

'Well, I never thought we'd get stopped by this.'

Oliver kept running on the spot as they waited for the farmer to transfer his flock of sheep from one field, across the road, to another field, whereas Lorna stopped, to catch her breath.

The animals filled the air with quite the fragrance as they baaed and bleated and jumped over imaginary obstacles on their way across the road, leaving a trail of mud behind. The farmer gave them both a wave of thanks as he closed the metal gate behind them and then he and Lorna were on their way again.

'Another hill? Fabulous!' she breathed.

'It's only a ten-per-cent incline. That's hardly anything,' he said, grinning.

'Doesn't make it easier.'

'You can do it!'

He could feel his leg muscles burning and his blood pumping as they neared the village of Todmore. Lorna told him, breathlessly, that it was just over the hill, about another half-mile and then they'd be there. That they could use the old stocks on the village green as a midpoint to turn around at and head back. He took a sip of his water and nodded, unable to speak right now as the hill rose before them, twisting through the trees.

He kept his eyes on the horizon that he could see, willing himself to get there, knowing that once they breached the top, it would be so much easier running down the other side, but he wasn't sure if his eyes were deceiving him or not, because he thought he could see some grey there amongst the blue sky that shone through the trees up ahead. Was that smoke? Or cloud? And what could he smell? Something metal. Something *burning*?

He glanced at Lorna to see if she'd noticed it too and realised that she was frowning as well. Somehow they picked up pace, sensing an urgency, and pushed the last fifty metres or so at speed, cresting the hill and stopping in shock at the sight of a car that had come off the road and hit a tree. Steam and something else were rising up from beneath the bonnet that was crumpled against a large tree trunk.

He and Lorna darted forward to render assistance. As

they ran to the car, he pulled his mobile from his running vest and dialled 999 to ask for ambulance and the police. He recognised this car. It had passed them just after the sheep had, blaring music with a heavy bassline. He and Lorna had tutted about the youth of today, then laughed at how they'd both sounded like old fuddy-duddies and watched the car roar up the hill, slightly jealous of the ease with which the engine took the car up, knowing it would not be as easy for them on two sets of fifty-one-year-old legs.

Lorna edged her way through the nettles and under-growth to reach the driver's door as Oliver finished re-laying the details of their location and the incident to the emergency services. Then, once that was done, he pushed further through the undergrowth, jumping a ditch to get to the other side of the car to check on any other passengers.

'Stay awake for me,' he heard Lorna say.

Glancing at the driver, he saw a young man, strapped into place behind the wheel, with blood running down his face from a large gash. The windscreen had been broken by a large protruding branch, that thankfully had come through the glass directly between the passenger and driver. Either a little to the left or a little to the right and one of them might have been impaled in their seat. In the confines of the car, he could smell alcohol and some-thing sweeter. Marijuana. The music continued to blare out from the speakers, so he reached forward to punch the buttons and silence it. The passenger, a young woman, was trembling and shaking in her seat. The two air bags had deployed, but they were both covered in small cuts and lacerations from the broken windshield.

The driver seemed to be losing consciousness, from the accident, the alcohol or drugs, they couldn't know.

'What's your name?' he asked the young woman, who had begun to cry.

'Carmel.'

'Okay, Carmel. And who is this next to you?'

'Andy. He's my boyfriend. Is he okay?' She tried to turn to look at him, but cried out in pain and stopped.

'Where does it hurt?'

'My neck and my back.'

'Okay. My name's Oliver and this is Lorna. We're both doctors. I think you drove past us on the hill.'

'I don't remember.'

'How much have you both drunk?'

'I don't know. A couple of cans?'

'Of beer?'

She tried to nod, but cried out again.

Oliver reached in to support her neck. 'I don't want you to nod or turn your head. I want you to try and keep still until the paramedics get here, okay? They should be here soon. What drugs have you taken?'

'We haven't.'

'I can smell it in the car, Carmel. What have you taken and how much?'

'Just a spliff. One. I promise. We shared it.'

'Okay. Okay.'

'Mine's drifting in and out,' Lorna said.

Oliver glanced past Carmel towards Andy. Like him, Lorna was trying to maintain Andy's cervical spine— keeping his neck in a neutral position to protect his air-way—but his head kept bobbing up and down and all the blood on his face was making it hard to see just what kind of injuries he'd received. They couldn't check his skull for a fracture, but he was developing dark circles under his eyes, which was not a good sign. It could indicate a skull fracture.

'Any blood in his ears?'

'None that I can see from this side.'

'Nor my side.'

'Just maintain that C-spine and airway. It's all we can do right now.'

He was impressed with how calm Lorna was. She'd totally switched into doctor mode. She was focused, level-headed and in control. And she was talking to Andy in a low voice, even though neither of them knew if Andy was even conscious enough to be aware of her words. But she did it anyway. Trying to sound soothing. Telling him that help was on the way and that he'd be okay.

Eventually they began to hear sirens that got closer and closer and soon enough a large yellow ambulance was pulling up on the road. It parked at the crest of the hill and put on its hazard lights, so that any traffic coming up the hill wouldn't speed up it, only to be confronted by a crash site. It would save any further accidents from happening.

Oliver told the paramedics what he knew and then he and Lorna stepped back and let them take over, placing cervical collars on Andy and Carmel. Their car doors still worked, so there was no need for any firemen to cut them out to get them placed on backboards, though firemen were now arriving, too.

'You okay?' Oliver asked Lorna.

'I'm fine. Well, apart from this little cut I got on my leg from going through that gorse bush, but I'm okay.'

He knelt to look at her leg and saw the cut. A small amount of blood had run down her calf towards her trainer. 'We'll get that sorted, don't worry.'

The first ambulance that had arrived had taken Carmel away already, as she'd been easily extracted first. Andy, as the more seriously hurt passenger, had been extracted second and now he was being loaded onto the emergency vehicle. Oliver knew he could have asked the paramedics for some gauze and saline for Lorna's leg, but they were busy sorting Andy and his injuries were more important, so he said nothing and watched them drive away. They gave statements to the police about what they'd witnessed and what Carmel and Andy had admitted to and then the police offered them lifts back to Clearbrook.

It felt strange being in the back of a police car.

But even stranger to be standing outside Lorna's cottage, watching her slide the key into the lock and invite him in.

He'd not been in before. They'd kept their relationship outside each other's homes since he'd been back in her life. They saw each other at work. They met in the village at a mutually agreed place before they started and ended their runs. Occasionally, they'd made it into a pub for a drink and their cheesecake date was coming up, which he knew wasn't a *date* per se. They'd meant to go before, but had been unable to secure a table. Verity had been so busy. Booked out, which was great for her business, whilst she'd begun her chemo.

'Come in. First-aid kit's in the kitchen.' She led him down a hallway and he glimpsed her living room and a downstairs bathroom briefly before he arrived in her kitchen. He'd heard of the term *'cottagecore'* before and, if he understood it correctly, her kitchen was a perfect example. A scrubbed stone floor, old wood units with gingham checked curtains, plates, cups and bowls stacked openly on a pastel-coloured dresser, each item mismatched, yet somehow perfectly matching its neighbours in colour or pattern. Lots of leafy green plants hung in corners: trailing ivy, spider plants, succulents. Herbs in pastel-coloured pots on the windowsill, glass jars full of cookies or flour, copper pans hanging from a rack above their heads. Something cooling on a wire rack, with a checked tea towel draped over it.

Strangely, he'd never imagined her as a baker, but now he was wondering if she was the source of all the wonderful baked goods that seemed to always be in a tin in the staffroom at work.

'Here we go. Gauze. Saline. Plaster.'

'Let me.'

'It's okay. I can do it.'

'I know you can, but isn't it always nice when someone else does it?' He smiled at her, taking the items from her hands as she pulled out a chair and sat down.

'Go on, then.' She held her leg out in front of her.

Oliver sat opposite her with a smile. He picked up her leg and placed it on his lap.

She had very nicely toned legs, but now he could see nettle stings and other scratches on her calf from pushing through the undergrowth to get to the crashed car. Sharp pink lines, one or two that had beaded blood, though not as bad as the main laceration. And now, in the light of the kitchen, he thought he could see something.

'Do you have tweezers in that first-aid kit?'

'Yes. Why?'

'There's something in the cut. A splinter? Something like that.'

Lorna passed him the tweezers and he poured some saline over the wound first, before carefully using the tweezers to grab hold of the offending item and pull it out. A thorn. 'Wow.'

Oliver smiled at her. Impressed that she hadn't flinched or made a sound. In fact, she'd been rather stoical, which she continued to be as he examined the rest of the cut to see if there was any other offending material that ought not to be there, but it looked clean. He used the rest of the saline to wash it out and then dried it with the gauze pad, until the blood stopped running, and applied a plaster. 'There you go. Good as new.'

She lowered her leg to the floor. Turning it this way and that. 'Did anyone tell you that you could be an excellent doctor?'

'Someone might have mentioned it.'

'I bet you have a wonderful bedside manner.' She smiled at him, met his gaze and then something strange happened.

It was as if the mention of the words 'bedside manner' had somehow made her imagine him standing by her bed. Being near her bed. Sitting on her bed. Because she blushed and looked away, got up and immediately began to occupy herself by picking up a tea towel and wiping an already clean surface. 'Tea?' she asked, not looking at him now.

He tried not to think of how he'd feel if he were ever close to Lorna in a bed. Would her hair look deliciously ruffled on her pillow? Would she be wearing pyjamas, or would her shoulders and arms be bare, hinting at nakedness beneath? The very idea of a naked Lorna lying on her bed and looking up at him made him glad that he was sitting down.

'Tea would be great,' he managed, trying to pull his focus back to the real world by eyeing up the array of cookbooks she had on a shelf nearby. 'You, er…do a lot of baking?' He wasn't ready to think of Lorna in such a way. He was in no hurry to rush headlong into another complicated relationship, because that was what it would be, considering their history and the fact that they worked together. Imagine if it all went wrong? He didn't want that and he didn't want complicated, either. He'd had enough of complicated.

She turned, smiling, grateful for the topic change. 'I try! I made this lemon drizzle earlier.' And she removed the tea towel from the loaf tin that had been cooling on the rack. 'It's *sans* drizzle at the moment.'

'So it's you that makes all the cakes and things at work?'

'Not always me. The cupcakes are usually Mia.' Mia was one of the receptionists.

'Who did that white-chocolate brownie thing the other week?'

'White-chocolate blondie. That was me.'

'It was delicious!'

'Thank you.' She seemed genuinely thankful for his compliment and looked as if she wanted to say something else, but, whatever it was, she stifled it and returned to making the tea.

Now it was safe to stand up, he got up and had a look out of her kitchen window. Her back garden, though small, or *bijou* as an estate agent might call it, was packed with flowers around a tiny patio and seating area.

'Did you do all of that yourself, too?' He was learning so much about Lorna. Things he didn't know. Things he'd never found out about her when they were at medical school all those years ago. Back then, she'd been so focused on her studies. On revision. She'd always had a book in her hand, or a pen and paper, making meticulous notes and researching study methods. But what had he actually known about her? She'd been good at pub quizzes, he remembered that, with a seemingly unfathomable amount of trivia knowledge. She'd put it down to the fact that her dad used to watch a lot of quiz shows on television and she would sit with him. She'd never seemed into fashion or music, but she would talk about books. Had she always baked? Did she like to garden? What else did she like?

'I did. It was an overgrown jungle when I first moved in, but whenever the weather was nice and I wasn't at work, I'd chip away at it.'

'Laying the patio? Everything?'

'Mmm-hmm. You see that large black pot there, next to the seat?'

'Yes.'

'It's a goldfish pond.'

'You're kidding.'

'No. Come and see.' She led him outside through two old French doors and into her garden and, sure enough, the large flowerpot was filled with water, plants and two perfect white and orange goldfish inside.

'And you did this all by yourself, too?'

'It's amazing what you can learn on the Internet.' She laughed at his shocked expression.

She was a marvel. 'You really are a woman of many talents, aren't you?'

'Well, I wouldn't say that,' she answered, blushing, though clearly pleased that he could see all that she had achieved.

He stared at her in amazement. She was wonderful. Beautiful. A talented and caring doctor. A runner for charity. A baker. A gardener. A DIYer. Self-deprecating. Funny. Kind. Caring. A phenomenal friend. With gorgeous eyes that looked at him now as if she loved him as much as he loved her. As a very good friend, obviously. With a wide smile that was generous and hypnotic and made him want to smile too.

The urge to pull her towards him and kiss her was so strong, so overwhelming, that he almost couldn't breathe. He felt trapped by her. By the sudden pull of her. He could imagine doing it. Reaching out for her hand and pulling her close. Feeling her body up against his. There would be uncertainty in her eyes at first, but then they would fall into the kiss and it would be amazing...

Or...she might laugh and pull her hand free and ask him, *What are you doing?* She would be embarrassed, afraid. Not sure how to handle the situation and say that she had a busy day the next day and then it would be awkward at work and their friendship wouldn't be the same and...

Oliver pushed the impulse down. Swallowed hard.

I will not kiss her. I will not ruin what we have.

They weren't young any more. They weren't foolish

and impulsive. They were adults. Grown-ups. People their age had grandkids.

'Well, this is all amazing.'

She looked around her, clearly pleased with his compliments. 'It was a lot of hard work, but when you do that, you get to reap the rewards, don't you?'

'You do.'

Lorna indicated the bench. 'Take a seat. I'll bring our tea out here.'

When she was in the kitchen, he let out a sigh and sank down onto the bench, thinking hard about life and the choices he'd made. He'd pushed to come here. Had pulled out all the stops to make sure he seemed to be the best candidate Priti could ever want for Clearbrook Medical Practice and all because he'd known Lorna was here.

What had been his *real* reason for that? What had been his intention?

To re-establish a decades-old friendship? To get his friend back?

Or had he *hoped* for something more? Without even thinking about the impact his return might have on her? Because he'd believed she was married. She might have been in a marriage that had lost the initial spark, but what if they had been comfortable? Happy? Settled, with grown-up children? Would he have caused issues in her marriage, the way Lorna had unwittingly caused problems in his relationship with Jo?

But he'd not thought of any of that. Not once. All he'd been able to think of was getting back in touch with the one woman whom he'd felt the most comfortable with. The one woman who had truly understood him. Who had seen his vulnerable side and given him her strength. If he was being honest with himself? Lorna made him feel good and he'd not felt good for a long, long time. Had he wanted her to see the new him? The free Oliver? The bachelor Oliver? And if so, why was that?

When Lorna came out with the tea and two slices of lemon drizzle cake on a tray, he smiled at her in thanks and resolved to himself that he would not use Lorna to make himself feel better. He'd suspected she might have liked him more than she'd ever let on and it had been a huge a boost to his ego to know that a woman like *her* might have had feelings for him.

But he wasn't a kid any more. He understood people. He knew how they had both been hurt by romantic relationships and he wouldn't do that to her. Or to himself. He'd never deliberately go out of his way to hurt her, of course not, but it happened in relationships. People got hurt. It was the way of the world.

He would never put Lorna in a position in which she felt uncomfortable. He would keep them strictly as friends and demand nothing more from her than that.

CHAPTER FIVE

OLLY WAS ACTING strangely since they'd come across that car accident. Lorna had felt him pull away from her and she wasn't sure why. Had he lost someone to a car accident? Were his nights haunted by bad dreams? She wanted to ask him, but she also didn't want to pry and, as his best friend, she also wanted to give him his space to work through whatever feelings he was having. He would tell her in his own time, when he was ready, but she just wanted him to know that she was there for him. She could be his comfort. His shoulder to cry on. She knew that, because she'd done it before.

So, that morning, at work, instead of waiting for him to bring her a cup of tea in their morning tea break, she made the tea and took it to his consulting room, knocking briefly on his door.

'Come in!'

Oliver was sitting at his desk, typing notes into the computer. He looked very handsome today. Dark trousers, soft pink shirt, open at the neck. He looked up at her in surprise. 'What's this?'

'I thought I'd bring you tea for a change. My last patient didn't show and I was free. I thought it might be nice to look after you.'

'That's very kind. Take a seat.' He indicated the patient's chair and she sat down with her own mug and had a brief look around the room. She'd not really been in here properly since Oliver had begun working in the practice. He had his certificates up on the wall. A couple of children's paintings and thank-you cards tacked to a notice-board. On his desk was a photo in a frame.

She leant forward, expecting to see a picture of Jo, but it wasn't. It was Oliver, with two older people that she guessed were his parents. Surprised, she sipped her tea and waited for him to finish.

His fingers moved swiftly over the keyboard. Then he hit the Enter key and turned to face her as he grabbed his mug. 'Well, this is nice. Thank you again.'

'No problem. You're always looking after me.'

He smiled and sipped his drink.

'And I like looking after you. Looking out for you. Making sure you're okay. It feels right.'

'I'm all right.'

'Are you? You seem a little…distant lately.'

'Me? No. I'm fine.'

'You're sure? I'm here, you know. Anytime you need to talk, I'm here for you.'

'I know that. What's prompted this?'

She shook her head. 'I don't know. But since that accident we came across, you haven't been the same.' She actually felt as though she missed him. Even though he was right there. It had been like the old days. The two of them against the world. He would make her laugh and she would enjoy being within his orbit. The day of the accident had changed everything. There'd been a moment afterwards, when he'd been tending to her leg and she'd felt his hands upon her, taking care of her, and she'd felt as if her heart might explode out of her chest. And then again, later, out in the back garden, she'd thought for a moment that…well, that he might kiss her, but she must have been mistaken.

She often realised much later that she had mistaken a man's desires. She'd thought Craig had loved her as much as she'd loved him and she'd been wrong. She'd thought he was still interested in being with his wife, but it had all been fake. She'd never been with anyone else, how on earth could she be qualified to know what a guy wanted? And what did she have to offer? Really? Dried-up eggs. Menopausal. Not as young as she used to be. Her own husband, who'd once loved her, had traded her in for a newer, younger model.

'Oh. Well, there's nothing wrong. Honestly.'

'You're sure?'

'Yes.' He smiled at her. A genuine smile that lit up his eyes and she felt reassured for the first time. There he was. Her best friend.

'Okay. It's a day off running today and I've managed to get us a table at Verity's cheesecake shop at six. She does late nights once a week.'

'I'm looking forward to it.'

'Great.' And yet somehow she still felt on edge. As if he wasn't talking to her the way he usually did. That he didn't sit next to her in staff meetings and give her a nudge with his elbow, so she would look at him and smile. That he didn't randomly message her with a funny joke or meme he found on the Internet. That their conversations of late didn't seem as deep as they usually did. 'Well, I'll let you get on. Busy morning.'

'You've got your Well Woman clinic this afternoon, haven't you?'

She nodded.

'I've got a patient on my schedule who's coming in because she's having bleeding after sex. Would I be able to get you to take a look if she wants to be examined?'

'You don't want to do it?'

'I'm happy to, but I know she asked the receptionist for a female doctor and you and Bella were both booked up, so they put her into my clinic for the consult, but told her that she could have a female doc do the examination if necessary.'

'Sure. No problem.' Lorna headed back to her own consulting room, sat down at her screen and stared at it. Her next patient was already here. Quentin Chiles. A man in his seventies, who was here about not being able to sleep. There was nothing in his record to state that he'd had issues before, so she was curious as to what was happening.

Quentin came in and sat opposite. 'Hello, Doctor.'

'Hello there, how can I help you today?'

Quentin sighed. 'I'm struggling, Doctor.'

'Okay, why don't you tell me a little about that?'

'I've lived alone all my life. I've never married, never had kids. It's never worked out for me, you know, and I thought I was fine about that, but I've met this woman at the church who seems wonderful. We get on great, she's a woman of God, she's kind, she's funny. A good friend, but... I think she wants more from me. Romantically, if you know what I mean, and I'm too set in my ways to be getting into all of that. I have my routines.

I'm happy. And I like her, but…she's asked me out and I said I'd think about it.

'But I'm getting stressed out about it and not sleeping very well, because if I say no, I'll hurt her feelings and I might lose my friend, but if I say yes, simply because I don't want to hurt her, when I'm not into it, then surely that's the wrong thing to do, too? I can't sleep over this. It's driving me nuts!'

She smiled at him in sympathy. This was more of a personal issue than a medical one, but perhaps he felt he didn't have anyone else to talk to about this. 'Have you considered talking to her about it? Tell her your worries? If she's as good a friend as you say she is, she'd probably be happy to listen to you.' Lorna felt for the guy and actually she didn't mind being his sounding board. Her afternoon wasn't jam-packed.

'That's not my way, Doctor. I was raised to believe that a man was a man and he didn't share his feelings with his significant other. She'll think me weak.'

'Are you sure?'

'The other thing is that she's a lot younger than me. By a good ten years and one of my good friends suggested she might be after my money. I have a good private pension and significant savings and she's always been, how to say this, less fortunate with money, if you get my drift?'

She nodded.

'The stress of it all is stopping me from sleeping and I need my sleep, Doctor. It's the one thing I look forward to of an evening.'

'Well, listening to you, it sounds like you want to say no and, if that's the case, honesty is the best policy here.

Why not sit down with this lady, tell her straight, but say you value her friendship?'

'But what if she gets upset? She seems very keen.'

'Then she'll be upset for a while, but she'll get over it.'

'Is it really that simple?'

'Absolutely! If you're the friends that you say you are and she likes you as much as you say, then I'm absolutely sure that she will understand, even if she does feel a little disappointed. She will value your friendship more and still get to have you in her life.'

He nodded. 'Maybe. I've been trying to avoid giving her an answer. Sticking my head in the sand and trying to ignore it. I haven't been to church in two weeks!'

'Then it's time to go back. This is hurting you. Stopping you from attending church, giving you stress, stopping you from sleeping. Just be honest with her. She'll appreciate it more than you know.' He definitely didn't need sleeping tablets, anyway.

He nodded. 'Thank you, Doctor. I appreciate you giving me the time today.'

'No problem. You take care.'

When he was gone, she couldn't help but think of the parallels with her own life. She had done what she had advised Quentin to do. She had spoken to Oliver. Asked him if everything was okay and let him know that she was always going to be there for him. It was what friends did.

The only question was whether she felt that Oliver had responded to her with the truth.

Verity's Cheesecake Emporium was on the high street of Clearbrook. It had Georgian windows and on display were cake stands filled with a variety of cheesecakes in highly polished glass domes. And after they'd decided to come here, they had finally got a reservation. He saw strawberries, blueberries, honey, lavender. Toffee, banoffee, crème caramel and chocolate. Sumptuous deliciousness no matter where he looked, and he finally understood why this cheesecake shop was as world-famous as Lorna had informed him.

When he opened the door, a little bell rang above his head and he was surprised to see the place was absolutely packed with people, talking, laughing, enjoying tea in delicate china cups and saucers alongside plates of all the sweet, culinary delights that this place had to offer.

He saw a hand rise and wave and he spotted Lorna over in one corner and he went over to join her, kissing her on the cheek in greeting. She'd changed out of her work clothes and wore a casual outfit of a moss-green tee shirt under loose denim dungarees. A polka-dotted hairband held her hair back from her face and she wore bright white trainers. She managed to pull off the look effortlessly and he was very impressed.

'You look great.'

In comparison he felt as if he'd not made any effort. He still wore the outfit he'd worn at work. Dark trousers. Shirt. Work shoes. Should he have gone casual too? Jeans and a tee?

'Thank you. Clothes may maketh man, but they certainly camouflage women.'

'Who are you hiding from?'

'Patients. They often don't recognise me if I put my hair up and wear something really casual.'

'Like Clark Kent. Maybe you should add glasses, too?'

She laughed and reached into a bag she had at her

side, pulling out a pair of black-framed glasses. 'Way ahead of you.'

He noticed she had a cup of tea in front of her that was now empty. She must have got here early. 'More tea?'

'They take orders at the table here.'

'All right.' He turned to get someone's attention. The girls behind the counter seemed to be whizzing about non-stop, but every now and again they looked up into the store and when they did he raised his hand and got a smile and a nod from a young girl with her hair twisted up into a messy bun.

Emilia—according to her name tag—arrived at their table, notepad and pencil in hand. 'What can I get you?'

'Two pots of tea, please.'

'Anything to eat?'

'What would you recommend?' he asked.

'Today's special is a toffee and honeycomb cheese-cake, but my personal recommendation is the limoncello and mascarpone cheesecake if you like something a lit-tle zesty.'

Oliver looked at Lorna. 'What do you fancy?'

'Do you have any of that chocolate hazelnut left?'

Emilia nodded. 'One slice.'

'I'll have that, please.'

'And I'll try the limoncello, thank you.'

'Great choice!' Emilia zoomed away to fill their order.

'She seems nice.'

'I think she's Verity's niece.'

'How is Verity doing?'

'I haven't seen her, but she's due a check-in with me in a week or so. Have you heard from Jo recently? I'm assuming she's still in the clear?'

He nodded. 'I don't hear from her often, but when she has a scan, she always emails me to let me know the results. Last time I heard from her everything was good.'

'That's great. I'm pleased for her. You both went through a really difficult time together. I guess that bonds people in ways that good times don't.'

'I guess it does.' His thoughts seemed to take him away and she wanted to pull him back.

'We went through a difficult time together, didn't we? Medical school, I mean. All those tests and assessments. Placements. All those times we worked into the early hours of the morning writing essays, losing sleep, and you had it worse than me. You had Jo to worry about.'

He laughed. 'Yeah. It wasn't a walk in the park. It would have been harder if I'd not had you. You got me through that.'

She shrugged. 'I just helped. You still had to put in the work and you had so much stress going on personally. You always impressed me with how you dealt with it. You were always upbeat. Making jokes.'

'Well, if I didn't laugh, I'd have probably cried.'

Lorna nodded. 'I always envied you, you know.'

'Envied me?'

'Absolutely! You seemed so laid-back about everything. Even with what was going on with Jo, you seemed so relaxed about it all. I wished I had that. I remember being tense a lot.'

'I was just projecting. I wasn't as relaxed as you thought I was. I remember thinking that if I just pretended that I didn't have to be stressed, then maybe I wouldn't be. I was trying to convince myself that everything was all right, when it wasn't. Some of those oncology classes were hard to get through.'

'But you and Jo...you were both very strong.'

'In public, maybe. But at home, in private...life was very tense.'

Emilia brought their pots of tea and two slices of cheesecake on a plate. 'Enjoy!' she said before disappearing quickly again.

'Well, these look great. Want to try a bite of mine?'

'Sure!'

He used his fork to slice a piece of his limoncello and raised the fork to her mouth. He tried not to think too hard of the way her lips opened and she accepted his offering, her lips sliding off the fork to consume the cheesecake.

'Mmm!' she said, her noises of pleasure doing strange things to his insides. 'Oh, my God, you forget how good the food is here. Try mine.' She made a forkful of her chocolate hazelnut and passed the fork over for him to hold.

He tasted the cheesecake, the smoothness, the softness. The bitter kick of the dark chocolate kicked into sweetness with the nutty taste of hazelnut. 'Oh, my God, that's amazing.'

'Isn't it?'

For a while the two of them were quiet whilst they devoured their desserts. But like all good things, they were gone too quickly and they were left to press their forks into the crumbly biscuit bottom to mop up all the crumbs. 'Now, if a plate of these were waiting for me at the end of that marathon we're going to do, then I think I'd get a record time,' Lorna said.

'Maybe we could dangle one at the end of a stick in front of you and you can chase it for twenty-six miles?'

She laughed. 'Sign me up! This is nice. Being here with you.'

He wanted to say the same thing, because it was true. He'd missed this. Sitting at a table with Lorna and spending time with her, only this time instead of there being a pile of textbooks in front of them, they could relax and enjoy the moment. As much as he would allow himself to relax. He didn't want to give her the wrong idea, even if his mind was making him think about her too much. 'So what do you do for fun? When you're not training for a marathon?'

Lorna shrugged. 'I read a lot. I garden. I bake. I've even learned how to sew with a machine and I made myself a pair of curtains for my bedroom. I've become a domestic goddess.'

He smiled at the image of Lorna in an apron, with sunlight streaming in behind her, surrounded by bluebirds and squirrels like some old-fashioned animation. 'That's amazing! But all of that—that's for your home. What do you do that's just *for you*? That broadens your horizons? That amazes you? How do you treat yourself?'

'I don't know. I'm not sure I ever have.'

'You haven't been travelling?'

'I've always been working.'

'You've never thought to take some time off and go and see the world?'

'No, I guess not. For a long time Craig and trying for a baby were my world. After I learned of the affair, healing myself by working was my world. What about you? Have you travelled?'

He nodded. 'I didn't realise how small my world had become until I'd travelled. I've watched the sun rise over the Great Pyramids of Egypt. I've ridden through a desert on a camel. I watched orangutans in Borneo. Swam with sharks off the coast of Australia. Watched the sunset in Tokyo. Millions of miles, through many, many countries and still all I wanted to do was come home.' He smiled ruefully. 'We're small creatures, with small lives and endless worries and concerns. We do what we can do to survive it.'

'Well, your travels sound amazing and I, for one, am glad you came home. This *is* home now, I take it?'

He made a show of looking around him. At the people at the next tables. Out of the window at Clearbrook village and finally back at the woman sitting opposite. 'It is.'

She beamed. 'Good. I hadn't realised how much I'd missed having you around, you know? We may have just started out as study buddies, but I really came to depend on you and, though I was excited to strike out into the world and try and make it on my own, I'm glad that we've found each other again.'

'Me too.' He'd not really thought too much about what Lorna had got out of their relationship. He'd known and understood what he'd got from it, but what had he given her in return? Some jokes? Comradeship? Someone else to bounce ideas off? Someone who had the same goals to share space with?

He'd known that she'd liked him, in spite of the fact that he'd been dedicated to Jo and nothing would ever have happened between them. Because he'd also known, deep down inside, that he *could* see himself with her. That he'd often wished that his life had been different and that when Lorna had come into his life, he could have been with her instead. He'd told himself it would be simpler. Easier. A relationship with Lorna would not have had cancer woes and chemo side effects. It would have been normal. And then he'd felt guilty about that.

And now here they were, early fifties, single, living in the same village, both divorced, both having gone through a fertility journey, both still really keen to renew a friendship that they'd started all those years ago.

The question was…how would it finish?

'So you're here for your six-week mother and baby check?' Lorna smiled.

Yasmin Groves was with her baby daughter, Daisy, who was just over six weeks old. Her special baby. A child she'd conceived after a stillbirth. This was the woman who had inspired Lorna to run for a stillbirth charity.

'Yes, that's right.'

'And how do you feel everything's going?'

'Great! Yeah. I could do with more sleep, but I guess every new mum says that, don't they?'

Lorna laughed. 'Most do, yes.'

'I think it's because I'm always up checking on her. We've got a monitor and all of that, but still, with what happened…'

Lorna nodded, understanding completely. 'Okay, let's take a look at you, Mum, first, whilst Daisy is still asleep and then we'll give her a look-over. Is that okay?'

'Yep.'

She glanced at her notes on the computer. 'So, it

says here you had a natural delivery with a second-degree tear.'

'Yeah.'

'Any problems going to the toilet?'

'No, not really. It stung to begin with, but that's stopped now.'

'Okay, and are you breastfeeding?'

Yasmin nodded.

'Okay, let's check your blood pressure.' Lorna wrapped the cuff around Yasmin's arm. She'd had a couple of episodes of high blood pressure during her pregnancy, but her reading today was back to normal. 'That all looks good. How are you managing with Daisy? Looking after her okay? Any problems?'

'She has a bit of colic sometimes, but mostly she's really good and doesn't cry much. Except at night.'

'Okay, and are you still bleeding?'

'No, that stopped a couple of days ago.'

'All right, well, I'd like to examine you, if that's okay? Check the stitches have healed well. If you'd like to go behind the curtain, I'll go get a chaperone.' Lorna managed to grab Bella. She explained the situation and Bella came in and introduced herself to Yasmin through the curtain.

'Ready.'

Lorna adjusted the light so that she could check the stitched area in the perineum. Yasmin had healed very well and Lorna couldn't see any reason as to why there might be any future problems. 'Have you abstained from sex since the birth?'

'Absolutely, yes! I haven't let Jase come near me, much to his dismay. Having these things blow up to twice their size hasn't helped.' She indicated her breasts.

'Well, everything looks okay down there and I'm giving you the all-clear for that, but don't feel like you have to have sex until you're ready and, when you do, go gently.'

Yasmin nodded.

'Are you happy for me to check your breasts?'

'Go ahead.'

Because Yasmin was breastfeeding, it was important for Lorna to check that her breasts and nipples were fine. First time breastfeeders could experience some discomfort and if baby wasn't latching correctly, it could sometimes cause damage to that sensitive area. 'Daisy latching on okay?'

'I think so. We did visit a lactation consultant right at the beginning and that helped with positioning.'

'Well, you look great, so why don't you get dressed? Thank you, Bella.'

Bella smiled and said goodbye and slipped from the room.

'Is that the other new doctor?'

'One of them, yes, though they've been here a few weeks now.'

'I met the other one the other day in the village. The guy? He's handsome.'

Lorna didn't want to ask her which one. Both Max and Oliver were handsome. So she simply smiled and waited for Yasmin to come out from behind the curtain before they could assess the baby.

'So, how is Daisy? Sleeping through the night?'

'Sometimes.'

'Feeding okay?'

'Yeah. I was alarmed at how often she was feeding to

begin with, but I think it was a comfort thing, so I got her a dummy, which has been better.'

'Lots of wet nappies?'

'Plenty. And why did no one tell me about the way poo changes colour in the beginning?'

Lorna smiled. 'Excellent. That all sounds normal. Does she follow your face and voice?'

'She seems to.'

'Okay, can you get her undressed for me and I'll perform a physical examination?'

She waited for Yasmin to undress her baby. Daisy wasn't fond of the idea of being undressed and began to cry as she was stripped down to her nappy.

'Oh, it's okay. It's okay.' Lorna picked the baby up and swayed a little with her to reassure her, enjoying the feel of a baby in her arms. These were always the best moments of a mother and baby check for her. When she got to be with the baby and imagine how her own life might have been different if she had fallen pregnant with a child. Would she have been a single mother because of Craig's affair? Or would she still be in a marriage, unaware of her husband's infidelity? Yearning for a child of her own made these moments special, when she could imagine, no matter how briefly, how things might have been.

Daisy gazed at her with wide blue eyes, her little tongue poking out of her mouth as she made a small noise. She was a beautiful baby and Lorna felt a longing ache. A grief for something she had never been given. A grief for something that had been stolen away from her.

All the baby's observations were normal. She had all the right reflexes, her chest and abdomen sounded good. Her umbilicus had healed well and her hips had good flexion and movement. 'She looks great.' Lorna handed Daisy back to her mum and told her she could dress her again. 'Well, I'm happy to sign both of you off as doing brilliantly.'

'Great! These first few weeks have been nerve-racking.'

'That's understandable, considering what you went through. You're booked in to have her first immunisations in two weeks.' Lorna checked her future appointments.

'Thank you.'

She waved Daisy and Yasmin goodbye, watching as Yasmin manoeuvred the pushchair through the doorway and out into the corridor. As she did so, she spotted Oliver saying goodbye to a patient. He stepped back so Yasmin could pass and she watched him look down at the baby and say hello.

Yasmin paused, politely, so Oliver could converse with Daisy in a baby voice and Lorna smiled, watching him. He would have made a good father.

What would their lives have been like if she'd married Oliver rather than Craig? Would they have still struggled with fertility? There was no medical reason why Oliver couldn't have kids and though she'd been diagnosed with a hostile uterus, it might have worked with him.

Maybe together they might have been amazing parents with a couple of kids by now? Maybe even thinking about grandchildren?

As Yasmin left, he turned and caught her gaze, smiling at her. 'She was beautiful. Did you see her?'

Lorna nodded. 'I did.'

And I held her in my arms and ached for all the babies I lost.

She'd also lost him. For a time. Yet now she had him back. Maybe they could be more than they were before? Having him here in Clearbrook brought all of the old feelings back.

Maybe Oliver could bring her happiness?

But she was too old to have babies now. He could still have them if he found someone a little younger. But it hurt to think that she could lose him to another woman.

That she had nothing to offer.

'You ever think of having kids?' Max asked Oliver.

Having a baby had been an obsession for Jo after her cancer treatment. She'd had her eggs frozen before she began chemotherapy and when she'd decided that she was ready to start trying for a child after it all, she'd been through so much—*they'd* been through so much—that he'd agreed. There had to be something good at the end of all of that.

Oliver had always wanted kids and he'd hoped for them after Jo's treatment was over. He'd always thought he would make a great father. Watching them grow. A little bit of him, maybe seeing his own eyes in someone else's face, noting similar mannerisms in his little miniature self. Wondering if they'd take after him or their mother more. Making them laugh, tickling their tummies, playing with them outdoors or taking them to after-school clubs, watching them become a person of their own and hopefully guiding them towards good life decisions.

There'd been many good days with Jo and he'd clung to those, telling himself that the reason their relationship had always been so strained was because of the cancer. But when the cancer had gone, they could move forwards.

What better way to do that than to cement their relationship with a baby?

IVF had been incredibly difficult. It had made their life all about Jo's health, all over again. Just as many tests and scans. Just as much bloodwork. Just as many needles and procedures, it seemed. The ovary hyperstimulation in one cycle had really knocked Jo for six. They'd stopped IVF for a bit to give her chance to recover, even though Jo had not wanted to wait, but Oliver had insisted upon it. For both of them. Of course, Jo had hoped that somehow, miraculously, she would get pregnant naturally in the meantime, even though that had been virtually impossible.

The stress of it all came back to him, every time he got to hold a baby in his arms, or stop to admire one. The drive to procreate, to have a child of their own, a symbol of their love, had been the thing to finally tear them apart. The resulting failure had caused recriminations and bitterness and so, since then, he was very often in awe and felt admiration and a little bit of envy for those who managed it so effortlessly.

But he'd given up on that dream now.

He caught sight of Max's face and realised he must have been daydreaming for a little while. 'Once, but it never worked out that way. What about you? Did you ever think you'd have more than one?'

'Before I met Anna, my wife, I kind of imagined I'd have two, maybe three, but I guess life teaches you to manage your expectations in new and cruel ways sometimes.'

'It certainly does. I was sorry to hear about what happened with your wife.'

Max acknowledged his sympathy with a nod. 'You faced cancer with your wife, too. Jo, wasn't it?'

'Yes.'

'And she's okay now?'

'I suppose. We don't really keep in contact except for Christmas cards, and she'll email me whenever she gets scan results.'

Max nodded. 'And you and Lorna? Friends for ever, I hear?'

Instantly, he smiled at the thought of her. 'Until death do us part.'

Max raised an eyebrow. 'Isn't that usually a vow said in marriage?'

As if summoned, Lorna entered the staffroom at that moment and smiled at them both. 'Hello. Max, did you get my email about Stella's results? They came through to me, rather than you.'

'I did, yes—I've given her a call to come in and see me about them.'

'Great. What a day, huh? I'm ready to go home, put my feet up and relax in front of the television with a bowl of popcorn.'

'No training tonight?' Max asked.

'Rest day,' said Oliver, smiling at Max, but his companion's attention was stolen by the arrival of Bella into the staffroom. Max excused himself and got up to go and talk to her.

Oliver went over to Lorna and nodded at the other two doctors. 'Think something's brewing there?'

Lorna raised an eyebrow. 'Since day one! They can't keep their eyes off one another.'

'Do they know it?'

'I'm not sure.' She gave a small laugh and glanced at him, her eyes twinkling with amusement. 'But they seem a nice couple, don't you think?'

'They have a lot in common.'

'So do we.'

Oliver smiled, but he felt afraid of what it would mean if he began to think of Lorna as a romantic partner. He'd be lying if he said he'd never thought of it. 'But we have decades of history. I'm not sure I'd want to be in the dating pool these days.'

'No? Why not?' She sounded curious. A little hurt.

'It sounds exhausting and I only have enough energy these days for work and practice runs with my marathon partner, who, let's face it, rewards me greatly with a large variety of baked goods.'

Lorna smiled. 'She sounds like a keeper.'

'She is.' And without thinking, he swooped in and dropped a kiss upon her cheek.

When he realised what he'd done, he felt himself colour as Lorna herself was too. He looked around them to make sure no one had noticed, but Max and Bella were too absorbed with one another to notice anything he and Lorna might have done. So he simply smiled. 'I guess I ought to head for home. Still have some boxes to unpack.'

'Need any help?'

'No, it's fine. Besides, you have a date with a bowl of popcorn and I wouldn't want to be the man to get in the way of that.'

'I'm happy to help if you'd like. I'm actually quite nerdy, would you believe? I love sorting and organising.'

He had a flash of memory. Of calling round to her new student digs once. Her old place had been closed due to a mould problem and she'd been assigned a new room. Her door had been propped open by a box, music had been blaring and she'd been arranging furniture and her possessions. Well, that had probably been the intention to begin with. But she'd been standing there, her back to him, not knowing he was there, headphones on, a wire trailing over half the room to a big old stereo and she'd been dancing, one hand on each headphone as if she were absorbed in the music. He'd stood there and watched her move, lost in the music, and he'd been a little hypnotised by the sway of her hips and the soft smile on her face.

She had given him so much and she wanted to help him now, too. Was that so wrong? 'Well, I guess I wouldn't say no to an extra pair of hands, if you really mean it?'

'Sure! I'll go home and change and then come round to yours.'

'I'll cook.'

'Perfect.'

CHAPTER SIX

SHE'D NEVER BEEN in Oliver's house before. She'd seen his student digs briefly once. She'd met him at the door and had only glimpsed inside and seen posters on the wall of some rock band and a messy bed. She could remember good-naturedly teasing him about tidying up, but, to be fair, he'd hardly ever been at his digs. He'd slept there, but not much else. He'd always been round at Jo's.

So knocking on his door this evening, brandishing a tub of apple turnover pastries that she'd baked the day before, made her curious and excited. Would he still be messy? What would his house, his choice of furnishings, his style, tell her about him?

When he opened the door to greet her, the first thing she noticed was that he'd changed into a pair of dark jeans and a black fitted tee. His hair looked damp and he was barefoot. And smelt great! He looked as if he were about to shoot a men's aftershave commercial.

'Hey, come on in.'

'I brought pastries for dessert.' She raised the tub.

'Great.' He stepped back to let her pass, dropping a kiss upon her cheek.

The hallway was dark enough to spare her blushes, but light enough to show the walls painted in a soft, light grey. There were two framed pictures on the walls—a graphite drawing of lions and another of elephants.

Oliver led her to the kitchen, where pots were bubbling away on the stove. It was a modern kitchen with white units and shiny countertops. The small round kitchen table was glass, with a succulent in a pot sitting in the middle. The kitchen screamed minimalism. Everything had its place, she noticed, when he reached into a cupboard and all the bottles, jars and cans inside were perfectly ordered. She was impressed. Not untidy any more...

'I'm cooking lobster linguine. Is that all right?'

'Great! Where did you get lobster from in Clearbrook?'

'I ordered it online.' He laughed. 'Can't go wrong with a bit of lobster tail. Take a seat. Drink?'

'Whatever you're having is fine.'

'I was just about to open a cheeky Sauvignon Blanc, but if you're driving...?'

'I walked here. Wine is fine.'

He opened the slimline wine cabinet and pulled out a bottle, which he opened and poured two glasses, handing her one. 'Thought we'd eat first before tackling those boxes, if that's okay?'

'Sure. How many are there?'

'About ten left over from the move. I've got most of the important stuff out now, so I'm sure this is just stuff from the old attic space, but it's worth going through to see if there's anything I can get rid of or donate.'

She nodded and sipped her wine. It was dry, yet fruity, leaving notes of citrus, tropical fruits and gooseberry. 'Mmm. This is lovely.'

He clinked her glass with his. 'To unpacking memories.'

'Unpacking memories.' She took another sip. 'You really have no idea what's in those boxes?'

'Nope. I just emptied the attic and they'd been in there for years.'

'Well, maybe I should let you open them first. Just in case, you know.'

'In case of what?'

'In case there's anything private or embarrassing in them.'

Oliver turned to look at her. 'Actually, that's a good idea. I did misplace that blow-up doll once...' He smirked.

Lorna smiled. 'Funny. You're a funny guy.'

He laughed and gave the pasta a swirl with a wooden spoon. 'This has got about five minutes. Let me give you the whistle-stop tour of the place.'

Holding her glass, she followed him around. The rest of the cottage was pretty much like the kitchen. Modern. Clean lines. No clutter. Everything perfectly organised. Even the books on his bookshelf had been arranged by colour.

'Who taught you to be so neat?' she asked.

'I taught myself.'

'Not Jo?'

'No. For the majority of our marriage, Jo was either resting in bed or sleeping on a couch. Her treatments made her exhausted and in the years in which she *seemed* well, she never really wanted to waste her precious time alive with simple, boring tasks like cleaning or organising, so I did it. We had enough chaos in our lives with health matters, without the house being a tip, too. The clarity of being in a clean space helped calm my mind when our world was being ripped apart.'

'I get that. When *we* were trying for a baby and going through IVF, it seemed all that mattered were my hormone levels, the thickness of my uterine lining, my blood results and whether that damned test would be positive or not. Everything else would fall by the wayside. We tried to be disciplined. Look after ourselves. Eat well. Keep the house right. But we were both working and busy and tired when we got home… I remember saying clearly that I wished we had a cleaner. Maybe I should have hired you?' she said with a smile as he led her up the stairs towards the bedrooms.

There were two bedrooms in this cottage. One was a small box room. Oliver had a desk in there, with a computer and a chair and a small bookcase with a pot plant on it. Then he led her to his bedroom. She stood in the doorway and looked around.

'We'd have had a lot to talk about if we'd known each other whilst we were each married, don't you think?'

'Heck, yeah.' She imagined what it would have been like to have sat down at night and shared her pain over IVF with Oliver. He would have got it. He would have understood. Craig had been there for her, of course he had, but, with hindsight now, she could sense that he'd been distracted. As if he'd been one step removed from all that had been going on, which he had been because he'd always been in another room texting his girlfriend. She'd thought he'd stayed up late at night, after she'd gone to bed, because the stress of the IVF had made it so he couldn't sleep, but he'd really been having late-night conversations with another woman he'd been trying to keep sweet.

If Oliver had been there, if he'd known Craig, would

he have liked him? Would he have noticed that something was awry with their relationship? Would he have tried to warn her? Or had a quiet chat with Craig, man to man? She liked the idea of him trying to protect her.

Oliver's bedroom was neat and uncluttered like the rest of the cottage. He had a double bed, with a soft, white duvet and cushions and a counterpane in a soft cream. A book sat on his nightstand, next to an alarm clock. There was a fluffy rug on the floor and stacked up against one wall were the last few boxes that she was here to help with.

'This is nice,' she said, trying not to imagine Oliver lying in the bed, half naked, with beckoning eyes. It was an image that was difficult to get out of her head.

'Thanks.' He glanced at his watch. 'Better get back to that lobster tail. We don't want to overcook it.'

No. That would be bad. Just as bad as imagining your best friend naked. She forcibly pushed the image from her mind and followed him down the stairs, trying not to notice the trimness of his waist, or the way the jeans moulded to his body. She knew he had good legs. She'd seen them when they'd gone on their training runs. He had great thighs. Strong. Powerful. Covered in a fine smattering of dark hair. Nothing too thick. He didn't look like a werewolf or anything.

As they reached the kitchen, he poked the lobster and declared it ready to serve.

They sat in the lounge to eat their lobster linguine. There was a film on the television that played low in the background as they chatted about their day and once Oliver had refilled their wine, they headed back upstairs to tackle the boxes.

'Okay, let's get this done.'

They'd brought up some bin bags and a few spare boxes—one labelled 'Recycle', one labelled 'Keep', another labelled 'Charity Shop'.

'Should we work on one box together or do one each?' she asked.

'One each? Might work quicker?' he suggested.

'Okay.' She pulled a box towards her. There was nothing written on the outside and the tape that held it together was so old, it tore off easily. Opening it up, she found a box of paper and card, with some stamps and ribbons inside.

'Ah, Jo's card-making phase,' Oliver said. 'She wanted something to do when she had no energy to go out and she thought it would save us money if she made her own. It didn't.' He smiled.

'Charity shop?'

He nodded.

She emptied all the things from the old box into the new one and then reached for another box. This one had writing on the side. It simply said 'uni'. Intrigued, she opened it up as Oliver worked his way through a box of books.

The box had a couple of old textbooks in it. Medical texts, obviously, but there was a photo album in there, too. She opened it up and smiled.

There were photos of the two of them from when they'd been friends before. It felt strange to be looking back at their youth. Oliver with no silver in his hair and no glasses. Her hiding in a big grey sweatshirt, holding an A4 folder to her chest as Oliver pulled a funny face behind her, his two fingers making bunny ears behind her head.

'What's so funny?' Oliver asked.

'Us. Look.' She turned the album round so he could see.

'Wow.'

There were pictures of their other classmates. Pictures taken in lecture theatres, labs. One of them all dressed in white coats and face masks. There was even a series of pictures from that time they'd done Halloween together and they'd all dressed up as zombie doctors and nurses and covered themselves in prosthetics and fake blood. She remembered that night. Lorna had actually fallen over and cut her knee for real and Oliver had used saline from the IV drip he'd been pushing around to clean it and then ripped more of his torn shirt to mop up the real blood and make sure she was okay.

'I remember thinking how you'd be a good doctor, even then. You had an amazing bedside manner.' The fact that they were now sitting beside his bed was not lost on her.

She turned more pages, got lost in even more memories and when the photos ran out, she noticed that there were other items in the slots where the photos ought to sit. A cinema stub ticket. A dried yellow flower. Odd. She looked at the stub. Realised it was for a film that she'd seen at the cinema with Oliver. A comedy to cheer him up.

But the flower?

'What was this?' she asked softly, touched that he had kept the cinema ticket stub.

Oliver looked over and smiled. 'You don't remember?'

She shook her head.

'It had been a really hot day. It was lunchtime. You'd been sitting out on the grass absorbing a few rays. You made a daisy chain as we were talking and I asked you if you could do one with buttercups. You said buttercups were for seeing if you loved butter and you plucked it from the grass and held it under my neck. Said I did and then passed me the flower.'

'And you kept it?' That was sweet.

'Of course. You gave it to me.' He looked away awkwardly. A little embarrassed.

He'd kept the buttercup. The cinema stub. The pictures in the album were of them. A few others, too, but mostly them. Oliver had cherished these items. They'd meant something to him.

'Keep?' she asked, feeling emotional at the thought of how he had kept the little things. To hold onto the memories that they'd had together.

'Keep.' He stared back at her. And for a moment they were both lost in *what-might-have-been*.

She felt a heat bloom begin in the centre of her chest and her first thought was, *Great, what a brilliant moment to experience a hot flush*, but it didn't rise up her neck and into her face the way her usual hot flushes did. This one sat in the centre of her chest and slowly worked its way *down*, making her aware of her entire body. An arousal, as her whole body became alive with anticipation.

She'd not wanted anybody physically for a long, long time. With Craig, sex had become something that was supposed to be functional but that didn't work. In the end, it had felt like something she ought to do. A responsibility to keep connected with her husband. Any conception had been going to take place in a lab and after each implantation they wouldn't sleep together, just in case. In the end, they'd got used to not sleeping with one another at all. So she'd stopped thinking of herself as a sexual being and then, after realising the betrayal, she'd been glad they hadn't been intimate for a long time.

But here it was. Those stirrings of lust and desire that she'd thought long gone. Not dormant at all, but alive, well and raging. For Oliver.

And he was looking at her in a way that made her think that perhaps he felt the same. They'd both had physicality removed from their relationships and to experience it again, to be aware, to want, to need, to *yearn* for touch, was a delicious sensation. And to experience it with Oliver was indescribable and as their fingers brushed as she passed him the pressed flower, they maintained the connection. As if neither of them wanted to part, as if the electricity that was racing up and down her arm was also racing around him and, together, they made a circuit. Apart, separate, they were nothing, but touching? Connected? They came alive! Fizzing and sparking and the intensity of it was so powerful!

He cleared his throat and looked away. Pulled his hand back. Clearly uncomfortable.

She was upset that she felt this way for her best friend in the whole world and yet, clearly, he did not feel the same way. She'd thought they'd had a moment over the buttercup. She'd thought they'd connected, shared a mutual recognition of desire, because she'd thought she'd seen something in his gaze, too. But he had pulled away. Now he was getting to his feet, suggesting he ought to fetch more wine as their glasses were empty.

When he'd gone downstairs, she let out a breath and

ran her hands through her hair. Maybe it was for the best? Because what if, after all this time, they were incompatible as partners? Maybe all they were destined to be was good friends and nothing more?

If I got together with him, he'd not be able to have children ever. And maybe I just imagined that moment? Seeing and feeling what I wanted to see? What I wanted him to be feeling?

She could not take the chance for him to have kids away from him. He deserved happiness. He deserved to find it and start a family, whilst he still had time and energy.

Reverently, she placed the album into the Keep box, broke down the old one so that it laid flat, ready for the recycling bin. She moved on to another box.

You can't lose your friend.

Downstairs in the kitchen, Oliver splashed cold water onto his face, then stood for a moment, bent over the sink, trying to rein in his feelings.

He'd forgotten about that photo album. About the cinema stub and the buttercup. Why had he kept that flower? It was just a buttercup! Hardly a rose or anything, a true flower of romance. Most people would consider a buttercup a weed. But he'd kept it, because in that moment back then, when Lorna had leaned in towards him, smiling, holding that flower next to his throat, he had felt something so strongly for her that he'd almost had to hold his breath. How she'd met his gaze, laughed and said, 'You *love* butter.' And she'd handed it to him, before glancing at her watch and running off to catch her next lecture, completely unaware of how much that moment had mattered to him. Those were the sorts of moments he'd wanted with Jo and to be having them with someone else had made him feel so...

That very same morning, he'd had a row with Jo. She'd accused him of spending too much time with Lorna. She'd yelled that he'd rather spend time with his class-mate than he would with her, his girlfriend. He'd known it was insecurity and he'd felt guilty that he'd caused her that. Jo had been struggling since the diagnosis of her breast cancer at such an early age, knowing she would have to have a mastectomy. She'd struggled with her idea of losing herself as a woman. He'd tried so hard to be supportive, but it had been difficult.

It had absolutely not been true that a mastectomy would make her any less of a woman. A woman was more than a pair of breasts. He'd not cared whether she'd had them or not—what he'd truly wanted was for her to be happy and healthy. It had been her character and her ability to make him laugh that had made him view Jo as a girlfriend. And they'd been together so long at that point.

But he'd begun to feel so alone. Jo had been down for months. He hadn't been able to touch her without her saying that he was pressuring her and, sure, it had probably been wrong for him to have felt something as Lorna had leant in with that buttercup, laughter in her eyes, but he hadn't been able to help it. The cancer had made him feel trapped. He'd been trying to be honour-able and gentlemanly by supporting Jo no matter what, but their moments together had been swathed in test re-sults and tumour markers and they hadn't been getting time to make happy memories and so when Lorna had leaned in like that...

It was a happy memory and, selfishly, he'd wanted to keep it.

He'd felt relief when she'd run off to a lecture, leaving him sitting there on that grass holding a buttercup. He'd wanted to remember the way Lorna had made him feel alive and he'd pressed the flower into a textbook, knowing he'd wanted to keep that moment for when things got tough.

It had been vanity. Seeing Lorna uncover it just now and the way she'd looked into his eyes after? He'd felt a surge of hormones, felt a need for Lorna in a way he'd been trying to control for some time now...

Oliver had played enough games. He'd been on an emotional roller coaster for too many years, way longer than he ought to have been. It was a ride he should have got off years ago. He didn't want to play games with Lorna.

Because he wasn't sure if he would win.

Or lose.

So, he would just have to remain her friend.

They were walking her home. Oliver had said it was the least he could do after she'd helped him finish unpacking those last few boxes.

They walked in a companionable silence through Clearbrook and Lorna's mind was filled with all that she had learned. She'd thought she was the one with hidden feelings for Oliver when they were younger. She'd thought that he had only ever seen her as a study partner and then a good friend. A best friend.

But what if she'd been wrong? What if Oliver had seen her as more than that?

Had he felt trapped in his relationship with Jo? She knew they'd had a few sticky moments, but she'd put that down to the stress of their situation. Cancer was a lot to grapple with at such a young age.

Her mind was awhirl with thoughts and unanswered questions. 'Can I ask you something?'

Oliver looked at her. Smiled. 'Sure. What's up?'

'It's about when we were at med school.'

He sucked in a breath. 'Okay.'

'Did you ever…?' She let out a small laugh, unable to believe that she was actually going to be brave enough to ask this question. 'Did you ever wonder what your life might have been like if you'd *not* been with Jo?'

He nodded. 'Of course. I think everybody at some point thinks about the road they didn't take. Or about how, if they went back in time, they'd make different choices with the benefit of hindsight. Why? What would you have changed?'

'Wow. Okay. Well, sometimes I think that… I wished I had been braver and spoken up more.'

'Okay.'

'That I would have been more aware of what Craig was up to and confronted him about it earlier instead of going through that whole pantomime.'

A pause. 'Oh.'

'Sometimes, I feel like I've been much too passive in life. Letting other people make my big decisions. So… yeah, I'd change that.' She laughed nervously, her face red and hot. 'Be more assertive.'

'I've thought about what it would have been like if we'd known each other when we were both facing the struggles that we did in trying to have our own families.'

'Oh. You have?' Now she truly didn't know what to say. She'd thought of this so often. She'd felt jealous of Jo having Oliver by her side as she'd been going through it. And she'd not felt proud of herself for having that emotion, or for thinking less of Craig at the time, because her own husband had been there for her physically at each appointment. He'd listened to her when she'd cried. Soothed her when she'd been sad. But had she truly felt that he'd been by her side one hundred per cent? No, she hadn't.

Especially in that last IVF cycle. That was the cycle where everything had slowly begun to fall apart and she'd felt his distance; she'd lain on those examining beds alone. Craig had sat on the opposite side of his room, tapping away at his phone. Had he been texting his mistress even then? He'd always denied it, but why should she believe him? He'd lied to her in the most terrible way possible.

'Do you ever think about...' she paused to take in a deep breath '...what it might have been like if we—?' She wasn't brave enough to finish her own sentence. She blushed madly. But then she thought about what she'd just said, about wishing she'd been braver, and she just blurted it out. 'If we had become a thing?'

Oliver sighed and looked down, formulating an answer.

His reaction made her nervous. As if he was trying to work out how to let her down gently and instantly she felt bad. She should never have asked. Never have shared.

'I think the best thing back then was for us to remain friends more than anything else. Don't get me wrong, Lorna, I did think about it. Of course I did! Every day that I saw you I had the feelings, but... I think it's best that we remained friends back then and I think it's best that we remain friends now, because I don't want to lose you again. I lost you for over half my life and, now that we're together again, I don't want to risk trying something that might make me lose you.'

Lorna stared back at him, feeling tears burn in her eyes at his words.

She simply nodded and said, 'Maybe you're right.'

CHAPTER SEVEN

THE NEXT MORNING, Lorna had a couple come into her surgery to see her together. Pauline and Avery Goodman were both in their nineties and were both struggling with getting rid of a cough.

She welcomed them both in. Avery walked slowly with a stick and his wife held onto his arm as they both ambled in.

'Please take a seat. It says here on your call note that you're both struggling with a cough, is that right?'

'Yes.' Pauline nodded as they both sank into chairs opposite. 'It won't go away. Avery seems worse than me. He coughs a lot at night and so neither of us are sleeping very well.'

'What sort of cough is it? Dry? Chesty? Are you producing any phlegm?'

'Sort of chesty, we think. Neither of us has sore throats, but we think it started as a cold, but the cough just won't go away.'

'Okay. Well, I'll do some observations and listen to both your chests and we'll decide on a treatment plan from there, is that okay?'

'Of course, Doctor.'

Lorna began her examination of Pauline first. Her

blood pressure was a little high, but nothing too concerning. Probably due to the doctor's visit and the walk in from the waiting room, and clearly she was concerned and stressed about her husband. Her chest actually sounded clear and she had no temperature either, so Lorna wasn't too worried about her.

Her husband, Avery, was a different story.

He had a low fever, his chest rattled, and he was clearly struggling to breathe. What he needed more than anything was a chest X-ray.

'I want to refer you for a chest X-ray, Mr Goodman. What with your fever and your breathlessness, I think you need to be looked at in hospital.'

'Oh, dear,' he managed.

'If it's all right with you, I'm going to call the hospital right now.'

Avery nodded, but clearly he was weary even from just speaking. He had no history of asthma, so that was good, but it was a worrying sight to see him breathing so badly. They shouldn't have left it so long to come in.

She messaged Reception and asked them to order her an ambulance to take Avery in. Normally, she would have asked Pauline and Avery to make their way in to hospital on their own, but Avery's breathing was so strained, Lorna wanted him to be with the right people en route in case things suddenly took a turn for the worse. His heart and his lungs were struggling to do their job and, at his advanced age, it was a huge worry.

'Will he have to stay in, Doctor?' Pauline asked.

'Possibly, yes.'

'Oh. We've never been apart. Not in seventy years.'

'I understand. But it's for the best if you want to see Avery up and about as normal.'

When she went out to ask a receptionist to call the ambulance, Oliver was at Reception.

'Need help?' he asked. 'I've had a no-show. I'm free to assist.'

'That'd be great, thanks.'

Whilst they waited for the ambulance to arrive, Lorna set Avery up with some oxygen as his oxygen saturation score was at eighty-eight. A healthy oxygen level was ninety-four and above. The oxygen brought his levels up a couple of points, but still not enough into healthy levels. Oliver made Pauline a cup of tea to steady her nerves as they waited, keeping her chatting and reassured about her husband, and when the paramedics arrived—two lovely young men—the paramedics loaded Avery into their truck and helped Pauline into the chair beside him.

She was so grateful for Oliver's assistance.

'Good luck,' they both said as the ambulance doors closed and the vehicle drove away.

Lorna stood there for a moment. 'What must it be like to have been with the love of your life for seventy years and to have never been apart?'

'I don't know. Makes you wonder, doesn't it?' Oliver turned to look at her. 'To have known someone for that long. To have been able to love them for so long.'

She stared back at him and nodded.

It made her ache for what she had lost.

Last night, after walking home from Oliver's, she had felt awkward. They'd had a lovely evening, and then, walking through the village with the scent of lavender in the air, gazing at people's wonderful gardens overflowing with blooms and colour, Oliver at her side, she'd begun to think that that was the very definition of happiness. That everything in her world was rosy. Until she'd stupidly told him that she'd thought about them being together. Or, at the very least, had asked him if he'd ever thought about it.

Her hopes had been high. That maybe he would say the words she so longed to hear. That maybe he would reach out for her hand and hold it in his. That maybe, just maybe, he would turn her to face him and kiss her!

But it hadn't happened that way. Oliver was too concerned about their friendship. About not wanting to ruin it if a relationship between them didn't work out, and she understood that. But still, it hurt.

Because she'd begun to have dreams. Dreams of the two of them sharing a life together. And he'd blown that idea out of the water.

He wasn't prepared to risk it.

She wasn't worth the risk.

And she'd been so sad, so upset, that she'd hurried indoors and cried afterwards. She'd lain in bed all night, staring at the ceiling, until exhaustion had snatched her into the realms of disturbing dreams. She'd woken this morning with the determination to give herself some distance from Oliver—personally, at least. To keep him firmly in the work-colleague zone. The friend zone.

As she walked back into Clearbrook Medical Practice with him, she felt so aware of their hands so close together. She could reach out and touch him. Entwine their fingers. A little gesture of togetherness. As if she felt the same things as him. But she couldn't bring herself to do so. What if he rejected her? What if he pulled away, as he had when they'd been sorting boxes? She headed straight for her room.

A rap of knuckles at the door made her heart sink. 'Yes?'

Oliver opened the door. 'May I come in?'

She nodded, but busied herself with signing a couple of prescriptions she'd printed out for patients to collect later.

'Are we okay?'

'Of course!'

'Only, after last night…'

He sounded concerned, but she didn't need him to be. 'I'm fine, Oliver. Honestly.'

'And we're still on for our training run this evening?'

The training run? Damn. She'd forgotten about that. 'Oh, right. Actually, I won't be able to make that. Something's come up.' She hated lying, but she wasn't sure she could handle a run with him tonight, knowing that he'd permanently friend-zoned *her*.

'Really? You're not avoiding me because of last night?'

She looked up at him. Put down her pen. 'Nothing happened last night.' And that was the problem. Because she'd been hoping that it might. 'And I really do have something to do. We can run tomorrow, okay? Missing one training session won't hurt.'

He nodded. 'Okay. Because the whole thing about making that decision was that I got to keep you as my friend. So that we didn't endanger that. We haven't, have we?'

She forced a smile. 'No, we haven't. I'm still your friend.'

He seemed to believe her.

Lorna was shocked that she could lie to him so well. So

believably. Or maybe it wasn't so strange. Hadn't she hidden her true feelings for him before, all those years ago?

'Good. Good. Well, you're still happy for me to bring you morning tea at break time?'

'Absolutely!' Another sweet—yet false—smile. It wasn't okay. It wasn't okay at all! But it was fifteen minutes at most. She could get through that, right?

'Great. Well… I'll see you later, then.'

The next day he decided to make an extra effort with her morning tea, because he felt guilty. Instead of just grabbing two mugs and carrying them through, he cleaned a tray and made a pot of tea. Organised a plate of biscuits and carried it down the corridor and knocked on her door, as he always did at morning breaktime.

'Come in!'

He pushed the door open with a smile, determined to be bright and bubbly. Determined to be his usual self when he was with her. Determined to enjoy their few minutes together, before the rest of the morning beckoned. He had a couple of patients left on his list, then his clinic finished earlier than the other doctors', because today he had an hour of admin scheduled for the morning, before he had to do a house visit.

'Here you go. This is for you.' He passed her a mug of tea. 'And these.' He passed over the plate of biscuits as well.

'Spoiling me.'

'I try.' He'd brought some fruit shortcake biscuits. Knowing that she favoured these over the plain ones in the staffroom.

He was still puzzling over the night before last. Running through her reaction to him saying he wanted to remain friends. It was clear that maybe she'd been hoping for another response and he got that. He understood that. He'd thought about it too.

But he'd already been through so much. Had already been in a relationship that had gone sour and it had been awful. He didn't want that for them. She was his North Star. She brightened his world. He didn't want to ruin that feeling because a little bit of lust or misplaced emotions told him to scratch that itch he so badly wanted to take care of. But a marriage that he'd thought would be for life had ended and he'd got that wrong—how could he be sure about anything any more?

He'd made a bad choice before and he didn't want to make a bad one now. Not this late in life. And he'd grown accustomed to being single. Had thrived in the freedom of it all and he wanted his remaining thirty or forty years of life to be the same. Right?

'So where are we running tonight?'

'Erm, I've worked out a route that takes us all around the outskirts of the village, around the borders of the lavender fields. We pass that castle that's in ruins, go past Eyersham Hall and then back down into Clearbrook.'

'Eyersham Hall? What's that?'

'It's a stately home. Used to belong to some lord. We'll skirt the edge of the property, but it's pretty nice up there.' She sipped at her tea.

He appreciated that she was talking to him as she normally did. Even if her tone sounded a little off. 'Not long until the big race. Think we'll do all right?'

She shrugged. 'I don't know. I guess we ought to talk race strategy. Your pace is sometimes faster than mine, so if you want to run ahead to forge your own time, don't feel like you have to hang back with me.'

He didn't like the sound of that. 'We *start* together, we'll *end* together. I want to cross that finishing line with you.'

Lorna gazed at him briefly, then looked away.

'You're sure we're okay?'

'We're fine.'

The next few days were pretty grim for Lorna. She felt as if she were moving through life in black and white. That she couldn't feel the joy that she usually felt. If a patient had come into her consulting room and said the same thing, she would probably diagnose depression, but she refused to believe it of herself.

She was an optimist. She always looked on the bright side and she tried to do that. Tried to find the joy. It wasn't as if Oliver had left—he was right there. Often in the next room. And she felt the creeping pain and hurt of discovering that the only thing they'd be with one another was friends. And she had to accept that. You couldn't make someone be with you, no matter how much you wanted it.

Colour began to return. She could smile again and when she really sat down and thought about it, she accepted that her friendship with Oliver was eternal. He was here and she was glad that he was and she began to enjoy her time spent with him once again.

Looking back, she could tell it was a grief process she'd had to go through. Grieving the idea of them being together. It was never going to happen, despite the way she still caught him glancing at her when he thought she wasn't looking. The way he'd smile at her, as if he truly loved her.

Those were good things, right? Because having Oliver as her very best friend in the whole world, right by her side, whenever she needed him, was like the next best thing. They continued working together. Running together. He continued to push her to run the next hill, even when she wanted to stop. He was there when, on one run, she tripped on a tree root. She smacked into the floor and winded herself, her knee ringing with initial pain. He got her to sit with her back to the tree trunk and examined her leg.

'What if I've damaged my knee and can't do the marathon? After all this training?' She began to cry, unexpectedly.

'You're going to be fine.'

He palpated the knee, washed it with water from his bottle and pulled off his own tee shirt to mop at the blood oozing from her capillaries.

Honestly, she wasn't bleeding that much, but she very much appreciated the view. Oliver had a nicely toned body. He didn't have a rippling six-pack, he didn't have pecs you could bounce an apple off, but he was handsomely muscled just enough for it to be seen.

He dabbed at her wound until she stopped oozing and got her to straighten and bend her leg to make sure nothing was broken.

It wasn't. But it still hurt, as did her palms from where she'd hit the dirt. Oliver helped her to her feet after a period of rest and draped her arm around his shoulder to support her, until she felt able to walk without assistance.

He helped her forge on when she was sore and in pain,

knowing that in the marathon she would hit a wall, both physically and emotionally, and she needed to know how to push on through. He brought her tea on their morning breaks, and the way he refused to give up on her when she was struggling in those early days meant the world to her.

He had her back.

He did love her.

He would always be by her side.

She signed them up for a competitive ten-kilometre race, in which there'd be hundreds of runners. It was a cross-country race and she thought it would be good practice for them to run with lots of other people.

They lined up at the starting line with over one hundred others and set off at a good pace when the whistle went.

It had been just over a week since the knee incident and she was feeling good, despite there being some bruising to it. It felt different to be running with others. The atmosphere of the race, the crowd cheering them on, actually made them run faster than their usual pace and they finished the race together, Oliver holding her hand raised high as they crossed the finish line in an excellent time of one hour and twenty-one minutes.

A marshal draped medals over their necks and it felt so good! The marathon itself was getting closer and closer and they were both feeling good about it.

Lorna still had *thoughts* about Oliver. *Emotions.* She loved him. She would always love him. But each time her heart decided to run away with all these fantasies about them being together, she would very firmly remind herself that they were just friends and fantasies were just that. A little bit of escapism. What mattered was that she was with him every single day and that they could laugh together and work together and that it was comfortable and good between them.

She'd not liked it when she'd felt a chasm developing between them and she refused to let one develop again. And though she'd vowed to put a distance between them, for the sake of her own sanity, she had tried and yet it had not worked. It had been impossible for her to achieve and, as she'd tried, she'd realised she did not want to achieve it.

Instead, she chose to look forward to work every day because he would be there. She chose to look forward to every evening because they'd be out on a training run or, if it was raining heavily, they'd sit in Oliver's house or her house, study the marathon route and talk strategy. Sometimes they'd order pizza and watch a movie. And at the end of every day, Oliver would kiss her goodnight.

A peck on the cheek. And that moment, every single time that he leant in to drop a kiss onto her cheek, she would close her eyes and soak up every precious moment.

Priti popped her head into his consulting room. 'Got a minute?'

'Sure. But just a minute. I'm about to pop out to do a house call,' Oliver said.

'That's exactly what I wanted to talk to you about.'

'Okay. What's up?'

'Melanie Brooker. Your patient. She was booked in by the trainee we have on Reception, so she didn't know Melanie's reputation, but Miss Brooker has a habit of trying to make complaints against staff. She's not meant to be put with male members of staff because of it, because she always makes allegations of impropriety afterwards.

There is a red flag on her record, but our new trainee didn't know to look for it.'

'I see.' Oliver had to admit, he'd not collected Miss Brooker's patient summary yet, let alone had a chance to read it. Whenever a doctor was requested to make a house visit, the practice would print out a patient summary detailing that patient's medications, their most recent history and any other pertinent information, so that the doctor might have some idea of what they were facing when they visited. 'But I'm on call today, so it is my duty to attend.'

'I know. And I'd go with you as a chaperone, but I've got a patient coming in and I can't reschedule. Might be worth seeing if Bella, Carrie or Lorna is free to go with you. Our nurse has already finished and gone home for the day.'

'I'll send a screen message. See who's free.'

'Great. Document everything, just to cover yourself.'

'Will do.'

It was a problem that could sometimes be faced as a doctor. You were there to help, the patient *needed* help usually, though sometimes the symptoms were bogus, but then they would attack the doctor with accusations afterwards. Sometimes, it could be a loneliness thing, or a mental health thing. It was annoying if the health complaint was a ruse, because that patient was taking up precious time that someone who really needed help could have used instead. The important thing to remember was that the patient still needed help, no matter what, and the only thing to do was be a consummate professional.

Oliver bent over his computer and typed a message that would appear on his colleagues' screens, asking if anyone was free to chaperone. The next thing he knew, Lorna had rapped her knuckles on his door and come in. 'I can come with you. Melanie and I rub along okay, so I can fill you in on the way.'

'Okay, great, thanks.' He sent another message to Bella and Carrie letting them know he had someone and then they grabbed their things and left in Oliver's car. Melanie lived on the outskirts of the village, just past the lavender farm, so they had about a ten-minute drive. It was a lovely day and they would have loved to have walked, but their lunch break was short and they still had afternoon clinics to get through.

'You need to take a left up here and then her house is a right turn on the crest of this hill.'

'Okay.' He pulled into Melanie's driveway. The house looked old, the garden unkempt and overgrown.

'Melanie was an only child, raised by two parents who were both unwell themselves. Her father had a history of back surgeries and lived his final years in a wheelchair. Her mother suffered with agoraphobia and never left the house and therefore Melanie had had to do everything for her parents.'

'Sounds like she never really had a childhood.'

'Not really, no. She missed a lot of school. She never really had a life of her own. When her parents passed, Melanie became a frequent flyer at the surgery. She was lonely. She had no friends and no one to talk to, so she would make up ailments just so she could see somebody. Most weeks, she was seen three or four times and was abusive to the reception team if they didn't give her an immediate appointment. Then the complaints began. We got the sense that complaining gave her an opportunity to feel important, and it also got her into mediation and meetings with the staff.

'Priti wanted to remove Melanie from the doctors' surgery and make her register somewhere else, but Melanie actually suffered a real-life medical emergency after falling down her stairs and broke her back. Like her father she ended up in a wheelchair, and like her mother she developed agoraphobia, so she began to require home visits. Priti agreed to keep her on the roll on the condition that Melanie could not ask for more than one appointment a week, which Melanie reluctantly agreed to.'

'Wow. That's a lot to unpack.' It was a tragic backstory and he had sympathy.

Knocking at the door, they waited for it to be opened and when it did, they smiled a greeting at Melanie.

'Come on in,' she grumbled, before turning her chair and leading the way to a darkened front room.

The house was quite dark. None of the curtains were open and it smelt a bit musty. Oliver wondered when she'd last opened a window. But this lack of care was typical of someone suffering from Melanie's list of complaints.

'Melanie, this is Dr Clandon. He's one of the new doctors that we have at Clearbrook. I don't think the two of you have met yet.'

Oliver felt Melanie look him up and down. 'No. We haven't.'

'It's very nice to meet you, Miss Brooker. How can we help you today?' Her hair wasn't combed. Her clothes were dirty and looked as if she'd been sleeping in them. He knew from the patient summary that Melanie had been given medication for depression.

'I'm not feeling great.'

'I'm sorry to hear that. Can you tell me a little more about not feeling great? Is it something physical? Or is it to do with your mood?'

Melanie shrugged. 'Both, I guess.'

'Okay, and how long have you been feeling a little different?'

'A few weeks. Those pills they gave me don't make no difference.'

'The antidepressants?'

Melanie nodded.

'All right. Sometimes it can take a little while to find the right antidepressant medication that works for you. Something we give commonly can work very well for lots of people, but it doesn't always mean it will be right for you, so it can be trial and error. Are you taking them regularly? It says in your history that you're to take one every day—are you doing that?'

'No. I just take 'em when I feel down, but nothing happens.'

He nodded. 'It can take a while for them to get into your system, but you must take them regularly every day, usually at the same time, or they just won't help you. Is there a reason you're not taking them every day?'

She shrugged. 'I forget. My memory ain't so good.'

'I understand.' He looked around the room, looking for clues that might help him, and couldn't help but spot a smart speaker perched on top of the television. He pointed at it. 'Maybe we could use this to remind you? Set up a repeating reminder alert so that it tells you every day to take your medication.'

'It can do that?'

'Absolutely.'

'All right.'

Oliver set up the reminder for her there and then, so that she would be reminded to take her medication every night at eight o'clock. 'Do you have any physical aches and pains?'

'Not really.'

He'd noticed on the summary that Melanie was also registered as having type two diabetes. 'Are you having your eyes and feet checked regularly? Do they send someone out?'

'I had me eyes tested the other week.'

'And your feet? Do you see a chiropodist? Or podiatrist?'

'No. Never have.'

Melanie was wearing socks, but, like the rest of her clothing, they looked grubby. As if they'd not been changed for weeks.

'Would you allow me to examine you? Perform a set of observations and give your feet a check?'

'All right. But I'm ticklish, mind.'

He smiled. 'I'll be gentle.'

Lorna engaged Melanie in conversation whilst he quietly performed a set of obs on her. They were talking about mundane matters—the weather, the tourists, if Melanie had heard from her aunt Brenda recently and if she was okay. Lorna kept Melanie engaged and focused on her. They only stopped talking when Oliver had to conduct a blood pressure test.

'Everything's looking good, Melanie. If you're agreeable, I'd like to take a set of basic bloods from you. We've not had a blood test for three years and I'd just like to check that everything's okay.'

'I don't like needles.'

'I can hold your hand, if you'd like?' Lorna suggested. 'Help you focus on something else.'

Melanie grudgingly nodded.

Oliver was so impressed with how Lorna was keeping Melanie calm. There was a framed picture on the television of a black Labrador and Lorna asked her about it. It turned out to be a dog she used to have that had died a couple of years ago.

'Two years ago?' Lorna clarified.

'Yeah.'

That was when the complaints had started. Maybe Melanie was grief-stricken?

'Have you ever thought about getting another dog?' Oliver asked, genuinely curious.

''Course I have. But because of the agoraphobia, I can't get out to the kennels or rescue places to have a look and I'm not sure I'd pass the home visit anyways.'

Oliver had got his blood sample and he sat back on his haunches and considered her. 'What if we could help arrange for someone—a charity maybe—to come and help you sort out the house and make the garden safe? Then you could pass a home visit and maybe get yourself a little dog to keep you company? Perhaps an older pooch that just wants to live its golden years out in relative peace and quiet?'

It was the first time he saw Melanie smile.

A real smile.

One that lit up her eyes.

'I'd like that.'

Oliver smiled back. 'When we get back to the practice,

I'll make some calls. Are you happy for me to give your contact details out, so people can call you?'

'I'm not good talking to strangers.'

'Then how about we liaise for you? Act as intermediaries? Then we could call you and let you know what's happening,' Lorna suggested.

'All right. You really think I could get meself another dog?' Melanie looked hopeful.

'We do.' Lorna smiled at Oliver and he smiled back.

'I just need to check your feet.'

Melanie nodded.

He pulled off her grubby socks. Her toenails were overgrown and needed cutting and she looked as though she had a bit of a fungal nail problem, but, thankfully, there were no wounds or damage to the feet that caused immediate concern. 'I'm going to arrange a house visit for a podiatrist, if that's okay? These nails need trimming, because if they curl much more, they're going to go into your foot and, with your diabetes, that could cause a problem for infection. Are you happy for me to arrange that?'

Melanie nodded. 'You two are nice.'

Oliver grinned. 'Thank you. Well, we're going to have to leave now and get back for our afternoon clinics, but I'll ring you later when I've spoken to a few people about helping you out. I'll keep you updated.'

'Thank you.'

'You're very welcome. You take care of yourself and we'll speak soon.'

Back in the car, as they drove away, Lorna let out a huge sigh.

'Did you notice how she opened up when we asked about the dog? I think grief and loneliness have really contributed to her problems, but I feel that we might have helped her today. Steered her towards a bit of optimism. What do you think?'

'Me too. If we can find someone to help her with the house and she can get herself another dog and she looks after it well enough, I think she'll feel less alone. Maybe we should get her some counselling, too, so that she can try and get outside with her dog. Take it for walks.'

'She's always refused counselling before, but maybe she will now. I really think you gave her hope today and saw her as a whole person, rather than just as someone who makes complaints.'

'That's the whole point of being a doctor. Looking at a patient holistically, rather than just as one set of symptoms that needs sorting.'

'You're a good doctor, Oliver.'

He appreciated her compliment. 'You are too. The way you kept her mind off the needle whilst she was having the blood test and holding her hand. A lot of doctors worried about complaints wouldn't have made any physical contact at all.'

'Like you say…she's a person. I've never been to her home before. Never seen how she lived since the accident, because she wouldn't let anybody in, no matter how hard we tried. All she'd do was have telephone appointments. To see her living like that…it made my heart ache for her.'

He wanted to reach for Lorna's hand. To squeeze it. To let her know he'd felt the same way. 'Well, we can help her now. We've seen what she needs.'

They drove back to Clearbrook, parking in a doctor's allotted bay and entering the building. Priti was in Reception and she wanted to hear how the home visit went.

When they told her, she was pleasantly surprised. 'That's great! Well done. But still, just to be on the safe side, I want you both to enter documentation of that visit onto her record, stating clearly what you each did and what was said and offered.'

'Will do.'

'And I just might know someone who can help her with the house and garden. Give me half an hour and I'll get their number to you.'

'That's great, thank you. And I'll make a referral to our talking therapy service. See if they can get someone out to her.'

'Make sure they send out two people. To protect them, as much as to protect Melanie.'

Oliver nodded and headed to the staffroom to grab his lunch. He'd brought it from home and left it in the fridge. A mixed chopped salad, topped with chunks of baked sweet potato and drizzled with tahini and sweet chilli sauce. It hit the spot nicely. Though there was more potato than salad, as he was trying to increase his carbohydrates before the marathon, as carbohydrates would break down into glucose and be stored as glycogen. The glycogen, he knew, would be the thing to give a runner energy for the race and it was important to have a good store of that, so that he didn't hit the wall mid-race. It was important to eat right for such a long race, as much as it was to train right. He was steadily increasing his calorie intake, as was Lorna.

'Last big run tonight,' she said, settling into a seat beside him.

'We're going to ache tomorrow.'

She smiled. 'But I feel confident about it. Don't you?'

'Absolutely. With you by my side? I could achieve anything. Perhaps we should climb Everest next year?' He grinned to show he was joking.

'Everest? I'm no good with heights. I think we should stay nice and close to the ground. How about an Ironman?'

He looked at her. 'You want to make this a regular thing? Every year we do something for charity?'

'Why not? It's been fun. And we've steadily raised money. Have you seen the sponsorship forms in Reception? They're nearly full!'

'People have been very generous. The people here in Clearbrook are very kind and welcoming.'

'They are.' Lorna finished her tuna and pasta dish and set it down on the table. 'Do you feel well settled in now?'

'I do. I can see myself being here as a very old man.'

She looked at him and smiled. 'What do you see yourself doing in ten years' time?'

He thought about it. 'I don't know. Maybe thinking about retirement? About travelling a little bit.'

'Alone?'

Oliver shrugged. 'You might be fed up with me by then.'

'Never.'

She said it so seriously and he knew that she meant it. He would love to think that she would go travelling with him. He'd loved seeing the world after his break-up with Jo, but he would love to show Lorna all the fabulous places he'd found. *Share* with her all the places that were important to him. He had an image then, in his mind, of them standing at the bow of a boat as it cruised down the River Nile. She would be standing there, billowing in white linen, the sun shining down on her smiling face and him stepping up behind her, kissing her neck...

He paused at the thought. He'd been trying so damned hard to keep her in the friend zone and it had been going so well. But, dammit, if his mind didn't have other ideas! It was always suggesting stuff like this to him and it really made his present situation difficult.

Because he could imagine it so clearly. The warmth of the setting sun. The sight of the city. The way her hair would dance in the breeze. Her smile as his lips caressed that softest of skin on the slope of her neck. How good she'd smell. How he'd want to wrap his arms around her and pull her close and...

He stood up and went to make a cup of tea. They had ten minutes before afternoon clinic began and he knew patients would already be in the waiting room early.

'What about you? Where do you see yourself in ten years?' he asked, turning her question back upon her.

She shrugged. 'I don't know. Probably still working, I guess. I try not to look too hard towards the future and make plans.'

'Why not?'

'Because every time I've done that I've only ever been disappointed.'

CHAPTER EIGHT

IT WAS A PERFECT, quiet country evening as they ran on
the trail about fifteen miles into their twenty-two. It was
balmy, no breeze. Shards of sunlight arced to the ground
through the tree canopy overhead as they ran through
the woods.

Lorna still felt strong. As if she still had gas in the
tank and that pleased her. Made her feel hopeful for the
marathon. 'I wonder if I'd be doing as well as this if I'd
still been training alone,' she said.

'Of course you would. I believe in you. You're running for someone else. You're running for that lost baby
and all the other families that might lose babies. That's
what's keeping you going.'

She glanced at Oliver beside her. He wore a navy running shirt, navy shorts, both with a red stripe down the
sides. Sweat had dampened the hair at the temples. He
looked dark and sexy and she loved how he had never
let her down on a training run. Not once had he dodged
one. Running for that baby, for those families affected
by stillbirth, was her main motivator, but Oliver beside
her was another.

'Maybe, but you've kept me going, too. Having someone to talk to and to share this experience with. Forced

me up those hills when I wanted to quit. I wonder if, on my own, I might've shortened some of my practice runs.'

'You've kept me going too, and not just during running.'

She slowed slightly. 'Really?'

'Sure. Look at how you got me through that whole experience with Jo. You got me through my studies. You got me through my tests and assessments. You've helped me settle in here. You've never given up on me and so I'll never give up on you. Ever.'

Lorna smiled. 'Well, I didn't get you through the *whole* cancer battle with Jo. You had years of that after we went our separate ways.'

Oliver laughed. 'Maybe, but you were still by my side, even if you weren't there.'

She risked another glance. 'Really?'

'Really. I could hear your voice. I could see your smile. Your words of wisdom. There was this one time when she told me that I could go if I wanted. The cancer had come back, she was fighting it again and she told me that I didn't have to stay if I didn't want to. That I'd not signed up for that and she didn't want to feel like she'd trapped me with her illness.'

'Really?'

He nodded. 'But I remembered one night that you and I had been together. It was when the chemo hadn't been going great and they were having to change her treatment protocols and Jo had been upset at the setback. How I'd not known what to say to her to keep her going. That the Jo I was hearing was frightened and that all I needed to do was be there and reassure her with my presence through all our difficult times. I kept hearing your voice.

Your words of encouragement. I kept thinking that we both just had to be strong enough to get through to the other side and then we'd find the happiness that we'd originally begun with.'

She remembered. She remembered saying that to him. He'd looked so lost, unable to help Jo. So frustrated. Because he'd sacrificed so much to be with Jo and yet there she had been, trying to push him away, when he'd been trying to do the right thing. And she'd so wanted, that night, to wrap him in her arms and tell him it would all be okay.

When she'd gone through her own fertility battle with Craig, she'd had no one to confide in. No one she could turn to for support. Oh, she'd had friends and colleagues and family, but they'd never been through it themselves, so she'd felt as though they didn't truly understand. Not really. And there'd been so many times when she'd thought of picking up the phone and trying to track Oliver down, but fear had always stopped her. Because she'd imagined him, back then, as being in happier times with Jo. That they'd be settled, with a family of their own and that he'd spent years watching a loved one go through a health battle. Did she really want to phone him and burden him with her own?

'You stood by her like a true gentleman. You were stoic and loyal. There were times in my past when I wanted to call *you* just to hear your reassuring voice. To make me feel better about what I was going through.'

He slowed to a stop and she slowed too, coming to stand opposite him. They were both out of breath from running *and* talking.

'I wish you had called me. It would have been great to have heard your voice. We should never have lost touch.'

'No,' she agreed. It had been the singularly biggest mistake of her life. It wouldn't have changed what had happened with Craig, but it might have been easier to get through afterwards, if she could have talked to Oliver.

'I take full responsibility. I should have called you.'

'The phone works both ways. You don't have to take full responsibility. Besides, I…' She swallowed hard at what she was about to admit. 'I lied to myself that I was too busy to keep in touch. I didn't phone because, well, I had feelings for you back then and seeing you with Jo, knowing you were with someone else—it broke me.'

Oliver stared at her. 'It broke me, too.'

She didn't know what else to say. Was he admitting that he'd had feelings for *her*? Back then? Had they been circling one another? 'You seemed so determined to be with Jo.'

'Of course. She needed me. I couldn't walk away in her hour of need and you—you being there—it kept me sane. You kept me happy. A reason to smile every day. Being with you soothed me. Strengthened me, so that I could face each day. When we parted to go our separate ways, to jobs, I…told myself I'd call you, but every time I went to pick up the phone, I stopped myself. Because I feared where it might lead and I didn't want to hurt either of you.'

She'd had no idea that Oliver's feelings towards her had been just as strong.

What had they lost? All those years they could have been together…

'We were both stuck.'

He nodded. 'I guess.'

'We're both free now.'

'I don't want to use you, Lorna, as a way to make myself feel better. I value our friendship way too much.'

'I value our friendship, too. So much! But I can't help but think about what might have been if we'd both made very different choices.'

'So do I.'

She stared at him then. Not sure what to do.

'We should start running again. Don't want to cool down. We've still got a few miles to go.'

He was right, of course, and so they set off at a good pace.

But her mind was awhirl with thoughts. How life might look now, if she and Oliver had got together instead of Oliver with Jo, or her with Craig. Would they have had many happy years? Children? Maybe even grandchildren by now? Would they be here in Clearbrook?

She felt an ache in her heart for what might have been. For what they had lost. It felt almost like the pain of grief. A mourning for something they'd never had but had wanted.

She knew she ought to feel good that she had him now as her friend. Fear had stopped them from becoming anything else before and fear was stopping them from crossing over that line now. There were no guarantees with relationships. Being the best of friends didn't automatically guarantee happiness.

But what if it was a great base they could build on, if only they were brave enough to try?

All their long runs were done now, it was time to relax, eat right, sleep well and maybe get in a small jog of just a couple of miles two or three days before the marathon.

He felt kind of odd having told Lorna how he'd once felt about her. He wondered what she'd think if he told her how he felt about her *now*?

They spoke a lot about their pasts. They talked a lot about their present, but hardly ever spoke of the future. Last night, on the run, she'd told him she didn't think of futures because she was always disappointed, and he didn't want that for her. He wanted her to be able to have dreams and make plans. He wanted her to look ahead and aspire to brilliance and happiness. Contentment.

Peace.

'We should go out for a meal,' he said, bringing her her morning cup of tea.

'We should?'

'Absolutely! To celebrate the end of the training, to celebrate our endurance, to celebrate…us. Our friendship.'

She smiled at him. 'Where do you want to go?'

'Somewhere special. Somewhere amazing. Where we both have to dress to impress. I'll get out my tux, you get out your heels, instead of your trainers…'

'Sounds nice.'

'I want this week to be amazing. A nice dinner. Marathon wins for the two of us…'

'We don't know if we're going to finish. I'll probably end up with a sprain halfway or something ridiculous. Wouldn't it be better to celebrate *after* the race?'

He pretended to think about it. 'No. It has to be before. One last pep talk.'

'Okay. Where would we go?'

Oliver sat back in his chair and took a sip of his tea. 'Leave it with me. I'll book somewhere and pick you up in my car.'

'All right.' She smiled back at him. 'I'll look forward to it.'

'That's all I want.'

Lydia Swann was Lorna's last patient of the day. Fifty-one years old, the same as Lorna, she came in looking a little pale and a little dishevelled.

'Take a seat, Lydia. How can I help you today?'

'I think I'm in menopause. I'm just so…' she shook her head as she struggled to gather the right words to explain her situation '…done in. Exhausted. And yet I'm sleeping really well. Last night? I went to bed at half past eight because I felt shattered and I didn't wake until eight o'clock this morning. Twelve hours! And yet I'm *still* tired. My brain is all foggy, I can't think straight. I'm bloated and I've gone off my food.' She looked directly at Lorna, with tears in her eyes. 'My mum suffered just like this.'

'It's certainly possible. You are of the age for menopause. Have you noticed any other symptoms? Any hot flashes? Night sweats? Any problems with intercourse?'

Lydia blushed slightly. 'I do get hot sometimes and, now that you mention it…sex has been a little uncomfortable, but I put that down to my new partner being a little, well, larger than I've had before.' Lydia blushed madly now.

'And he's a new partner, you say?'

'Yes. But we've known each other for a long time, we just never got together before now. There were always other partners, you know?'

She did know.

'And are you using any lubricants to help with that?'

'Sometimes. You don't always think about it in the moment, do you? Not until after when it hurts. If I'm honest, he can be a little rough, which surprises me, because otherwise he's such a nice man. I guess you can never quite know someone until you actually do.'

Lorna smiled. 'Maybe sitting down with him and talking to him about what you like in the bedroom might help. What your expectations are. Your turn-ons. To help him understand your needs and boundaries.'

'I know I should, but it's all so new and exciting that I don't want to spoil anything, you know?'

'I understand. Have you noticed any change with your breasts?'

'Well, that's the thing that's odd. I have. And they're bigger than they were before. I thought a lack of oestrogen from menopause would make them a little *less* full. A bit droopier, if you catch my drift?'

Lorna nodded. 'And when was your last menstrual period?'

'They've always been irregular, but I think about three months ago.'

'Is there any chance you could be pregnant?'

'At my age?' Lydia seemed surprised. 'I don't… I'm not sure. Can you fall pregnant when you're menopausal?'

'If you're in menopause, then no. Menopause means that you stop producing eggs, so it would be impossible to get pregnant. But it is still possible when you're in perimenopause, which I suspect is the stage you are in. We'll need to do a blood test to confirm.'

'I'm fifty-one, Lorna!'

'I know, but I think it's worth checking, considering your symptoms, before we start thinking about menopause or HRT, or anything like that. Have you been using protection with your new partner?'

'Yes! Except…there was this one time we didn't.'

'One time is all it takes.'

'But I have grown-up children. I have a granddaughter!'

'Look, I don't want to worry you unnecessarily. We're just checking. Ruling things out.'

'But you really think I could be pregnant?'

'Maybe. Like I said, let's rule it out.'

'And if I am?'

'Then you come back in and talk to me again. I can give you your options and choices, but obviously, if you were to be pregnant, your pregnancy would be considered high risk.'

'Because of my age.'

'Yes.'

Lydia rolled up her sleeve. 'Then let's do this. I need to know.'

'I know this is scary, but you did say your new partner was a good man. Do you think he'd make a good father?'

'He already is. He has three boys and they all adore him.'

'Okay. So let's wait and see what the blood test says and we'll go from there. It can take a little longer to get the results, but they're more reliable. I'll book an appointment for you in two days' time and that way, whatever the result, we can be sure to meet up again and discuss options for moving forward.'

When Lydia was gone, Lorna couldn't help but wonder what her results would be. Was this simply menopause, or could she be pregnant? The odds were very small, but not impossible.

Lorna tried to imagine how she would cope if the same thing happened to her. They were the same age. But her situation was different. Lorna knew her periods had stopped. She was in full menopause—there was no chance of getting pregnant.

She'd always yearned for a family, to have a baby, so despite all the risks of having a baby aged fifty, if she were in Lydia's position, she knew she'd go through with it. But who would be the father? Oliver?

She knew instinctively that he'd make a good father. In the same way that she'd always imagined herself as a good mother. They both had so much to give.

But it's too late for me, anyway.

She'd accepted the fact that her dreams had changed. That her time for achieving them had passed. But what if she could have a new dream? To still dream of and aspire to a happy future? She could have that still. She just had to find a way to make it happen.

Going out for dinner with Oliver this Friday was something nice to look forward to. The marathon was something that she was excited for, even though she knew it was going to be tough. Anything worth having you had to fight for.

Should she fight for Oliver to see her as more than just a friend? Or was that being selfish? That dream to have a child could still be in his grasp if he went with someone other than her and she wanted him to achieve his dreams. That was if he wanted it. Should she ask him? Directly? Because if he said he did, would she be able to bear hearing that, knowing it would end her hopes? But if he said no...

He was worried that if it didn't work, if it went wrong, then their friendship would not be the same. It was a possibility. They worked together. People might take sides. It might make the work environment uncomfortable. Look at how it had felt when they'd had that little snafu a while back...

But we overcame it. Because we loved each other so much. Maybe we could overcome anything?

She thought about what a life with Oliver would look like. Waking up together. Having breakfast together. Being at work all day with each other. Coming home in the same car, or running in together. Cooking meals that the other liked. Sharing a bed. Day after day after day.

She felt a warm glow at the thought and then a wave of sadness. For she knew it was something she would never have, unless Oliver changed his mind. Her dreams never ever came true. And she'd grown to accept that.

When she opened her front door, Oliver presented her with a small bouquet of flowers.

'Oliver! What are these for?' Lorna gasped with delight and then held them to her nose. 'They're beautiful!'

'Beautiful flowers for a beautiful lady.'

He loved it when she blushed like that. Loved how much she was surprised by the flowers. Had her husband ever bought her flowers? Had she ever had romantic treats from him? He'd been thinking a lot lately about the guy Lorna had married and what Craig had done to her at the end. Discovering his ultimate betrayal on that devastating day when she'd learned that their last attempt at IVF had failed.

He simply could not imagine doing that to her. The man had to have been crazy not to have known what he'd had right in front of him.

'You look stunning, by the way.' Lorna was wearing a beautiful cocktail dress, in the softest, palest blue. Chiffon? Or maybe silk?

'You don't scrub up too badly yourself.'

He laughed and gave her a twirl, to show off his tux to the best effect. 'Thank you.' He held out his arm, so she could slip her hand through, and then he escorted her to his car, waiting by the kerb.

He'd had it detailed. Buffed to the highest shine, inside and out. Soft jazz played on the stereo as he drove them to their destination—Marič's, a Croatian restaurant situated in the next town over.

'Have you been there before?' she asked him.

'No. But I've heard great things about it and the online reviews are glowing. The food is out of this world, apparently.'

'I don't think I've had traditional Croatian food before.'

'Nor me. But I'm hoping to find my next great taste sensation.'

The roads were pretty quiet as they drove through villages and countryside. The restaurant had ample parking and he found a spot out back, near the river that actually fed into the brook that ran through their own village.

'Stay there.' Oliver got out and walked around the car to open her door and held out a hand to help her alight.

'Thank you.'

'You're welcome. Ready?'

'I am. I'm really hungry, too.'

'Great.'

They walked to the front door and when they walked inside, they were greeted by a waitress who took them to their table by the window. Violin music played softly in the background as the waitress poured water for their table and took their drinks order.

They took a moment to look around. The restaurant was busy, almost full. The aromas from the food were making them salivate. 'Let's choose something. I'm starving.' They picked up the menus and considered everything. 'I like the sound of the *girice*.' That was deep fried whitebait fish with mayo.

'Mmm. Think I'll go for the—hmm, I don't know how to pronounce it—*dagnje pedoče*.'

'The mussels in garlic and lemon?'

'Mmm.'

'What were you thinking for a main?'

'I think the chicken breast with the wild mushroom sauce. It says there it's served with potatoes.'

'Sounds amazing. I'm not sure what to choose, it all sounds so delicious. Maybe the slow-cooked beef in wine and gnocchi?'

Lorna looked at him and laughed. 'We're going to have to be rolled out of here!'

They gave their orders to the waitress and clinked their wine glasses together. 'To the big race.'

'The big race.' He sipped his drink. 'Are you nervous?'

'A little. We've been waiting for it for a long time.'

'We have, and the big day is nearly upon us.'

'I think as long as I get a decent sleep the night before, I'll feel more confident. What are you going to eat the night before?'

'A big bowl of pasta with a tomato and mushroom sauce. I'm sticking to carbs and food I'm familiar with. No point in upsetting my stomach right before the race.'

She nodded. 'That's why I'm not having anything too spicy today, either.'

They chatted about the race until their food arrived. The mussels and the whitebait looked delicious and they tucked in with gusto. 'This is amazing.'

'I can see why this place has such good reviews.'

'Talking of amazing…have you noticed what's going on between Bella and Max?'

'There's definitely something. The way they look at one another.'

Lorna laughed. 'I think they think they're hiding it quite well.'

Oliver smiled and nodded. 'But they make a great couple, don't you think?'

'I do. I hope they can work out whatever's stopping them from being together.'

'Me too. They're a good match and I can't think of any couple that deserve to be together more.'

She looked at him, thoughtfully.

She could.

CHAPTER NINE

IT WAS THE day of the marathon and Lorna had not got as much sleep as she'd wanted. She'd not slept well the last two nights. Not since that meal with Oliver. Him arriving with flowers, walking her to his car as if she were some kind of lady. Opening the door for her. Getting to the restaurant.

The restaurant itself had been gorgeous. Bijou. Candlelit. Soft violin music playing in the background. Their seats by the window, perfect. And then they'd got to talking about relationships. Bella and Max's.

She'd felt so close to happiness. So close to getting a chance at pursuing a romantic relationship with him, the way she'd always dreamed. But Oliver, as always, had been cautious. Hesitant.

Had she been pushing for something that might ruin them? And if so, what did that mean? Was she trying to sabotage her own happiness? Because for a long time after Craig, she'd told herself that she was not destined for happiness. She was not destined to be happy. But that, instead, she would live a life alone.

Maybe Oliver was right to hesitate?

When he'd pulled up in front of her cottage, she'd thanked him for the ride home and got out of the car.

'Thank you for a lovely evening,' she'd said, before walking back into the cottage and closing the door.

But things felt half finished between them. Incomplete. They should have talked more about themselves, but she'd not had the courage of her convictions to do so. Doubting herself as usual.

And so, no, she hadn't slept well. Saturday morning, she'd gone out to collect her race kit and fill in any last-minute race registration forms, before coming home again. Spending all day inside, staring at the television, but not really listening to what was being said.

It was really early. Six a.m. Oliver was meant to be picking her up at six-thirty. They were going to drive to the race together. They had looked forward to this. Trained hard for this. Could she run twenty-six miles with him by her side, feeling this way? She needed to be focused on her run. Her timing. Her nutrition. Her gels. Her hydration. Pace. Not whatever this was.

Her doorbell rang and her heart thudded.

Lorna unlocked the door and pulled it open.

Oliver stood outside in a tracksuit over his race gear. She saw his number pinned to his chest. The same number would be pinned to his shorts on the leg. Like hers. 'Good morning.'

'Morning.'

'It's good weather, at least.'

'Yeah.' It wasn't brilliantly sunny. The sky was blue, but there were plenty of white clouds and there was a cool breeze.

'Ready?'

'I guess so.'

He offered to carry her kit to the car and she watched

him pack it into the back and then he opened the passenger door for her. Two days ago, he'd opened the car door for her, treated her like a lady, and he was still doing it today. He'd never let her down or treated her differently.

She smiled at him.

He closed the door as she was putting on her seat belt.

Smiling, she settled into her seat and they drove out of Clearbrook, heading for the marathon.

There were hundreds of people waiting to run, dressed in all colours. Neon orange, bright pinks, blues, greens, yellows. There were even some people in fancy-dress outfits. Oliver saw one guy dressed as a teddy bear, and another on stilts. He admired their bravery to add an extra element of difficulty onto what was already a difficult race.

He and Lorna stood a little way back from the starting line, the faster professional runners and running clubs near the front. He felt apprehensive about the race, about how they'd both do. There'd been a few niggles, some slight injuries during training sessions. He felt a lot of tension and nerves and had to keep shaking out his leg and arm muscles, as if warming them up. Glancing at her, he thought Lorna seemed just as nervous. Just as uncertain. He knew she'd struggled with her self-belief during this and he wanted her to feel as if she could do anything.

'We're going to climb mountains today.'

'As well as a marathon? I didn't sign up for that.' She laughed, nervous.

'Metaphorical mountains. We're ready. We can do this. We've trained hard.'

'I don't want to let anyone down. You. Me. Yasmin. My charity.'

'You won't.'

'How do you know?'

'Because I know you. And you're not doing this for yourself. You're doing it for others and you will kill yourself to finish this race for them and for all those families that your sponsorship money will help.'

She nodded, but he could see that she still didn't believe it. Maybe she wouldn't until she'd crossed the finishing line? He'd always considered himself a good support, a great partner, but what if he wasn't as good as he thought? Look at how much support and advice he'd given Jo. And look at how that ultimately ended.

His one main relationship in life had begun on unsteady ground and it had ended badly. That was his experience. That relationships ended badly. That he wasn't good enough. What if he wasn't enough for Lorna, either?

He didn't want to let her down and nor did he want to enter a relationship with Lorna with a clause going into it about what would happen if it ended. It felt almost fatalistic. Pessimistic. But he was just being practical. Sensible. Trying to stop the hurt before it began, just in case. Though maybe, like a marathon, you had to go through the pain to feel the joy?

He wanted the race to be a success, but he also wanted any future relationship he got involved in to be a success, because it was something he had waited for his whole life.

He reached for her hand and squeezed it. 'Ready?'

'As I'll ever be. You?'

'I'm good.' He squeezed her hand again, raised it to his lips and kissed it.

She smiled at him.

He loved the way she smiled at him. The way she

blushed. That coy look she did. It was beautiful. She was beautiful. She always had been.

'Runners! The race begins in ten! Nine! Eight!'

Maybe the marathon, this long race they were about to enter, was some sort of metaphor for them. Their relationship, their friendship, had been like a marathon. Long. Sometimes difficult. Occasionally they'd hit a wall, but they'd always found strength in the other. Running by her side and keeping her safe and strong and supported and loved was just like a relationship itself.

He knew he would stay by her side.

'Seven! Six! Five!'

The crowd joined in with the countdown. Onlookers, those not running, stood behind metal barriers and clanged bells and blew whistles and cheered. Some held cardboard signs above their heads with messages of hope. Everyone here wanted everyone else to finish. To do well.

'Four! Three! Two! One! Go!' A horn blared and the runners in front of them surged forwards and he let go of Lorna's hand and began to run beside her.

They would get through this. He had no doubt in his mind at all.

They would cross the line *together*.

The first ten miles went by easily. Lorna felt strong. Powerful. As if her stamina would last for ever with Oliver at her side. But in mile eleven, there was a series of hills and the initial excitement of starting the race was over and she began to think about how many miles were left.

Another fifteen miles!

But she kept going. She kept thinking about Yasmin and the baby she'd lost to stillbirth. That was who she was running for. To raise money for a charity to help Yasmin and other families like theirs, who had lost a precious baby.

She understood their pain. Yasmin and her husband had also gone through IVF to fall pregnant with their son, Adam. He had been a most wanted child and once Yasmin had fallen pregnant after months of trying, she had sailed through her pregnancy as if she had been born to do it. Like all prospective new parents, they had begun to plan for their child. Bought pushchairs and a car seat, a crib, a Moses basket. They'd spent hours deciding on names, had even sent Lorna pictures of the nursery when it had been completed. They'd hired an artist to paint a mural on the wall. The room had looked amazing. When Yasmin had gone into labour naturally, she and her husband had excitedly gone into hospital, preparing for their lives to change in the most dramatic way possible—through the joy that was new life.

Yasmin had been monitored through some of her contractions and the midwives had noticed one or two decelerations of the baby's heartbeat. They'd turned up her synthetic oxytocin, a drug used to increase strength and rhythm of contractions. She'd bounced on a ball. She'd walked and paced around her bed. She'd sucked on gas and air, but her cervix hadn't been dilating as well as it ought to. Baby Adam's heart had kept slowing and it had become an emergency and Yasmin had been rushed into surgery for an emergency caesarean, where she'd been put to sleep. She'd not wanted that, but had been willing to forgo the moments after birth holding her child, if it had meant they would both survive.

By the time the surgeons had opened her up, Adam

had been floppy and blue and, despite efforts to revive him, he had been born sleeping. Yasmin had woken expecting to see her baby in a cot beside her bed. Instead, she'd found her husband red-eyed and pale. In shock. And no crib beside her bed.

She'd been devastated. She'd screamed and blamed herself. She'd sunk into depression for a while, but Lorna had been there for her, as much as she'd been able, encouraging them to feel whatever they'd needed to feel to deal with their grief.

She'd sat with Yasmin for many hours and she hated the fact that this still happened to so many babies every year. Born sleeping, with no reason why. An autopsy on Adam had discovered a coarctic aorta that hadn't been picked up on scans. A narrowing of this vital main artery. His heart hadn't been strong enough to deal with the contractions and birth process. Yasmin had a reason, but so many parents did not.

It happened to far too many. Nearly two hundred families who would suddenly find themselves bereft.

Adam's death had occurred just over a year ago. Yasmin and her husband had been terrified to try again and Lorna understood that fear that conflicted with the powerful need to hold a baby in your arms. And so she was running for them and, no matter how hard this race got, no matter how steep the hills or rough the trails, she would keep going.

'You okay?' Oliver asked.

'Yeah. You?'

'I'm good. But I think we might have run the last two miles too quickly. We need to slow our pace a bit if we're going to finish strong.'

'All right.' It felt good to ease off a little. She pulled a gel from her pack and ripped it open. The gels helped with energy levels on long runs, providing high carbohydrates and essential electrolytes to keep her fuelled. Plus, they were easy on the stomach. She passed one to him.

'Apple?'

'Of course.' She knew what his favourite flavour was. They'd practised. Tried out many different varieties and stuck to the ones they had tried and tested.

The crowds were good. Kept them going for the next few miles. Lorna recognised one or two faces, smiling and waving and cheering as she and Oliver passed.

By mile twenty, her legs ached, her feet hurt and her ankle was throbbing and she pulled up. Oliver came to a stop beside her. 'What's wrong?'

'My ankle.' She turned it this way. That. Rubbed at it. 'Something's wrong.'

'Sprained?'

'No, just…hurts. What if I can't keep going?'

'We've not got far to go! You can do this! Even if we walk over that line, you're going to finish this race!'

She was grateful for his confidence, but she wasn't feeling it. The roads seemed endless and her thoughts had been on Yasmin and baby Adam and her own lost chance at a family and here she was, yet again, putting others first and not herself by trying to push through the pain. Was it so wrong to want to feel selfish on occasion? 'You go on, without me. I'll catch up.'

'Not a chance! Here.' He grabbed her arm and draped it around his shoulder. 'I'll support you, but we're not stopping. Come on. Walk with me.'

They walked for a mile. The pain began to ease a

bit and the awkwardness of being this close to him felt uncomfortable.

If he were mine, I could cry!

She had to stop again briefly to rearrange her socks that had begun to fall down. The temptation to stop and sit for a while was huge. Especially because they were near someone's house and the aroma of fried bacon was issuing from the windows and all Lorna could think of was a bacon sandwich. Instead, she took her last gel and ploughed on, with Oliver's encouragement.

By mile twenty-four, she looked at him, realising they'd never run this far together, ever, and there were only a couple of miles to go. Two more miles and then they could stop. Two more miles and she would have achieved something she had never achieved before and she would have raised a couple of thousand pounds for a charity to help families going through the worst pain ever. Her legs might hurt. Her body might hurt, but that pain was temporary. It would pass. The pain of families that lost their precious babies would never go away.

I think I can do this!

Lorna felt a surge of adrenaline and she and Oliver began to pick up their pace. They were going to finish around the five-and-a-half-hour mark, which was amazing, because she'd thought it might be six hours or more.

Eventually, the finish line was in sight. An arch of balloons in red, white and blue and a huge crowd of cheering onlookers.

Lorna reached for Oliver's hand and grasped it as they ran towards the line, picking up their pace for a final surge of excited energy, and as they crossed, they raised their hands high and whooped and hollered and slowed to a stop, instantly being draped with a foil-like wrap by race marshals and helpers. The foil wrap helped them keep warm as their body temperatures dropped once the race was done and then someone was there draping a medal around each of their necks.

'We did it!' she gasped.

'We did it!'

She fell into his arms. Clung to him. Kissed his cheek and never wanted to let go. But race marshals moved them on and slowly they made their way to the recovery area.

Oliver had driven her home and when they'd got to her cottage, she'd invited him in to celebrate their triumphant completion of the marathon. They'd drunk some wine, ordered pizza, and eaten it whilst watching some rom-com on television. Now they sat beside each other on the sofa, tired and aching.

'What a day.' They both still wore their medals. The pizza-delivery guy had looked confused when he'd seen them hanging around their necks. But now Lorna held hers up in front of her. 'First medal I've ever won.'

'I think I got a medal once before. Winning a rounders competition against a neighbouring school. Wasn't as posh as this, though.'

'I'm thinking of getting one of those box frames, putting in my running top, my number and this medal so I can put it out on display. Maybe at work?'

'Good idea.' He reached for her hand. 'But I have a better idea.'

'What's that?' she asked as he turned to face her on the couch.

Oliver reached up to stroke her cheek and she smiled. She felt content. Happy. Tired. But not too tired for Oliver to be touching her. To be showing her affection. Love. She was pleasantly surprised, but she wouldn't question it.

'Are you happy?'

She nodded. 'I am. Are you?'

He looked thoughtful. 'Today was incredible. To achieve what we did today made me realise what a great partnership we are. What a great team we have always been.'

She smiled. 'I'm glad.'

'I know I said before that I didn't think we should be any more than friends, but twenty-six miles is a lot of thinking time and running by your side, being there with you, being a part of something amazing with you, made me realise how I always wanted that to be true.'

'We are amazing,' she said. 'Amazing friends.'

'We could be more.'

Lorna stared hard at him. Did he truly mean it? Was this their moment? 'I need you to be clear.' She thought she knew what he meant, but she didn't want to make a move and be wrong! To be rejected right now would be too much.

'I think that... I'd like to try and be more than friends.'

Lorna stared, heart pounding in a way it hadn't during the marathon!

She gazed into his eyes. She gazed at his lips. How often had she dreamed of kissing him? Or knowing him physically? Intimately? 'You mean it?'

He nodded. 'I want you.'

Lorna could hold back no longer. She leaned in and

wrapped herself around him and she held him. Enjoying the feel of him in her arms. Why had he resisted for so long? Yes, he'd wanted freedom and not to feel restricted by another romantic relationship, but when had Lorna ever made him feel restricted? With her, he could be free! And able to do anything!

'You and I have had a long day. I don't want to push for something whilst you're tired.'

'I don't feel tired any more!' She sat back and looked at him, her eyes sparkling with happiness. 'I feel like I could run another marathon.'

He laughed at her joy. Loving it.

'I do need a shower, though. I'm stinky and I have mud on my legs.'

He smiled, and she could see he was picturing her in the cascading water. 'A shower sounds good.'

'Do you…want to join me?'

Oliver stood and offered her his hand. 'That sounds even better.'

Okay. She definitely liked where this was heading. Lorna took his hand and led him up the stairs. The delicious anticipation of what was ahead of her caused her heart to race, her skin to grow hot and every nerve ending to come alive. Moments ago, she'd felt herself sated and maybe she was in some ways. Her hunger was satisfied. Her conscience clear now that she had run that big race and satisfied all the people that had sponsored her and offered money to a good cause.

But sexually?

She'd not been sexually satisfied for a long time. So many nights she had spent alone in the last few years. Occasionally dating. But never tempted enough to bring anyone back or to go to theirs, so she'd learned to satisfy herself.

But it was never the same. Never the same as someone else's touch.

She walked him through her bedroom and towards the en suite. It wasn't a huge bathroom, but the shower was large enough to fit two quite nicely.

Lorna switched on the shower and then turned to face him, suddenly feeling apprehensive. Almost shy. It had been so long since she'd last undressed in front of a man and to undress in front of Oliver...

But he must have sensed her nerves for he stepped towards her and took her face in his hands and kissed her gently. 'We don't have to do anything you don't want to do.'

'That's just it. I want to do it all.' She flushed with heat, her desire for him, her need for him, pulsing through her body. She'd waited for him for so long. They'd both waited. And the sweetest, *best* things came to those who waited.

And she knew she needed to show that, because Oliver was a gentleman. He had always been a gentleman and he would never force her to do anything that she wasn't comfortable with.

Yet she was comfortable. She was excited. She just couldn't believe the time was now. That she was about to have the man she had wanted for years. That they were going to take their relationship to the next level. And so she reached for his tee shirt and lifted it slowly above his head, revealing his chest and stomach.

She was so used to seeing him in a shirt and tie. Or a tee. But he had a fine body. A perfect body, in that it wasn't ripped or overly muscular. It was just right. A broad chest, the shape of strong muscles in his arms, a stomach that wasn't washboard flat, but like hers.

He's made for me.

And then she took hold of the bottom of her own tee and raised it over her head, exposing herself in her running bra. Exposing her midriff, that she knew had got a little added extra, a little mid-life padding since menopause had hit, but that didn't matter. She was who she was and when she looked into his eyes, she saw admiration and desire.

'You're beautiful,' he whispered.

'So are you.' She laid her hands upon his chest, trailing them down over his stomach, admiring every inch. Taking in how he felt. Then she reached his shorts and saw his arousal for her. She ran her hands over him and he closed his eyes and let out a soft sigh of pleasure.

It made her feel good to see the effect her touch had on *him*. She marvelled at it. She wanted to see more. She wanted to hear him groan. Gasp. All the things. And so she slipped her hand inside his shorts and he pulled her towards him and began to kiss her.

He was hot and heavy in her hand. She could feel the heft of him, the weight. The solidity. She wanted it for herself and she let go, slipping off her own shorts and underwear and pushing herself up against him. Rubbing. Pressing. Teasing.

'Wait.' Oliver pulled off the rest of his clothes and took her hand, pulling her into the shower, gasping as the steamy water hit their bodies.

She felt his hands upon her. Exploring. Discovering. She felt as if she might explode if she didn't feel him inside her, but he turned her so her back was to him and his hands explored her breasts, her waist, her sex, as his lips caressed the side of her neck.

Lorna pressed herself back against him, opening her legs to give him better access.

It had never been like this with Craig. And if it had been, she couldn't remember it. Sex might have been fun for them once, but then conception had become all about laboratories and petri dishes and her legs up in stirrups with doctors between them, rather than her husband. It had become a clinical thing. A procedure, rather than a sexual experience.

They'd begun to abstain, because Craig had said he was frightened after each implantation to damage her or disturb the pregnancy and so he'd stayed away from her, the distance between them becoming a chasm, so that physical need had got lost in the infertility journey they had been on. She'd noticed the distance between them but had considered it normal. They had been under stress. They hadn't been trying to get pregnant the same way that other couples did. They had needed help. The act of conception had not been about two people any more, but about many—fertility specialists, doctors, nurses, lab techs, phlebotomists.

But what she was doing now was just about them. About her and Oliver and as the hot water and his hands and mouth continued to explore her, she knew she was going to one hundred per cent own it. Live every second. Devour sensation and arousal and pleasure as Oliver gave it to her. As she took it for herself. Because this was just about them.

In that moment.

Together, as they'd always been meant to be.

CHAPTER TEN

HE COULD HAVE stayed in Lorna's bed for ever. Last night had been…

Well, there are no words.

Everything he'd ever done in his life, every choice that he had made, even if he'd felt ninety-nine per cent sure of something, there had always been a voice of doubt, but not last night. Last night he had been more sure of being with Lorna than he ever had about anything and he couldn't quite believe he had made himself wait that long, until he could be sure.

But he'd *had* to be sure, because any doubt would have ruined the moment and he'd not wanted anything to ruin that.

Last night had been the most singularly beautiful night of his entire life.

They'd enjoyed a huge amount of foreplay in the shower, exploring one another's bodies, but then they'd moved into the bedroom to make love, which they had done, once, twice, three times, before he'd snuggled into her, being the big spoon, and fallen asleep with her in his arms. They both must have been so exhausted, because they were still like that when he woke.

He was used to waking early. It was Monday and they

both had to be at work, but first, he wanted to do one last special thing before they had to return to work and reality hit.

So he reluctantly pulled himself from between the sheets and sneaked downstairs to make them breakfast. He wanted to give her breakfast in bed. After yesterday? They were both physically spent and then, after last night's extra-curricular exercise, they both needed to replenish some much-needed and valued calories, if they were to get through a long work day.

Her fridge was well stocked. Healthy. As he'd expected it would be. Lorna was always making sure she ate right. So he made them both pancakes and drizzled them with maple syrup and fresh berries and took up a tray, laden with coffee and fresh fruit juice, too.

Lorna was just sitting up in bed as he pushed open the bedroom door. 'Good morning!'

She smiled hesitantly and looked so beautiful, with her sleep-swollen face and mussed hair. 'Is that for me?'

'It's for us both. I hope you're hungry?'

Lorna nodded, pulling the covers up over her.

'We had quite the workout yesterday.'

She smiled as if agreeing.

'Finishing that race was amazing. Crossing the line with you? Superb. But being with you, physically, was just on another level for me.' And he meant it. It was. And he wanted this for the rest of his life.

'My legs hurt.' She reached out to massage them through the bedsheet.

He laughed. 'Anything else?' He couldn't help it. He felt as if he was on a high. Nothing could bring him down.

She shook her head. She was being very quiet. A little subdued. Maybe this was how she was in the morning?

He poured her coffee into her cup, trying not to spill it. 'I've been thinking. Thinking *a lot*. Because I want to feel this good all the time and I want us to have this for ever. Feel this way together, for ever.'

Lorna smiled and deliberately forked in a mouthful of pancake as if she couldn't respond because she was eating.

'And so I'm just going to be crazy here, Lorna, and leap in with both feet, because I think we've both waited long enough.'

'Long enough for what?' She frowned at him, unsure.

'To move in with one another. To be a real couple. Get married, eventually.'

She looked at him in shock. 'What?'

'I mean it, Lorna. I love you and I want to be with you. For ever.'

She stared back at him. 'What are you saying?'

'I love you, Lorna Hudson. I think I've always loved you, but I know now that I am *in love* with you.'

Lorna seemed to stop breathing. 'What?'

He nodded, smiling at her. 'You are beautiful. Strong. Incredible. Enduring. You've never let me down and you're always ready with a smile and a hug and I want that for ever. But not as friends. As something more. If you're ready for that, too?'

She stared at him in horror. 'You said…*married*. Are you asking me to marry you?'

He guessed he was. 'Yes.'

Lorna swallowed her pancake and looked away, as if suddenly nervous.

Her response scared him. Wasn't this what she'd wanted? She'd pushed for this. For them to have a relationship. *He'd* been the hesitant one.

'We ought to get ready for work.'

'But—'

She suddenly threw back the duvet and got up and headed into the en suite. He heard her lock the door.

It wasn't the reaction he'd expected.

Had he judged this incredibly wrong?

Cursing, he got off the bed and began to get dressed.

Lorna stood in the bathroom. Completely still. In shock. Her mind replaying his words for her over and over again.

Move in with one another. Be a real couple. Get married.

A couple of days ago he'd not wanted to move beyond friendship and today he wanted to get married?

She ought to be happy, she knew. All of yesterday, during the race, she had been strengthened with him by her side, and last night? Last night had been incredible. She'd not known it was possible to love someone like that. Be loved by someone like that and for something to feel so right!

But his words scared her. If she said yes, she was dooming him to the prospect of no children ever. Not naturally, anyway, and she couldn't imagine either of them would then want to go through a long adoptive or fostering process, or anything like that. What they'd begun last night, finally, after so long…and she could have a real chance of happiness here!

Yet he had a chance at a real family with someone else. She'd not thought he would move so fast as this. Why hadn't she asked him about children? Why didn't she know? Would she be enough for him? Just him and her?

She'd thought she'd wanted that. To be with Oliver. They'd lost so much time apart already and she did want to be with him.

But marriage scared her. She could only think about what he would be losing by choosing her. She'd been married before and it had all gone wrong. Going through a divorce had been one of the worst things to ever happen to her, but, more than that, the feeling that she just wasn't enough to have kept her husband had left her self-esteem reeling.

What if she said yes to Oliver and the same thing happened? What if he left because they couldn't have a child?

He knows my age. He knows I'm menopausal. He knows what being with me would mean. Maybe it could be okay?

She couldn't bear to not be enough for him.

To lose him again.

Oh, why did I push for this? For a relationship? How did I think it was going to go?

'Lorna…' Oliver said her name softly. He had to be standing on the other side of the door. 'Lorna. Please come out and speak to me. We need to talk about this, before we go in to work.'

She didn't know if she was strong enough just yet. She needed to gather her thoughts. 'You go. I'll meet you there,' she called out.

There was silence for a moment and then he said, 'I'm worried, Lorna. Are you okay?'

'I'm fine. Just please go and I'll see you later.'

'I don't want to go. We need to talk about this.'

'You've already said too much.'

'What do you mean? Please come out and talk to me. Face to face.'

But she knew that she couldn't. She couldn't face him. Not right now. She needed space, she needed time. To breathe. To compose herself so that she could react in a less emotionally distraught manner. Not right now. Not when it was all so raw. 'Please, Oliver. Please just go! I'm begging you.'

He must have heard the pain and upset in her voice, because she heard a whispered, *'All right...'* Then she heard his footsteps leave the room and head downstairs.

Softly she opened the bathroom door and listened to him moving around downstairs and then the opening and closing of her front door.

The finality of that front door closing broke her.

She gazed at the running gear on the floor and she remembered what it had been like to start the marathon with him. The way he had supported her and not left her side. The smile on his face every time he brought her tea in the morning at work, how good she felt when he sat down in the patient's chair in her room and they chatted about their day. She remembered how he'd helped Melanie, how he'd taken extra time to make sure he was doing the right thing by a patient that many had wanted to dismiss. The fun they'd had at medical school. The date at Verity's. His consistency at always being there for her.

Was she going to let him walk away?

She imagined him walking out on her for ever and never again having a night like they'd shared last night. Never being with the guy that had kept a buttercup she'd once held under his throat because he considered it special. The ache she felt in her heart made her realise that she couldn't do it. She couldn't lose him. Not this quickly. And he'd not said that they ought to get married straight away. He'd said *eventually*. Giving them both time to adjust to a second chance. A new beginning, with an old friend. An old love. A timeless and eternal love. Because she had always loved him and her reaction just now... had that hurt him? Had it made him feel rejected? She didn't want him to feel that way—she'd just been scared. And she was human. She was allowed a moment of hesitation, right?

Lorna rushed down the stairs and yanked open the front door. 'Oliver!'

He was about to pull away from her kerb when he saw her. He switched off the engine and got out of the car. 'Lorna. Are you okay?'

'I'm good. I'm fine. Look, I'm sorry, just now, for how I reacted—you scared me. Talking of moving in and marriage. All the things I'd failed at before. I got scared because I don't want to fail at them with you. Not *you*. You're my world. My everything. I couldn't bear to fail at something as big as marriage with you. I've had one big failure in life and it took me a long time to get over it.'

'I don't want to fail either.'

'But I'm not sure you've properly thought this through.' She had to be sure. She had to.

'I've thought of nothing else.'

'But...' She looked down, could feel her heart breaking at what she was doing. 'You could still have a real family with someone else. You can't do that with me. I'm in menopause, my periods have stopped, but with someone else...you could.'

She had to say it. Finally. After all this time, she had to remind him. Just in case. Because before he'd come here, she'd been ambling along through life just fine, thank you very much, and she'd been content enough. She'd never been a roller-coaster girl. She didn't need peaks of excitement and troughs of despair in her life. She needed to keep things on an even keel.

'Is that what you think I want?'

'I don't know! All I know is that I still think about what *I've* lost. What I will never have. You went through the same thing, so you know that pain. That agony. But you still could try. I can't believe I'm saying this after last night, which was wonderful and amazing and a night I will never, ever forget, but I need to tell you. Remind you. I couldn't bear it if you were to walk away from me because you realised you were trapped in a situation you hadn't fully thought through.'

'I have thought it through. Having a child was my dream once upon a time, but I've moved past that. Have I mentioned it since? Kids are wonderful, but I don't judge you or your worth on whether you can provide me with a child. I just want you to let me love you, and allow yourself to be loved in return. Can you do that?'

'Of course I can!'

'Then that's all I need.'

'Then I'm out here...' she looked down at herself, clad in only a vest top and her underwear '...wearing next to nothing because I couldn't let you leave without telling you that I love you, too.' She smiled. 'If you'll have me.'

The postman was coming up the road. Oliver shrugged off his jacket and wrapped it around her, pulling her towards him. He let out a sigh of relief. 'You scared me for a minute there. So…you're saying that you want to? Be with me? Officially?'

'Yes. If you want to be with me too, we can do this. Day by day. Week by week and all the big things, moving in, getting engaged, married. All of it. Eventually.'

He kissed the tip of her nose. 'Then I can't wait for eventually! I love you, Lorna Hudson.'

She kissed him properly, not caring that the postman was standing there waiting to give her some letters. She laughed at the postman's expression, then turned back to Oliver. 'And I love you, too.'

EPILOGUE

OLIVER WAS MOVING IN. A lorry turned up in front of her cottage and he got out of his car and came into the house. 'Ready for your plus one?'

Lorna laughed. 'Always. I can't believe we're doing this!'

'You know, our weekends are turning out to be pretty spectacular. Last weekend we ran a marathon, this weekend I'm moving in...what's going to happen next week?'

'I don't know. Something just as good, I'm sure.'

'Let's hope.'

They spent some time directing the movers, instructing them about where the boxes should go. She and Olly had spent the week at his place deciding which furniture he would bring with him. Thankfully there wasn't too much, because when he'd rented the property it had already been partly furnished. But he had his favourite chair, a wardrobe, some bookcases and books. His guitar. His bike. His training gear. A few bits and bobs that he'd stored in the loft. His memory boxes that they'd sorted together all those weeks ago.

'Drink?'

'Love one. Oh! Whilst I think about it, I saw this.' He pulled a leaflet from his back pocket, advertising an

Ironman competition next year, open to everyone, consisting of a two-point-four-mile swim, a one-hundred-and-twelve-mile bicycle ride and a marathon run at the end.

'Wow! Okay. You think this should be our event for next year?'

'Could be fun.'

She looked at him and smiled. 'I really think you and I ought to check the dictionary for the real definition of fun, because I'm not sure I remember reading about an Ironman being an example.'

He kissed the tip of her nose. 'No, but you'd look cute in bike shorts.'

She looked him up and down, pressed herself against him and stroked the front of his trousers provocatively. 'So would you.'

Oliver smiled and turned his body so that the movers couldn't see what she was doing with her hand. 'In front of strangers, Dr Hudson?'

'Want me to stop, Dr Clandon?'

'Want? No. Need? Reluctantly, yes. But hold that thought and we could pick it up again after these guys have gone.'

'Won't you want to unpack?' She continued to stroke him.

'It can wait.' He kissed her. Deeply.

She savoured every moment, still in disbelief at what was happening and how their lives were changing. There was so much to tell everyone! They'd tried to keep it secret until Oliver had moved in, but everyone at work had already guessed, so...maybe they weren't as discreet as they'd thought they were. But there was still family to tell and, though they had no doubts that everyone would be thrilled for them, they wanted the move done before telling everyone else. They wanted to keep their little bubble for as long as they could.

Lorna let him go with a sigh. 'Tea, then?'

'Great.' Oliver adjusted his trousers with a smile and went to direct a mover who was trying to bring in the wardrobe.

She gazed at Oliver. At this man who had made her the happiest woman on the planet. Good things came to those who waited, but had the world really needed to make them wait this long?

Perhaps so. They'd both still needed to grow before they could be together. To work out any last remaining baggage they had each been carrying.

Oliver was worth the wait.

This amount of happiness had been worth the wait.

And she knew she would spend the rest of her days being in love and smiling because of this man. Her soul-mate.

Her guy.

As the removal guy trotted upstairs with a large box, Oliver turned to her, holding another. He smiled and passed it to her. 'I think you need to unpack this one.'

She raised an eyebrow. 'What's in it?'

'Open it and see.'

Smiling she took it into the kitchen, slicing open the tape with a knife, only to find another box inside. 'What is this?'

'So many questions.' He laughed.

She sliced open the next box. And then the next. And the next, until finally she sliced open the tape on a small box that revealed a small, velvet-lined box, wrapped in tissue paper. 'Oliver?'

'Just open it.'

Her hands were trembling. She thought she knew what it might be, but she didn't want to leap to any conclusions. Making assumptions had almost made her lose him and she didn't want to make those same mistakes. Not with him.

So she delicately unpeeled the tissue paper and slid out the blue velvet box. It had a gold catch, which she flicked open with her finger and, taking a deep breath, she pushed open the lid.

As she did so, Oliver went down on one knee. 'Lorna… you have made me complete and I love you more than I ever thought it was possible. Will you do me the honour of becoming my wife?'

Lorna gasped at the diamond solitaire ring that sat nestled within the dark blue velvet. Almost stopped breathing as Oliver took the ring from the box and held it to her finger.

He looked up at her, his gaze filled with love.

'Yes! Yes, I will marry you!'

Oliver slid the ring onto her finger and then he was standing and pulling her into his arms for a celebratory kiss.

'This is your version of eventually?' She laughed.

'I waited a week. How much longer did you think I could wait?'

She laughed and kissed him, knowing that they had the rest of their lives to be together. And it would all be absolutely perfect.

* * * * *

*Look out for the next story in the
Cotswold Docs duet*
Finding a Family Next Door

*And, if you enjoyed this story,
check out these other great reads from
Louisa Heaton*

Resisting the Single Dad Surgeon
A Mistletoe Marriage Reunion
Finding Forever with the Firefighter

All available now!

FINDING A FAMILY NEXT DOOR

LOUISA HEATON

MILLS & BOON

To Nick, James, Becca, Jared and Jack. x

CHAPTER ONE

CLEARBROOK INFANTS' SCHOOL was situated down a small narrow lane and Bella could see that parking was a nightmare. She was glad that she had decided to walk Ewan in for his first day as everywhere she looked people were double parking, or patiently waiting, or even doing three-point turns when they realised there was nowhere to go. It was the first day back after the May half-term for most children, but the first day for Ewan, here at his new school.

It was a lovely day, the air filled with the scent of lavender from the fields all around. It was something that had surprised her when she'd come to Clearbrook for her own job interview. That rich, floral scent, the air so thick with it, it had almost made her feel sleepy. Even Priti, the practice manager, had joked that no one in Clearbrook suffered from insomnia.

The lavender helped some towards her nerves. Towards her headache. She was anxious for two reasons. It was her first day at Clearbrook Medical Practice as a new GP, but it was also Ewan's first day away from her for a whole day. Nine till three-thirty for school and then he was in the after-school club until six p.m. It was a heck of a long day. It had been him and her against the world for the last four years and, though she'd loved every moment of it with him, she couldn't wait to see what schooling would do to his character. What his favourite subjects would be. Who his friends would be. What he would want to be when he grew up.

Ewan was already good at reading. Bella had been reading to him since he was a baby and he already knew his alphabet and the ten times table. She'd been determined to raise a good boy, an educated, well-behaved, respectful boy, and the act of letting go and letting someone else teach him, someone else *influence* him, was terrifying.

But that was part of being a parent—letting go. Trusting in the system. Of course, she'd scanned the school OFSTED reports. Talked to the governors. Met the teachers. Ewan's first teacher was a lovely young woman called Miss Celic. She'd given off good vibes. Seemed warm and welcoming. Bella had been happy he was going into her class. She felt confident about it.

But she was still nervous. She had tried to prep Ewan for what would happen. Had even created a book for him, with photos of his school and his teacher that she'd copied from the school website. Shown him the playground and the corridors where he would hang his coat and bag, where he would go for his dinner and how to go to the after-school club when the bell rang at three-thirty and most of the other kids went home.

She knew what he would be eating—Monday was vegetable lasagne midday. The after-school club would give him toast and fruit to tide him over until he got home.

Bella knew he would be okay. He was a confident little boy—just as she'd raised him to be—but a tiny part of her, strangely, wanted him to resist going in. Part of her wanted him to cling to her and not let go when it was time to part and say goodbye.

As she entered the playground with the other parents, she could see a mass of children. Happy, playing. Some clinging to their parent's legs. She saw one guy standing alone, talking to his young daughter, who looked to be on the verge of tears. He was trying to calm her. Smiling. Soothing her. Wiping away her tears with a handkerchief. Was he a single dad? A stay-at-home dad? Maybe he had a job to go to after drop-off?

The little girl was beautiful. Hair a dark blonde, like her father's. Her eyes were large and blue. He was dressed for work. Dark trousers, a pale blue shirt, open at the neck. A suit jacket. He was handsome. Far too handsome, to be fair, and he probably knew it. The kind of man that could simply smile and easily schmooze you with his good looks and twinkling charm, bedazzling you with his beauty so much that it would be too late before you noticed the red flags of his behaviour.

She knew the type. Ewan's father had been like that and she refused to be pulled in by one ever again.

Mind you, she thought, *can't tar all guys with the same brush. Maybe this one's a unicorn?*

She imagined this handsome man prancing around in front of her, wearing hooves on his hands, a multicoloured tail swishing around behind him and a giant sparkling horn protruding from his head. Bella smiled to herself, then dismissed the image, far more interested in watching the guy be so tender and kind to his upset daughter. His face was the picture of patience and love and when he reached up to wipe away a tear from his daughter's face, she felt an ache.

Bella turned away from their private moment as the man then reached out to his daughter to give her a hug. 'Are you ready?' she asked Ewan, smiling, trying to look and sound confident with her decision to put him in for a full day straight away. The school had suggested that, until Ewan got used to the place, he only come part time for the first couple of days. Mornings only. Or afternoons only. But, as she'd explained to them, she couldn't do that with her job. Her job was full time and so she needed him in full time. She'd promised them that he would be fine, because she would prepare him for it. Ewan was strong, she'd told them. He'd be all right.

Ewan nodded, smiling.

He held her hand, but she could feel him trying to let go as he gazed at a group of boys playing on the playground equipment. There were rope bridges, a climbing frame, a slide, a circle of tyres, swings and what looked like a low climbing wall. The group of boys were having fun.

'Can I go and play, Mum?'

He'd be going in any minute and, though she wanted to stay every second she could with him before she'd have to let him go, she knew that he would need to make friends and so she nodded, reluctantly, and let him go. She watched him run away from her, without a care in the world as he joined the other boys. He seemed to seamlessly join in and was laughing and playing, clearly not worrying about her.

She felt a pang in her heart. Had she raised him to be *too* confident?

No. This is a good thing.

She was happy to know that she'd successfully raised him to be confident and outgoing—it was what she'd wanted. Being this way meant that he would cope with the long days apart from her and therefore it would make her life easier. She turned to look at all the other parents, her eyes falling again on the man, with his daughter, that she'd seen before. The man was standing now. He'd lifted his daughter into his arms and was hugging her, whispering soothing words into her ear. He was smiling. He kissed her ear and put her down again, the little girl slipping her hand into his and nodding to him, trying to be brave.

Part of her wanted that moment with Ewan. To give him one last moment of encouragement, one last pearl of wisdom that would make him feel brave enough to go into school without her. To have that experience that all the other parents talked about. But she wasn't going to get that and that was okay, too, because she would rather see him happy and smiling and enjoying himself than have him clinging to her leg and making her feel awful to leave him behind.

A whistle blew and the doors opened and teachers appeared.

Bella saw Miss Celic standing there in a pink summer dress and white bolero cardigan. She was greeting parents and children alike as they began to file past her towards their classroom and Bella turned to call for Ewan. To kiss him goodbye before he went in, but he was already past her, grabbing at his bag and lining up for his teacher.

She stood there, feeling proud of him for being so brave, so carefree. She'd wanted one last word to wish him good luck, but he was already gone. She laughed to herself instead. She was proud of a job well done. This was how she'd raised him to be. Confident. Brave. Outgoing. She'd raised a good boy and the evidence was there to see. She could go into work now and not worry about him.

Instead, she watched the man walk his daughter towards Miss Celic, saw him kneel, kiss his daughter's cheek one last time, saw him mouth the words *I love you* as his daughter gave him one last desperate hug. Miss Celic took the little girl's hand and led her wards into the school, the doors closing shut behind them, and then all the parents began to file away.

The man gave one last wave and blew a kiss, before his daughter disappeared from sight.

She knew he would remember this last moment. That memory that he would keep for ever now. Maybe something that he might bring up one day, say, at her wedding, talking of the moment he knew he had to let go of his daughter the first time, to make her own way in the world?

He disappeared into the migrating crowd of parents and she knew she had to get to work now. Had to face her own first day. It was a day that she'd been looking forward to for a long time.

This was the beginning of the fresh start. No more would she just be a locum GP, travelling here, there and everywhere to work the odd day, leaving Ewan behind with her own father, or with a childminder. No more would she face let-downs and disappointments and be cheated of the chance to gain a long-term relationship with a set of patients.

Today, she began her role as a *permanent* member of staff at a surgery. A place where she could build relationships for the first time. A place where she would put down roots. Where she would raise her son to be a man. A good man. A strong man, who was respectful and kind and loving and loyal. She hoped to make good friends here, too.

It was a three-minute walk from the school to the medical centre. Not far. And what a beautiful walk it was. Down the lane, across the village green, a little way down the main street and there it was, on the left. Surrounded by old stone cottages, thatched rooves and gardens full of blooms. A fat ginger cat sat on top of the post box next door, surveying the green. She reached up to stroke it and the feline allowed it, head bumping into her hand with a loud purr.

'What's your name?' she asked, knowing she might sound silly, talking to a cat, but she loved cats and she'd promised Ewan they might get one, once they'd settled in properly. A rescue cat, maybe? Something older, that was just looking for someone's lap to sleep on every night?

And then she was there, standing outside the doors of Clearbrook Medical Practice, and she was straightening her clothes and checking her hair and sucking in a deep breath. The doors slid open at her approach and she stepped inside and headed to Reception, frowning as she approached, noticing the man that had said goodbye to his daughter standing right in front.

Was he a patient here?

She tried not to take in more details about him, because she didn't want to, but her eyes seemed to do their own thing and she couldn't help but notice how much taller he was, now that he was closer to her. How his shoes were perfectly buffed, the confidence with which he stood there as he waited for the receptionist to be free from her patient with a prescription enquiry. Then her nose betrayed her by noticing how good he smelt. Something masculine. Sandalwood? Neroli? Bergamot? She was never very good at identifying specific aftershaves or lotions that men wore.

And then the patient went to sit in the waiting room and the man in front stepped forward and she heard him say, 'Hello. I'm Dr Moore.'

Dr Moore? Dr Max Moore? Priti had told her that there were going to be three new doctors starting at the practice. A Dr Oliver Clandon, herself and a Dr Max Moore. She'd just expected, though she didn't know why, that the two men would be older. She wondered where his wife was and why she wasn't at school drop-off this morning. Maybe she started work earlier than him and it had just been more convenient for him to take their daughter in for her first day?

That had to be it, so it didn't matter that she was going to have to work with this guy that was way too handsome for his own good. He was already taken.

She stepped forward to speak to the receptionist. 'And I'm Dr Nightingale. I'm expected, too.'

Dr Moore turned to look at her, his face breaking into a friendly smile as he held out his hand for her to shake. 'Hello! It's Max.'

She took his hand and shook, but broke contact as quickly as she could without being rude. Ignoring the tingles in her hand, the shiver that ran up her arm. 'Annabella. But everyone calls me Bella.'

There was a strange pause. 'Very pleased to meet you. I guess we're going to be working together?'

She nodded. Smiled. 'I guess we are.'

Annabella. But everyone calls me Bella.
Max had been able to breathe then.

Bella. Not *Anna.* She didn't have the same name as his dead wife. And she looked nothing like her, either. His wife had been blonde, like him, Bella was dark-haired. Hair like dark chocolate. Smooth, silky. Piercing blue eyes.

He'd noticed her earlier at the school, of course. How could he not have? She'd looked so lost and alone, her son having gone to play with some other boys on the climbing frames, and Dr Nightingale—*Bella*—had stood there in the centre of the yard, arms locked around her body, gazing at her son and looking a little unwanted.

He'd felt her pain.

Max knew the feeling. Saying goodbye to Rosie this morning had been incredibly painful. His daughter had not wanted to say goodbye. She'd wanted to hold onto him. She'd been scared. She hadn't known anybody.

She'd begged him to stay with her.

His heart had ached for her. Knowing she had such a long day ahead of her. Not only a full day of school, but also an after-school club, but Miss Celic, his daughter's teacher, had reassured him that Rosie would not be the only one to do that. There were going to be others having a long day, too, but they'd be okay, once they settled into it.

It had been hard to say goodbye. It had been hard to let her go. He'd protected her so much from the world, it felt wrong to let someone else protect her, even if they were teachers. Trained professionals. But he'd been her everything since Anna's parents had emigrated to Spain, in search of warmer climes for their health. He'd promised he'd visit them every summer holidays. Stay for a couple of weeks, so they could continue to know their granddaughter and be a part of her life. But, needing support, he'd moved here, closer to his own parents, so that they could be involved with Rosie, too. His daughter had lost a mother, much too soon. She needed as many people as possible.

Max wondered if Dr Nightingale's—Bella's—son was in the after-school club, too.

He must have asked the question out loud, because she was nodding. 'Yes, he is, but I'm not sure he's that worried about it. He couldn't wait to get into school this morning.'

'I had the opposite. I think Rosie wanted to stay with me.'

At that moment, the practice manager, Priti, arrived and welcomed them both. 'Let me introduce you to the other doctors. I think they're between patients right now.'

They met Dr Oliver Clandon first. He was an older gentleman. Distinguished. Seemed really nice and friendly. Then they were introduced to Dr Lorna Hudson. Again, older, but she had stunning red hair, wavy. Kind eyes and a bright smile. She shook their hands. 'Did you find us all right?'

'It was easy enough. Thankfully the clinic is near the infant school.'

'Oh, that's right. Priti said you'd both got young kids. How old?'

They kept their conversation short, as Lorna's computer beeped to let her know her next patient had arrived and so Priti took them to their consulting rooms. Bella first and then his room, next door to Dr Nightingale's. 'There's a welcome pack on your desk. ID card and passcode information for the computer is in the pack. You'll want to create your own password.'

'Thank you.'

'First patient is at ten o'clock. We've allocated both you and Bella twenty-minute consultations for the first day, just until you get into the swing of things and begin to learn where everything is.'

'Sounds great.'

'I'll leave you to it, but my office is just at the end of the hall. I'm on an admin day, so, any problems, don't hesitate to knock.'

'Will do. And thank you again.'

Priti left him to it and he sat down at his desk, switched on the computer and, whilst he waited for it to boot up, he opened his backpack and removed the framed picture he'd brought with him of Anna holding Rosie in her arms, when she was just a few hours old. It was one of the few pictures he had of them together, where Anna looked well. When she still had her hair. He treasured it. Looking at it, he could almost pretend that it was just a normal picture. A mother with her newborn child. The glow and exhaustion on her face from happiness, before more horrible news hit them.

He wondered how Rosie was doing. If she'd settled. If she was okay.

He had to trust that she was, if he was going to do his job. But it felt as if a part of him were missing. Max glanced at the wall that separated him from Bella. Dr Nightingale.

She was probably feeling the exact same way.

Bella called through her first patient of the day. Her first patient ever at Clearbrook, knowing that she would remember this patient over any other, because of it.

Dorothea Godwin ambled down the corridor towards

her, leaning heavily on a walking stick and carrying a wicker bag in her other hand. 'Hello, Doctor. How are you?'

'I'm very well, thank you! Pleased to meet you. I'm Dr Nightingale.'

Behind her, the door to Max's room opened and she turned to see him waiting for his own first patient to make it down the corridor, too. Automatically, she smiled at him and his own smile was warm and comforting. Genuine. Reassuring. She felt a little bad about jumping to conclusions about him earlier, just because he was attractive. His looks didn't mean he'd be like her ex and the trust issues she'd developed since that past fiasco would need some work if she was going to make friends here. She had plans, beyond her job and Ewan's success at school, of really becoming part of the community. Of becoming social, and she knew she needed to work on herself first.

She nodded her greeting and closed the door behind her, waiting for Dorothea to settle into her chair before she took her own seat. 'It says here that you're concerned about some breathing issues you've been having?'

Every time a patient booked an appointment, the reception staff had to ask what the consultation was for, so they could make a note and add it to the clinic list. That way, the consulting physician could check the history before the appointment to see if there was anything similar in the patient's previous history, what comorbidities there might be, but also to prepare themselves for the consult.

'That's right.'

Dorothea was breathing heavily from the short walk down the corridor from the waiting room. 'I'm just breathless a lot lately and I've never been like this before. I did have a spring cold a week ago and I wondered if it was something to do with that.'

'It's possible that a viral infection could have caused a residual lung issue, but let's have a chat first and then I'll do some obs, if that's okay with you, and see where we go from there. How does that sound?'

'Marvellous.'

'Is the breathlessness worse after movement, or is it like this all the time?'

'Both, really.'

'And you've never had any issues with asthma, or your lungs, before?'

'No. Fit as a fiddle.'

Bella performed some observations on Dorothea. Her blood pressure was a little raised, but to be expected. Her pulse was a little fast and she had a slight temperature. 'What sort of symptoms did the cold give you?'

'Well, this breathing issue. I coughed a lot. A dreadful cough for the first few days and I felt so tired.'

'Blocked nose? Headaches?'

'No, not really.'

'Okay. I'd like to do a quick swab, if that's okay? To check to see if you have Covid.' She swabbed Dorothea's nose, dipped the swab in the solution, mixed it and then added a couple of drops to the testing stick. Whilst she waited for the results, she listened to her patient's chest. She had equal sounds. No crackling. So no chest infection and her heart sounded good, no arrhythmias, or murmurs. She had no swelling in her ankles, no puffiness, no water retention. Her oxygen saturations were at ninety-three, just under what they should be at ninety-four. 'Do you live with anyone?'

'No. I enjoy my freedom too much. Believe it or not, but I used to be quite the vixen in my youth. Got plenty of offers, but never really wanted to be tied down by a man. I do have a gentleman caller, though, so I get to have some fun when I want it. On my terms!' Dorothea laughed, then coughed.

'Sounds like you have it all worked out. Good for you.'

Dorothea chuckled. 'Indeed. I saw what my own mother went through and knew I didn't want that for myself. It was odd for women, back in my day, to not want marriage, but I made it work and all those people who thought I was odd are a little bit jealous now.'

Bella nodded. She could remember her own mum telling her that little girls grew up to get married and have children of their own and it would bring her happiness, but all her own personal heartbreak had come from romantic relationships. 'You have Covid.'

'No! But I'm vaccinated!'

'The vaccination doesn't stop you from getting Covid. It just stops it from getting really bad and putting you in hospital.'

'So the breathlessness is down to that little bugger, then, is it?'

'I'm afraid so. You might just need to take it easy for a little while. But I can prescribe you an inhaler to use that should help things, if you feel like you'd need it.'

Dorothea nodded. 'Better to have something and not need it than need something and not have it.'

'My thoughts exactly.' Bella made up the prescription. 'I've sent that order through to your named chemist. You should be able to pick it up this afternoon.' She paused.

'Maybe get your gentleman caller to look after you a little bit.'

'Ernest would love to move in and nurse me, I'll give you that, but what about my social life?'

'How do you mean?'

'I go to a lot of clubs and groups. I have an art class every Monday evening. I have that tonight. So far, it's been fruit in bowls and still life and all that.' Dorothea leaned in. 'But tonight, we've got a life model. A male life model!'

Bella laughed. 'Good thing I've prescribed you that inhaler, then!'

'Can I go to the class with this Covid thing?'

'People aren't that upset about it these days. It would be best for you to stay in, to help prevent spread, but no one's going to stop you. You could always wear a mask and warn everyone.'

'Ooh, good! I'll do that, then! Let the male model think I'm breathless from Covid. You've been very nice.' Dorothea's gaze dropped to her hand. 'I don't see a ring. Are you not married either?'

Bella didn't like to discuss her own life with her patients. Not if she could help it. 'No, but I do have a little boy who is the love of my life and that's all I need.'

Dorothea stood. 'Motherly love is a wonderful thing, but—' she winked '—no substitute for a warm body in bed with you! That wonderful little boy will grow into a man and will *leave you* for someone else. If you don't want to be alone, you have to get out there.'

Bella laughed awkwardly and said goodbye to Dorothea and watched her walk down the corridor back out to Reception and then she went back into her consulting room and closed the door.

She'd never minded being alone. Had sworn off the idea of marriage. Had sworn off the idea of men completely. But Dorothea was right. It had been a long time since a man had lain in a bed with her. Since she had allowed a man to be with her. Since she'd had someone to be vulnerable with.

She thought of Max's smiling face, lying on a pillow next to hers, and instantly she stopped typing.

I can't think of him like that! He's married.

Probably. And even if he wasn't, he'd no doubt have a long line of women who would be more than happy to jump into bed with him and he would not consider an insecure single mother with trust issues.

That wasn't sexy.

Bella had Ewan and, yes, one day he would move out. One day he *would* start a life of his own, but he would always *come back* and visit his mum, because they were close and had a strong bond and that would never change.

And it would be enough.

It would always be enough.

She reached for her bag and found the paracetamol. Her headache was bad today and so she took two, hoping they would help.

They usually did.

CHAPTER TWO

MAX'S FIRST PATIENT, a Mr Robert Heaney, came down the corridor, limping. The consult note said 'pain in left leg' and it was vague enough to be any number of possible reasons. So he invited Mr Heaney in and settled down into his seat. 'How can I help you today?'

'It's my leg. This one.' Mr Heaney patted his left knee. 'Been causing me a problem for about a week now with this pain in my calf.'

Max nodded. 'Is it something that's come on suddenly?'

'I guess. One day it was fine and I could get about no problem, the next day, it's hurting me.'

'And have you banged the leg? Had a fall? Injured it in any way?'

'No, nothing like that. I am an active man, so I've noticed it a lot. I do a lot of walking and a lot of gardening and when it first started, I just imagined I'd maybe pulled it or something and imagined it would go away, but it hasn't.'

'And would you say the leg looks different? Is it swollen, or red, or hot?'

'A bit.'

'And what is the pain like? Is it a sharp, stabbing pain, or more like an ache?'

'It throbs. Like in pulses.'

'All right, well, maybe we ought to take a look at it. Can you raise your trouser leg above it, or would it be better for you to remove them?'

'I'll have to take them off.' Mr Heaney stood and began to drop his trousers, before Max could offer him a chaperone.

His patient's left calf muscle did look more swollen than the right and there was a redness and a heat to it. Max took a tape measure and measured the circumference of both calf muscles and the left one was a couple of inches larger than the right. 'Well, this could be a simple infection, but the thing we're worried about the most with symptoms like this is a DVT. A deep vein thrombosis.' A blood clot. It could be worrying in case the clot spread to the lungs and caused a pulmonary embolism. It could be life-threatening. 'Any chest pains? Any breathlessness?'

'No.' Mr Heaney shook his head. 'Is this because I went on holiday to Barcelona?'

'When was that?'

'Just over a week ago. Went on a stag do. My future son-in-law's.'

'If it is a blood clot, then that is possible. What I'd like to do is refer you to hospital immediately for an ultrasound scan. Would you be able to get there? Is there someone who could drive you?'

'My wife.'

'Good. I'll print out this letter for you to take with you and you'll be seen as quickly as they can. I'll call through to them now.' Max found the details for the local hospital and followed the protocols for a DVT referral.

'And if it is?' Mr Heaney asked when Max got off the phone. 'Is that surgery?'

'It can be. They'll also prescribe blood thinners for you to take afterwards. Maybe warfarin or rivaroxaban.'

'Never thought I'd get something like this.' He seemed shocked.

'It can happen to anyone. Any time and sometimes for no reason at all that we can determine.' He passed his patient the letter. 'Good luck. I hope they're able to sort it out for you quickly.'

'Thank you, Doctor.'

'Bye.'

That was the thing with many health conditions. You could feel perfectly fine, completely unaware of something malignant growing inside. He remembered a great aunt of his own, who had lived to the grand old age of ninety-four. She'd seemed fine. Healthy as a horse. Had never been sick a day in her life. Then one day, right after lunch, she'd passed out. Hit her head on the way down and was taken to hospital and there, during a scan, they'd discovered that her body was riddled with tumours and she'd passed away two weeks later.

But she'd had no pain. No discomfort to tell her that something was wrong. She'd still been attending all her groups. Still laughing. Still enjoying her nightly tipple of whisky before bed—her only vice. In those last two weeks, the whisky had been exchanged for morphine.

And then there was his own wife, Anna. She'd been the picture of health. Glowing. Happy. She'd fallen pregnant—accidentally, but they'd adapted to the news. And then, at four months, she'd discovered a lump. Thought it nothing more than a cyst.

But it hadn't been.

You never know what life might suddenly throw at you. What curveballs you'll have to deal with.

Max picked up the framed picture of his wife and baby daughter. How much he wished they could have had more time. But it had been short. Fleeting. And now he was alone with Rosie, trying to be the best father he could be.

He had four more patients to see before morning break. He met a very nice young lady who wanted to discuss going on the contraceptive pill. A young boy of four with chicken pox. An elderly gent with back pain, having spent too long in the garden over the weekend, and his last patient before break was a young woman who came in looking pale and red-eyed, pushing a pram with her three-week-old baby son in.

'I feel nothing,' she said, before she burst into tears and he had to pass her the box of tissues that had been sitting on the window ledge.

Max waited for her tears to dry up and encouraged her to speak more.

'Since having baby Hayden, I just… I don't feel any joy. I don't feel anything…for him.' She indicated the baby and began to cry some more. 'I should, right? I should feel something! I should be totally in love with him and yet all I feel is numbness and sometimes resentment that my life has changed and what for? My life is harder now. I'm not sleeping. I'm not eating. Hayden cries all the time. I'm left alone all day with the baby, because my husband works and I can't tell *him* how I feel.'

At that moment, Hayden seemed to wake and began to fuss and so Max got up and scooped the baby out of his pram and gently began to sway with him and pat his back in case he had trapped wind, and waited for his mother, Rachel, to stop crying.

'What you're feeling is totally normal. Bonds don't always immediately appear because you want them to, or because the media or online influencers paint a picture of domestic and maternal bliss with their babies. Your body has been through an enormous change. You're flooded with hormones and you're adapting to a new dynamic, whilst trying to take care of a brand-new baby human. It's okay to feel this way, to feel a little blue after birth. We call it postnatal depression and it's normal, but it doesn't mean it'll last and it doesn't mean you will always feel this way. Now, let me assess little Hayden to see if there's a reason for the crying.'

Baby Hayden was fine. He'd put on a few ounces since his birth weight, his reflexes were good, his chest and tummy sounded fine and Rachel said he was having wet nappies and breastfeeding well.

'He could just be a little colicky, which is common.' Colic was when a baby cried a lot for no apparent reason. It made them hard to soothe, they'd clench their fists, go red in the face and bring their knees up, indicating perhaps a little discomfort in their stomach. 'It does pass, usually around three to four months. You can get anti-colic drops and you can make sure you're not eating spicy foods or anything that might upset him, but honestly? I can't promise you that these things will work. What you need to do more than anything else is to give yourself a lot more grace. Make sure you rest. Nap when Hayden sleeps. Eat well. Drink plenty. Try and get outside each day if you can—the exercise and fresh air will do you both good.'

Max remembered the first few weeks after Rosie's

birth, when the bad news of Anna's condition had got worse and instead of being allowed to enjoy those first few weeks with her baby, she'd got to sit in hospitals, enduring chemotherapy.

He'd taken Rosie on those outdoor walks alone. They'd spent many hours in the parks, or walking the trails, and he'd talk to his daughter as they went, telling her all about the ducks and the trees and the flowers, but most of all, about the beautiful and wondrous person that was Rosie's mother. How he hoped that Rosie would be able to form memories with her mother that she would be able to remember for herself. A hope that she was never able to accomplish.

Rosie had no memory of her mother. She'd been too young when Anna had passed and he'd had to raise his daughter alone. Fiercely loving her and protecting her and making sure she wanted for nothing, but fearing all the time that he wasn't enough for her. That her lack of a mother in her life would somehow hold her back. Make her less confident. As she had been that morning about going into school.

'Are you able to sit down with your husband and tell him how you're feeling? I think you'll be surprised that he probably feels just as overwhelmed as you do.'

'But I'm meant to know what to do as a mother. How to soothe my baby and I can't sometimes. It's like he hates me.'

'And it bothers you. You care about it. Which shows that you *do* have feelings. You are attached. You do love your baby, it just takes time, sometimes, before that bond blooms and you'll reach a point where you can't remember not loving him.'

'I hope so.'

'Is there the possibility that your husband can give you some alone time? So you get a break? Time to shower? To meet with friends?'

'We haven't spoken about it.'

'Perhaps you should try. I'm sure he'd understand. Have you spoken to your health visitor about this?'

Rachel shook her head.

'Well, I'll inform her for you. Get her to check in on you a little more often, but I'd also like to see you, maybe in another week? See how you are? And if you feel like it's getting worse, or you're not coping at all, you ring the surgery and I'll see you, all right? I'll leave word with Reception that if you call, they're to fit you in somehow. I'll make time for you.'

'Thank you.' She burst into tears again. As if that one small act of kindness was all too much.

He bid her farewell, wishing that there'd been some sort of magic button he could press to make her world all right again. *He* knew she would get over this. He knew there was light on the other side for Rachel. But she couldn't see it yet, because she was still in the trenches, feeling guilty that she wasn't being the mother she imagined she was meant to be.

He felt her pain.

Max made his way to the staffroom. He was the only person there and so he rummaged in the cupboards and found a box of peppermint teabags and switched on the kettle. As he waited for it to boil, he picked up a magazine off the low coffee table and began to read, putting it down again when Dr Nightingale—Bella—entered.

'Hey. How's it going?' he asked.

'Good, I think. You?'

'Same.'

'Feels good to finally be putting down some personal roots and not living the locum life any more.'

'I know exactly what you mean. I felt like a jobbing doctor, picking up the occasional shift here and there, but never staying in one place long enough to make any real friends at work. Fancy a tea? I've got the kettle on.'

'Do they have anything herbal?'

'There's peppermint. That's what I'm having and I think I saw a lemon and ginger one in there, too.'

'Peppermint will be great, thanks.' She sat down beside him, looking quite nervous and apprehensive, tucking her long, dark hair behind one ear.

She had beautiful skin, he noticed. Like porcelain. If she'd been an actress, she'd have made an excellent vampire. He smiled.

'What?' She caught him smiling.

'Nothing. Peppermint, you say?' he said, trying to distract as he got up to make her drink, too.

'Yes. Please. No sign of Lorna or Oliver?'

'I think I heard him take a drink down to her room.'

'Oh. Do they know each other, then?'

'Erm, I think I remember Priti saying something along the lines of them knowing each other at medical school.'

'Wow. They must have a lot to catch up on, then.'

'Yep.'

'Must be strange for the two of them to meet up again after all those years.'

It had to be. But kind of nice, too, he thought. 'How do you think our kids are getting on?'

Bella laughed. 'Ewan's probably taken over the whole

school by now. I'd hoped for a wistful cuddle before he went in, but he couldn't wait to get in there. Don't think he's even thought about me. He couldn't wait to be off.'

'But that's good, right? That you've imbued him with such confidence? I wish Rosie had a little of that. Might put my mind at rest, knowing she's got such a long day ahead of her without me.'

'Have you ever been apart?'

'She's spent some time with her grandparents. The occasional sleepover, you know, but that's with people that she's grown up with. That she knows. Miss Celic, the school, all those other kids, they're all strange.'

'She'll be okay. Even if she doesn't think so right now, she will be.'

'It's hard though. Being a single parent. Trying to be both a mother and a father to your child. Rosie's mum, she…er…she died. When Rosie was one year old.'

'I'm so sorry to hear that.' She looked surprised too. Her sympathy sincere. 'What happened? If you don't mind me asking?'

'Anna discovered she had breast cancer at the beginning of her pregnancy. It was aggressive and we were actually advised to terminate, so that she could receive treatment.'

'Oh. That must have been awful for you both.'

The way she was looking at him was intense. He was taken in by the inviting blue of her eyes. The way she seemed to understand the pain they'd been in at being told such a thing. 'It was. I told Anna I'd support her either way, but that I agreed with the doctors. Anna though? She didn't. She wanted to be a mother and she felt so well she didn't want to terminate, convinced she could beat the cancer. She was induced early. Thirty-six weeks, but tests afterwards showed that the cancer had metastasised and that all they could offer her was palliative chemotherapy.'

'My God…' Bella looked down at the floor. 'I'm so sorry.'

'It's been me and Rosie ever since. It's been hard, but I think we're doing okay. Anna's parents emigrated recently, due to their own health, seeking warmer climes, and so, knowing I wanted to give Rosie some stability, I moved here to be closer to my parents, so that she had family that wasn't just me.'

He paused, thinking about all the stress he'd gone through when he'd heard that Morag and Jim, Anna's parents, were leaving. They'd been his rock. His connection to Anna and now even they were gone.

'What about you? Are you here with Ewan's dad?'

Bella smiled and shook her head sadly. 'No, I'm not. I'm a single parent like you.'

He nodded. 'I see. Does Ewan get to see his dad?'

'No.' Bella sucked in a deep breath and looked everywhere but at him.

Had he overstepped?

'Blake was cheating on me. I found that out the day I discovered I was pregnant with Ewan. I moved out—we'd been living together, and I left the door open for him to be a part of Ewan's life, but he didn't want to know. He pays child support, but that's all we get from him. Not a card, not a present. He didn't even come to see his son when he was born. But, you know, we've accepted that and moved on and I think I'm doing a half-decent job at raising a little boy that will grow up to respect women and not cheat on them. And…' she laughed '…he's clearly confident.'

Max smiled. 'Well, from what I saw today, you've raised a very happy little boy.'

'Thank you.'

He passed her a mug of peppermint tea. 'And what do you do when you're not raising a man of the future?'

'Sleep!' She laughed, accepting it. 'I like to read. Fiction. I also dabble with drawing and painting, but I'm not very good.'

'Seriously? I like doing that, too. You should show me your work.'

'Oh, I don't think it's anything that should be endured by the public.'

'You show me yours. I'll show you mine.' He winked at her and laughed when she blushed and looked away.

He loved the way she blushed. That creamy porcelain skin gently glowed with a hint of pink. A small bloom of warmth on each cheek that slowly dissipated again back to the vampire white.

'I guess we'd better get back to it?'

She nodded. 'Yes.'

'I'll see you later.'

She raised her mug. 'Yes. And thank you. For my peppermint tea.'

'You're welcome, Bella. You're very welcome.'

Even though she'd enjoyed her first day, her heart ached for Ewan. She had missed him so much. And once her admin for the day and her telephone appointments had been completed, she grabbed her things from the staffroom and hurried to the infants' school to collect from the after-school club.

She imagined she'd find a very tired young boy. She

imagined that when she walked through the door to collect him, he would see her and run into her arms for a kiss and a big hug. And then he would babble excitedly about all the things he'd done that day as they walked home and maybe she'd have some art to pin up on the fridge.

But when she arrived at the school, the kids were all outside playing in the playground on the climbing equipment and she could see Ewan at the top of the climbing frame, laughing with his new friends and, though she hated to call him down, she knew she had to get his attention. 'Ewan! Ewan, I'm here now. We can go home!'

One of the staff came over to her. 'You're Ewan's mum?'

'Yes, that's right. How's he been?'

'Brilliant. That's a happy boy you've got there. Very confident. Wasn't shy about joining in or leading the group.'

Bella was glad to hear it. 'Has he eaten?'

'Just some fruit slices. He was more interested in playing pirates with the other boys over there.'

She nodded, watching as Ewan reluctantly began his climb down. She couldn't see Rosie and she had to be here, because when Bella had left work, Max had still been working on some prescription requests.

'I'll take you in, so you can pick up his coat and bag,' said the staff member.

'Oh, right. Of course.' Reluctantly, she headed inside, feeling as though she'd have to postpone that hug and kiss for a little while longer.

Inside, there was a small kitchenette, where another member of staff was washing some multicoloured plastic plates and forks and spoons. She wore a tabard with teddy bears on it. 'This is Ewan's mum.'

The tabard lady nodded and smiled.

Past the kitchenette was a room filled with lumpy sofas, beanbags and boxes of toys and puzzles, a TV in a corner, with a games console and a messy bookshelf. Next to the bookshelf was Rosie. Curled up on a chair with a member of staff, having a story read to her. The little girl looked so tired. So overwhelmed, her cheeks red, her eyes puffy, as if she'd been crying for a long time, that even Bella felt her heart ache for her.

Once she'd collected Ewan's coat and bag, she took a moment to go over to her. 'It's Rosie, isn't it?' Bella knelt down, to be on the little girl's level.

Rosie nodded, uncertainly.

'My name's Bella and I work with your dad. He'll be here soon. You won't have to wait too much longer.'

'Really?' Rosie looked hopeful, the hint of a smile breaking across her face as she glanced at the doorway, as if expecting her dad to walk through any moment.

Bella smiled back. 'Really. I'm Ewan's mummy. My name's Bella. I'm a doctor, like your dad.'

At that moment, the door swung open and in walked Ewan. 'Mummy!'

She stood and held out her arms as he ran straight into them for a hug, a hug that she hoped would last for minutes, if not hours, as she so needed to feel his body pressed against hers. But the second he held her, the second he let go to reel off an impressive list of all the things that he'd got up to that day. 'Slow down, slow down! Wow. Okay. First things first. Coat on.'

He slid his arms into his coat and she passed him his bag. 'Ewan, have you met Rosie?'

Ewan glanced at the little girl. 'No.'

'I need you to be friends with her, okay? Look after her.'

He nodded. 'Okay.' And then he did something that was very sweet. He walked over to her and held out his hand. Just as she'd taught him to. 'Hello, Rosie. My name's Ewan. Do you want to be my friend?'

Very shyly, Rosie nodded and shook his hand.

Then Ewan turned to her. 'Can we go home now? I'm *starving*!'

She chuckled. 'Yes. Me too, but…' She turned back to Rosie. 'Do you want us to wait with you until your dad gets here?'

Rosie shook her head. 'I'm okay.'

'All right. Well, we'll see you tomorrow?'

Rosie nodded.

When Max arrived at the school, he found his daughter snuggled into a member of staff on the couch, being read a story. Her cheeks were flushed and she looked so very tired and instantly he felt guilty for subjecting her to such a long day.

Maybe it was too soon?

Maybe going back to work like this, accepting a full-time job like this, wasn't fair on her? But the second she saw him, her face brightened and she ran across the floor to him and threw herself into his arms as he scooped her up and swung her around, before pulling her in for a long, long hug. 'Oh, I've missed you! Are you okay?'

The staff member who'd been reading her the story got

up and smiled at him. 'She's been fine. A little teary to start with, but that's to be expected. We've just been enjoying this story. Do you want to take it home with you? Finish it at bedtime?'

It felt good to hold Rosie in his arms. Her little, light-weight body. He'd missed her so much. Had worried about her all day. Had she thought he'd abandoned her? Despite all the talks they'd had about what this day would look like? Feel like? 'Thank you.' He took the book and kissed his daughter's cheek. 'Ready to go home?' he whispered.

He felt her nod and so, without putting her down, he grabbed her coat and the teacher put the book into her bag and passed him that and she mouthed goodbye and he left, feeling his heart lighten the further and further away they got.

He would get her home, feed her, bathe her, put her to bed.

And do it all again tomorrow.

Would it get easier?

Max stroked her back as he walked with her in his arms. He didn't care what anyone might think, he would carry his daughter for as long as she would let him, because one day she'd be too old for it and he never wanted to think about that. Or those difficult teenager years when perhaps she might be embarrassed by him and ask him to walk about ten yards behind her to pretend they weren't together.

When they got back to their new home, a cottage on Field Lane, he finally put her down to search for his keys and open the door.

Rosie ran inside and headed for the kitchen.

'Hungry?'

She nodded.

He opened the fridge. 'We've got…pizza? How does that sound?'

She beamed. 'Pizza! Pepperoni?'

'Is there any other kind?' He grabbed the pizza and placed it in the oven and, whilst it was cooking, he got some salad bits out and began to prepare a side. 'So, how was your first day?'

'Okay.'

'You make any friends?'

'A boy.'

'A boy?' He turned around, surprised. He'd always viewed Rosie as a girl's girl. He'd never imagined her making friends with a boy first. 'What's his name?'

'Ewan.'

Max smiled. Bella's son. 'Okay. Is he nice?'

Rosie nodded. 'Mmm-hmm. Can I help you cut things up?'

He had some child-friendly knives, so he let her slice the cucumber.

'Bella's nice, too.'

He stopped to look at her. 'You met Bella?'

'She said hello to me. She's a doctor, too. Like you.'

'That's right. You liked her?'

Another nod. 'Did she offer to be your friend, too?'

Max smiled. 'Yes. Yes, she did. I think we're going to be very good friends.'

'So you had a good first day, too?'

He kissed the top of her head. She was saying she had a good first day. It helped leach away some of the guilt he'd been feeling. 'Yeah. A great first day.'

CHAPTER THREE

BELLA HAD SLEPT much better last night than she had the night before, but still she woke with one of her usual headaches she'd been having lately. Sighing, she popped a couple of painkillers whilst Ewan ate his breakfast and then checked his bag to make sure he had everything he needed for the day.

'Where are your plimsolls?'

'I don't know.'

'They were in here yesterday. How could they have disappeared?'

'I don't know.' He wasn't really listening. He was watching cartoons whilst spooning cereal into his mouth.

Bella sighed. She'd have to ask at the school, or check the lost-property box, but it was annoying, because they were brand new. 'Ten minutes!' she called, as post dropped through the letter box and she headed down the hallway to collect it.

Two letters confirming that she was now a new customer of a couple of utility companies and one letter that looked as if it was from the hospital. Before they'd moved here, she'd been to see her own doctor about the headaches she'd been having. She was sure they were just migraines, but, better to be safe than sorry, her GP had referred her to a neurologist. The neurologist in question worked at three different hospitals and one of them happened to be at the hospital closest to Clearbrook.

Opening the envelope, she discovered that she had an appointment in a few weeks' time. She made a note of the date and time in her phone, so that she could inform Priti that she wouldn't be in that afternoon and to rearrange her clinic for that day. It said on the letter to allow three hours for the appointment, in case she had to have a scan, so unfortunately it would mean missing half a day.

'Come on, we don't want to be late. Go brush your teeth.' Ewan scampered upstairs and Bella turned off the television and checked her own bag and reflection in the mirror. Pale, as always, though the bags under her eyes looked the same. She dabbed some concealer on them and hoped for the best. No one wanted to visit a doctor who looked ill themselves. It hardly inspired confidence.

The concealer helped and she told herself that all she needed were a few more decent nights' sleep. It was stressful—moving home to a new area where you knew no one. Starting a new job. A full-time job. Sending your kid to school for the first time. They'd both been through some big changes. She was trying to separate herself from the past. Their last home had been nice, but it had been the place where everything had gone wrong and it felt tainted somehow.

Starting anew, turning over a new page, felt like the start they both needed. The doctors at Clearbrook were great and Max was… She flushed, pushing the image of his face on her pillow away. Max was a nice guy, but she had zero intentions of getting involved with him. What she needed to do was find a way to integrate into the rest of Clearbrook society. Maybe there was a book club or supper club she could join.

That might be good. Maybe an art class? I ought to have asked Dorothea for the details...

Ewan came running back downstairs, full of beans and ready for a new day.

'You get the teeth at the back?'

'Yes, Mummy.'

'You brushed for two minutes?'

'Yes.'

'You set the timer?'

'Yes!'

She smiled at him and ruffled his dark hair, before helping him on with his coat. Then she grabbed her own bag and jacket and headed on out.

They were walking down their front path, when Bella spotted movement at the cottage opposite and slowed down, unable to believe her eyes.

Max? And Rosie?

He'd spotted her, too, and had the same look on his face that she must have had on her own. Surprise. Shock. But pleasant surprise, at least.

She'd just been thinking about him. Embarrassed, she hoped she wasn't flushed in the face.

'Hello, you two. What are you doing here?' Max asked.

'We live here.'

'So do we.'

'What, here? On Field Lane?' She couldn't quite believe it.

'We're renting from Dr Mossman, who used to work at the practice.'

'So am I!' She remembered the kindly old gentleman

telling her as she signed the rental agreement that he had a few cottages that he owned in the village. That he'd bought them when he was in his fifties, to help fund his retirement. That his wife had enjoyed doing up the properties, because she used to be an interior designer and so it had become a project for them both.

Rosie was clinging to her dad's leg, but she peered from behind him and gave Bella a shy smile.

'Morning, Rosie.'

'Hi,' she answered, shyly.

'Are you on your way to school?' Max asked.

'Yes.'

'We might as well walk together, then, if that's okay?'

She couldn't think of a way to say no without being rude, but it unnerved her. Working with Max was one thing. There was a distance that was created, a line that was drawn, when someone was your colleague. But being with them away from work? In your free time? And doing so willingly? That made him more than a colleague, somehow, and his dashing good looks and easy charm made her uneasy. She was already drawn to his friendly warmth. His smile. His twinkling eyes. And she didn't want to be. Before, she'd allowed a man's dashing good looks to blind her to the small red flags and she didn't want to make that mistake again.

Her ex, Blake, had been handsome and effortlessly charming. He'd been that way with every woman, but he'd made her feel as if she were his whole world and she'd been the one he'd come home to at night. But he'd been the ultimate snake and the worst of it was—she'd been totally blindsided by him. He'd told her she was beautiful, whispered sweet nothings into her ears most nights, but it had all been part of his ruse. To make her feel as though she didn't have to worry about him. That she didn't have to doubt the strength of his love.

And so when he'd started going to the gym three times a week, she'd been happy that he'd found something else he'd loved. But he hadn't just been working out with weights, but with another woman. He'd come back buffed, but that was because his physical workouts had been sexually athletic, as well as on the elliptical. And he'd always come back so pleased with himself, telling her about his gains and what he'd managed to lift, and she'd been so happy for him. Even encouraged him to go more, seeing as he'd been enjoying it so much.

I was such a fool.

Bella had felt humiliated when she'd discovered the truth of his deception. Belittled. Naïve. And she'd sworn to herself never to be taken in by a handsome man with a stunning countenance ever again.

Glancing sideways, she stole a glance at Max as if to see if she could see anything about him that might give away secrets and lies, but there was nothing there. He seemed genuine, but she couldn't possibly risk it.

Ewan and Rosie walked together, ahead of them. She could hear him babbling away to Rosie about the biggest worm he'd ever found and she couldn't help but smile at him.

'Rosie told me you met yesterday,' Max said.

'Oh, yes. At the after-school club. She looked so tired, bless her, and I just wanted her to know that you were right behind me and she wouldn't have to wait much longer. I offered to wait with her.'

'She told me. She liked you. That you were very nice to her.'

Bella smiled. 'I told Ewan to be her friend. I hope that's okay?'

'Of course, it is!'

'I still can't quite believe that we're neighbours.'

He laughed. 'No. Nor me. But I guess we should have figured it out. Trying to buy a place in Clearbrook is incredibly difficult. The fact that we've both managed to rent somewhere should have been a clue. Dr Mossman told he owns almost the whole street in Field Lane.'

'He's probably got a nice comfy retirement ahead of him, then.'

'Probably. You know what would be nice? And we only have to do it if you're okay with it, but we'll both be walking to school each morning before work—we could arrange to meet up each time and walk in together. That way the kids can get to know one another more.'

It seemed such a simple, nice and easy suggestion. And he meant it as friends and neighbours, surely nothing more than that? But could it be a ruse for something else? They would spend all day with each other at work anyway…

Relax, Bella. Remember those trust issues you promised yourself you'd work on?

'Erm…okay.'

Max glanced at his watch. 'Eight-fifteen each day?'

'Sure.' She nodded and smiled, her heart fluttering in her chest at the idea of meeting up with him every day to walk into school and then—*oh, my goodness, on our own*—walking into work! 'We'd better tell people at work we're neighbours. Don't want them thinking the wrong thing!' She could just imagine the awful gossip that might start if they didn't make it clear to everyone.

'I'm sure they wouldn't think anything untoward. Lorna and Oliver are good friends and that's understandable—they know one another from way back—and you and I are good friends because we're living opposite one another, we work together and we're both pretty much the same age and single parents. It just makes sense.'

When he put it like that, of course it made sense. But Blake used to make things sound like good sense, too. Make things sound reasonable when all along he was a cheating, lying scumbag, seeing another woman behind her back. The people at work could still jump to conclusions about them. People naturally tried to matchmake. They couldn't help it.

But I should give him the chance to be my friend, right?

Wasn't that why she was here in Clearbrook? To make a fresh start? To make friends and connections? Max could become a very valuable friend, if she just allowed herself to give him the chance and ignored how handsome he was. How drawn she was to stare into his eyes.

As they reached the school, they stood by the gates and watched as Ewan introduced Rosie to some of the friends he'd made the day before and Rosie got invited to play on the climbing frame with the others. She glanced back at her dad, as if asking for permission. He gave her a thumbs up and she smiled and hurried after Ewan.

'She's going to get braver every day,' Max said, watching his daughter with pride in his smile. 'Makes me feel better about leaving her today. Yesterday was so hard, knowing she didn't want to go in, but she told me later that their teacher is nice.'

'Ewan said the same thing about Miss Celic.'

They stood together watching the kids play for a while, then the bell rang and the teachers came out to gather the children to their individual classes. Rosie came back to give her dad a hug and walked over to join the line. Ewan didn't come back for a hug. He just lined up behind Rosie and turned to give his mum a wave.

'How easily they let you go,' she said.

'It's because you did such a great job raising him.' Max touched her arm, probably without thinking. Probably casually, without any intent for its meaning. Just a *Hey, I see you, fellow single parent. You've done a great job.*

But Bella felt a frisson of something tremble through her. An awakening. An awareness. Of course, she found Max attractive. Maybe that was the problem! And no man had touched her for years. And it wasn't as if she were bereft of contact. Ewan hugged her all the time. He climbed into bed with her in the mornings, sometimes, but that was different. Innocent. Her son. Her little boy showing his mummy some love and she loved their snuggles that they had.

But it didn't stop her from feeling lonely. It didn't stop her from craving the touch of a lover. That was a different kind of touch. A touch that told her she mattered in a different kind of way. That she was important to someone else. A touch that was just for her and nobody else.

Having Max touch her, however innocently, reminded her of the ache that she felt at losing the father of her child. At losing a relationship that she'd thought would end with her walking down an aisle in a white dress. His touch reminded her of all that she had lost and yearned for, yet was scared to have.

When the kids disappeared inside, they turned and began to walk to work. It was only a few minutes' walk, but she felt as if it would feel like aeons.

'So, tell me more about your art,' Max asked her.

Bella laughed. 'You make me sound like a professional painter.'

Max laughed. 'Aren't you?'

'Do zentangles count?' She smiled, thinking of the type of art she did like to indulge in.

Zentangles were a collection of structured patterns. Those patterns were called tangles and you could create combinations of tangles such as lines, cross-hatching, dots, curves and shapes. No great skill was required, which was why she liked it.

'Absolutely! Are they like mandalas?'

'Kind of.' She pulled out her phone and did an Internet image search for zentangles and showed him the screen.

'Cool.'

'I find it relaxing, especially if I'm feeling a little stressed.'

'You feel stressed often?'

She laughed. 'You sound like a doctor.'

He laughed, too. 'That's good. I'm glad that I do. Do you think we get stressed because we're single parents and we have no one to share the burden with?'

'Possibly.'

'I read to get rid of stress. Reading is huge for me. I've always got a book on the go. Try to read a chapter or two before bed each night. And you're not going to believe this, but I once fancied myself a bit of an artist. You should come over one night and look at my etchings.' He laughed out loud and she blushed, madly, but laughed, too. 'Seriously, I have one or two of my drawings up on the walls in the hallway.'

'Seriously?'

'Yep.'

'What are they?'

'Wild animals, mostly. I used art as a way to escape the reality of what Rosie's mum was going through. There were many long hours spent in oncology wards and treatment rooms.'

'It must have been incredibly hard for you both.'

He shrugged. 'It was harder for Anna. When you get pregnant and have a baby, everyone expects you to be happy. To be in celebratory mood. Or sleep-deprived. Our families wanted to celebrate Rosie's arrival, but felt like they couldn't fully, because of what Anna was going through.'

'How did your wife deal with it? The new baby and fighting cancer?'

He smiled. 'She was strong. Stronger than me, that's for sure. Never complained. Not once. She said that she felt that she couldn't, because she'd made the choice to continue with the pregnancy, rather than start treatment early, and so it was all on her and she would take the consequences.' He sighed. 'I used to tell her that she was allowed to be angry. That if she needed to shout and scream, then she could, but she never did. She just wanted to hold Rosie as much as she could and love her as much as she could. Until she couldn't.'

Bella turned to look at the man beside her. The widower. The single father. A doctor. Her colleague. Neighbour. *Friend.* She couldn't imagine going through such pain. Couldn't imagine having to make a choice between continuing with a pregnancy, or aborting it to fight for her own life. To hope for a future pregnancy much further down the line. What kind of strength had it taken, in the face of all those doctors advising her to terminate, to say, *'No. I'm keeping it.'*?

She cast her mind back to the day she'd discovered she was pregnant with Ewan. Discovered that Blake had been cheating on her and that he didn't want to be a father. A friend had asked her, in the days after the break-up, when she'd still been reeling from having moved out, if she was going to keep the baby. There'd been absolutely no doubt in her mind that she was going to continue with the pregnancy. The baby had not cheated on her. It wasn't the baby's fault and, though she'd worried about the future, though she'd worried that every time she'd look at her child, she'd see Blake, it had not been enough to deter her. The second that line had turned pink, she had felt protective of the tiny bean growing deep in her womb and her protective instincts had appeared as if from nowhere.

Maybe Anna had felt the same? Bella couldn't imagine being placed in Anna's situation. What would she have done?

I'd have done the same.

She felt a strange connection to Anna, then. A unity. An understanding. And she knew without a doubt that Anna Moore, Max's wife, must have been one hell of a brave woman.

When they arrived at work, they said hello to everyone. Lorna had brought in some lemon drizzle cake that she'd baked for everyone and it sat neatly by the kettle, in a cake tin, ready for everyone to enjoy at morning break.

'Let's see what today brings!' said Max.

She'd nodded and smiled at him. How quickly a single day could change things. Yesterday, she'd been worried about him being so attractive. Had worried about her attraction to him. Had told herself she would keep him at arm's length, because of it. And yet today, in the matter of an hour, she'd discovered that they were neighbours and she'd learned more of his past, connected with his wife and suddenly he didn't seem such a threat to her any more.

She'd thought, because of his looks, that he must have led a charmed life. That it was easy for him and good things happened to him and that he probably took what he wanted and life just gave it to him.

But he was just as tortured and damaged as everyone else and she felt bad for judging him.

Turns out you never can tell what someone is going through.

He wasn't narcissistic. He wasn't Blake.

He was like her. Just trying to get through each day.

And Bella resolved, there and then, not to be so standoffish and to enjoy being his friend. On her way to her own room, she knocked on Priti's door and went in to tell her about needing the afternoon off in a few weeks' time.

He'd not mentioned to Bella that when he'd told her that he'd encouraged Anna to be angry about her prognosis, he himself had been angry.

Anger was not an attractive quality, especially in a man, and a lot of people could be scared about it, but he remembered being immensely angry at discovering his wife's cancer had spread during the months of her pregnancy and had become terminal.

He'd been angry at himself, for not persuading Anna

more to terminate the pregnancy. He'd been angry at the world for threatening to take his wife from him. And yes, he'd been angry at the idea that he would eventually be left alone to raise a child whose life had caused Anna to lose her own.

Max had not wanted to resent Rosie. Of course not. It wasn't her fault. She'd not made the choice to stay and it had taken both he and Anna to make a baby, no matter how accidentally. And Anna had only examined her breasts so early in the pregnancy because a midwife had mentioned it.

As Rosie had thrived, getting bigger and glowing with health, his wife had got sicker, thinner, paler. Weaker. As Rosie had begun to develop, learning how to sit, crawl, walk, Anna had begun to be more bedbound. It had almost been as if the umbilical cord had still been there and that somehow Rosie were taking all of Anna's vitality.

It had been a difficult year and then, days after Rosie had turned one and they'd celebrated her birthday in Anna's hospice room, surrounded by balloons still, his wife had finally passed away. Quietly. Without fanfare. In her sleep.

Three had become two.

He'd not known how to be. How to get through the days. Anna's parents had helped as much as they could, but they'd been grieving too. The days had seemed difficult for them all, even for Rosie, who had clearly noticed her mum was no longer around to snuggle with in a bed.

But it had been Rosie who got him through the worst of it. Her smile, her chuckles, her laughter. The way her eyes were exactly like her mother's, it was as if Anna still lived on, only in her daughter.

Max had found the strength to continue. His wife had made this choice for a reason. She'd told him, towards the end, that she'd never wanted to leave him alone and she had kept that promise. His desire to love and protect his daughter had driven him through every day and somehow the days had become less about survival and getting through them without crying and more about enjoying the time that they had together, as life was precious. It was a gift and you had to live in the present. Not worry about the past, or tremble at the future, because no one knew how much of that you had.

He was glad he'd told Anna's story to Bella. Because now it was in the open, it wasn't a painful secret that lurked in his past. He'd talked about it and it was done. Of course, Bella had made it so easy for him to say. There was something about her that made talking all the easier. Maybe because she'd been hurt, too? Maybe because she walked this path of single parenthood as well, and that made her a fellow traveller?

Max called his first patient of the day through. The note on the computer simply said 'numb hand'. A glance through the patient's history told him that this patient, Mary Connor, was sixty-two years of age and had been diagnosed with a tremor before, but Parkinson's tests had been negative.

Mary walked through his door with a smile and sat down in the chair beside his desk. 'Morning, Doctor! I'm Mary, pleased to meet you.' She held out her hand.

Max shook it. 'Hello. I'm Dr Moore, how can I help you today?'

'Well, it's this hand, Doctor.' She held out her left hand. Same side as her tremor. He could see that her arm was still trembling and he'd also noticed a slight slur to her voice as she spoke. But, having never met the patient before, he didn't know if this was usual, or new. 'It feels a bit numb and my grip isn't what it used to be. I keep dropping things.'

He frowned. 'Okay, and how long has it been feeling like this?'

'A couple of weeks. Not long. I waited because I thought maybe I'd banged it and the numbness would go away, but it's not.'

'Is it getting worse? Spreading?'

'No. It's just the same.'

'And can you point out for me where the numbness is?'

Mary indicated the areas around her thumb and forefingers and near the wrist.

'And can you remember banging it?'

'No, but that doesn't mean I didn't. My husband, Tom, he says I'd forget my head if it wasn't screwed on, just lately.' Mary laughed, but he could hear behind that laughter that there was a very worried woman, trying to act as if it didn't bother her, when it clearly did.

He examined her hand, wrist and arm. Palpating it, checking the joints, rolling and flexing them, asking if anything hurt. There were no bruises that he could see. No cuts. No swelling. But clearly she had lost sensation. He got her to try holding different things, from a thin slip of paper to a pen, to a book, and clearly her strength of grasp was lacking and the slip of paper fell to the floor instantly.

He'd been hearing the slur, more, too. 'Can I ask you, Mary, about your speech?'

'My speech?'

'Yes, I can't help but hear a bit of a slur, sometimes. Is that new, or is that something you've always had?'

She seemed to think. 'I don't know. I think it's come on in the last few months. Gradually, I think, but I've not had a stroke or anything, have I?'

'I can't rule it out at this stage. But if the slurring has been there the last few months, then it's possible that you had a mini stroke or TIA, a transient-ischaemic attack, but those don't usually leave you with symptoms. They're transient. They don't stay. Regarding your arm and hand issues... I think we need to do further tests. You also mention that your husband has noticed your memory isn't very good at the moment, so I think, if you're happy for me to do so, I'd like to refer you to a neurologist.'

'You think it's serious, then?'

'I think I'd like to rule out certain conditions, but, at this stage, it could be anything. A specialist will be able to narrow down what it is we're looking at, so that we can treat you effectively and as early as we can.'

'Right. I see. Am I going to get better?'

'I'd like to think so, but we need to do these tests to ascertain what we are working with.'

Mary looked concerned. 'I thought maybe I just had a bit of nerve damage in my old age.'

'Well, perhaps it is, but let's get you seen by someone with a more specialist knowledge, just in case.'

His patient nodded her agreement.

When she was gone, he wrote up her notes and made the referral. There was an excellent neurologist at the local hospital and he would be able to put Mary through some tests, maybe an MRI or CT scan, to ascertain what was going on. Max had seen a case like this once before, years ago, and it had turned out to be nothing but old age settling in and he hoped that this was the case here, but he had a bad feeling and he didn't like it. He knew, more than anyone else, how important it was that symptoms and diseases were caught early, so that something could be done. Even if it was for an illness that had no cure, sometimes they could slow its progression to give patients a greater quality of life, for a lot longer than they would have had if they'd left it late, or not bothered to mention it.

His next patient was a much simpler case. An obvious urine infection, for which he prescribed antibiotics. After that he saw a gentleman who thought he'd detected a lump on his testicle, but it was actually just a cyst on his cauda epididymis. A place in the testicle that stored mature sperm cells. Occasionally, this area could become filled with fluid, but it was common and often resolved itself. He checked to make sure this patient didn't have a urine infection—he didn't—and told the patient to call again if it wasn't gone by the end of the month. If it wasn't, they'd refer him for an ultrasound, just to be sure.

Max went into his morning break and cut himself a thin slice of Lorna's lemon drizzle and waited for Bella. He was looking forward to talking to her again. He felt as if she understood him. Understood the struggles of being a single parent.

But when she came into the staff area, her eyes looked red, as if she'd been crying.

Instantly, he was alarmed and got up. 'Hey, you okay?'

Bella had thought she looked okay. She'd thought all traces of her crying had to be gone.

Damn it! I waited before I came out here, too!

'I'm fine. Honestly.' She smiled, feeling embarrassed that Max had noticed. At least Lorna and Oliver weren't here too, but they'd be in Lorna's room together again, probably. 'It's nothing.'

'You're sure? Here. You sit down and I'll make you a tea. Start on my cake. I haven't touched it yet. I'll cut myself another slice.'

She eyed the cake on the low coffee table. It did look good and a hit of sugar would feel nice. She sat down and forked a mouthful of cake. It was delicious! Moist and lemony. Exactly as it ought to be.

Lorna, this is amazing.

Max handed her a mug of tea and settled opposite. 'Difficult case?'

She nodded and tried her hardest not to think about Tansy Jenkins. Or the look in her eyes. 'I don't know why some cases hit so hard. They just do. And I don't even know the young woman! I met her just this morning for the first time and have to give her the worst news in the world.'

Max nodded.

'This patient and her husband had been trying for a baby for two years. They were on the waiting list to start IVF. They even had an appointment for two months' time to start the process. Meet with a fertility specialist. But discovered they were pregnant a couple of weeks ago. But this morning, she woke up and she was bleeding and had pains, so she came to see me and...'

Bella could hear her voice tremble and, not wanting to cry, she stopped speaking for a minute, so that she could breathe. Regain control of her voice and be professional. But it was hard sometimes as a doctor to have that emotional distance. You could try as much as you wanted but at the end of the day you were dealing with real people. And you were human, too, with empathy and sometimes the empathy won.

'I had to tell her she was probably miscarrying. Losing the most precious thing in the world to her. She couldn't stop crying. Couldn't stop blaming herself for having done a bit of gardening yesterday. Couldn't bear the idea of having to tell her husband, who'd left for work early and had no idea.' Bella let out a long breath. 'I helped her make that call. I spoke to him, too, and he cried. She cried. I cried. I mean… I was not the professional, distanced doctor that they needed in that moment.'

'You were the perfect doctor for them in that moment,' Max replied. 'You showed them that they mattered. That you cared. That they weren't just another number. Another loss. Another statistic.'

'I hope they saw it that way. But worst of all is that I felt aware of the time factor. That people in the waiting room were being kept waiting, but I couldn't do anything about that as I needed to give my patient and her husband as much time as they needed. I just felt so bad. So guilty.' Bella forked in another mouthful of lemony deliciousness and before she knew it, she'd finished the slice. Drowning her emotions with a citrus sponge cake. 'I ought to go back now, miss my break and try to catch up.' She stood to go.

Max stood with her. 'Let me take a couple off your hands.'

'Thanks, but you should take your break.'

'And so should you, after such an emotional appointment. Let me help you. Who do you have on your list?'

'A wart removal and a mole check.'

Max smiled. 'I'll take the wart, if you want.'

Bella smiled back at him. He was so kind. So thoughtful. She had completely misjudged him yesterday. He was nothing like the vain, charming Lothario she'd first imagined he might be. She'd been so unfair when she'd first met him. Judging him wrongly and all because of what had happened with Blake. She'd never have been like that before. 'Okay, thanks. You're very kind.'

'Take your tea back with you. Drink it when you can.' He passed her her drink in its mug.

She felt her fingers brush his, felt a small blush fill her cheeks at the contact. 'I will.'

They both finished work that evening at the same time, meeting each other coming out of their consultation rooms and so they headed to the infants' school to pick up Rosie and Ewan together.

Once again Bella felt extremely aware of Max at her side as they walked. He was a very handsome man and she would be lying to herself to say she wasn't attracted to him. She just knew she wouldn't act on it. She could look, but not touch. As her mum used to say, there's nothing wrong with browsing the menu, you just don't order the delicious dish.

He'd been so kind to her today. Thoughtful at her being upset, offering her his own slice of cake, taking her patients so that she didn't overrun. Little things, but they mattered. He seemed a genuinely nice guy. A gentleman. But she still felt cautious. She'd not known a single man in her life who had not let her down. Who had not lied to her. Who had not cheated, and that list included her own father. Men always wanted something and very often did not feel satisfied with what they had.

She really wanted to believe that Max was different and maybe he was, but her experience dictated to her that he wouldn't be. Somehow, he would let her down. Hurt her, if she allowed him, so that it was best to keep him at arm's length. A friend. A colleague. A neighbour. Nothing more than that.

Besides, work relationships were complicated. Nobody wanted to mess in the company ink. And she had Ewan to think about. Ewan to be a role model for. If Bella was going to invite any man into her life, to be someone that Ewan could look up to, he had to be stellar in his behaviour. He had to be something that all men had proved to her they were not. Loyal. Honest. True. Plus Max had Rosie, he had his own worries to fret about. No. She and Max were too complicated to do anything about any attraction she might feel and that was all it was. A physical attraction. It would pass. And she didn't have to worry about it any more than that.

At the school, Ewan and Rosie came running to greet them. They'd both been playing outside on the rope bridge and even Bella noticed the difference in Max's daughter today from yesterday. Her confidence was growing and that was nice to see.

'Had a fun day?' she asked Ewan.

'Great! Me and Rosie are guinea pig monitors!'

Guinea pigs? 'Really?'

'Yes!' Rosie grinned. 'Their names are Monty and Tommy!'

'Wow.'

'We get to bring them home during the school holidays and look after them!'

'Do you?' Bella raised an eyebrow at Max, who laughed at her horrified expression. She didn't mind cats or dogs, but little things that scurried? No, sir!

'Get your bookbags, you two,' reminded the staff member of the after-school club. They'd learned her name was Lynne.

'Any problems?' Bella asked.

'None at all. Those two are really blooming and Rosie's come completely out of her shell since Ewan became her friend. He's very popular.'

Bella beamed. That was good. That was exactly what she wanted for her son.

'You can't split them up. They do everything together. It's lovely to see,' Lynne continued.

Bella couldn't help but notice that Ewan held Rosie's hand as they walked home together. It was innocent and sweet and reminded her of when she was a child and they'd gone anywhere with school, you had to hold hands with your walking partner, whether you liked them or not. She'd once had to hold hands with a young boy called Glen, who'd taken great pleasure in teasing her and pulling on her hair in assemblies. His hand had always been sweaty and she'd hated it. But Rosie and Ewan looked very happy indeed. Chattering away to one another about stuff they'd done at school that day.

She was so proud of her son. She'd spoken to him so much about this before starting school, about making sure he had friends that were girls, as much as he had friendships with boys. That he was always to be respectful and kind, no matter what, and if he ever heard his friends making fun of someone else, then he was to stop them or walk away. Bella wanted to raise a man of the future.

The lavender scent in the air added to the warm, balmy feel of the evening and they even saw, heading out of the village, Lorna and Oliver in running gear.

'I didn't know they were into running,' Max said.

'Lorna mentioned she's training for a marathon. Maybe he's helping her?' She turned to look at Max. 'What about you? Do you work out? Go to the gym?'

'Not really. I know I should, but I've always wanted to prioritise any spare time I had by spending it with Rosie, or making sure she had a relationship with Anna's parents. I've always liked walking though. Country trails, that kind of thing. I've often thought about getting a dog. I think Rosie would love it, but it wouldn't be fair on the dog to be cooped up all day.'

'*You'll* just have to make do with the school guinea pigs, then!' She laughed.

'Hmm. Not sure how I'll feel about that. But I'd imagine that would only be during school breaks. Is Ewan going to attend the after-school club during the holidays, same as Rosie? Or have you made other plans?'

'No, he'll be at the school. It seemed easiest. Less disruptive. I've got him signed up already.'

'I've done the same, too. But…how do you deal with the guilt? I'm feeling a lot of that right now.'

'I think it's to be expected. We've been their whole world for so long and then they reach four years old and suddenly we hand them off to someone else. They learn as much from their teachers and friends as they used to from us. I think it's about letting go. Accepting that this is a part of their development.'

'And do you find that easy?'

'Are you kidding me?' Bella laughed. 'I'm always worrying about Ewan getting the right messages. All I can do is give him a base to work from, but it's up to him who his friends are, which lessons he likes the best, which teachers he dislikes, how he feels he might have to change to fit in with everyone else.' She shook her head. 'I'd love to explain to him that, at school, you try your hardest to fit in and be like everyone else, because you think it's the most important thing in the world. But then, you leave school, become an adult and realise that being an individual is far, far more important and all the quirky stuff that made you stand out, or all the strange stuff you get teased for, are what make you you! And you learn to treasure it, rather than hide it. But I think he's too young for all of that.'

'Yeah.'

Bella shrugged. 'He's four. He's more interested in cartoons and animals right now.' She smiled ruefully. 'But I'll help him understand it when he's older, if there are any problems that develop.'

They reached Field Lane and began to walk up it towards their homes.

'I like talking to you,' Max said.

She smiled. Strangely, considering her feelings yesterday, she liked talking to him, too. 'Well, don't be too impressed. I only have one or two pearls of wisdom and I think I've shared them already. After this? It's all trivia and bad celebrity impressions.'

'That sounds great, too. We must get you drunk one day, so I get to see and hear them all.'

'Good luck with that.' Bella didn't drink alcohol. She'd seen how alcohol had affected her father whenever he drank, which hadn't been often, but when he had? It had been horrible. She never wanted to be that out of control.

She was all Ewan had to take care of him. There was no time for getting drunk, or lying in bed. Besides, she had enough bad headaches as it was, without adding hangovers to them.

'Well, maybe one night you two should come over to ours for a pizza night. Might be fun one weekend or something? I think the kids would like it.'

Pizza? With Max and Rosie? At their cottage? The kids would love it. But was he asking her as a neighbour? A colleague? A friend? Or something else? She felt a frisson of anticipation wash over her. The thought that he might find her attractive felt quite delicious.

'Just friends,' he said, smiling. 'Obviously.'

Just friends. Obviously.

Disappointment washed over her and suddenly she felt embarrassed and silly. She was reading too much into their friendship. 'Um…this weekend?'

'How about Friday night? Come over to ours about seven p.m.? We'll do pizza, then a movie or something?'

'Okay.' She nodded, trying to control the tingles in her tummy at the idea of going over to Max's place. But it would be okay, right, because the kids would be there. No funny business would happen—*just friends, obviously*—and they'd be so close to their own home, if they had to make a rapid exit for whatever reason.

Not that there will be one, because nothing will happen. Just friends.

Obviously.

'Great. And preference in the pizza?'

'Any kind is great.' She didn't want to seem a bother.

'Okay. It's a date. Kind of.' He frowned, then laughed. 'Rosie? Say goodbye to Ewan.'

'Bye, Ewan!' said Rosie.

'Bye, Rosie.'

She walked Ewan across the road, looking both ways before they crossed, even though Field Lane was a very quiet road and not really used except by the people who lived on it, and let Ewan into their cottage. As she turned around to close the front door, she noticed Max was waiting on his doorstep, checking to make sure they got in okay. Even though she lived only a couple of metres from his own place, he still waited to make sure she was in safely.

That's really sweet.

She gave him a smile and a quick wave and then closed the door. Bella stood there for a moment, thinking of what a nice guy Max was turning out to be, and then that evil little voice in her head that made her doubt everything spoke up.

But he's not interested in you. You've been friend-zoned. So deal with it.

Friday night had arrived and Max had managed to pick up a couple of things for pizza and movie night. He'd bought a selection of pizzas with different toppings. He'd bought popcorn for the movie and even mini ice creams for pudding, if anyone had room. He'd sorted through his extensive DVD collection and got out all the ones that Ewan might possibly choose, but, even he had to admit, Rosie's taste in movies was very rooted in princesses and fairy tales and he wasn't sure how much Ewan would like that, so he'd made sure to pop out to the Clearbrook Library at his lunchbreak that day and borrowed a range of other DVDs that might interest him.

He'd bought a bottle of wine for himself and Bella and he'd even dawdled over the flowers and wondered if he ought to buy her a bouquet. A gift of some sort. But then he'd remembered that look of fear in her eyes, when she'd thought he was asking her over as some sort of date, and so he'd forgone the flowers totally.

Not that he wouldn't have minded dating Bella if he were in a totally different situation. He liked her a lot. Being a single parent, like himself, she understood the struggles of that, but he also felt they connected on another level. This past week, with every conversation they'd had, he'd begun to like her more and more. Seeing past that beautiful exterior that she clearly wasn't aware of, to the beauty of her soul. Bella cared deeply about her job, her patients and most especially Ewan and she was doing an amazing job of raising a fabulous little boy, if Rosie's tales were anything to go by.

He wished he'd known Bella before. At medical school, the way Lorna and Oliver had known each other. He just knew, deep in his heart, that she and Anna would have loved one another and been the best of friends. They were so alike in spirit and character.

'When are they coming?' Rosie asked. She'd got changed out of her school uniform and had put on a pink tee shirt with a denim overall dress and white frilly socks.

He checked his watch. 'Any minute now, I should think. Now remember, they're our guests, so they get to choose the pizza and the movie.'

'Okay. Can I help?'

He was putting out some snacks. Crisps. Crudités. Hummus. 'Sure. Want to get the cucumber from the fridge?'

It didn't take long to finish chopping up the cucumber, carrots and putting out the mangetout. The wine was chilling nicely in the fridge, the kettle was full and he'd even managed a quick tidy. The place didn't look too bad. They'd unpacked most things, but he did still have a few boxes of Anna's things that he couldn't bring himself to get rid of. Her favourite dress. Books that she'd loved. Little bits of memorabilia. Her wedding ring. Jewellery. That he thought Rosie might like when she was older.

The doorbell rang and Rosie leapt up. 'They're here!' and she raced for the front door.

'Wait for me.' He didn't like Rosie opening the door without him there. You never knew who could be on the other side, even if you were expecting someone.

But then he was swinging the door wide and in rushed Ewan and behind him, looking awkward, but stunningly beautiful in a sun dress, was Bella. She looked completely different from how she dressed for work. This dress was very summery. Not work attire at all. It was a pale blue, with tiny daisies on it, and her hair was down and loose and he thought he could even detect some kind of perfume, which she never wore for work.

'Come in!' He stepped back and kind of held his breath as she came in. She had a diamond clip in her hair to one side and as she passed, he couldn't help but notice the long, smooth length of her neck and a hint of clavicle and he was so struck by it, he almost found himself staring and had to remind himself to close his mouth and shut the door.

Thankfully, she didn't notice him being dumbstruck by his physical reaction to her. It was disturbing to him, too. He'd not had a physical reaction to any woman since losing Anna. He'd noticed beautiful women, of course.

He could appreciate them, but he'd never felt such a raw, physical disturbance at being so attracted to one.

A pang of guilt washed over him and his gaze instantly went to a picture of himself and Anna that sat on the hallway table. It was a candid shot. One that he'd always loved. Taken before they'd known she had cancer. Before she'd got pregnant. They'd gone to the seaside, despite the rain and the gloom, and had fish and chips on a beach. The picture was of them both, but in it, Anna had a cagoule hood around her face, desperately trying to keep the rain off, and she'd been laughing heartily and he'd quickly snapped it with his phone to capture the moment.

It was the last time they'd ever been to the seaside. The last time they'd ever gone away together. Weeks later, she'd fallen pregnant and the whole cancer nightmare had begun.

Max closed the door and followed Bella and Ewan into the kitchen. Rosie had already invited Ewan to go and play in the garden and the two kids had disappeared out of the back door.

'I brought you this.' Bella smiled and passed him a small gift bag.

'Oh! You didn't have to bring anything.'

'It's just a small thank you for inviting us over.'

He opened the bag and found a small box of ornate, but very expensive chocolates. 'Wow. Thank you. That's very kind.' He pondered about whether he should lean in to give her a thank-you peck on the cheek, but after what he'd felt in the hallway? He wasn't sure he wanted to feel any more guilt and so he simply smiled and said, 'Wine?'

'I don't drink, but tea would be lovely.'

'Tea, it is.' He smiled again, broader this time, and

started to make them both a cup of tea. 'You'd think those two would be exhausted after a long day, wouldn't you?'

Bella laughed. 'I think kids have different fuel packs from adults. When do we lose it, do you think? That endless energy?'

'Erm…when responsibilities begin to weigh us down?'

'Maybe. Can I help with anything?'

'It's all done. Why don't you take a seat? Or would you like a tour of the place?'

'A tour would be great!'

Max gave her a quick tour of the cottage. It didn't take long—it was only two-bedroomed. But apparently, his place was nothing like hers, even though they looked the same from the outside. Her kitchen had a separate, smaller dining area, whereas his was combined, but upstairs, she thought that maybe her bedroom was bigger and it had an en suite, whereas he had a separate dressing area.

Back in the kitchen, he stood by the back door and asked the kids what kind of pizza they wanted. They settled on ham and pineapple and whilst it was in the oven he set about making a home-made coleslaw.

'Have you always liked to cook?' Bella asked.

'I learned to. I'm afraid I was your typical barbecue man, standing over the fire in my pinny and tongs cooking sausages, until Anna got sick. Then she didn't have the energy and so I learned to cook and found I rather enjoyed it. What about you?'

'I love food, don't get me wrong, but I actually hate the whole business of cooking. The end result is wonderful, but I hate all that cleaning up you have to do. How much mess it makes, how much extra work it creates. What I need in my life is a personal chef and kitchen maid, then I'd be happy.'

'I think we all would be!' he agreed, smiling.

'Staff. I think I just need staff. To be honest, I thought working full time in a job at last and not being a locum would feel so good, and it does, but I hadn't taken into account how exhausted I'd feel at the end of each day. I just want to flop on the sofa, yet there's cleaning to do, cooking, shopping, laundry, spending quality time with Ewan. Making sure he's bathed before bed, reading him a story. It's a lot, you know?'

'You need me time. Time to recharge?'

'Yes! Oh, listen to me! I never thought I'd complain about being a mum and having a great job, yet here I am.' She sounded embarrassed and he didn't want her to feel that way.

'You're human and there are only so many hours in the day. It's natural and you're *not* complaining. Just stating facts. I feel the same sometimes. When do we find time for friends? For ourselves? Going out? Visiting family? It all comes at a cost. A cost of time and energy. We're allowed to feel like we're flagging at some point, when there's just one of us holding down the fort. Other people have partners to share the load, remember?' He placed the bowl of freshly prepared coleslaw on the table and got out the salad he'd made with Rosie earlier, from the fridge.

'You're right.'

Ewan and Rosie came bursting through the back door then, full of smiles.

'Go wash your hands, you two. Pizza will be ready in two minutes.'

Rosie grabbed Ewan's hand and pulled him towards a bathroom.

'I love how easy they are together. It's like they've known one another for ages.'

'They have. A whole week!'

Bella smiled.

He liked her smile. The way it lit her eyes. The way her cheeks rounded. The softness of her lips.

I must stop focusing on her lips!

But it was difficult not to. Especially when he liked to make her smile, too. It made him feel good. It made him feel as if he was doing something right. He used to try so hard to make Anna smile when she was going through treatment, but she'd felt so ill and so weak most days, it had been difficult. He'd felt as though he was failing her. Rosie had been able to make his wife smile. Or maybe she'd just saved her strength for her daughter? When he'd sat by Anna's bedside and reminisced with her, trying to make her remember happier times, he'd smiled himself and held her hand and tried to make her comfortable and fetched her whatever she'd needed.

So, yes, he felt good that he could make Bella smile and he told himself not to feel guilty about doing so. He'd been starved of it for so long.

Her happiness made him feel better about himself and that was worth its weight in gold.

They'd had a lovely evening together. Bella couldn't remember the last time she'd been at a friend's house with her son, laughing so hard and just enjoying another person's company. These last few difficult years as she'd struggled to raise Ewan on her own, she'd often felt iso-

lated and alone. So, to be invited out, to be asked to bring
Ewan along, to sit and watch some silly cartoon movie
about anthropomorphised cars, whilst eating the most delicious pizza—had been wonderful.

She knew the evening had to draw to a close when
Ewan couldn't stop yawning. It was nearing nine o'clock
at night and it was a whole hour past his usual bedtime.
There'd be no time for a bath before bed, but she figured
she could let it go for one night.

'All right. Time for bed, you,' she said, stroking his
thick mop of hair.

'Can we stay a little longer, Mummy, please?' Ewan
begged.

She considered it. But a brief look at Rosie and she
could see that Max's daughter had tired eyes too, and she
didn't want to outstay their welcome, even though she
also didn't want to bring this brilliant time together to an
end. Because once she got back home and Ewan was in
bed, she'd be alone again.

'I think we all need to get some rest. Come on!'

They got up and headed to the front door, thanking
Max and Rosie profusely for having them over and welcoming them to their home.

'You're very welcome! We've loved every minute of it
and we must do it again.'

She found herself agreeing. 'Absolutely! But you must
come over to ours next time.'

'Sounds like a plan,' Max agreed, opening the door as
Ewan gave Rosie a hug goodbye.

Seeing her son hug Rosie, Bella figured that she ought
to thank Max, too, in a similar way. It would be harmless,
right? A hug, a peck on the cheek from a friend, that was

all. But she felt herself blushing as she leaned in to give him a quick hug, felt a heat suffuse her body at the feel of him taking her in his arms, and when she pressed her lips to his cheek? Felt the brief brush of bristles against her own skin? She felt alarm at how much she wanted to stay there. Within his grasp. With his hands still upon her.

Bella pulled away, blushing. 'Well, thanks again. Goodnight.'

'Goodnight.'

She blew out a breath as she and Ewan crossed the street to their own cottage and once again she couldn't help but notice that Max didn't close his front door until she'd gone inside and closed her own.

He'd given her one last beaming smile and a wave and she'd waved back, feeling her heart thumping madly in her chest.

Something was happening here between her and Max. Was it just friendship? It felt that way and she wasn't sure where all these other feelings were coming from. He'd given her no sign he wanted anything else and yet her mind was awhirl.

She'd so fiercely kept herself away from men since the break-up with Blake. Had told herself that she would remain single for ever now, until her dying day, because she could never imagine trusting a man ever again. And yet here she was, developing feelings for Max. A guy!

The stress of it all was bringing on another headache. She rubbed at her forehead and looked at herself in the hall mirror as Ewan headed upstairs to brush his teeth before bed.

I look tired. Are those bags I'm getting?

She rubbed at her face and let out a heavy sigh, before

kicking off her shoes and heading upstairs to hopefully read Ewan a very short story before he'd fall asleep.

Bella thought about what it must feel like to be a parent if you could share the burden with someone else. She pictured putting Ewan to bed. Then Rosie, and going downstairs to find Max on her sofa. How she'd sink into his welcoming arms and they'd snuggle. Watch a bit of television, before suggesting they go to bed themselves. Watching him undress. Feeling the mattress sink as he got in beside her. The warmth of his long, hard body pressed up against hers as they spooned. The feel of his hand gently stroking down her side, smoothing over her hip, sliding up her thigh...

But what if it wasn't all it was cracked up to be? Like on social media where everyone always posted pics and videos of their amazing, happy lives. It wasn't always like that. It couldn't be. Behind the scenes there were probably arguments and upsets. Strained silences. Betrayals.

It couldn't be perfect. She might envy couples who could share the load, but did she envy them everything else? The wondering if the late night at work meant something else? Whether taking his phone outside meant he was having a call with someone he shouldn't? Whether the flowers he brought home really were for the fact that he simply loved her?

Max seemed wonderful.

Perfect.

But would that all change if they took their relationship beyond friendship?

She had to accept that it could.

But she couldn't accept the risk that it might...

CHAPTER FOUR

MAX HAD RACHEL and baby Hayden back in his clinic first thing for her check-up since she'd seen him last time for possible postnatal depression. When she came into his room, she looked just as hassled and just as pale as she had done before.

'How's the past few days been?'

'Difficult, if I'm honest. I'm still not sleeping great and Hayden is still colicky. It got really bad a couple of nights ago. I had to hand him off to my husband and go into another room, just to gather myself.'

'So you've spoken to your husband about the difficulties you've been having?'

She nodded. 'He's trying to understand, but I'm not sure that he does. He's smitten with Hayden. Perfect with him. Hayden doesn't cry as much for him. It's like he's better at being a parent than me.' Rachel began to cry and he passed her the tissue box, letting her cry, letting her get out this frustration that she was feeling. 'I just feel so sad all the time. It never goes away and I feel like I'm failing my baby.'

This most definitely was not baby blues. This tiredness, guilt, sadness that Rachel was feeling, all pointed to a case of postnatal depression. He was so glad that Anna had never had to go through this, too.

'I just…wake every day and before I even open my eyes, I feel this sense of doom. Like this thought going round and round in my head of how on earth am I going to get through the day, today? I've stopped going out. I avoid people. I don't answer the phone, because everyone expects me to be happy.'

Max nodded. 'I understand. And I think it's really important that we get you feeling better. I'd like to refer you to a counselling service. They can come to your home, if you can't make it out and about, though I think they prefer it if you can try and make it to them. I'd also like to prescribe an antidepressant to help with your mood. How do you feel about doing that?'

'Fine. I need to feel better. I can't keep going on like this.'

'It's important for me to ask though, Rachel. Have you ever had any thoughts of harming yourself, or Hayden?'

She looked shocked. 'No! I'd never!'

'Okay.' He smiled soothingly. 'I had to ask. Now there's no shame in having postnatal depression. It affects at least one in ten women after birth. It's not a weakness. It doesn't mean something is wrong with you and we don't know why it affects some women and not others. Do you write a diary or a journal?'

'I used to.'

'Do you think you could keep one? Maybe write in it each day about how you've felt? Maybe have a mood tracker? You can download various templates from the Internet. But try to keep track of your mood and emotions daily. It will help to spot some triggers and will also help the counsellor that sees you.'

'All right.'

'The important thing to understand right now is that this is treatable. And it is temporary. You *will* start to feel better and it might help to write that on the first page, so that every time you open your notebook or journal, you see that.'

'Okay. That sounds a good idea.'

'Now, I know you're breastfeeding, so I'm going to prescribe a medicine that will not pass through the breast milk, so it will be totally safe for you to take.'

Rachel nodded. 'Okay.'

'And I want you to try and get outside for a walk every day if you feel you can manage that. Fresh air and exercise will help you, and I want you to take this leaflet.' He passed her a leaflet from his desk. 'It lists all the places where you can get help, and that one on the bottom? Puts you in touch with another mother who's been through the same thing. Like a buddy, or sponsor.'

'That sounds helpful.'

'It can take the antidepressants a few weeks to start working, so shall I see you again in about two weeks? See how you're doing? But again, if you feel you need to be seen sooner, or things get worse in any way, you call immediately, okay?'

'Thank you, Dr Moore. You've been very kind and understanding.'

'It all just takes a little time, okay? But everyone, me, your husband, your health visitor, your family, they all want the best for you and we're all here to listen and to help. This isn't a burden you should feel you're shouldering alone.'

Her eyes welled up at that, but she simply nodded, thanked him again and left. Max wished there were a magic button he could push to make her see that the clouds would lift. That would improve her mood and make her feel connected with her baby. He hoped she wouldn't look back on this period and hate the fact that she missed out on enjoying her son's early weeks. But there was no magic button. If there were, he would have pressed it a long time ago, to take away his wife's cancer because, by rights, she should have been here to enjoy Rosie. To see the beautiful young girl she had grown into. He wasn't meant to be alone, either. They were supposed to be on this parenthood road together. That was the deal.

His mind drifted to Bella and Ewan.

When they'd come round for pizza and a movie, had been wonderful. Sitting there, in the dark, laughing, enjoying the film. It had felt like family. Had given him a taste of what could have been.

I wonder if Bella felt the same way, too?

Them getting up to go had broken the spell.

Left him wanting.

And then, when Bella had kissed him goodbye on the cheek? He'd felt a pull. Wanted more. Wanted to hold onto her and never let go. To squeeze her tight. To breathe her in.

To not feel alone any more.

He'd honestly not realised how lonely he'd been lately. He'd thought he was fine. Him and Rosie against the world.

But there was so much that he missed. So much that he needed.

Could he find that with Bella? He knew she liked him, but that was as friends and neighbours and colleagues. And it wouldn't be simple for either of them. They were both single parents, they each had a responsibility to their child first. And what if he asked for more and she wasn't willing to give it? How would that affect them at work? How would that affect their friendship, if Bella knew he'd wanted more, but she wasn't ready to give it? Bella had been cheated on. She'd be wary, he knew that. So was he. He'd had his heart broken in the worst possible way and he wasn't sure he could go through something like that again. No. He could never go through that again. He'd already made so many sacrifices in his life, he would not do so again. They would have to remain friends.

He went to the staffroom to fill up his water bottle and noticed a leaflet on the side for a travelling fair that was coming to just outside Clearbrook. It would be a lovely place to take Rosie. Every child should go to a funfair at least once.

He couldn't help but think, *I wonder if Bella and Ewan would like to go, too?*

Bella was saying goodbye to a patient who'd been in to see her and walked out with a diagnosis of tennis elbow, or lateral epicondylitis, to give it its clinical name, when Max caught her attention as he was heading to his consultation room. He held a leaflet in his hand.

'Just saw this. Fancy taking the kids to it?'

She took the leaflet and saw *Lawton's Family Fair! Coming Soon!* The fair seemed to promise fun rides, inflatables, games, hot food and drinks and the admission prices seemed pretty reasonable too. 'It's this weekend.'

'Looks fun. What do you think?'

'Can I think about it? Check my diary?' she asked.

'Sure. Let me know.' And he gave her a smile and disappeared into his room.

Bella did not need to check her diary. She knew her weekend was clear. Her weekends were always clear, because they were the days she dedicated to Ewan and Ewan would *love* to go to the fair!

But she did need to think about it. Her headaches were still bad and she imagined that at the fair there'd be lots of loud music pumping from speakers at various stalls. There'd be flashing lights and strong smells and that wouldn't help any. But the biggest thing she felt was wariness. Fear. Doubt. Last Friday, they'd met up for pizza night. Somehow, she'd offered to host next time.

Next time? What am I doing?

Going to the fair together? Was it too much? Were they doing too many things together? They already walked to school together every day. Often went to pick up the kids together—only one night had one of them had a heavier admin load than the other and that had been that first night. When Bella had met Rosie in the after-school club.

Would he read too much into it?

Will I?

Because the more time she spent in Max's company, the more she found herself stealing glances. Wondering what he was thinking. What he thought of her. What it might feel like to kiss him. What it might feel like to not be a single parent and not have issues with trust and how crazy it would be to throw caution to the wind and just pull him towards her and kiss him so passionately that the rest of the world would disappear.

She had crazy flights of fancy like that.

Who wouldn't with a guy like Max?

Bella couldn't believe she was even considering it. Going with him to the fair. Max was dangerous. A threat to her emotional well-being, because he was so easy to like. So warm. She'd not got involved with anyone since Blake and she'd seriously believed that she never would again. But here she was. Thinking about saying yes.

I'm probably reading too much into it anyway! He's just a single parent, like me, looking to take his kid somewhere fun, and he knows how much Ewan would enjoy it, too.

Bella looked down at the leaflet. Was she even seriously considering keeping Ewan away from this, just so that no one else got the wrong idea about what was happening between them? She'd always tried to make the best decisions for her son and he'd never been to a funfair before. And she would not keep him away from this. Imagine him going to school and discovering all his friends had been and he had not?

I'm sure I'm perfectly capable of staying away from Max. I've had years of practice of keeping myself apart from guys.

Bella found herself standing outside Max's door. She rapped her knuckles against the wood.

'Come in!'

She opened the door and wafted the leaflet in front of him. 'I checked my diary and we can go. When's best for you?'

His smile, when it broke across his face, made her feel good. Clearly, she'd made him very happy indeed. 'How about the Sunday afternoon? If we go about two o'clock? That should give us a couple of hours there and have them both home in time for tea, bath and bed at a reasonable hour before school the next day.'

She gave a nod. 'Sounds like a plan. Two o'clock it is.'

'Can't wait.'

Bella smiled and closed his door, letting out a breath. She didn't understand why she was so worked up about this. Why did it feel as if it were a date? Because it wasn't. A date usually involved just two consenting adults—they didn't bring their kids along.

Or maybe they do, if they're single parents?

Bella had no idea. She'd never done this before. Dating Blake had seemed much easier. Simpler. They'd gone to pubs and restaurants. Once they'd even gone to see a show in London at the West End. Blake had turned up at her house with a stretch limo once and taken her to a ball. That had been an amazing night. A night she could spend proudly on his arm. Feeling the eyes of everyone on them as they'd arrived. The way he'd held her hand as she'd alighted from the car. He'd been so wonderful to her in those early weeks of their courtship. He'd been wonderful for what she'd thought was years, until she'd realised it had all been a hoax and that he'd completely pulled the wool over her eyes.

She'd been so blind and she didn't want to make the same mistakes again. Wouldn't let any dashing charmer humiliate her like that again. And though she felt in her heart that Max wouldn't do that, she'd believed the same thing once about Blake.

Was there any way to be sure? To know?

All I can do is be sensible, and if I feel that this thing

*begins to run away with me, then I'll just have to be strong
enough to put a stop to it.*

Bella nodded to herself and began working through a
referral to physio for her last patient.

The Lawton Family Funfair was situated in a couple of
farmer's fields just outside Clearbrook.

Rosie and Ewan were getting so excited and they hadn't
even got there yet, but as they parked up they could hear
the loud music being blasted from large speakers and the
lavender scent that usually pervaded the air was taken
up instead by the twin aromas of fried onions and candy
floss.

Families, couples, groups of kids were all making
their way along the road towards the fair, the entrance-
way marked by an arch of lights and a clown figure holding a big bunch of helium balloons shaped like cartoon
characters and superheroes.

'What do you fancy going on first?' Max asked Rosie,
who was holding his hand.

Rosie shrugged, uncertain.

But Ewan, who was raring to go, said, 'Everything!'

Max turned to Bella and laughed. 'I think it's going to
be an expensive afternoon for you!'

She nodded. 'Tell me about it.'

As they passed the clown, they headed into a line of
game stalls. Hook a duck. Another where you could try
and throw ping-pong balls into goldfish bowls. Another
where you could throw darts at playing cards. A coconut
shy. A shooting range. A basketball net. All the stallhold-
ers happily called out to attract newcomers to part with
their cash. Beyond them, they saw rides—teacups, a small

carousel, a ghost train, a big wheel. Horns blared, music blasted, people screamed and laughed.

Max felt Rosie cling more tightly to him. 'Shall we try to hook a duck?' he said, kneeling down to be on her level.

She nodded and he paid for them all to have a go. It was quite easy to hook a duck, but only ducks with odd numbers on the bottom would win a prize and they had no idea how many ducks actually had those. Max hooked a duck with an even number, as did Ewan and Rosie, but Bella selected a duck with the number seven on it and got to choose a prize from the shelf of cuddly toys. Bella smiled at Ewan and said, 'You pick one.'

Ewan eyed the soft toys. 'Rosie can pick.'

Rosie pointed at a pink teddy bear no bigger than her hand and Bella gave it to her. 'Here you go!'

Rosie beamed. 'Thank you!'

Max smiled, too. That was so thoughtful of Ewan and her to do that.

His daughter clung to her teddy and his hand as they reached the teacups. 'Can we go on this, Daddy?'

'Absolutely.' He and Rosie climbed into one teacup, Bella and Ewan the next. It was so nice to see the kids' faces so lit up with joy and happiness. As the music played and he showed Rosie how to turn the cups, gently, because he didn't want her to feel ill, he couldn't help but glimpse Bella and Ewan in theirs, next to them, and Ewan was spinning them like crazy! Bella's face was an absolute picture and he couldn't help but laugh out loud. When the ride stopped, he held his hand out to her, to help her out of the teacup, and she took his hand in hers with relief.

'Thank you!'

'You're welcome.' And he realised, in that moment, that

he didn't actually want to let go of her hand. Only he had to. Guiltily, he let go, but it was as if he could still feel her hand in his. As if the imprint of it were seared into his memory. He tried not to think too hard about it. Tried to lose himself in watching Rosie ride the carousel. Taking pictures of her each time she came around, capturing her happiness for ever in an image that would later become his next screensaver.

Bella took Ewan on the ghost train, but Rosie didn't fancy that one, so they waited for them, watching them disappear through two doors that hooted and hollered ghost noises, as sirens blared and horns hooted and they eventually came blasting through two black doors on the other side, looking exhilarated and happy.

'Again! Again!' yelled Ewan.

'Maybe later.' Bella laughed, clambering out of the car.

They stopped briefly to get hot dogs for them all and they sat down at a set of benches to eat their food. They were delicious. Frankfurters on long, fluffy, white finger rolls, covered with caramelised onions and drizzled with tomato sauce and mustard. They all must have been really hungry, because everyone ate every bite. After, they played at a few more stalls. Ewan won a yo-yo that whistled, Max won his daughter another teddy and Bella won a stuffed dog after knocking over a pile of cans with little bean bags.

'Mummy, can we go on the big wheel?' Ewan asked.

'I guess. How about you guys?' Bella looked to him and Rosie.

'Why not?'

They got into the queue and that was when Ewan said, 'Can Rosie and me go in one and you two go in another?'

Max looked at Bella with one eyebrow raised. Alone in a big wheel? It did have pods designed for little kids interspersed with larger ones for adults and there was a sign at the bottom saying that it was safe. 'What do you say, Rosie?'

She nodded.

'Okay,' Bella said. 'But you must behave yourself with Rosie. No swinging the pod and scaring her. You hear me?'

'I won't.'

'Cross your heart.'

Ewan mimed crossing his heart.

'We'll be in the pod behind you, so we'll see if you do!' Bella warned.

He trusted her and he trusted Ewan. So far, Bella's son had looked out for Rosie at school and so he was also going to trust him here. Rosie did, too, so this was going to be a big test for them all.

But the last week or so had shown Max that he could leave his daughter to be looked after and protected by someone else and if Rosie felt confident about it, then so would he.

They watched and waited patiently as the previous riders disembarked and then, pod by pod, they loaded up. Rosie and Ewan got into a red pod, with white stars on it, the door clanking shut behind them as they took their seats and got strapped in. Then their pod moved forward and he and Bella stepped into a blue pod that had big white polka dots on it and he couldn't help it, but he kind of felt a little nervous. Sitting this close to her, in such a confined space. Just the two of them.

The pod had open windows either side and they could

hear the music being piped in, as slowly they began to ascend. Ahead of them, they could see Ewan and Rosie waving to people as they got higher and higher.

'This is amazing,' Bella said. 'I don't think I've ever been on a big wheel before.'

He was surprised and turned to look at her. 'You haven't?'

'No. Have you?'

'A long time ago. With friends. But I have to admit that we were maybe a little too drunk to have appreciated it properly. My friend, Matty, kept trying to roll the pod and thought it was hilarious. By the time we got off, I was almost ill.'

She laughed. 'Are you still in touch?'

'Sometimes. He's an army doctor, so I occasionally get a postcard or two. Oh, my God, look at that! Doesn't Clearbrook look amazing from up here?' The pod had risen above the fair, higher into the sky, and now they could see across the fields, past the lavender farms, towards the village. It looked picture-postcard perfect. Thatched roofs, and quaint roads dotted by colourful flowers, and the north side of the village, flanked by huge fields of purple lavender.

It was almost romantic.

'It looks amazing! Where's Field Lane? Can we see our cottages from here?'

Max had to lean over her way to look out of Bella's window to check. Trying to orient himself from the sky, like a bird, was weird, but eventually he worked out which road was theirs. 'There, see? By that big oak tree, over to the left?'

She nodded, turning to him, smiling. 'I see it.'

And that was when he realised that he was mere inches from her face. Her smiling, happy face. Her beautiful, gorgeous face. Her mouth. Her lips. This woman whom he had only just begun to know. Whom he worked with every day. Who seemed to adore his daughter, just as much as he did. This beautiful soul. He felt himself staring at her, hesitant, afraid to make a move, but considering one.

She looked back at him, realising the intent in his gaze.

And if he'd thought for any moment, that she did not want him to kiss her, he would not have done so. But she didn't look that way. She looked…breathless, apprehensive, yes, but…as if she was ready to try a kiss, too.

It shocked him. Surprised him, but the look in her eyes told him that he could do this and, feeling emboldened, he leaned in a little further, their lips millimetres apart. One last bit of eye contact. One last check that this was okay, that she gave her consent—that was incredibly important to him—and it was all he could think of. All the other stuff between them was forgotten. That this was his co-worker. That this was his neighbour. That this was his good friend. That was all gone. All that mattered, in that intimate moment, was the fact that he wanted, needed, to kiss her. To see how it felt. To see how she tasted.

The sounds of the funfair were gone. The aromas. The rest of the world. All there was were him and her, pressed tightly together in that pod. Her mouth near his. Her lips parted in expectation.

He pressed a hand to the side of her face and leaned in for the kiss.

For a moment, he was lost. Fireworks could have gone off, bombs could have exploded and he wouldn't have noticed, because all that mattered was her. The feel of her.

Her softness. The way she gently kissed him back, losing herself, too, the way her tongue gently caressed his and then was gone again. The heat that flared in his body, the way his body stirred in response to her touch, her taste, her softness and suddenly, they were breaking apart and staring into each other's eyes and looking shocked at each other. At what had just happened. At what they had both just felt.

CHAPTER FIVE

MAX DIDN'T KNOW whether to apologise, or to make a joke, or to say nothing. He didn't want to break the spell, he didn't want the pod to reach the ground and put them back into the real world again. The real world had been suspended whilst they were in the pod, isolated, in their own self-made world, where there was nothing but each other.

He wanted to kiss her again. To try it again, to see if the second time would feel just as magical as the first.

And then, before he could say anything, they were at the bottom of the ride and the big-wheel guy was clanking open their pod and he stepped out and there were Rosie and Ewan waiting for them and he scooped his daughter up into his arms.

'Did you enjoy that?' It seemed easier to pretend that nothing had happened right there and then. The kids hadn't seen, it would have been impossible for them to have seen, and if he pretended everything was normal, then maybe it would be and he would realise that he hadn't made a huge mistake and risked their friendship, or anything like that.

'You could see the whole world!' Rosie exclaimed.

Max smiled and kissed his daughter's cheek. He glanced at Bella, feeling a little embarrassed. A little guilty. How was she feeling? But she was kneeling down, away from him, straightening her son's collar on his jacket and smiling as Ewan babbled on about a bird they'd seen fly past.

Maybe the whole world could stay the same.

Maybe they could pretend the kiss hadn't happened.

Because miracles happened, right?

They had to.

They just had to.

What madness had overtaken him to do such a thing? They could have carried on as they always had, but an impulsiveness had overtaken him, because of what? The way her eyes had looked in the shadow of the pod? The proximity?

No. It was more than that. They weren't strangers, they'd slowly become friends, and he had come to look forward to every walk to school each morning and after work. He'd gone to her house this Friday just gone, her turn, she'd said, and he'd had a wonderful time. The kids had sat at a table completing a jigsaw puzzle together and he and Bella had sat next to each other on the couch, talking, laughing, sharing stories. *Bonding*.

And he'd realised that he really, really liked her. How much they had in common. She'd shown him some of her paintings that she'd done. Mostly watercolour, and she was talented. She'd been most self-deprecating and couldn't see her own talent, but she had it. There was even a huge canvas above her fireplace of a watercolour that she'd done of a giant amaryllis flower and it was stunningly beautiful. Graceful, light of touch, the pinks and yellows flowing into each other seamlessly.

He'd noticed his hand just inches away from hers and he'd had to pull it away, because the temptation to reach out and fold her hand within his had been too much. Instead, he'd laughed to himself, embarrassed, frozen, and he'd stood up as if to examine the painting more intensely, but in reality he'd needed to get away from her, to stop himself from touching her. From reaching out to feel her skin against his.

The kids had been oblivious to the tension. Had Bella? His body hadn't felt like his own, so he'd shoved his hands into his jeans pockets where they'd been safe and unlikely to reach out without his permission. But then she'd got up from the sofa and come to stand beside him and she'd begun to talk about how she'd painted the amaryllis and all he could do had been stare at her profile and gaze at her lips and her eyes and the way her dark hair fell about her shoulders and he'd known he couldn't stay a moment longer. Because if he had? Something would have happened. He would not have been able to stop himself.

As he hadn't on the big wheel.

Getting in the big-wheel pod with Max had felt unnerving, because it would be the first time the two of them would be together, hidden away from the world, in an enclosed space. They were together at work, but there were always other colleagues around and they had a job to do and of course they were professionals. When they were walking the kids to school, Ewan and Rosie were there. Walking to school together to pick up the kids at the end of the day? They were out in public and she felt relatively at ease.

But getting into that pod?

At first, she had been incredibly nervous. Her stomach dancing with butterflies and her blood pulsing through her ears louder than the music that had been blaring from the speakers, or so it had seemed. But then she'd begun to relax as they'd marvelled at how the fair and Clearbrook looked so beautiful from such a height. It had been like looking down on a cute model village and the lights from the fair had sparkled and dazzled and, for a moment, it had felt as though they were in another world!

They'd tried to spot their own cottages and Max had leaned across to point and something had shifted. Whether it had been the press of him up against her, or the way the multitudes of light had been reflecting off his face, but she'd suddenly found that she couldn't stop staring at him. Marvelling at his broad smile, feeling the attraction for him well up and spill over whatever walls she'd put up to protect herself from this very kind of thing.

It had almost been like not having control over her own body—it had simply reacted to him. She might have told her mind that she would never allow anything to happen with Max, but it was as if the rest of her hadn't got that memo.

She liked Max. A lot. He was funny. Charming. Handsome. Kind. A great dad and, yes, even though she'd only known him for a short period of time, she'd begun to think of him as a wonderful new friend.

And that kiss…

Wow. I mean… I cannot deal!

His kiss had been tender, yet passionate. Intense and yet gentle. He'd cradled her face and she had felt her heart melt, being made to feel as if she were something precious, something fragile, something that he cherished, because she'd not been made to feel that way for a long time.

When had she last had anything, or experienced anything, that was uniquely just for her? That had nothing to do with being a mum, or a doctor, or a friend? That kiss had been something special and that kiss had also changed everything, because when they'd breathlessly broken apart, she'd not known what to say. And he'd looked at her as if he'd been just as shocked at what had happened and he'd even looked a little guilty.

Of course. The last woman he probably kissed like that was Anna.

And he felt bad.

I'm the other woman still, even though his wife is dead.

She sensed his regret and it made her clam up and so the second the pod revolved to the floor and the door was opened, she got out as quickly as she could to make sure the kids were okay and fuss with Ewan's top, and asked him if he needed the loo, or whether he wanted to go home yet.

Bella hoped and prayed that Ewan *would* want to go home. Because she needed some space. Some time to breathe and process what had just happened between herself and Max.

Would they be able to ignore it, then? Pretend it never happened? That would be easiest, wouldn't it?

Ewan yawned. 'I want to stay.'

'Hmm. You look tired.'

I'm shaking. Look at my hands trembling!

'I think we ought to make a move,' she said, louder, for the benefit of Max, who she could not bring herself to look at yet. She didn't want to see the regret in his eyes again. Clearly he wasn't ready for anything else.

'You're going? I'll drive us back.'

Damn. She'd forgotten that they'd come out here in his car. 'No! You stay and enjoy yourselves, we'll walk, or grab a taxi.' Finally she managed to look at him. Briefly, but she managed eye contact. She could see he looked pained and interpreted it as apology. He'd not meant to kiss her. It was a mistake. Of course it was a mistake!

And here she was again, feeling hurt because of a guy.

I knew I should have kept my distance!

'No. Let me drive you,' Max insisted.

So she let him drive them home. As usual, the two kids chatted away quite happily in the back seat of the car, but up front it was uncomfortably quiet. When he parked up in Field Lane, he turned to her. 'Bella, I—'

She pushed open the car door and got out, without waiting to hear what he was going to say. 'Thanks for the lift.' She helped Ewan out, let him say goodbye to Rosie and then they were marching across the road to their own cottage.

This time, she didn't turn to check if he was waiting to make sure she got inside safely. She didn't turn at all. Not even to wave to Rosie, which she felt bad about. She just wanted to get indoors and hide.

And breathe.

And *think*.

Too easily she'd allowed herself to get close to another guy. Why had she allowed it to happen? Because they worked together? Because they were both single parents with kids in the same class, who lived opposite one another? It was hardly the basis for a relationship now, was it? She'd let herself be taken in by a handsome guy, again. And she'd felt his rejection of her, almost instantly, when she'd seen the regret of his actions in his eyes.

I'm a fool!

How on earth was she going to face him tomorrow on the walk to school? The entire day at work?

How would she ever face him again?

When Max woke the next day, after a night of stunted and disturbed sleep, his stomach was a bundle of nerves. He'd wanted to try to explain to Bella how he felt, how he didn't want anything to change between them, but she'd not given him the chance.

Not in front of the kids anyway and he could respect that, so maybe at work today, they could talk? He hoped that he would give her the chance to talk. Maybe after they'd dropped the kids off at school and on their way to the practice?

He let Rosie knock on Bella's door. Max stood out on the lane and waited, holding Rosie's bookbag and PE kit that she needed that day.

Bella and Ewan came out and he looked at her to try and gauge how she was feeling. She managed a tight smile at him. 'Morning.'

'Morning.'

He hated that he'd made her feel any particular way. He didn't want her to feel bad about this. This was something that he had done. She was not in any way to blame for anything.

The kids ran ahead and he unexpectedly got some alone time with her.

'How are you?'

'Good. I'm good. How are you?' she asked, looking at anything that wasn't him.

'Fine. Listen…about yesterday…'

She stopped walking, turned to face him. 'Let's just

forget about it. Let's just forget it ever happened and we'll just move on, okay?' Her voice sounded bright. As if she was trying to convince herself as much as she was trying to convince him.

'If that's what you want?' He felt hurt, even though he wanted them to move on and pretend everything was normal, too. Hurt because he'd felt something during that kiss. Something that had disturbed him so greatly that it had almost caused him to be mute. He'd not expected such a strong connection, had not expected to feel so much for Bella, this soon. How long had they known each other? Was it possible to feel this much for someone so quickly?

Of course, he'd heard of people who reportedly fell in love at first sight. Or couples who said they just knew the second they met their person. Or couples who moved in with one another after a week and were still together forty-odd years later, with children and grandchildren. But they were all *stories*.

Stuff like that had never happened to him. Even with Anna, who'd he'd believed to be the one and only love of his life, ever.

It was the shock of what he'd felt for Bella in that kiss, in that moment in which the world had paused, that had stunned him into silence. That had caused him to realise that he'd been wrong about that prior belief.

'It is. We'll just carry on like it never happened, okay?'

'Okay.' It wasn't okay. Not really. But if she wasn't willing to explore this, then maybe she thought the kiss was a horrendous mistake. And he had to respect her wishes. He wasn't sure how he was going to be able to tell himself that he could not pursue this, but he would. Somehow. Having her as his friend, neighbour, colleague, would be enough, right? It wasn't as though she was going to walk away and disappear from his life. He needed her. Wanted her, by his side as all of those things. His connection to Bella was so strong already and it grew every day and there was nothing he could do about it. And he'd nearly ruined it with an impulsive act.

They dropped the kids off and began their walk to work. It was a beautiful day and the lavender scent filled the air again and Bella chatted on about endless things— the weather, the flowers in people's gardens, how beautiful the ginger cat was that they often saw here sitting on a low stone wall.

He would smile. Nod. Occasionally answer in monosyllabic words. But he wanted to say so much more. He felt as if he might burst if he couldn't fully apologise for his actions. If he couldn't explain properly what had happened. But that was his fault. He was the one that had kissed her, not the other way around, and if this was how she chose to deal with this, then he would go along with it.

When they got to work, Lorna was just coming out of the bathroom, having changed into her work clothes after running in. They both said hello to her and then Bella grabbed a mug of tea and disappeared into her room.

'Everything okay with Bella?' Lorna asked.

'Er…. Yeah, I think so. Why?'

'I don't know, she just seemed a little unsettled.'

'No. Everything's fine.'

'Well, I might pop my head around her door. Check on her, just in case.'

He smiled, wondering if Bella would confide in Lorna about what had happened yesterday.

If she does, I'll just admit to it, if Lorna asks. Be honest.

Honesty was always the best policy. Even when it was painful. When Anna had discovered she had cancer early on in her pregnancy and the doctors had advised her to terminate, because her type of cancer was aggressive, they had taken some time to make their decision. Anna had wanted to continue with the pregnancy and, though he'd wanted to be the good guy and support her one hundred per cent in a decision about her own body and for their child, his honest opinion? Agreed with the doctors. And so he'd told her.

'I don't want you to die. Your cancer is aggressive, and if you wait to give birth who knows what will happen in those short months?'

'So what are you saying? I should terminate our child?'

'To give you the best chance of survival. We can always try for another child... We can't try for another you.'

She'd told him that by saying that he'd made her feel all alone. Abandoned almost, when he'd not wanted her to feel that way at all. But he'd been trying to do the best thing for her and this child was as much his as it was hers. He'd had to have his say, right? He was allowed an opinion.

And, of course, she'd continued with the pregnancy. He'd tried to marvel at every stage. The way her belly had grown. The first flutterings of movement. The feel of a first kick. Buying baby clothes in pink when they'd discovered it was a girl.

But as she'd grown, so had the cancer and though Anna had bloomed, he'd known something dark and insidious had also been growing within her and the doctors' decision to deliver her early had been a good one, even though Anna had wanted to go to term to give her child the best chance of health and life. His decision to be honest about his feelings had caused an upset in their relationship, but he'd believed it vital to be honest. He'd always prided himself on it.

Surely he should be honest with Bella about his feelings, too? So that she was clear on how he felt? But what if she rejected his feelings, the way Anna had, to do her own thing?

Max headed into his own consultation room, closing the door behind him. Booting up his computer, settling into his chair, checking on results and letters that had come in overnight. He'd been given an admin hour first thing. His clinic didn't start until ten.

He saw that his patient Robert Heaney had been diagnosed with a DVT, as expected. That some bloods showed other patients were iron deficient and that another had pernicious anaemia. He called through to the reception manager, Saskia, and asked her to call the patient to arrange an appointment to discuss the results and come in for a B12 injection.

He lost himself in the paperwork, but couldn't help but think about Bella in the next room.

CHAPTER SIX

BELLA WAS JUST settling in, when there was a knock on her door.

Please don't be Max. Please don't be Max!

'Come in!' She forced a smile and relaxed her shoulders and beamed when she realised it was only Lorna. 'Hey. What's up?'

Lorna settled into a chair. 'Well, to be honest with you, that was going to be my question to you. Is everything all right?'

'Fine! Why?'

'I don't know, you just seemed a little…unsettled out there. Terse. Bad weekend?'

'No! Just a little…miscommunication, that's all. It's nothing. It's passed now.'

'Oh. Anything I can help with?'

'No. It's done. Honestly, everything is fine.'

'Weren't you and Max going to the funfair at the weekend? Did something happen between you two? The atmosphere was a little awkward out there and I only ask because, well, this is a small practice and, as the lead partner, I need to make sure that my doctors are all getting on okay.'

'I'm fine. Honestly. Like I say, it was just a miscommunication.'

'Between you and Max, or…?'

'We've settled it.'

'You're sure?'

'Yes.'

'You don't need a mediation, or anything?'

'No.' Bella smiled. 'It's not like we're married!' She laughed, imagining Max sliding a ring onto her finger. His eyes staring into hers. Stepping forward to seal their marriage with a kiss. 'It was something silly and I overreacted, that's all.'

'Okay. Well, I just want you to know that I'm here if you ever need to talk. I know I'm your boss and colleague, but I'd like to think that I'm here as your friend, too, so if at any time you want a chat…then I'm here. My door is always open, as they say.'

'Thanks, Lorna.'

She watched Lorna go, hoping that that would be the end of the matter. She didn't need her and Max's kiss to become a work issue, where Lorna got to weigh in. She'd only been in the job a couple of weeks and didn't want to cause trouble for anyone. Especially not this early. She wanted to put her roots down here. Raise Ewan in this peaceful and beautiful village.

I'm going to make a concerted effort to let Max know that everything is all right between us, because I can't have it going any other way.

Mr Colin Gatsby was her first patient of the day. Aged fifty-one, he came in with a smile and ruddy cheeks.

'Hello, I'm Dr Nightingale. How can I help you today?'

'It's this redness on my face, Doctor. Itching like crazy, it is, and I can't stop scratching at it.'

It did look quite sore and red. 'And how long has it been like this?'

'Three days. I thought maybe it was too much sun, but I've never had anything like this before. The occasional blotch on a cheek, when I've been stressed or something, but it's never itched like this. I couldn't enjoy the fair yesterday, because all I wanted to do was scratch.'

'Okay, is it just on your face, or anywhere else?'

'Just my face. Mainly my cheeks. It goes up to my temples and a little down my neck. I put some aloe vera on it, but it just burned every time.'

'Is it all right if I examine you?'

He nodded.

Bella washed her hands and then put on some gloves and examined Colin's face. The skin was extremely dry and rough. 'What's your cleaning routine?'

'Soap and water. Always has been.'

'You shouldn't be using soap. Not with your skin, it's very dry. You've got something called rosacea. It's common and it can come and go, but certain things can trigger it. Sunlight, heat, exercise, hot drinks, spicy food... We need to change your skin routine.'

'Skin routine? I'm not sure I've ever had one!'

'Well, we need to change that, Mr Gatsby, if you want the itching to stop and to keep control of this.'

'Like what?'

'Well, your skin is very dry and so we need you to start using a moisturiser, every day. Preferably twice a day, morning and night, before bed.'

'Like what the wife uses?'

'You can, but I could also prescribe a specific one that's for sensitive skin, that doesn't contain any perfumes or unnecessary ingredients that might antagonise your skin.'

'All right. Is that all I have to do?'

'No. I'm going to prescribe some metronidazole gel. It's an antibiotic gel that you apply to the reddened area each day, after you've washed and moisturised, and then, after that, I want you to use a suncream, every day. Nothing less than factor fifty. Every time you go out. Whether it's sunny and hot, or the middle of winter and foggy. *Every time* you go out.'

'Really?'

'Yes. Wait for the gel to dry properly, before you use the suncream.'

'That sounds like an awful lot to do, Doc.'

'It won't take you a minute or so more than your ordinary wash in the morning, but it's important, Mr Gatsby. Believe you me, if you lived in Spain or another hot country with your skin, it would look and feel a lot worse. The UV light aggravates rosacea.'

'Oh, I didn't know that. And with all these creams and potions, it should get better, should it?'

'Yes. You can use the metronidazole gel for a few months, but, after that, moisturising and protecting your skin with suncream every day should help a great deal and if it comes back or gets worse, you come and see me again.'

'Right. Okay. Well, thanks.'

'No problem at all. I've sent a script for those items to your usual chemist.'

'Lovely. All right, thanks, Doc. And thanks for seeing me.'

'It was a pleasure to meet you.'

She wished she could get rid of her own blushing every time she interacted with Max. Imagine how much easier life would be if she could just apply a cream that would stop him from being able to see how interested she was in him. How he made her feel.

It would certainly have made yesterday easier to bear.

Max was just finishing for lunch, when there was a knock at his door. When it opened, he was surprised to see Bella standing there with a tray. Two mugs of tea, two red velvet cupcakes and their lunchboxes from the fridge. 'Care to accept an olive branch?' she asked, smiling, her face full of hope.

How could he say no? And he was delighted that she had come to him and made this move. 'Gladly! Come on in!'

She smiled. 'I thought I'd take a leaf out of Oliver's book. He always takes Lorna a cup of tea in the morning and so I stole the idea and thought I'd bring you lunch, tea and dessert.' She placed the tray on his table.

'This looks great! But it's such a lovely day outside. What do you say we pack this up and go sit on the green? There's a bench under that big horse-chestnut tree, so there'll be shade.'

She glanced out of the window. 'Sounds like a plan.'

They transferred the tea into two travel mugs, wrapped the cupcakes and carried their lunches outside to the green. As expected in the middle of the day, it was popular and there were a couple of other people spread out on a blanket in the shade, reading books.

He also thought that Bella might feel a little more com-

fortable out here in public. Though he greatly appreciated her action to bring his lunch to his room, where they
would have been in private, he saw no reason as to why
they couldn't still have a private conversation out in public. And this way, they got to enjoy the warm, sunny day
and the fresh air, after being cooped up in their consulting rooms. Made everything a little less intense.

'This is wonderful,' she said, sitting down on the bench.

'Perfect spot,' he agreed. Was now the time to try and
apologise?

'Lorna spoke to me earlier today.'

'Oh?'

'Asked if there was a problem between us.' She gave
him a quick glance. Smiled. Looked away and bit into her
sandwich. When she'd finished chewing, she said, 'I told
her it was settled.'

'Okay. I mean, it is, right? I'd hate to think that what I
did yesterday would ruin anything here. This is an amazing place, with amazing people, and I want to settle here
and feel good here and I'd never forgive myself if I'd
screwed that up for you.'

She looked at him. 'You didn't screw it up.'

'I am sorry about what happened.'

Her cheeks coloured. 'It was just a kiss, right?'

He nodded. 'Right.' He could certainly view it that way,
even if he didn't want to. That kiss had meant something
for him. He'd never kissed another woman since Anna
and yet he'd felt able to kiss Bella. Had wanted to kiss
Bella. Over and over again. She stirred feelings within
him. Feelings that he couldn't contain, but tried to.

'Something spontaneous. Unplanned. And I could have

stopped it, too. I also hold responsibility here, and for that? I apologise.'

She was right. She could have stopped it, could have pushed him away, only she hadn't.

She'd kissed him back!

Why hadn't he thought about that? He'd been so busy blaming himself, he'd not thought too much about her response to the kiss. But then again, he was good at blaming himself. He blamed himself for getting Anna pregnant. If she'd not been pregnant, then she would have fought her cancer before it spread and she might not have died. He blamed himself for not fighting harder for a termination. He blamed himself for not enjoying her pregnancy and feeling anger towards an innocent baby. And he blamed himself that his wonderful daughter didn't have a mother.

He was good at laying the blame for everything at his own doorstep. Maybe he ought to try not to do that any more. Maybe with Bella, life could be different. She was certainly making him see things from another viewpoint.

Somehow, he felt a little lighter.

Max smiled his thanks for her apology, even though he felt as though she didn't have to make it.

'You know, in the spirit of goodwill and friendship and getting us both back on an even keel, I had an interesting email arrive in my inbox today.'

'Oh?' He was all for getting them back on an even keel. He'd not liked how it had felt for them not to be getting along. It had felt at odds with his contentment and happiness.

'I'm on the mailing list for the Todmore Maltings in the next village. It used to be an old Victorian factory building, but now it's a set of artists' studios, alongside a pottery, a gallery and a café. But every month, they do public events and things and I noticed in the email today that they're holding a pottery experience for beginners next Friday afternoon.'

'You should do it! You told me you always fancied doing pottery.'

She nodded, smiling. 'And you did, too. We both have an early finish next Friday and it just seems meant to be, so, as friends, would you like to go with me? I'll happily go on my own, but it's nice to have someone there that you know.'

Bella really was offering him the olive branch. She'd meant it when she came to his consulting room.

Well, if she could put all that upset behind her, then so could he! 'Er, sure. Would we be back in time to pick up the kids from school?'

'Easily. Want me to forward you the email, so you can see the details of it?'

'That would be great.'

'I just thought it might be a fun thing to do and…well, I can't think of anyone else who would like to go with me.'

'Ah. A pity invite.' He laughed.

'A hundred per cent!' She laughed, too. 'No, seriously, just…de-escalating a situation is all.'

'Well, as long as you can restrain yourself, you know.'

She gave him a playful shove and he laughed.

This was better. This was much better. He almost felt as if they were back to normal, as long as he didn't allow his mind to go off on flights of fancy of the two of them shaping bowls on the same pottery wheel, as it was in that film. What was it called?

Max couldn't remember and that part didn't really matter. What mattered was that everything was fine between them again.

Just as it was meant to be.

Bella was glad that they'd talked. That the white flag of truce had been shown, the olive branch accepted and now they were back to normal.

She'd debated mentioning the pottery experience, but she remembered he'd mentioned wanting to give it a try and how else could she prove to him that she wanted to put the kiss behind them and just move on?

By showing I was happy to spend some time with him.

And unlike in the pod, they would not be alone. They would be in a class, with other people, out in public. It would be fine. No accidental kisses. No forced proximity. No opportunity to stare into each other's eyes and forget the world.

It would be fun. Light-hearted. A laugh. Maybe they'd both get to make something they'd be proud of. And once it was done, they would have moved past the awkwardness of the weekend and how it had felt to walk to school with him this morning.

Eva Watts was her first patient of the afternoon. She came in looking pale, with dark circles under her eyes. 'I'm just so tired all the time. It's like I've got no energy to do anything.'

'How long have you felt this way?'

'A couple of months, to be honest. I kept thinking it would get better, but it just seems to be getting worse. I'm having headaches, too, and I've got this weird tingling in my fingers.'

Bella examined her, noting her pallor, her low blood

pressure and the fact that Eva seemed a little underweight for her height. And she had bruising on her forearms that looked as though she'd been held down. It was worrying. 'How's your appetite?'

'Not great, to be honest.'

'Do you eat red meat? Leafy greens?'

'No. Chicken and fish usually, with rice or pasta, that kind of thing. My boyfriend is on this health kick. He goes to the gym, he's training to be a bodybuilder and he didn't want to be tempted by bad things in the house, so we eat a very simple diet.'

The boyfriend sounded as if he might be much stronger than her, then. 'Does he take supplements?'

'There's a cupboard full.'

'Do you take any?'

She shook her head. 'I'm not training and he doesn't like muscly women.'

'What are your periods like?'

She sighed. 'Heavy. Painful. Like clots. I flood a lot.'

Bella nodded. 'I think you might be anaemic, Eva. I'd like to do a blood test to confirm.'

'Oh. Okay.'

'We'll do it now, if that's all right?'

Eva nodded.

Bella opened her cupboard, where she kept her blood-test equipment, but she was all out of purple vials and needed to go to the stockroom to get some more. 'I won't be a moment.' She excused herself and headed to the room where they kept everything a surgery could need—blood-sampling equipment, the emergency bag with defibrillator, oxygen canisters, swabs, pads, bandages, saline, tongue depressors, tools used for IUD insertions, scissors, tweezers, everything and anything was kept in there in neatly labelled drawers and maintained by their health care assistant, Carrie, who ordered the stock.

The purple vials were on the back wall, with all the other colours. She was getting a very bad feeling about Eva and her boyfriend. Those bruises looked painful and as if fingers had been squeezed tightly about her wrists. As she reached for a tray of tubes, the door behind her opened.

'Oh! Hi.'

Max.

She turned and smiled. 'Hi! What have you run out of?'

He laughed, nervously. 'Oh! Um…plasters, of all things. Paper cut.' He held up his finger, which was bleeding.

She knew where the plasters were and she was closest to them. She pulled open the drawer. 'How did you do that?'

'Refilling the printer with blood forms.'

'Ouch. Been there. You'll need an antiseptic wipe, too, hold on.' The box of wipes was in the same drawer as the plasters and she pulled one out and ripped open the packet and took hold of his hand without thinking about it. In doctor mode. Fixer mode.

Not until she was holding his hand and wiping away the blood did she think about where they were and what they were doing. In a store cupboard. Alone. Up close. Holding his hand!

Bella swallowed hard and tried not to blush, focusing intently on cleaning his wound, which was just over a centimetre in length. He'd really sliced himself well. It occurred to her that maybe she ought to have put gloves on, but it was too late now, and she just figured she'd wash her hands really well when she got back to her room, where her patient was waiting.

My patient!

'I…er…' She backed away and handed him the plaster, blushing furiously. 'You can do this part. I have a patient waiting, sorry.'

And she rushed past him, pulling open the stockroom door and leaving as quickly as she could. She blew out her cheeks and felt the coolness of the air in the corridor.

Wow. That was close.

Not that anything had been going to happen. More that they had been in forced proximity again, so quickly after the kiss, and it had simply reminded her—her body being an absolute traitor!—that another kiss would be a wonderful thing.

Bella apologised to Eva when she got back to the room and washed her hands. 'Now, about your heavy periods you mentioned…did you want to try something to help with those?'

'Like what?'

'Well, it's been shown that going on the contraceptive pill can help lighten periods, though obviously not everyone wants to take hormones.'

'That might be helpful, actually. My boyfriend, he doesn't like wearing condoms and I don't want to get pregnant, so…'

'Is there any chance you could be pregnant now?'

Eva shrugged. 'Maybe.'

'Okay. I'll add hCG testing to the blood test as well just to confirm.' She put on gloves and took her patient's sample. 'We should have the results for this back in one or two days, but in the meantime I'm going to prescribe you some iron tablets to take, just to be on the safe side. It's best to take them with food and if you can swallow them with orange juice then that helps with the absorption. If you are pregnant, then it's totally fine to take.'

'Do I have to call to get the results?'

'We'll text you with the results.' She checked that they had the correct mobile number, which they did. 'If the pregnancy test is positive, then I'll call to talk to you. I take it it's safe to call you on that number?'

'Why wouldn't it be?'

'I couldn't help but notice your bruising, Eva.'

Eva instantly looked down and pulled down her sleeves. 'It's nothing. I ran into a door.'

'I understand, but…a door doesn't make bruises like that. Fingertips do. Hands do. Does your boyfriend have any…anger issues?'

Eva looked down at the ground, utterly defeated. 'He doesn't mean it,' she said quietly. 'I get things wrong and he gets upset.'

'If you're in danger, Eva, I can help you.'

'I'm not.'

'I can put you in touch with people who can help.'

'I'm fine. Can I go now? He's waiting for me outside.'

Bella didn't want to let her go, but what could she do? She had no idea how bad things were, or if this was an isolated incident. 'All right. But I want to see you again in a week's time. You can tell him it's to discuss your results, but I'd like to check on you and, if you're willing to consent, I'd like to disclose details of this consultation with my designated adult safeguarding lead.'

'Why?'

'Because I have an ethical duty of care to you and

you've told me that your partner mishandles his anger and I've seen evidence of bruising on your arms, which will go onto your legal medical record, detailing my concerns.'

'What will this other person do?'

'They'll read my report. They may get in touch with you to talk further about your needs and your safety.'

Eva looked uncomfortable, but curious. 'But who is it?'

'It's Dr Lorna Hudson.'

'I know her. She's nice.'

Bella smiled. 'She's very nice and is extremely good at what she does.'

'What if…what if Ben finds out?'

'We would do our absolute utmost to ensure that only you are spoken to about this in a safe way that would not endanger you to any further harm.'

She nodded.

'You're giving me consent? To talk to Lorna? To see what help we can give you?'

She nodded again. 'I'm so tired.'

Bella reached forward and placed her hand on Eva's. 'I understand. But we know now and we can help you. Let me make an appointment for you. Same time, next week?'

'That'll be fine. He's away next week on a training camp.'

'Perfect.'

Eva Watts' blood-test results came back showing that, yes, she was very anaemic, so Bella was glad that she'd already got her on iron tablets. The medication should help her feel better and hopefully give her more energy, by correcting the imbalance in her system. Thankfully, she wasn't pregnant, either.

She spoke to Lorna and informed her of her safeguarding concerns for her patient.

In the meantime, Bella tried to continue as normal. Working with Max. Walking to school with him each day. He was so easy to talk to when they kept their conversations light-hearted and they both intensely avoided talking about the funfair kiss.

The kids were getting on great at school and party invites and sleepover invites were starting to come in from other kids, as their friendship group expanded.

She was beginning to feel settled in Clearbrook and was happy. As Friday rolled around and she and Max could go to Todmore for the pottery class, she was excited and nervous. Max offered to drive and it took them about twenty minutes to drive there. When they got to Todmore Maltings, they were given directions to their class and found a room filled with a variety of people, old and young alike. Their instructor was a middle-aged woman called Celia and she told them that today they would construct a decorated tile, using a technique called slip and score. Slip and score allowed for joining two pieces of clay together. The potter would scratch marks on the surfaces to be joined and then a liquid mixture of clay and water would be applied to join them together.

Celia showed them a variety of tiles made by previous students to give them an idea of what they could achieve and set them to work, with paper and pencils first, so they could draw their designs.

Bella decided to make a tile with fruit on it. An apple. A banana. Cherries. Max was bolder. He wanted a cat and a mouse. Once they'd drawn out their pieces, they were left to try and shape the clay and discovered it was a lot harder than it looked. Their first attempts looked like something a child had tried to create and they couldn't help but laugh at each other's attempts. It was kind of freeing to play with clay and it was almost like being back at school, but eventually they got there and attached their pieces of shaped clay to the tile.

Not bad for first-timers, she thought, glancing at Max, noticing that he had a smudge of clay on his face, just above his beard line. 'You've got something here,' she said, pointing at her own face for comparison.

'Oh, thanks.' Max tried to wipe at the mark but it wasn't coming off.

'Here. Let me.' She grabbed a clean cloth, dipped it in water and then leaned towards him to help wipe away the clay. One hand on his jaw to position his face so she could see what she was doing. It felt weirdly exciting to be staring at him so intently like this. Touching his face. Wiping at the clay smudge. So close to his mouth.

His lips. She knew how his mouth had felt upon her own. The heat of their kiss. How it had made her feel. Awakening her body for the first time in a long time, and now that Max had woken the beast? It wanted feeding.

Part of her more sensible, logical mind told her to be more forceful, to get it done quickly, to not drag this out, but that voice got drowned out.

Bella took her time. Dabbing gently. Not wanting to give him a red mark. Wanting to be gentle. Softly wiping his face, trying to focus on the clay mark, rather than the fact that she knew he was staring at her face, his lips parted, breathing hesitantly.

She was fascinated by the way his beard grew. Looking at every bristle. At the tones of his skin, the way his cheekbone shaped his face. Her fingertips on his jaw held him gently, but she wondered how fast his pulse would be going if she could press the flats of her fingertips to his neck. Very fast, no doubt. As her own was.

The clay was coming off. It had dried upon his face, so had been difficult to begin with, but now it was coming off more easily and she realised, very quickly, that she didn't want this moment to end, but end it had to. 'There you go. All done.' She managed a smile, but her insides were in turmoil. Her blood felt hot. As if it were fizzing with sparks of electricity, and she was so aware of him.

'Thanks.' His voice sounded gruff and he had to clear his throat and say it again.

Celia told them the work would go into the drying room and they could come back for next week's class, where they could be painted and then fired.

Bella and Max were working the next week, so Celia told them they could take their pieces home as they were.

'Shaping clay was harder than I thought. I would have liked to have had a go on a potter's wheel, though,' Bella said, laughing nervously.

'You can never have enough wonky bowls in the house,' he mused.

'Absolutely.' She smiled at him in amused agreement. She could remember as a child making an ashtray out of clay for her dad once, at school. It had been the ugliest thing ever, but her father had treasured it and used it as a place to drop his house keys every time he came in from work. Maybe one day, Ewan would make something for her and she would treasure it.

Travelling back to Clearbrook, she was very aware of

Max in the seat next to her. The way his hands held the steering wheel. How, on occasion, when he changed gear, his hand came close to her thigh, and she found herself imagining how it might feel to have Max's hands trace up her thighs. How it would feel to have him stroke that soft, sensitive skin on her inner thigh…

It made her heart pound and she couldn't believe she was having such thoughts. When she'd first seen him at the school, he'd looked like the exact kind of guy that would be dangerous to her. Of course, she hadn't really known him then and, since then, they'd become very close—working with one another, living near one another, spending time in each other's houses… The situation had changed and she thought that maybe, just maybe, he might be different.

Why? She wasn't sure. But she knew she was incredibly attracted to him and since the kiss, there had been moments—in the store cupboard, at the pottery class, in the car—when she'd found herself wishing that she weren't so afraid. Weren't so wary. So that she could allow herself to indulge. Perhaps in just the physical? Keep emotions out of it, but allow herself to sate her lust, because what would be wrong in that? People did it all the time.

But not people who work closely together.
Not people who are neighbours.
Not people who ought to know better.
Then who?

As they waited for Ewan and Rosie to grab their coats at pickup time, they were given paintings that the kids had completed that day. Ewan had painted a rocket going up into space and Rosie had painted a garden full of flowers.

'Those are amazing, guys,' Max said, admiring them both.

'What's for dinner? I'm starving!' Ewan asked.

It was Max's turn to host. 'Fajitas. Is that okay?'

'Yum!'

Bella was beginning to feel that everything was becoming complicated with Max again after that little blip at the funfair. She'd tried being in his company, pretending that everything was fine, and she'd almost made herself believe it, but was it really? She'd sat next to him at pottery today and they'd been laughing and enjoying each other's company and, yes, he'd given her all the warm, wonderful feelings, but that was okay, because, she'd told herself, nothing was going to happen.

And then she'd helped to clean his face. Had glanced once into his eyes and seen something reflected back that had told her that even he was struggling to pretend that nothing had happened between them. She'd seen wonder and want in his eyes, too. He was handsome. Sexy. But neither of them could dare to overstep the mark. She could still appreciate his beauty. Could still steal glances at him when he wasn't looking. Could wonder as to why he was still single. A guy like him…should have been snapped up by now, surely?

He was a dedicated father. A professional. Gorgeous. Clever. Kind. Why hadn't he sought out another relationship? Had he really been alone since his wife died? It almost didn't seem possible. She was curious about him and her curiosity didn't seem to want to fade. She needed to know more about him and what he wanted from the future. A headache was beginning to form. Tension? Stress? From all the frowning as she tried to work him out?

As they stood in the kitchen together, she chopping up salad, he warming the tortilla wraps in the oven, she found herself asking him exactly that. 'Do you think you'll ever settle down again? Like, get married, again?'

He turned to look at her. 'Why are you asking that?'

'I don't know. It's just that, you know, clearly you have a lot to offer someone. I just wondered why you'd not pursued settling down again. Or have you?'

Max let out a heavy sigh. 'I don't know. I always told myself I could never, but, as Rosie gets older, I have thought about what it might be like to be with someone again. I haven't before because, well, it was just too soon. Everything I've been through makes you wary of wanting to get close to someone else again. I mean, imagine if they got sick? I'd panic straight away.'

'So you're looking for someone who has one hundred per cent of their health?' She smiled.

He laughed. 'Yes. And someone who loves Rosie as much as I do. Someone who doesn't mind my long hours.' He shook his head. 'Basically, I'm looking for the impossible. How about you? You ever considered it?'

'Wow. Um… I hadn't. Being betrayed like that, abandoned like that, with no support for his own child, I… It kind of interfered with the way that I view guys. I mean, honestly? I do not know a single guy that has never let down a woman. My dad let down my mother. My brothers haven't always stayed true to their partners. I had Blake, who cheated on me. Friends whose marriages have broken down because of cheating, too. I just… I'd need a guy who couldn't ever possibly let me down.'

He smiled at her. 'Are you looking for the impossible, too?'

'Maybe. Is that so wrong, though? To want to protect yourself from future hurt?'

'No. It isn't. I get it. We're all vulnerable, but I guess, if we both want to be with someone in the future, we're just going to have to have faith and place our trust in them.'

'How do you do that, exactly? When you've been as hurt as I have? As you have?'

Max shook his head. 'I don't know. But if you find out, promise you'll let me know.'

She smiled, sadly. 'I promise.' The conversation had got serious. Asking him about whether he'd get into another serious relationship. Was she curious in general, or for herself? Could she see herself with Max and Rosie? As a blended family?

It was a weighty topic and worthy of further consideration, but Bella honestly didn't know where to go from here. Say something more? Make a joke to break the tension?

Luckily, Max came to the rescue. 'Okay! The fajitas are done. Want to call the kids in?'

She was grateful to him for changing the subject. 'Sure.'

Max had struggled to get that conversation out of his head all weekend. He was only willing to settle down with someone who technically couldn't possibly exist. How could he guarantee that the person he chose would be free of any health concerns, now or in the future?

He couldn't.

That wasn't how humans worked. They were made up of many moving parts. Filled with trillions of cells, fuelled by hormones and blood, and anything could go wrong with any singular part at any time in their lives.

So, was he doomed to failure? Doomed to be alone? Not willing to risk his heart in case someone got sick?

And Bella. She was looking for someone who wouldn't let her down. Wouldn't cheat on her. He would like to think that person existed. He would like to think that he was the type of guy that wouldn't let her down, but was it possible? Human beings were fallible. They made mistakes. They made sacrifices, they told white lies in the hopes of protecting someone. Sometimes bigger lies, to protect themselves. He wasn't a cheat and never could be. It went against all he held dear, but would he disappoint her in other ways? Upset her? Break her heart by directly opposing her own wishes?

They were being honest with each other now, but what about later on? And the reason he kept thinking about whether he could be with Bella was what he'd felt during that kiss. And again in the stockroom when she'd tended his cut. In the pottery class when she'd cleaned his face of clay.

Those moments, short as they were, had been so intense and all he'd been able to do, in that pottery class as she'd dabbed at his face with a cloth, was to think of that kiss. To look into her face and see her eyes so dark with concentration and secrets that he'd wanted the world to stop, so that he could find out what they were. What she was thinking, because he could see that she was just as discombobulated as he was!

Every spare moment, he spent thinking about Bella. About how well the two of them got on, about how good the two of them might be together. The kids got along, they were the best of friends. He and Bella were clearly attracted to one another. Surely they could be something amazing? If they were both brave enough to take the risk?

Were they brave enough? Could he be that brave so that he could have Bella? Could she be that brave to have him? To risk it all on the possibility of happiness? Was possibility enough?

His first patient of the day was Mary Connor, who'd come to see him after receiving her results from her scan at the neurologist.

She sat in front of him, holding the letter. 'It says it's corti…cortico…' She sighed and struggled with the pronunciation.

'Corticobasal degeneration.'

'I'm not sure I fully understand what that is. I did speak to him briefly at a consultation when he gave me the results, but I was just so overwhelmed and I'm not sure I took anything in. Can you tell me just exactly what this is?'

'Sure. It's a condition that is a type of dementia and it's something we can manage, but not cure.'

'Dementia, yes. I got that. So I'm going to lose my memory, then?'

'It's more than that, I'm afraid. This condition is caused by the body failing to break down a particular protein called tau. When tau builds up in the brain, it forms these clumps that can be quite obstructive and it leads to a person being unable to move well, speak or swallow, as well as affecting memory.'

'Oh, my goodness…'

'You remember you came because of problems with your arm and you mentioned your memory issues. These are early symptoms you've been having and it's good that it's been caught early, because we can give you preventative medicine.'

'The doc gave me pregabalin.'

'Yes. It should help with any pains you feel.'

'But that's all? Just pain? It won't stop anything else?'

'I'm afraid that we don't have much to prevent this disease, but we can treat the more symptomatic issues.'

'But I'm going to most likely end up in a wheelchair? Or in a bed? Unable to think? Or speak? Or swallow?' Mary's eyes welled up.

Max passed her the tissues and she took one, blowing her nose.

'We can't be sure how the disease will progress in individuals and not everyone gets all the same symptoms. We will meet up regularly though and monitor you and do what we can, as and when the need to step in is required. I can also put you in touch with support groups and talking therapies, if you or your husband need it.'

'I just never thought a little tremor would succeed in telling me my life could soon be over. There's so much I still wanted to do.'

'And there's no reason why you shouldn't still do them.'

She nodded and dabbed at her eyes. 'You never think it's going to end like this, huh? You think you'll live for ever and then, maybe when you're in your eighties or nineties, you'll go to sleep one night and just never wake up. Go peacefully. That's what I always wanted. But it turns out in this life you don't get what you expect.'

'I guess not.' He felt bad. He felt that he ought to be comforting her in many more ways, but right now, whilst she was upset, he felt as if his words might be empty.

'I guess I could make arrangements for that clinic. The one that helps people pass in the way that they choose. Peaceably and in control, whilst they still have it.'

He didn't know what to say. His calling to be a doctor was to help people and to prevent suffering. But he was subject to laws and guidelines.

'And this isn't fair on my husband! What he'll have to watch me go through, because this, my illness, it doesn't just affect me, does it? It affects him, too.'

He understood her anger and her frustration. He'd always thought he would be married to Anna his entire life. That they would share memories. Make memories. Travel. Raise a family. Have grandchildren and great-grandchildren and, as Mary suggested, live into their golden years together and fall asleep holding hands.

But life hadn't given him or Anna that. Life had taken Anna from him, cruelly. And much too soon. At the end she'd slipped away quietly in her sleep. But not before he'd seen her moaning in pain. Not before he'd seen her crying about leaving Rosie. Had endured long hours at her bedside holding her hand with her unaware because the morphine had knocked her out so well. He'd listened to those last breaths and then the silence that had followed and there'd been nothing easy about that. Not for either of them.

He didn't want to go through that with anyone ever again and he felt for Mary that she possibly faced such an ending, too.

What was the lesson from that? To take happiness whenever he could get it? To treasure every moment and stop second-guessing himself? Why was he torturing himself over Bella? They could be happy, couldn't they? They just had to try. Better to have loved and lost than never to have loved at all.

At morning break, he stepped outside to grab some fresh air and found Bella standing outside, too. She hadn't seen him, but she stood over in the small practice garden, her back to him, one hand up against her head.

'Hey.'

She turned, looking pale, with dark shadows under her eyes.

Instantly, he was alarmed. 'Are you all right?'

'Just a headache. I've taken some paracetamol, but this one's not shifting. Probably because I didn't get much sleep last night—I'm just tired.' She smiled a soothing, dreamy smile.

'Have you been drinking enough water? Most headaches are caused by dehydration.'

'I know. I read that study too and, yes, I have, I just needed some fresh air.'

He felt reassured. 'It is beautiful out here, isn't it?'

The garden was small and private and had a wooden bench dedicated to a doctor long gone.

Dr Bartleby. Who loved this garden.

There was a cherry tree. Hollyhocks that stood tall and proud, brandishing their dark, scarlet blooms, foxgloves in lilac that were feeding the bees. Dwarf sunflowers and lupins and chrysanthemums. A small rockery with heathers and a tiny water feature, so that they could hear the soothing sound of babbling water, even though they were nowhere near the brook that ran through the village.

'It is. I'm so grateful we have this space at work.'

He stared at her for a moment. 'Can I ask you a question?'

She turned to him, smiled. 'Of course.'

'We all get trained on how to deliver bad news to a patient. How to be professional. How to maintain that emotional distance, so that you can be clear, but also friendly and approachable, but they never teach you how to deal with afterwards. For the medic, I mean. I had to explain to a patient today that she isn't most likely going to die in the way that she would like, but instead in a much more difficult and distressing way, and sometimes, I just…' He sighed. 'I can't reconcile that in my mind. She's such a sweet lady and she doesn't deserve what's going to happen to her!'

'Does anybody? I'm sorry you've had to do that.'

'Every time I do, I remember what it was like to sit in that room at the hospital and be told by doctors that Anna's cancer was terminal. I know what it's like to be the one in the chair. I know what it's like to have your world, your future, turned upside down and I just wonder how that doctor felt when they left us, afterwards. Left us sitting in that room, holding our newborn daughter. Did they get upset? Did they have to take a break? Or did they just go right into the next room and deliver much happier news to someone else?'

She took a step towards him. 'This world will always be filled with unanswered questions. We won't ever get the answers we truly seek and maybe that's the whole point? Isn't life supposed to be a mystery and an enigma and we all just do our best to bumble our way through it and hope that we don't get hurt too much in the process?'

'And what if you have been hurt?' he asked, his voice low and soft. 'How do you get brave enough to try again?'

She looked deeply into his eyes. Standing close now.

'I guess you try and find ways to heal yourself. The best you can.'

He stared back. She had such beautiful eyes. Soft and alluring. A deep blue. Her skin looking so perfectly pale and creamy in the sunlight that shone down into the garden. The sun highlighting her cheekbones. Causing a perfect shadow just beneath her full lower lip.

He couldn't help himself. He reached up to rub his thumb over it and her lips parted. Max wanted to kiss her so badly, but he remembered what had happened the last time that he'd just followed his impulses and he didn't like how it had gone.

But something surprising happened instead.

Bella stepped *towards* him. She laid a hand upon *his* chest. She paused briefly, her eyes glazed with desire, and suddenly her lips were upon his and she was kissing him and the world turned upside down and inside out as he kissed her back, pulling her into his arms and allowing the kiss to become deeper. More intense.

The same thing happened as before. The world went silent and stopped. The noise from cars in the distance disappeared. The sound of bumblebees silenced. The aroma from the lavender fields was no longer there. It was just the two of them, standing in a void, bodies pressed up against one another, and Bella felt wonderful in his arms. Her softness, her curves. The way she tasted, the way she made him feel.

Alive again! After so long of living in a strange half-existence that he'd once thought was fine.

This was what had been missing from his life. This connection that you could only feel with another person who cared for you as much as you cared for them. This meeting of spirits. This coming together, and all from the power of a simple kiss.

When it ended, the world returned and part of him hesitated, unsure of what to say, wondering if she would panic again and blank him, or act embarrassed, or say it was a mistake.

Please don't say that, Bella! I couldn't bear to hear you say that what I just experienced with you was a mistake.

She looked up at him nervously, then a smile crept across her face. She blushed.

And he smiled, too. Maybe everything would be all right, after all? 'Are you okay?'

'Yes. Are you?'

'Yes. I'm feeling…apprehensive. I don't know what this means, but I know I don't want to mess this up.'

She sucked in a deep breath and nodded. 'Nor me.'

'So, how do we proceed? I mean…how do you want this to go? We both have so much at stake here. It's complicated.'

'It is. I guess we…take it slow. We don't rush things. Or miss steps. We go slow and carefully.'

'Yes.' He wanted to kiss her again. But there were patients waiting and they had a job to do. 'We should get back to work for now.'

She nodded.

'You're definitely okay?'

A smile. 'Yes.'

She'd been hesitant to kiss him, but had been compelled to, unable to stop herself, ignoring the fierce headache that still raged in her skull, making her feel nauseous. *Damn these migraines I keep having.*

The pain in her head had almost ruined the perfection of that kiss.

This second kiss had been everything she had imagined it would be like, after her experience at the funfair. She'd held back from kissing him so many times since that day and she'd been proud of her self-control, despite her physical and emotional attraction to Max. But today? She just hadn't been able to hold back. He'd looked and sounded so beat. That appointment that he'd had had really upset him. It might surprise the general public to realise that GPs were not automatons that sat in a room with patients for ten minutes, listened to their symptoms, gave them a prescription and sent them on their merry way.

GPs were human, too. And they felt patients' pain and they empathised with them sometimes, on levels the public could never know. Because they had to be professional, but sometimes, when patients left the room and the GP was alone again...

It could hurt.

Perhaps because that patient's situation mirrored an experience the doctor had faced, or one of their family members had faced, either in the past, or much more recently.

Clearly, Max had had one of those today and she'd wanted to make him feel better, yes, but she'd also wanted to let him know that she was there for him.

She liked him very much. Rosie, too. But that didn't make any of this less scary. Would he come to disappoint her as all other guys had? Would he ever walk away and leave her because she wasn't enough?

Back in her room, she took more paracetamol, glad that her neurology appointment was soon so they could rule some conditions out. Bella was sure it was just tension headaches. Stress headaches. Migraines. Her father had always had bad heads, she'd probably just taken after him. And doctors made the worst patients anyway, because they knew all the horrors and were brilliant at leaping to conclusions. 'If it looks like a horse and it sounds like a horse, then think horse, not zebras.' That was what her mum had always said and it was true.

It had to be migraines. All the symptoms were there and she'd been under a lot of stress, lately. Her blood pressure had shown that. A house-move. A new job. Making sure that Ewan was settled and happy. Her tensions with Max. She'd been putting herself on the back burner a little too much.

All I need to do now is be happy and enjoy my life.

CHAPTER SEVEN

IN THE SPIRIT of taking care of herself, that weekend, whilst Ewan was watching cartoons inside, Bella took a chair into her small back garden, along with a sketch-pad and a pencil, and began to draw the flowers that she could see.

There was a beautiful calla lily that had flowered, its white bloom reaching for the sky, having launched from a plethora of long green leaves. At its heart was a long yellow spadix, powdered with pollen, awaiting a bee.

It was a beautiful, graceful plant and she could feel herself relaxing as she drew it, long, free strokes of the pencil filling the page to capture the plant's elegance.

'You know that's highly poisonous, right?'

She turned at Max's voice, surprise crossing her face. 'How did you get out here?'

'Ewan let me in.'

'What? I've told him to not answer the door without my permission.' She knew she would have to have words with him later on. It was fine this time—after all, her guest was Max. 'But what if you'd been someone else? Someone dangerous?'

Max raised an eyebrow. 'In Clearbrook?'

'You never know. Do you let Rosie open the door without checking?'

Max smiled. 'Touché.'

She got up out of her chair and peered behind him. 'Where's Rosie?'

'Watching the cartoons with Ewan.'

'Oh.' She smiled at him and stepped towards him, pulling him to one side, away from the gaze of the windows and back door, and sneaked a kiss from him. 'Hi.'

'Hi.'

'Is it really poisonous?' She lifted up her pad and gazed at her drawing of the lily.

'It surely is. I did a shift in an A & E once—triaging minors—some kid came in with his parents. His mouth was all red and looked burned and raw. It was swollen and he had some difficulty breathing and he also kept being sick.'

'Poor kid!'

'We weren't sure what it was. We figured that maybe he'd ingested something, but even the parents were clueless. Said he'd been out playing in the garden. The dad had recently filmed a video in their back garden and showed us, so we could see what was there, and he had calla lilies. The kid had eaten one as a bet with his brother.'

'I don't think Ewan would do that, but maybe I should get rid of that one.' She turned to look at the plant that just a moment ago she'd thought was graceful and beautiful, eyeing it with distaste now and concern. 'Was the kid okay?'

Max nodded. 'He'd not eaten too much before he realised he was in trouble. The calla lily contains calcium oxalate crystals that feel like microscopic needles. Thankfully the crystals don't break down in the human body, so he couldn't suffer from whole body poisoning. He'd not eaten enough for that to happen. We gave him cooling things—milk, yoghurt and prescribed his parents to allow him to have lots of ice lollies to soothe his throat of damage—but we kept him in for a little while to observe his breathing. Then he went home.'

'Scary.' She looked him up and down, admiring him. 'Did you need something?'

'I did, yes.'

'What was it?'

He smiled. 'To see you.'

Bella chuckled. 'Oh. I see. Well…mission accomplished.'

He leaned in for another kiss, after checking they weren't being observed. The press of his lips upon hers caused her heart to race and her temperature to rise.

'Actually, there was something,' he said.

She looked up at him, smiling.

'I wondered if you'd like to go out for a meal with me one evening.'

'A meal?'

'Yes, it's this event in which two people, who like each other very much, spend time together getting to know one another more over the consumption of food, deliciously prepared by someone else.' He laughed at the face she pulled. 'I want to do this right, Bella. And neither of us want to rush into anything and I've been given the name of a well-respected babysitter who could look after the kids for us and put them to bed.'

'Who?'

'You know Verity, the lady that owns the local cheesecake shop? She's dealing with cancer at the moment, remember, from the team meeting?'

'Mmm-hmm.'

'It's her niece. She's twenty, looking to earn some extra pennies whilst she's on break from uni.'

'What's she studying?'

'I think Lorna said she was studying Economics.'

'How does Lorna know a babysitter?'

'She knows Verity and they talk a lot, from what I understand.' He tilted his head to one side. 'That's a lot of questions and not an answer. Are you stalling because you don't want to go, or is something else worrying you?'

'Of course I'd love to go! I'm just nervous, that's all. Starting something, the two of us. This part's all exciting, it's brand new and exciting, but what about afterwards? When it gets more complicated?'

He held her face gently in both hands. 'We take this one day at a time. We're not rushing. We're getting to know one another. Taking it slow. But I'd dearly love to spend some more alone time with you, without having to worry about the kids.'

She nodded. 'Me too.' It was nerve-wracking. Exposing herself to possible hurt again, but she had very strong feelings for Max already. How would she feel if she just kept trying to ignore them? That would hurt, too. 'Okay. When?'

'Probably a school night. How about I invite Ewan over to ours for a sleepover? I've got an air mattress he can use, or he can sleep in the lounge on a pull-out sofa bed. In the morning, we meet for our walk into school as normal. Neither of us stays out too late, we don't get carried away and no one turns into a pumpkin.'

'Great! Let's do it. Where shall we go?'

'Jasper's is meant to be good and that way it's in the village and we're close if either of us has to rush back for the kids or something.'

Bella smiled. 'You've thought this through!'

'I'm very thorough when it comes to planning.'

'I'm very impressed. How good are you at gardening?'

'I know my way around a rose or two.'

'Great. Want to help me uproot a lily?'

Bella sat nervously in the waiting room. It always felt strange to be the patient. Sitting out here, with all the other patients. She'd brought a book to read, in case of a long wait, but she couldn't concentrate. She'd woken with a slight headache today but she put that down to the stress of the appointment.

She'd told Max about it. Told him that she wouldn't be at work that afternoon, as she was seeing a neurologist for her headaches, but that she'd see him that evening for their dinner date and tell him all about it. But that he wasn't to worry. She wasn't. Which was a slight fib, because she was always going to worry until she got the all-clear and the professor diagnosed her with migraines.

He'd been worried, bless him. Of course he had. But she hoped she'd put his mind at rest. And they'd had a great afternoon in the garden, pulling out that lily and then pottering about doing little jobs together and she'd felt right at home with him. Doing things like that together. She could almost pretend they were a real family. The kids inside watching cartoons whilst Mum and Dad got some jobs about the house done...

The afternoon ranked right up there with one of the best

ones that she'd had. For something simple like that. She didn't need expensive dinners, or posh cars or expensive holidays. Bella just wanted to enjoy the simple things in life. And there was something special about beginnings. The excitement. The hope. The trepidation of what might be. What this might evolve into. Something grand? Something long-lasting? Was she with the guy who would become the love of her life? She tried not to think that way, but she was a romantic at heart and couldn't help herself.

Max was a good contender, that was for sure.

He seemed honest. Kind. True. She knew about his life already and there was nothing there that he was hiding. Nothing that would creep out of the woodwork at a later date to ruin everything. No ex-wives. No ex-girlfriends that still had issues with him. No weird behaviour. He was a straightforward guy. Open. Everything laid out on the table for her to view and assess. He'd told her—*'My life is an open book. Ask me anything.'*

She'd appreciated the gesture. Appreciated that he understood her fears and that he wanted to be as open with her as he possibly could. They'd talked about Anna. Blake. The kids. Their job. They'd talked of future aspirations and dreams and he really was on the same page as her.

They both wanted happiness and security and love. The possibility of one day having more children.

It didn't seem too much to ask.

He'd put his head around the door of her consultation room before she'd left. Wished her the best. She'd thanked him. Told him she'd see him tonight and that she promised she would tell him everything that happened. Best to be as honest with him as he was being with her. The headaches were no surprise. He knew she had them and he believed, the same as her, that it was most likely migraines. They were common, even if they were a pain, but she'd told him that as soon as she had any details, she would let him know, because she understood his fears, too.

Bella put her book away. It was useless. She kept reading the same paragraph over and over again. It looked as though she was one of the only patients to have arrived without someone accompanying her. Max was at work with everyone else and, anyway, it was fine. She wasn't afraid of coming to see a doctor.

'Bella Nightingale?'

She looked over at the door and saw a nurse, holding a clipboard, who smiled at her. When she got closer, the nurse said, 'Hi, I'm Heather and I'm just going to do a short set of obs on you and take some bloods, if that's okay?'

Bella nodded. 'Fine!'

She followed Heather down a pristine corridor and into a small side room, where her observations were taken. Blood pressure, which was normal. Oxygen saturations, perfect. Pulse and respirations, normal. Blood sugar, normal. Chest and lungs, clear. Ears, clear. Then Heather took a blood sample and placed a cotton swab over the needle site and taped it into place. 'If you'd like to go back into the waiting room and Professor Helberg will call you through.'

Bella had researched Professor Helberg, of course. It made sense to, if she was going to place her trust in him. He specialised in treating patients with headaches, all types of migraines, especially hemiplegic, as well as movement disorders and Parkinson's. He had a ninety-eight per cent approval rating on the Internet, with lots of five-star reviews from previous patients. He was pleasant. Kind. Gave clear explanations about diagnoses and what next steps to take. He was happy to consult with other professionals and gave patients great confidence in his ability.

In short, the kind of doctor she was more than happy to see.

Bella was happy that all her obs had been normal. It boded well. And she felt confident when her name got called again and she went into the professor's consulting room. She shook hands with him, said hello and sat down.

Professor Helberg smiled a warm, friendly smile. 'Good afternoon. It's *Dr* Nightingale, isn't it?'

'Yes. I'm a GP in Clearbrook.'

'Ah! I was going to choose general practice one time of day, until neurology grabbed my fascination.'

'Really?'

'Oh, yes. Now then, let's see.' He tapped away at his keyboard. 'I've received a letter from your own GP that states you've been suffering from some intense headaches of late. Now, he's given me details, but I'd like to hear all about it in your own words, if you don't mind?'

'Of course. Well, they started about six months ago, to be honest. I've had headaches before, but nothing that's required me to take painkillers, they've mainly been just from tiredness or dehydration and a quick guzzle of water usually sorted them out, but in the last half-year or so I've noticed these more intense headaches. I've been keeping a diary, to see if there's some sort of trigger—either emotional, hormonal, physical or food-based—but I can't seem to find a pattern or anything I can point my finger at.'

'And do these headaches always require painkillers?'

She nodded. 'Yes.'

'And how would you describe them? Are they always in the same place, for example?'

'Yes. Always here, just above my eyes.' She pointed to the spot.

'And what sort of pain is it? Burning? Stabbing? Sharp?'

'All of those.'

'And do you get any other symptoms with them? An aura? Nausea?'

'I feel nauseated sometimes. Tired.'

'Ever been sick?'

She nodded. 'Once.'

'Did it make you feel better?'

'No.'

'And you've not noticed any weakness with these head-aches? Nothing one-sided? No muscle weakness or dif-ficulty with the limbs?'

'No.'

'All right. Well, I'd like to do a brief physical assess-ment, if that's all right with you? I'll call my nurse in to chaperone. I just want to test your reflexes and run through some neuro obs.'

'That's fine.'

'If you'd like to hop up onto the bed, I'll fetch Heather.'

'Okay.'

The professor worked his way through a standard set of neuro observations, including checking her pupillary response to light, using a hammer to check her reflexes, which would help identify any abnormalities of her ner-vous system. He checked her motor skills, her coordina-tion and balance, but everything seemed pretty standard, as far as Bella could see.

'And remind me, you've not had any recent head injury? Even something small?'

'No.'

'No falls, or anything like that?'

'No.'

'No loss of consciousness with your headaches?'

'No.'

'And you don't seem to have any shaking or tremors, which is all good. No numbness or tingling in any of your extremities?'

'I don't think so, but I'm very busy, so I might not always notice.'

'Hmm. And no history of stroke, or TIAs or seizures?'

'No and nothing like that in my family.'

'And you're not taking any medications or herbs or other supplements?'

'I take a vitamin supplement. Just a standard one.'

'And everything else about your health seems normal? Periods regular?'

'Yes.'

'Okay. Why don't you take a seat back over by my desk?'

Bella went to sit down.

'All of your findings seem absolutely fine and I'm happy that, from what we've covered today, I can't seem to actually find anything physically wrong with you, which is good.'

'Great!'

'But, as a doctor, you also know that that doesn't always mean that there isn't anything wrong. This could just be migraines, as I'm sure you expect, but it would be remiss of me not to make sure, so what I'd like to do is refer you for a scan, just to make sure that there's nothing going on in the brain that should alarm us.'

Bella sucked in a breath. 'Okay.' She knew what that meant. Professor Helberg was going to check for anomalies such as aneurysm, tumour or lesions.

'And it's to rule things out, as much as it is to rule things in. You're having headaches for a reason and the fact that they've become bad only in the last six months or so suggests some sort of change. Now, it could be environmental, for all we know, and nothing to worry about at all, but I think, due to their severity, that we should get a scan and just double-check. How does that sound?'

'Would that be today?'

'Yes. Or we can arrange it for another day, if you have to be somewhere?'

She checked her watch. She should still make her date with Max in plenty of time. 'No, no. That's fine.'

'Excellent. Okay. Heather will take you through to the scanning department. When you've had the scan done, go home, relax or go and do something that's fun to take your mind off it and if, when I review it, I see anything disturbing—which I honestly don't expect to find—I'll give you a call in the morning. Does that sound like a good plan to you, Dr Nightingale?'

'Call me Bella. And yes, that sounds perfect.'

'Great. I'll call you tomorrow, but, like I say, go out tonight. Have some fun. There's nothing worse than staying in fretting about these things. At this point, I'm not worried and I don't think you should be either.'

'Thank you, Professor.'

'Call me Martin.'

* * *

It had been a long time since Max had taken a woman on a date. His last date had been with Anna. Nothing spectacular. Nothing that had cost a lot of money, but one that had meant a lot to the two of them.

He'd taken Anna to the beach. She'd wanted to watch a sunrise and so he'd figured out all the logistics himself. Picking a beach that had sand, rather than stones. Checking the meteorological websites to make sure the skies would be clear and what the sunrise times were. When to set their alarms, so he could pack Anna and baby Rosie into the car and get to the beach in good time.

It had been a lovely morning. A summer morning, so it hadn't been cold. Rosie had stayed fast asleep in her car seat for the majority of it, not even waking when Max had lifted her from the car and taken her down to the sand, where he'd placed her on a blanket, next to her mother.

Anna, despite the warmth of the day, had been quite thin and not able to regulate her temperature very well, so she'd been bundled up in blankets and had even worn a beanie to hide her bald head. And he'd sat and held his wife and sipped at coffee from a travel mug as the bluish sky had begun to change colour to molten golds and orange.

It had been a beautiful moment watching the sunrise. Awe-inspiring. He'd never really sat and watched one before, but it had taken his breath away. To watch something so wonderful. So commonplace, really, in that it happened every single day, but he had never woken early enough to watch one. Or if he had, he'd been in a city, on his way to work and juggling traffic, his mind elsewhere.

After that, Anna had become too weak to leave the

house, really. But she'd spoken of that sunrise often and had told him that, when she was finally gone, when she had breathed her last, if he ever wanted to find her, all he had to do was watch another sunrise and she would be there, in all of those glorious colours.

So, it felt strange now to be dressing up and getting ready. He hoped everything had gone okay at Bella's appointment that afternoon.

I mean, it had to, or she would have cancelled.

The babysitter was already here, downstairs watching Rosie, and Bella would be here any minute to bring Ewan across.

He felt as if he was stepping into a new world.

Dating again?

He'd once thought all of that behind him, but he had a good feeling about where he and Bella were going. He felt as though he was willing to risk his heart again for her, which was a huge step for him. He was ready and he couldn't think of anyone better, who made him feel the way that he did when he was with her. He missed her when she was gone. Looked forward to seeing her every morning, without fail. She brightened his day and he hoped that he, in turn, brightened hers.

This blip with her headaches...it had to be nothing, right? If the neurologist had found anything of concern today, he would have told her and Bella would have told him and then...well, he would have had to deal with it somehow. But she'd not cancelled, so that was good news and good news was great.

He heard a knock at the door and he heard the babysitter answer it and invite Bella and Ewan in. 'Max? They're here!' she called up the stairs.

'Okay, thanks. Down in one second.' He took that second to just stand in front of the mirror. Not to check his appearance, but to look himself square in the eye and give himself a little pep talk.

I can do this.

Bella is everything I could possibly want.

Enjoy tonight.

Make something good happen.

He smiled at himself then went trotting down the stairs. He could hear the kids in the kitchen and as he reached the hallway, he turned and saw Bella standing in the doorway.

She looked breathtaking. Beautiful. Her long dark hair was swept up into some complicated twist, revealing the long, smooth curve of her neck. She wore a body-hugging dress in a cobalt blue that stopped just above the knee and the fancy black heels she wore made her legs look shapely and simply stunning.

'Wow. You look amazing.'

She turned and dazzled him with her smile as she looked him up and down. 'So do you.'

'Are you ready to go?'

She nodded, holding onto a small black clutch bag that had a fringe.

'We won't be too late,' he assured the babysitter.

'It's fine. You two go and enjoy yourselves.'

'Thanks.'

He held out his arm for Bella and walked her out to his car. Jasper's wasn't that far, to be fair, and they could have walked it, but he wasn't sure how comfortable those heels were that Bella was wearing, so it seemed the right thing to do. 'Everything okay?'

'Everything's great.'

'How'd your appointment go?'

'He didn't find anything and he's not worried. I passed all the tests and we did a scan to be on the safe side, but he told me to enjoy myself tonight, so that's what I'm doing. Let's not talk about it.'

He felt greatly reassured. 'Perfect.' He wanted to give her a night to remember.

Jasper's was a stunning building. A real look of history about it, so that he felt it must have been here for a few hundred years. It seemed to have a lot of original features, but had been adorned with modern ones, such as hanging baskets filled with overflowing flowers, and window boxes. A wide pavement in front allowed for some outdoor tables and benches and a few people sat at those enjoying a nice beer or wine.

Stepping inside, he heard the soft piano music and marvelled at the low lighting provided by wall sconces. Again, there was a mix of old and new. Original features of wooden oak beams and whitewashed walls sat adjacent to round tables with perfectly white tablecloths and bud vases filled with local lavender. Historic photos of times past adorned the walls in matching black frames and he noticed, up in the ceiling, old farming tools. A scythe. Rakes. Even a pitchfork.

'Good evening. My name is Rupert. May I help you?' A man approached them, dressed neatly all in black.

'I have a reservation for a table for two? Name's Moore.'

Rupert didn't even have to check his list. He must have had it memorised or something. 'Of course. *Dr* Moore, isn't it? We have a beautiful table for you. Follow me.'

They followed Rupert through the tables towards the

rear of the restaurant, going up a couple of steps and being presented with a table by a window that overlooked a lake.

'Madam.' Rupert pulled Bella's chair out for her and waited for her to sit and when Max sat opposite her, the waiter presented them with drinks menus. 'It is an absolute pleasure to have now hosted all of the doctors from the local practice. Here's to a pleasant evening for you both. Tonight's drink special is a beautiful burgundy wine, Roja St Georges. I'll be back in a moment to take your order.'

When he'd gone, Max smiled at her. 'He seems nice. And isn't this place stunning? I'd heard good things, but never imagined it would look like this inside.'

'I think Lorna and Oliver came here. I remember her telling me one lunchtime about it and she had nothing but good things to say. She recommends the beef wellington.'

Max smiled. 'I'll keep that in mind.' He glanced out of the window at the smooth, still lake, then back to Bella. 'Beautiful view, inside and out.'

She blushed. 'I don't know what to order. It all sounds delicious.'

'Shall we go with the Roja St Georges?'

'I don't normally drink alcohol.'

'Okay, we can have soft drinks.'

'You know what? No. We should celebrate today. One glass won't hurt me.'

Rupert took their drinks order and brought them their burgundy, presenting a sample into Max's glass to taste first. Max took a sip and nodded. It was delightful. Smoky. Oak laced with hints of dark cherry. When the drinks were fully poured, Rupert presented them with food menus and disappeared again. He was the perfect host. Knowing when to stay and when to go. Knowing that people preferred to chat with each other, rather than with their server, unless he was invited into the conversation.

'I'm so glad you asked me out here tonight.'

'Me too.'

'I can't remember the last date I went on.'

He had an image of a sunrise. Of a sleeping Rosie, completely unaware of the glorious colours above her. Of how Anna had felt in his arms, all bones and angles. 'I think it's probably been a long time for the both of us.'

'True. Tell me about your best date ever.' She leaned forward, interested.

'Isn't it bad form to talk about a past connection with a current one?'

'Only if you go on about it non-stop. But I've asked and I'm interested.'

He nodded. Thinking. 'Okay. Well, I guess it was the first ever date I had with Anna.'

'What did you do?'

He laughed. 'We went tenpin bowling and I very quickly learned that she was extremely clumsy and much preferred to roll her ball into the gutter than strike a pin! It doesn't sound like much, but I don't remember laughing as hard as I did that night. She was cute and funny and she made me smile so hard, my face ached the next day and I just knew I had to see her again. What about you? What was your best date?'

'Erm…probably with Blake. We went to one of those escape-room things with a bunch of our mutual friends. I just remember that whilst everyone else was trying to solve puzzles, all I could think of was to steal glances at this man that kept trying to smile at me and I just knew, in that moment, that something special was happening. Something was being created. Forged between us. It was electric. Exciting. I've never forgotten it.' She smiled and sipped her wine, nodding appreciatively.

'When you know, you know,' he agreed.

'Absolutely.' She smiled back at him, eyes gleaming.

He was beginning to feel that he knew now. Looking at her, right at this moment in the candlelight, with the piano in the background and the delicious scent of lavender and food in the air. Something was being created now. Forged now. Just as she'd said.

And the evening had barely begun.

They chatted for a while about the menu and placed their orders and after about fifteen minutes or so, their starters arrived. Scallops for Max and a seared tuna for Bella.

'This is delicious,' she said and offered him a taste. They sampled each other's food, laughing and joking, and before they knew it, their mains arrived—a chicken saltimbocca for Bella, served on broad beans with a garlic and thyme fondant potato, with a chicken jus, whereas Max had ordered the dry-aged sirloin, served with a celeriac purée, roasted baby potatoes, salsa verde and samphire.

'How's Rosie doing now? I remember how shy and uncertain she was on her very first day. Is she enjoying school much better?'

'Absolutely. She loves it. In fact, I think she prefers being at school than at home!' He laughed. 'I think because Ewan and all her friends are there, whereas at home it's just me and, let's face it, I'm not as fun as those other guys.'

'It's great that she's gained so much confidence.'

'I'm a very proud dad. She got a handwriting certificate the other day. Did I tell you?'

'No. That's amazing! Maybe we should get handwriting certificates?' Bella laughed.

'Probably!'

'Or perhaps we should get star charts? That might be fun.'

'What would we get stars for?' Max asked.

'Hmm…' She seemed to really think about it. 'Injecting babies without making them cry? Getting through the day without crying ourselves?'

He nodded. 'I don't think I'd get many stars.'

'I do think there's a website, though, for people to rate their doctors. Have you ever looked at that? Checked out your reviews?'

'I don't think I've ever been anywhere long enough for people to remember my name.'

'Well, you have. I've looked.'

'Really? What did it say?'

'That you're amazing. Kind. Helpful. That you listen well and are thorough. And one person wrote that you were sexy.'

Okay. He wasn't sure how he felt about patients saying that about him, though he knew that some patients could form affections for their care givers. For people seemingly in authority who could take care of them. He winked. 'Thanks for writing that. What do yours say?'

Bella laughed. 'Well, no one's called me sexy, but one did say that I had nice warm hands.'

He reached for her hand then. Impulsively. Framed it with his own, as if judging them for himself. He made a big show of it. Made humming noises. Turned her hands this way, then that. 'Okay. I agree with that one hundred per cent.'

She laughed and her cheeks were pink with delight.

And he didn't want to let go of her hand. It felt so good in his own. Smaller than his. Her fingernails painted a soft, shell pink. Her middle finger adorned with a gold ring, with a small blue stone. A sapphire? Topaz? Tanzanite?

His gaze met hers. 'I'm very glad that we're doing this.'

'So am I,' she said softly.

'I'd better let go, so you can eat your food,' he joked and released her hand, shaking his head at how quickly he was falling for this woman. They were meant to be taking it slow. To be enjoying each delicious moment. But all his mind wanted to do was run away with all these crazy images of what could be in the future for them. He imagined waking up with her, going downstairs and their two kids in the kitchen eating breakfast together, a little yappy dog around their feet, as sunshine streamed in through the windows as they enjoyed being the perfect, happy, blended family.

He would scare her off with all of that. It scared him and yet he yearned for it. He'd thought that he was building a family and a future once before, but then fate had cruelly pulled the rug from under him. He'd made plans and life had laughed at him.

He needed to move much slower this time.

'Is everything to your satisfaction?' Rupert had arrived at their table.

'Everything's perfect.' Max smiled at Bella. Knowing that if anyone asked him about his most perfect date from now on, he'd talk about this one.

CHAPTER EIGHT

THEY HAD A lovely meal, sitting at their beautiful table in Jasper's, sharing the most delicious food. Bella had looked beautiful and all he'd wanted to do was sit opposite and gaze at her. But main courses led to desserts and after desserts there was only so long you could linger over coffees before you had to spoil the moment and get up and leave.

When they reached Field Lane, Max walked her to her door. 'I've had a wonderful time tonight. Thank you.'

She smiled up at him. 'Me too. I'm glad we had this planned so that I didn't have to sit in all evening worrying about...well, you know.'

'You'll get his call tomorrow and I bet everything's fine.'

She nodded. 'I'm sure it will be.' She glanced at her cottage, turned back to look at him, smiling. 'You know... with Ewan at yours, we don't have to say goodnight just yet. I don't know about you, but I'm not ready for this evening to end.'

He didn't want it to end either. 'Nor me.'

'Want to come in for a bit?'

'I'd like that very much,' he said, feeling his blood begin to race.

'Good.' She unlocked the door, stepping back to invite

him in, closing it softly behind him and placing her bag on the hall table. Then she looked at him, her eyes full of longing and desire, and he couldn't resist.

Instantly, they were kissing, searching, grasping at each other's clothes, gasping, moaning as he pushed her back against the wall and held her hands above her head as his lips found her throat and his hard body pressed against her soft, pliant one.

He wanted to consume her and be consumed by her. Her taste, her scent, was driving him wild and he found the clasps of her dress and pulled them free, groaning with delight as his hands found her skin, her waist, her hips, her breasts, wrapped in slips of silk and lace.

Scooping her up into his arms, he began to carry her up the stairs, towards the bedrooms. She laughed and laid her head against his chest as he located her bedroom, where he laid her down on the bedspread and stood there for a moment, gazing at her, his desire for her almost bursting from his trousers as he undid the button, the zip, to release the pressure. She got to her knees and helped him unbutton his shirt and then his clothes were being tossed to the floor and he pushed her back against the pillows and lost himself in her.

There was no more taking it slow. Not now. How could he? He was due back at the house. He needed to let the babysitter go, so, though he wanted more than anything to savour every moment and take his time and explore her, his need for her, her desire for him, drove him onwards. They could savour each other another time. This time was for something else. Something passionate and powerful and animalistic.

He bit, he licked, he kissed, he stroked. His hands found

with a smile, thinking of how her dinner date with Max had ended.

He was the first guy she'd been with since Blake and she'd never believed that she would be falling hard for the next guy she slept with. Realistically, it shouldn't have been a surprise to her. She'd never been a woman who'd indulged in casual flings, or one-night stands.

Max? Was special and she woke this morning feeling hopeful for the future. Happy. Contented. And looking forward to more nights like that!

Ewan had had a great sleepover at Rosie's and when Bella and Max met again in the morning to take the kids into school, they kept giving each other secret glances. Smiling. Holding each other's hands as they walked, when the kids weren't looking, and then breaking apart whenever one of the kids looked back to say something. It felt special, their little secret. It felt powerful and positive and she'd not walked with such a bounce in her step for years. And each time their hands crept back together, their fingers entwining, it felt right and wonderful and Bella felt as though she was glowing.

Eva Watts was back in her clinic for a follow-up. The lady with low iron and a domestic abuse case. When she sat down in Bella's clinic, Bella was glad that she couldn't see any new, obvious bruising, but, as Eva had said, this week Ben was away at a training camp.

'So, you received your blood results?'

Eva nodded. 'I'm glad I wasn't pregnant.'

'But your iron was low, so have you been taking the tablets I prescribed?'

'Yes.'

'You should start feeling a lot better very quickly, if

you continue to use those. How are you getting on with the contraceptive?'

'Good.'

'No side effects?'

'No.'

'And did you tell Ben you were going to start taking them?'

'I told him that they were women's vitamins, to help with my heavy periods.'

Bella nodded. 'I understand. How's everything going with the relationship?'

'Well, he's away, like I said, but after talking to you, I spoke to Lorna on the phone, who's also been amazing, by the way. It's made me think about my relationship and I, er, changed the locks on the house. He won't be able to get in, when he comes back. My name's on the deeds, so he can't say it's his place. I've packed up his stuff and put it in the garden shed out back, so he can collect it, and my brother's moved in to stay with me, so I'm not alone when he gets back.'

'Wow. Okay. I was not expecting that, but I have to say I'm happy to hear that you've felt strong enough to take action and let Ben know that how he treats you is not reasonable.'

'Well, he doesn't know yet. I haven't told him. I'm going to ring him, later. I just wanted all the door locks done and secured first.'

'How do you think he'll react?'

'Badly. But he won't do anything with my brother there. Cam's a civilian that works in the police emergency room, taking calls, so he's got connections within the force, you know? He's a big guy, same as Ben, but Ben's a coward that can only take on women, so...'

'How long can your brother stay for?'

'Long enough. I'm going to tell Ben tonight. I'm scared about it, but I know it's the best thing for me. I don't deserve to be treated as anything less than amazing.'

'Agreed. I'm so proud of you, Eva.'

'I knew what was happening. I saw all the red flags, but I just couldn't do anything about it. I felt like I needed him. He made me feel that no one else would want me, because I was useless, and I lost touch with family, who'd all been wondering what the hell was going on.'

'And you told them.'

'Yes. I was terrified, but everyone was there for me. They all wanted to help and I realised just how much I was loved and how their love came without conditions, because that's what it should be like, right? A person deserves to be loved one hundred per cent. Not only when they do or behave like someone else expects.'

'That's right.'

She spent a little while longer with Eva and then waved goodbye to bring in her next patient. She was so happy for Eva and she was right. A person deserved to be loved unconditionally. They deserved happiness. As she herself had found with Max.

Her internal phone rang. A call from Reception. 'Hello?'

'Dr Nightingale? It's Saskia on Reception. I've got the secretary of a Professor Helberg on the line, who says she needs to speak to you urgently.'

Bella instantly felt sick. Her heart began thudding in her chest and her mouth went dry. 'Put them through.'

There was a click and a pause and then a woman's voice. 'Dr Nightingale?'

'Yes.'

'Can you just confirm your date of birth and first line of your address for me?'

She did so.

'Thank you. I'm Rebecca and I'm calling on behalf of Professor Helberg. He wonders if you could possibly call in today at all.'

'Call in? Does he have my scan results?'

'I don't know. All I've been asked is that I contact you and ask you to come in. He'd like to see you in person.'

In person.

Doctors preferred to deliver bad news in person. If her scan had been clear, she'd have received a text or a call, as he'd promised. Having to go back in meant it was something else.

Oh, my God, what is wrong with me? Why is everything going wrong now? Just as everything was starting to be perfect?

'Erm… I'm at work. I'm a GP. I've a clinic of my own.' She brought up her patient list. It was full, as expected. 'Can't he call me?'

'He'd like you to come in,' Rebecca insisted.

Clearly she didn't have any more information than that and this was important. 'Let me talk to my practice manager and my colleagues.' Lorna had an admin afternoon. Maybe she could take her patients? 'See if anyone can take my list.'

'Thanks. We'll see you later on, then.'

Bella was left holding onto the phone, staring into space. There was something wrong with her. Something the professor wanted to talk to her about in person. He'd found something in the scans. Something that was causing her headaches, but what was it?

Numbly, she got up and headed for Priti's office. Knocked.

'Come in!'

She must have looked white as a sheet, because when Priti looked up, she did a double take and then was up on her feet, closing the door behind a stunned Bella and helping her into her seat. 'Tell me.'

She explained as best she could. Saw realisation in Priti's eyes. Priti wasn't a doctor, but she understood. Knew the subtext.

'Don't worry about your clinic. I'll divide your patients up between Oliver, Lorna and Max. We'll carry the load. You go and find out what's happening.'

'Okay. Thanks. Will you do me one other favour?'

'Of course.'

'Don't tell Max where I'm going. He'll panic. Just say I've got a bad headache and I've gone home early, or something.'

'I don't like lying to my doctors, Bella.'

'Just if he asks. Please.'

'And are you sleeping?' Max asked his patient, Mrs Clara Dewberry.

'No. I'm not! Even though I feel shattered and everything aches. Is it supposed to feel this way?'

Clara had been into the surgery two days ago to see the nurse, as she'd received a text from the surgery asking her to arrange a shingles vaccination. Even though Clara was only fifty-one, she had an auto-immune condition that required her to be vaccinated at fifty, rather than waiting until she was seventy.

'Side effects from the vaccine can feel very flu-like. But rest assured, you don't have the flu.'

'What about the fever and the shivering?'

'Unfortunately, they are expected side effects of the vaccination and they can last up to five days afterwards. The shot really wakes up your immune system, so that it can respond to this infection.'

'So you're saying I just need to push through it and then I won't have to suffer with shingles?'

'Yes, you have to push through it, but no, it doesn't mean you won't get shingles. It works similar to the Covid vaccines, in that it can't stop you from having the condition, but it should stop the complications that come with it. With shingles, there's a real risk—especially if you get shingles on the face, head or neck—of real complications. In some people it has been known to cause blindness or deafness. Others that get it elsewhere can suffer with a peripheral neuropathy that could last years, or even a lifetime. The vaccination is there to stop that from happening.'

Clara sighed. 'So just keep pushing through?'

'Take painkillers. Paracetamol every four hours and you could take ibuprofen in between to keep you topped up and stave off the fever and body aches. How's your arm feel where the injection site is?'

'Bloody painful! I can't lie on it.'

'I'm sorry to hear you're having a difficult time, but I'm afraid you're just going to have to soldier through it. Have you someone at home who can support you?'

'My husband. He works from home, so he's always there.'

'Well, that's good.'

He spent some more time reassuring Clara and eventually she left, feeling better that her symptoms were only temporary and led to a greater good. As she exited the room, Priti popped her head in. 'Max, are you able to take on a couple of extra patients? I need you to take two more.'

He checked his list. One, according to the records, was notorious for never showing up at all, so he probably had time, and the others all seemed to be coming in with considerably minor things. He just didn't want to run late picking up Rosie from school. 'Er…sure, should be fine.'

'Great. I'll give you Maxine Riker and George Potter.'

Max nodded, then frowned. 'Aren't they Bella's patients?'

'She…er…had to leave early.'

He looked up, frowning. 'Why?'

'I'm not at liberty to say.'

'Priti—'

'As my employee, I have to protect her confidentiality, Max. You know the rules,' she said quietly.

'But…' He knew it was useless and Priti was right. Though he didn't like the look on her face. Something was going on. Had Bella heard from the professor? His stomach lurched at the thought. Surely if it had been good news, Bella simply would have just come in to tell him? 'Ask Maxine and George to come in as early as they can and I'll slot them in between patients.'

'Thank you.'

When she was gone, he instinctively picked up his mobile phone and dialled Bella, hoping to find out more information. If she'd heard from the professor and gone home because the news was upsetting, then…

Had she gone back to see the professor at his clinic? Why? Further tests?

There's no need to panic just yet. Perhaps her scans were inconclusive. Sometimes they might not be all that clear if the patient moved in the scanner.

She'd been nervous. She might have fidgeted.

But what if it wasn't nerves and a blurred set of images? What if they'd found something?

What if there was something seriously wrong with her?

Traffic had been heavy getting to the professor's clinic and when she finally arrived and got inside, she found the waiting room busy. She sat down, full of nerves, wondering what the hell was going on? What had been found? What was she dealing with?

If there's something seriously wrong...

Her first concern was for Ewan. If she was sick, if she needed to go into hospital for some sort of treatment, surgery perhaps, then who would look after her precious little boy? She supposed she could call one of her brothers, but they had their own lives and Ewan didn't actually know them all that well. They'd never been a close family.

Which left Max.

Ewan knew Max and if he had to stay round at their house, he'd have his best friend, Rosie, to play with too. But that was an incredible assumption she was making, because would Max be able to do that? She'd never asked him, or talked to him about this possibility, because she'd just assumed it would be headaches. Migraines, at the most. Nothing serious.

And Max...how would he react?

If she went into the professor's room and discovered it

was something bad, something terrifying, life-threatening, then would Max want nothing to do with her? Would he run a mile in the other direction? This was his greatest fear, right? To be involved with someone who was sick again? The thought horrified her. She couldn't lose him. They'd taken their relationship to the next level. Yesterday had been...well, amazing. Yesterday, she'd felt so good. So happy. So hopeful. As if finally the world was being nice to her and that she just might get her happy ever after, but now?

Why am I being kept waiting?

She knew it couldn't be helped. All these other people here had official appointments. They were meant to be here. She'd been told she would be fitted in and, being a doctor herself, she knew that meant making a patient wait, sometimes. She didn't like it, but that was how it was. She'd not brought her book to read, so she had nothing to concentrate on...

Then she noticed the coffee table. Filled with magazines. She went to grab one, picking one randomly, knowing that she wouldn't be able to focus on anything inside it at all. Not one jot.

It appeared to be some sort of women's magazine with lots of lurid, gossipy headlines. Not her usual type of thing, but she began to flick through and her eyes were caught by the very first story: *My fiancé dumped me after my stroke!*

Drawn in, horrified, she began to read. This young woman, relatively fit and healthy, had taken ill at her local gym, falling to the ground with a splitting headache and losing consciousness. She'd woken in hospital, days later, to discover her left side didn't work very well after a cerebral stroke had left her with deficits. She'd had brain surgery to remove a large clot and been told that she'd probably not gain full function again, but that she'd be offered a full physiotherapy regime. The fiancé, a six-foot stud, with ripped abs, who earned a living as a male underwear model, had dumped her after she'd woken still slurring her words.

Bella closed the magazine and let out a tortured sigh. Why had she chosen to read that story? Why? What good had it done? All it had done was reinforce the idea that Max would leave her as soon as he found out about this. It wasn't fair. She wanted to cry. These were just meant to be migraines and if he left her...

She wiped her eyes and checked her watch. She checked her phone.

A missed call from Max.

Her heart sank. She couldn't call him back. Not yet. Not until she knew what was going on. Maybe this wouldn't be as bad as she feared. Maybe Professor Helberg just wanted to deliver the good news in person, rather than over the phone. There was a chance of that, right?

Wasn't there?

'Bella?'

She heard the dulcet tones of the professor himself and looked up. Throwing the magazine into her seat behind her, she scurried from the waiting room and followed him into his consulting room.

'Do take a seat.'

'What is it? What have you found?' She didn't need him beating around the bush. She needed to know. Right away.

Professor Helberg nodded and turned his computer screen so he could show her directly.

* * *

'Everything okay, Max?' Oliver had found him out in the practice's garden, after they'd all taken on an extra couple of patients to cover Bella's surgery.

'Not great, no.'

Oliver came level with him and passed him a mug of tea.

'Thanks.'

'A problem shared? You know…if you want to.'

He wasn't sure of what to say. What to share. He didn't even know if Bella had told either Lorna or Oliver about her headaches.

'I'm worried about Bella.'

Oliver nodded sagely. 'I guessed so. Is this about her neurology appointment?'

Max turned to look at him. He did know?

'She mentioned she'd booked that afternoon off for it. Has she had to go for a follow-up?'

'I don't know. She won't answer her phone. She could just be at home, but I don't know, because she won't answer.'

'It must be difficult for you, not knowing.'

Max groaned. 'I just… I just don't know how I've managed to find myself here all over again, Ols. I went through torment with Anna. I'm not sure I have the strength to go through something like that again.'

Oliver was quiet for a moment. 'You know I went through something similar with my wife? Jo?'

'I heard something about it, yeah.'

'She fought breast cancer, same as your wife, Anna. We caught it early. Stage Two. We thought it would be an easy fight, you know. It hadn't spread, she'd go on chemo, maybe radiation, have a little surgery and it would all be over. Only it wasn't like that. Her body didn't cope well with the chemotherapy and it didn't seem to do anything to the tumour and we had to keep changing regimens, but eventually she was cancer free and we felt strong, you know? We celebrated and I told myself it was all over and thank God, because I couldn't go through that again. You think you won't have the strength. But you find it. You dig deep and you find it, because you love that person.'

'Are you saying I love Bella?'

'Don't you?'

He laughed. 'We were meant to be taking it slow, but…' Max sucked in a breath and thought about it. He had to admit his feelings for Bella ran very deep. Incredibly so. Was it love? Already? He couldn't resist her. He thought of her all the time. She made him happy just being in the same room. Last night had proved to him just how much he felt for her.

'You know, you watch someone you love be ravaged by a health condition or disease and you just know you'll do anything to help them feel better. It's all you can do. Be by their side and love them. It's all they need from you. A simple thing, really. You get the easiest job. They're the ones truly fighting.'

'I don't know if I can. It nearly destroyed me last time.'

'She just needs you by her side, Max. Whatever this turns out to be. She just needs your love and support. If you can't give her that, then tell her straight away, because she'll be fighting enough, without having to fight for you, too.'

'Can you do that to someone? Someone who's scared?'

'Jo offered me an out once. When it came back in her

lung. Said I didn't have to stay with her, if I didn't want to go through that again. If I didn't have the strength.'

Max stared at him. 'And did you consider it? Leaving?'

Oliver looked down at the ground. 'Honestly? I thought about it. For a *microsecond*. I knew I wasn't going to, but still, a voice pulled at me, told me that if I did, I could walk away and be free of it all. All the stress. All the heartache. All the grief. That I could have a different life and I'd be a fool to not take that opportunity. I'm human. As a species we generally prefer the easier life.'

'But you stayed?'

Oliver smiled. 'I stayed.'

Max sighed.

'She has a young son and she's going to be frightened. Decide what you can give and don't mess her about.' Oliver clamped his hand on Max's shoulder in a show of solidarity and then left him to his pondering.

Birds were singing brightly in the trees. As if they had no cares in the world at all. Perhaps they didn't.

Perhaps everything would be easier if he could just fly away and never look back.

CHAPTER NINE

Bella made it back in time to pick up Ewan from after-school club. After her consult with the professor, being stunned into shock with all the details, she had noticed the time and rushed back through heavy traffic to make it to Clearbrook Infant School.

She left her car outside her house and hurried to collect her son, her mind reeling with information, and she just couldn't think straight. She didn't remember the car journey at all. She'd driven on autopilot and it was lucky she'd made it back in one piece.

As she opened the door, she saw Max helping Rosie on with her coat.

Max.

He'd want to know where she'd been. He'd been calling her. Had left four messages on her voicemail, calmly and kindly asking her to please ring him and just let him know that she was all right.

Well, she wasn't all right and the news that she had, the diagnosis that she had, was not something she wanted to tell him over the phone. It would have to be done in person. Face to face. Knowing it could end everything that they had together.

He stood and turned. Saw her. 'Bella!' He glanced at Rosie, then at Ewan, and silently mouthed, *Are you okay?*

'Get your things, baby,' she said to Ewan.

As her son ran to get his bookbag and PE kit, Max came up to her. 'Where have you been?'

'I...er...had to go and see Professor Helberg.'

'And?'

Ewan came running up to show her a collage he'd made. A castle, made of pasta pieces and cloth, paint and glue. 'Wow! That's amazing!' She turned to Max. 'Not here. I can't talk about it here.'

He flinched and she felt her heart sink. If there was one thing that Max hadn't wanted to sign up for, it was another unwell partner. This was a man that did not want to have to sit beside another partner's bedside.

She was most likely going to lose him. Her one shot of happiness, of love, that she'd had in recent days, already threatening to fade away and disappear.

They walked the kids home, Ewan and Rosie babbling away together as usual, without a care in the world. Bella gazed at her son, marvelling at his perfect little happy face, free of frown lines, or dark circles or any kind of life worry. Because that was how childhood was meant to be. Carefree. Happy. How was he going to deal with a sick mother? Or worse than that? Her darling little boy. How could she prepare him for any of that?

She felt tears prick at her eyes and she quickly wiped them away.

'We need to talk, Bella,' he said quietly.

'I know! But not now, not in front of the kids.'

'Then when?'

'When they're in bed.'

'I can't leave Rosie alone in the house to come over to talk to you. Let me come back with you. The kids can go play in the back garden and we can have some privacy to talk.'

She looked at him. Felt her heart aching. He deserved answers, of course he did. 'All right.' But she didn't want to. Didn't want to impart the news that would destroy everything.

'Good. Rosie? We're going to go in with Ewan and his mummy for a bit. We need to talk about work.'

'Yay!' The two kids skipped ahead as they turned into Field Lane and before Bella knew it, they were back home.

It had been only a few hours since she'd left here this morning, but it felt as if so much had happened in the last few hours. Her whole life had changed. Done an abrupt one-eighty. She'd thought this was simply migraines. Migraines!

How wrong I was.

She unlocked the back door and the kids hurried into the garden, Ewan picking up a football and promising to show Rosie how to score a goal between two flowerpots.

'Bella.' Max went to her and crushed her into his arms. Just holding her. Squeezing her.

She soaked up every moment of that hug, just in case it was their last. Tears escaping from her eyes.

And then he let her go. Sat her down at the round pine table in the kitchen and asked her what had happened.

'Professor Helberg's clinic called asking me to go in and see him face to face.'

'Okay. And what did he say?'

'He had my scan results back and they found something. The reason for my headaches.' She didn't want to meet his eye. Didn't want to see the moment he would back away from her.

Max sucked in a breath and nodded. Girding himself for the truth. 'What was it?'

She thought back to that moment in the clinic. Of the professor turning his screen towards her so that she could see the scan image for herself. How her stomach had plummeted to the floor and she'd wanted to throw up right there in his office. 'It showed that I have a three-centimetre pituitary tumour.' A tumour that was growing on her pituitary gland, located in a hollow, just behind her eyes, which explained the headaches.

'Pituitary? So that means it's benign, right?'

'Most likely.' She nodded. 'Professor Helberg thinks it's the non-secreting type. He doesn't think that it's producing hormones.'

'Okay, and what's the treatment plan?'

'He's taken extra bloods and I'm booked in for a more detailed MRI scan, but, basically, he wants to operate and try to debulk it.'

'Debulk? So he doesn't think he'll be able to take the whole thing?'

She shook her head. 'It will mean future surgeries throughout my life, but he reassured me it's slow growing, so they wouldn't be all that often, but...' Her gaze went to her son in the garden, laughing and happy with Rosie. 'How do I tell Ewan his mummy's got a brain tumour?' She began to cry, but her tears weren't just for Ewan. They were for herself. For Max. For what she was about to lose. How endangered her future happiness was.

Max stared at her from the opposite side of the table and she'd never felt so far apart from him.

'Helberg said he'd go in trans-nasally. It's called an endoscopic transsphenoidal resection. Forceps go in here…' she pointed at her nose '…through the sphenoid sinus and to the tumour. I've got to go in tomorrow to have my eyes tested, too, check there's no pressure on my optic nerves.'

Max sighed. 'Okay. Well, at least we know that pituitary tumours don't usually spread. They're benign and don't grow fast, so that's good, right?'

'But he's going to have to keep going in, if he doesn't get it all. That means lifetime treatment. Lifetime monitoring and there could be complications with the surgery.' She looked at him, considering him. 'Look, I know you didn't sign up for this. Neither did I, quite frankly, but it is what it is and I need to deal with it and look after my son. I can't be looking after you too, so if you're not strong enough for this, then I'm giving you an out and I'm begging you to take it. It's not fair on you, to put you through something like this again.'

He stared at her. 'Do you want me to go?'

'It's not about what I want, but I need to concentrate on me and Ewan right now. I can't be distracted by you, if you're going to be hovering in doorways, not sure whether you're staying with me or not.'

'You think I'd leave you like this?'

She met his gaze then. 'Yes. Because I know you don't want this.'

He looked hurt, shocked. Then he looked down and away. Guilty.

It was enough. It told her all she needed to know. If she was going to have to get through this alone, then she needed a clean break from him. Not have it be long drawn out and painful. 'Maybe you and Rosie should go now. I need to spend time with Ewan.'

'But, Bella—'

'No, Max!' She got to her feet and physically pushed him away, her hands on his chest, her voice breaking as she erupted into tears. 'Don't make this any more painful than it has to be! You didn't sign up for this! You didn't sign up to look after me and I could be sick for the rest of my life! And you know what other detail came up from this? I may not be able to have another baby naturally, because the pituitary controls ovulation and without a pituitary then I'm screwed!'

She stood in front of him now, feeling rage and upset and grief that she now found herself in this position. 'And I don't have the strength to look after you right now! I can't watch you agonise over whether to step away! So just go! Go and leave me be!' And she stalked away and into the garden, wiping her eyes and forcing a smile and calling out to Rosie that her daddy was waiting for her in the house and was ready to go.

She didn't want to see him walk away.

Didn't want to have to close the door behind him as he walked out of her life.

There was too much going on already and she needed to be selfish right now.

Selfish for her and Ewan.

He hated how they'd left things. Bella had done her best to push him away, getting this look in her eyes that had practically told him she'd accepted it alread,y and she'd got up from that table and gone into the garden with Ewan, brooking no further conversation on the topic.

So, he'd called for Rosie and headed home. Feeling hurt. Called out. Betrayed. Yes, he'd said what he'd said before, but did she really think so badly of him that she honestly thought he could walk away from her now? He was hurt that she felt that about him. Maybe before, it might have been true, but that was before they'd got serious. Before she'd become an all-consuming force in his life.

He was already reeling from the diagnosis. A brain tumour. A pituitary tumour. Once he'd fed Rosie and she was sitting watching some kids' channel on television, he'd got out his tablet and begun doing some research.

Pituitary tumours meant that Bella could no longer drive, now that she'd been diagnosed. He read that surgery was the most common treatment for them. That recovery was quick, because the surgeon did not have to cut into the skull, unless a craniotomy was needed. That even though it was benign, she would still receive radiation treatment afterwards, especially if they couldn't remove the whole thing. That with the removal of her pituitary gland, she would have to take hormones for the rest of her life. That, yes, it could affect her fertility.

He did want more kids, of course he did, and he'd imagined that happening with her.

He closed the tablet and pushed it away and stared up at the ceiling.

Oliver had been right. When Bella had offered him that out, a part of him had considered it. The part of him that had been destroyed by Anna's passing. By watching her suffer. By sitting by her hospital bedside, praying each time she'd fall asleep that this wouldn't be the time where she didn't wake up. Where he'd watched expectantly for every breath that she took, praying to keep her with him for longer. Praying to keep her here for Rosie.

It had been selfish. Totally selfish and he'd recognised that selfishness towards the end and he'd felt guilty for it, the way he felt guilty now, because, sure, life would be easier if he didn't have to deal with all of this, right?

But I am dealing with it. I am a part of it.

Had she pushed him away because she felt in her heart that he wasn't strong enough? Had he already shown to her that he wasn't strong enough for this?

Max hated being on this side of the street. He hated the fact that there was a road that separated them, because he wanted to be with her, holding her, telling her it would be all right. And yes, if he was being honest, he did already feel exhausted at the prospect of having to go through something traumatic all over again, but that didn't matter. Not truly. He could push it to one side, because he knew he could be there for her. He loved her.

He just had to prove it to her.

She heard Max knocking on her door in the morning, ready for the walk to school with him and Rosie, but she refused to answer. Yesterday had been a huge day for her and she just wanted some time for herself and Ewan. She wanted to take the day for themselves, so that she could talk to him about what was going to happen. She'd already called Priti, the night before, to say she wouldn't be in and, just a minute ago, she'd left a message on the school's answerphone, to say that Ewan would not be attending that day.

She'd texted Max, too. Told him not to call round, but he was knocking anyway, and then she heard her letter box flap open. 'Bella? You there? I just want to make sure you're okay.'

Maybe he did, maybe he didn't, but she just didn't have the energy for him. She'd lain awake all night, curled around Ewan in his bed, silently crying. She didn't have the headspace to watch him walk away, because she knew, deep down, that this was not what he wanted or needed. Because this wasn't just about him and her, was it? There were Ewan and Rosie, too.

And she'd become part of Rosie's life and Rosie had come to love her and now he was going to have to explain that she was sick. Would be going into hospital. Having surgery. That she could die. Of course he wouldn't want to put his daughter through that. She'd already lost her own mother, why would Max want to let her lose anyone else?

No. It was better this way. Quicker. Easier. Less painful.

Rip off the Band-Aid.

A clean cut was better than one that was slow, blunt and horrific.

She loved them both, Max and Rosie, and in her own way she was trying to protect them, too, but most of all she was trying to protect herself. She was going to undergo a major surgical procedure that could change her life for ever and she didn't want to see them get hurt. It was too heavy a load for her to carry. She, Ewan, Max and Rosie had become a little blended unit. Ewan loved having Max in his life—that paternal figure she'd always wanted for him. Max was a good role model for her son and if she and Max were over now, would he lose that?

She heard nothing more from the letter box and assumed he had headed off to school. Ewan was still upstairs, brushing his teeth, and she planned to take him out today. Maybe to a play park. Treat him. Buy him something new and then, when they got home, she would try to tell him that Mummy was sick and would need to go into hospital soon.

Bella knew she needed to call her family and tell them the news. She'd need someone to look after Ewan whilst she was having surgery and then afterwards, hopefully, recovering. Even though they weren't all that close, she figured her brothers would help her. Maybe one of them would move in for a bit, because she'd hate to send Ewan away to somewhere strange. His life was about to be turned upside down—she didn't want him to have to go through the stress of being somewhere new.

Besides, she also wanted his routine to remain. Going to school each day, being with his friends and not always worrying about his mum. But how did you tell a four-year-old about something like this? Would he even understand what a brain tumour was? Should she leave out that scary word and just say Mummy needed to go into hospital for a bit and she'd be back soon?

Her phone beeped to announce the arrival of a text message.

It was from Max.

Hope you're okay. I'd like to talk to you. Please call me. Max x

Bella gazed at that little x on the end of his message. She knew this wasn't easy for him, either. She was about to put so many people through so much stress and she hated every moment of it. 'Ewan? Come on, honey, we need to go!'

Professor Helberg didn't want to wait. He'd got her scheduled for an eye test and a full MRI tomorrow back at his clinic and, once that was done, he'd said he wanted to get her in as quickly as possible to remove as much of the tumour as he could. Debulk it, if he couldn't remove the whole thing. Remove her pituitary gland and afterwards place her on hormones for life to replace those that the gland naturally made: thyroid-stimulating hormone, which did what it said on the tin, stimulated the thyroid to make more hormones; follicle-stimulating hormone, which affected the ovaries; luteinising hormone, which helped with ovulation; adrenocorticotrophic hormone, which told the adrenal glands to make its hormones. Plus there was antidiuretic hormone, which helped the body to regulate the balance of sodium and water in the body.

It was a busy gland and did a lot of things. Professor Helberg had described it as the body's thermostat.

Ewan's footsteps came thumping down the stairs. 'Where are we going?'

'To the park.'

'Why aren't we going to school?'

'Because Mummy asked them if I could take you out for the day and they said yes, as it was a special day.'

'But I was going to have a special day at school. They're bringing in animals. All kinds, Miss Celic said—donkeys, goats, sheep and a llama!'

Bella's heart sank. She remembered getting that letter now. She'd had to sign something giving Ewan permission to pet the animals.

Was she being selfish? Taking him away from something he'd been looking forward to? 'Would you prefer to go to school, then?'

Ewan nodded emphatically.

He looked so happy, bless him, she just couldn't take him away from that. And keeping his routine was very important right now. Letting out a sigh, she smiled at him and said, 'Okay. Go put your uniform on, then. I'll take you in and give the school a call. I'm sure they'll be fine about me changing my mind.'

'Yay!' Ewan went hurtling back up the stairs.

Priti couldn't tell him anything, which frustrated him. He got why. She was protecting Bella's privacy, and he liked that Priti had their backs, but this was Bella and he needed to talk about what was happening.

Both Lorna and Oliver came to his room to check that he was okay, knowing what he'd gone through in the past and asking how Bella was. It made him feel ridiculous to say he didn't know, because she wouldn't let him in.

'She offered me an out, just like we talked about the other day, and then told me to take it. Said I wasn't strong enough.'

Oliver clapped him on the shoulder. Said he'd be there for him with anything he needed. Lorna said she'd call Bella, offer her love and support.

He felt jealous of the two older doctors. They seemed like they had no problems at all. They were finding happiness a second time around. Max had thought that he'd found the same thing. But Bella had pushed him away.

Was she right to?

Could she see him better than he could see himself?

Had she pushed him away because she sensed a weakness in him? An approach in which he'd always been on the back foot?

He thought he'd given her everything, made her feel safe and secure, but maybe he hadn't done that at all. It was all about perception and hers was different from his.

Yes, this scared him. He could admit that.

Bella needed surgery for a tumour. Benign, but still. If the professor couldn't get the whole thing out, then Bella would be under his care for the rest of her life, constantly returning for multiple debulking surgeries and each surgery carried a risk. That meant him and Rosie sitting by her bedside, hoping for good news each and every time.

Could he imagine doing that?

Again?

The alternative was what? A life alone. Just him and Rosie, knowing that he wasn't strong enough for Bella? How awful he would feel, if he allowed her to push him away like this?

So this is when you show her that you're not weak. That you want to fight for her.

Because he knew his life could only be better by having her in it. Her and Ewan! And if that meant they had to go to hospital on occasion for check-ups and surgery, then he would do it, because he loved her! And he wanted— needed—her in his life.

Max glanced at the clock.

He could not go to find her. He had a full list. Again, they were seeing patients that had already pre-booked for Bella's list, sharing the names out amongst themselves. They were all pulling double duty so that patient care did not get disrupted.

He would have to wait for this evening and he would pack a lunch and sit on her doorstep with Rosie, if he had to, until she let him in.

Because he would not let her go.

Not ever.

They were meant to be. He was sure of it. Both of them having been given a second chance of happiness after going through so much trauma.

He was not going to let a three-centimetre tumour stand in his way!

Bella had felt so alone all day. Her mobile hadn't stopped ringing—Max, Lorna, Oliver, Priti, her brothers. Her dad. She'd not answered any, feeling the need to cocoon herself and shut herself away from people. She didn't know why she felt that way. Only that she somehow felt that if she withdrew, it would somehow hurt them less if something horrible happened.

So, when the time came for school to end, rather than need Ewan to go to his after-school club, she picked him up at the school gate at the normal time of three-thirty. Plus, she reasoned, it meant that she wouldn't see Max.

She appreciated that he had called more than most, but if it was only to confirm what she already felt was true— that it would be better for him to walk away and just be a friend—then why did she need to hear it? She was doing him a favour. Rosie, too. That precious little girl didn't need to be worrying about her either.

Ewan was full of the animal day exploits and wouldn't stop talking all the way home. She let him chatter about how soft the fur was on a llama, but how greasy it was on a sheep, and how he'd had to wash his hands after touching them all. He'd beamed with joy telling about how he'd fed lambs with a bottle of milk, how their greedy little mouths had chugged away at the teats and almost pulled the bottle from his hands. How he'd laughed. How he'd wrinkled his nose at the initial smell of farm animals.

It was a joy to listen to him. A joy to see his happiness, and she didn't want to ruin it, so she let him carry on. Let him be a little boy for just a little while longer.

At home, she started to cook his dinner and whilst the vegetables were in the steamer and the potatoes were boiling, she sat him down at the kitchen table and told him that in a couple of days, she would be going into hospital.

'Why? Are you sick?'

'Just a little bit. But I don't want you to worry, because I've got an amazing doctor who is going to look after me.'

'And you'll come home?'

'I'll come home,' she said, hoping it was true. Hoping her procedure went smoothly and without complications. All surgery came with a risk, no matter how run-of-the-mill it was. But the idea that her son might be left alone, if the worst happened…it almost broke her heart.

A knock at her door made her jump. Then her letter box rattled and she heard Rosie's voice. 'Hello?'

She couldn't ignore that little girl, could she? Even though she knew that Rosie would not be standing on her doorstep alone.

Time to face reality.

Bella sucked in a deep breath and walked down the short hallway to the front door. She placed her hand on the handle, let out the breath and let it swing wide.

Rosie beamed and ran right past, finding Ewan immediately as Bella had known she would, leaving Bella to look at Max. He held a bunch of wildflowers in his hand and proffered them to her. 'Rosie picked you these.'

'Oh. They're beautiful. I must thank her.'

'Can I come in?'

She nodded and stepped back. Knowing this conversation needed to happen. Knowing that, at some point, she'd like to ask him for a favour, even if he was going to try and keep his distance from her. She wanted to ask him to still let Rosie play with Ewan. To check in on him, to keep things normal for him.

Max walked into her kitchen and turned to wait for her.

She'd never felt so nervous in all of her life. Even more so than when she'd waited in Professor Helberg's waiting room. 'How have things been at work?'

'Fine. Everyone sends their love.'

She smiled. Grateful. 'I got a lot of texts today. You must thank them for me.'

'I will. I'll do anything for you. Except one thing.'

Here it is. The thanks, but no, thanks.

'I will not walk away. I will not be accepting your get-out clause. I am here. For you. And Ewan. But understand this. I am not here for you and Ewan as a friend, or as a neighbour, or as a colleague. I am here for you as your partner. Your lover. Your boyfriend, or whatever else you wish to call us. I am in this. One hundred per cent. I can't be anything else, so don't try to tell me that I am. I love you, Bella Nightingale, and I want to be there with you, every step of the way, no matter what.'

She stared at him. Hardly daring to breathe. Hardly daring to interrupt this moment of absolute shock and wonder and joy that she had not been expecting. 'You…mean it?'

'Of course! I'd hardly joke about it!'

'But you said that—'

'I know what I said, but that was before and I should never have said it. We were making silly wishes. And when people wish they often ask for the impossible. I never thought I could find anybody again as wonderful as you and I don't care if I'm going to have to sit by your hospital bedside. I don't care if I'm going to have to worry about you. What I care about is *you*. Being with you. Getting to *love you*. And if that means in sickness or in health, then I will still take sickness, because it will mean that I am *with you*. Getting to love you, and that's far better than not getting to love you at all. But…can we try for health, if at all possible?' He winked at her, his face beaming.

'But…you want more kids. So do I. That might be something that's off the table for me after the surgery.'

'There are many ways to make a family.'

'It's easy to say, Max.'

'And harder to go through. You think I don't know that? But I was a guy that would have ended my family, ended my chance of having Rosie, if it meant keeping the woman I loved and I can do that again. I love you, Bella, and if we struggle to have more kids, then we struggle, but I know we will find a way. Together. I just need you to believe.'

'I want to. But I'm so scared, Max.'

'I know you are, but let's be scared together.'

Bella rushed into his arms and squeezed him tightly. 'Oh, my God… I can't believe it. You're sure? You're absolutely sure?'

'One hundred per cent. We already have an amazing family. You, me, Rosie, Ewan. Anything else from hereon in is a wonderful bonus. I could never regret a thing with you.'

She gazed up into his eyes. His beautiful eyes. 'I love you.'

'And I love you.'

And he pulled her in for a kiss.

The kids, watching from the window, made 'yuck' noises and then laughed.

EPILOGUE

'AW, THESE ARE CUTE!' Bella lifted the little hanger from the rack and showed the set of three pink Babygros to Max. 'Can we get these?'

He smiled. 'They're very cute. But we don't even know if we're having a girl.'

'We can get those blue ones, too. Hedge our bets.'

'Why not just wait for the ultrasound?'

'Hmm, sensible. But something tells me it's a girl.'

'Maternal instinct?'

'No, Rosie keeps calling the baby a girl and I agree with her. Besides, I'm carrying high and the heartbeat is faster and…' She smiled at the Babygros again. 'These are just so cute!'

He laughed and kissed her. 'You know you're a doctor, right? You don't have to believe in old wives' tales.'

'You know I'm pregnant, right? You're meant to indulge me.'

'I do indulge you. Didn't I rub your feet last night? Didn't I go out and fetch you mint choc ice cream at midnight?'

'You did.' She laughed. 'All right. It's just… I'm excited, you know? I never thought this day would come and Rosie really wants a little sister, so…'

They'd been through so much together. So many scary days. The surgery had gone well to remove her tumour. Remarkably well. Professor Helberg had got it all. No need for her to go back and have further surgeries. She'd undergone some radiation, which had made her feel unwell, but she'd been so grateful for Max's presence. Watching over her. Caring for her. Holding her hand and listening to her fears. Making sure that Ewan was okay.

Max had held the fort and had never wavered. Never doubted.

He was the strongest man that she knew.

And afterwards? They'd had a little help to fall pregnant. IVF. Only needing one cycle and falling pregnant right away. It had been miraculous and Bella wanted to enjoy every minute of it.

She hung the Babygros back on the rack in the hospital shop. They would wait. Wait to see what the twenty-week scan said. Everything had been going perfectly up until now. She checked her watch. 'Nearly time. Shall we go?'

Max nodded and hand in hand they made their way to the maternity ultrasound department. Ewan and Rosie were in school and getting on better than ever. They'd been so chuffed to learn that they would be moving in together and becoming brother and sister and had adapted to that so easily. She and Max had found a wonderful house to buy in the village and had moved out of their respective cottages on Field Lane and bought something a little more on the outskirts. They even had views of the lavender fields from their windows.

They sat and waited in the waiting room for a little while, feeling excited. Nervous. Desperate to know which colours to paint the nursery. And when they were called through, Bella clambered onto the examination bed and lay down, tucking blue paper into the top of her underwear to protect her clothes from the cold gel that was about to be applied.

'Do you want to know the sex?' the ultrasound tech asked.

'We do.' Bella clasped Max's hand and squeezed it tight. It didn't matter what sex the baby was. Not really. They already had one of each. Whatever this baby was would be a beautiful bonus.

Life was turning out perfect for them. Yes, they'd been through their hard times, but maybe they were done with those now. Now their lives were about starting something new. Something hopeful. Something wonderful. She was deeply in love. Happy. She could not ask for anything more.

'It's a girl.'

Bella beamed and gazed with love at Max. 'I knew it.'

'I love you so much,' he said.

I love you too, she mouthed and turned back to look at their daughter on the screen.

* * * * *

*If you missed the previous story in
the Cotswold Docs duet,
then check out*
Best Friend to Husband?

*And, if you enjoyed this story,
check out these other great reads from
Louisa Heaton*

Resisting the Single Dad Surgeon
A Mistletoe Marriage Reunion
Finding Forever with the Firefighter

All available now!

MILLS & BOON®

Coming next month

NURSE'S TWIN PREGNANCY SURPRISE
Becca McKay

'What are you talking about?' Hazel asked.

But as she neared the urine specimen container set neatly on the side, alongside two testing strips, understanding quickly began to dawn on Hazel.

One strip to test her urine for blood, glucose, ketones...all the usual suspects. The other strip to test for a very specific suspect. The kind of suspect that Libby dealt with day-in, day-out. *Pregnancy*.

Hazel was hardly breathing as she approached the testing strip but even from a foot away she knew the result. She could see the two pink lines as clear as day.

'Libby is this a joke? Because...' but Hazel couldn't finish and from Libby's expression, and the vehement shake of her head, she knew this wasn't the kind of prank her friend would pull.

Hazel picked up the pregnancy test with shaking hands and tilted it towards the light as though that might change the result somehow. But of course, it didn't. Nothing would. Because Hazel was pregnant.

And when it came to the father, there was only one possibility. *Dr Garrett Buchanan*.

Continue reading

NURSE'S TWIN PREGNANCY SURPRISE
Becca McKay

Available next month
millsandboon.co.uk

COMING SOON!

We really hope you enjoyed reading this book.
If you're looking for more romance
be sure to head to the shops when
new books are available on

Thursday 27th March

To see which titles are coming soon, please visit
millsandboon.co.uk/nextmonth

MILLS & BOON

LET'S TALK

Romance

For exclusive extracts, competitions and special offers, find us online:

f MillsandBoon

X @MillsandBoon

⊙ @MillsandBoonUK

♪ @MillsandBoonUK

Get in touch on 01413 063 232

Afterglow Books is a trend-led, trope-filled list of books with diverse, authentic and relatable characters, a wide array of voices and representations, plus real world trials and tribulations. Featuring all the tropes you could possibly want (think small-town settings, fake relationships, grumpy vs sunshine, enemies to lovers) and all with a generous dose of spice in every story.

♪ @millsandboonuk
© @millsandboonuk
afterglowbooks.co.uk
#AfterglowBooks

For all the latest book news, exclusive content and giveaways scan the QR code below to sign up to the Afterglow newsletter:

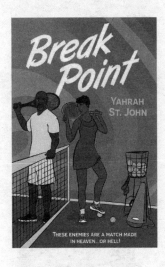

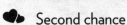
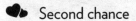
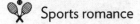

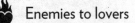
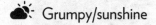

FOUR BRAND NEW BOOKS FROM
MILLS & BOON MODERN

The same great stories you love, a stylish new look!

OUT NOW

Eight Modern stories published every month, find them all at:

millsandboon.co.uk

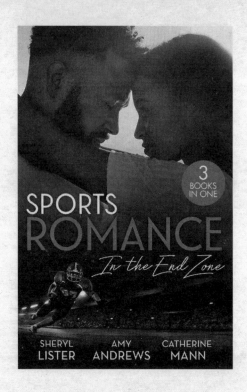